CAPTURED IMMUNE

A ZORDI WORLD NOVEL

SECRETS TRILOGY
—2—

CAPTURED IMMUNE

MELISSA LAM

12Bunnies
Publishing

Developmental editing by: R. D. Langr
Editing, cover design, and proofreading by: Enchanted Ink Publishing
Author photo by: AB-Photography.us
Logo art by: A. Krause Studio

www.authormelissalam.com

For Rennie, my baby sister.
I admire your strength and confidence.
When I grow up, I want to be like you.

CONTENTS

SCRUBBED MIND

PLAYLIST

Chapter 1: "When You're Gone" Avril Lavigne
Chapter 1: "Falling" Harry Styles
Chapter 2: "These Four Walls" Little Mix
Chapter 3: "HALF HEARTED" We Three
Chapter 4: "I Almost Forgot" NIGHTBREAKERS
Chapter 19: "Only You (Acoustic)" Little Mix
Chapter 20: "You Are The Reason" Calum Scott
Chapter 21: "Lose Control" Teddy Swims
Chapter 25: "Avalanche" James Arthur
Chapter 26: "When You Look Me In the Eyes" Jonas Brothers
Chapter 27: "Say You Won't Let Go" James Arthur
Chapter 28: "I'll Be" Edwin McCain
Chapter 28: "Until The End" Dean Lewis
Chapter 29: "Like I'm Gonna Lose You (feat. John Legend)" Meghan Trainor
Chapter 29: "Fight For You" Jason Derulo
Chapter 31: "Infinity" Jaymes Young

CONTENT WARNING

Buckle up, peeps! This wild ride is packed with death, violence, explicit sex (the best kind!), pregnancy loss (sniffle sniffle), kidnapping (because why not?), and enough swearing to make even the dirtiest sailors blush. As if the twists and turns aren't crazy enough, the cliff-hanger will make you drop to your knees yelling, "Nooooo!" to the sky.

This is a roller coaster of chaos, so keep your arms and legs inside the ride at all times! We are not responsible for any sleep deprivation or wall damage from book-throwing. Enjoy the thrill!

1

———

TREY

She knew that word would crush me. She knew, and she used it anyway. *Goodbye* is the word my mother taught me to use only when I'd never see someone again.

"*Goodbye* means forever. *Bye* is just for now," my mother said to me countless times when I was a kid.

Exactly nineteen years ago, on a rainy night in September, she said goodbye to me. I never saw her again.

Arella purposely used that word to hurt me, and it worked. I'm so wrecked by it, I haven't found the strength to move yet. My bare feet are standing where her car stood in my driveway a minute ago. Where we both stood a minute ago, shouting at each other, saying things we didn't mean. *At least, I didn't mean them.*

Rain pelts my bare back like little bullets shooting from the sky. The hems of my workout shorts drip water down my legs. I'm not even wearing shoes, because I didn't have time to put any on before chasing after Arella.

I tried getting her to stay. I wanted to explain and make things right, but she refused to listen.

So now I'm here . . .

Alone . . .

With a wallet-size photo of Arella and me gazing deeply into each other's eyes.

It's slowly curling in my hand. She shoved it at me right before taking off. I want the happiness we had when we took this photo. The happiness I have whenever I'm with her. Whenever we're cuddling until the very last second we have to get out of bed. Whenever we're exchanging looks from across the room that say *I admire everything about you* without actually saying it.

I've got half a mind to mount my Harley and chase after her right now—after the only person who's ever made me feel whole. I'll come clean. I'll tell her everything. I'll confess that the flat tire that brought us together wasn't an accident and tell her what Zordinaries are. I'll show her my powers and explain how I know for a fact that the baby growing inside her isn't mine.

Am I risking going to z-prison? *Yes.*

Do I care? If it'll get me my girl back, *no.*

Even knowing she's pregnant by another man, I still want to be with her. I love her too much to not forgive her. I'll raise that baby like it's mine, if that's what it takes for her to forgive me too. *Will she?*

She was pretty upset after finding me shirtless with another woman. But she was off sleeping with another guy for who knows how long, so what's the difference? I guess the difference is that she *saw* me. I suppose if I saw her half-naked with someone else, she'd be harder to forgive. But I'd forgive her—after bashing the other guy's face in.

No one touches my girl.

No one.

Except, she's not my girl anymore. *Was she ever?*

"What happened?" Jess asks when I step back into my house. She's draped over my couch with a slight grin on her face.

I wasn't in the mood for her when she showed up unannounced, and I'm definitely not in the mood for her now, so my tone comes out rough. "Cut the shit. I know you heard everything." *Or did she?*

With her enhanced hearing, Jess can hear something as small as dust fall. Arella's immunity probably blocks Jess's power like it blocks mine.

"Okay, fine." She perks up. "Was that the Ordinary you've been fucking around with?"

I hate the way she says that, as if my relationship with Arella was only "fucking around." Arella means a hell of a lot more to me than that.

"How well could you hear our conversation?" My soaked workout shorts cool against my skin as I drag my feet behind the couch. I'm dripping water all over my clean carpet, and I don't care.

Jess twists to face me. "As well as any other person can hear. I didn't need my gift to catch what you guys were saying. You were screaming at each other so loud, I'm sure the moon people heard y'all."

Dammit. I didn't mean to shout at Arella. I just couldn't control myself when she kept lying to my face, demanding that I pay child support for another man's child.

Okay, technically, she wasn't demanding anything. What she actually said was that she'll be taking a DNA test to prove that I am the father and that I should be *prepared* to pay child support. Because I'm an asshole and was pissed off to shit, I told her she'd be stupid to think she's getting a dime from me, when in reality, I'd give that woman anything she wants.

Money? *Done.*

My house? *Take it.*

My car? *Here ya go.*

Just be with me.

With a sigh, I scold myself. I shouldn't have let her go. I

especially shouldn't have grabbed her the forceful way I had. Add those to my long list of mistakes.

Jess continues with a sparkling grin. "Sooo, she's pregnant?"

"Yep." Admitting it out loud to another person makes it more real.

"Who's the father?"

Isn't that the million-dollar question? I wish I knew. At the same time, I don't think I want to know. I'll obsess over it, and I'll want to know everything about him so I can figure out why she chose him over me. "I dunno, but she tried to tell me it's mine."

Low laughter bellows from Jess's gut. "Wow! I'm so glad I was here to witness this. An Ordi trying to convince a Zordi she's carrying his child? Holy shit! This is better than TV."

Seriously? I glare at her. "Get out."

"What?"

With the fingers not holding my precious photo, I point at the front door. It swings wide open, coming to a firm stop just before hitting the wall. "Get the fuck out."

"Hell no! I need to know all the deets! Like, what's her motive? Is she trying to get your money?"

"Out! Now!" I give her two seconds. When she still doesn't move, I lose it. With a flick of my wrist, the couch shoots toward the door with her still on it.

"Whoa! All right, all right. I'm leaving. No need to be such an ass."

She's right. I am an ass, and she's a bitch, so I don't give a flying fuck what she thinks of me. I just lost the most important person in my life, and she's laughing about it like I'm on some stupid reality TV show. I'm done being her entertainment, and I'm done being her last-minute rebound. *Just get out!*

Once she stands, I point at the couch and fly it back to where it belongs. The second Jess has crossed the threshold, I wave a hand at the door. It slams shut behind her, and the bolt lock clicks. I hope I never have to see her face again. Ever.

I push the sopping strands of dark hair away from my face as I storm into my music room.

Minutes later, my pen flies messily across notebook paper as lyrics tumble from my mind. It's not long before I've got two new verses and a chorus written. I grab my guitar to play some chords along to the melody.

When I was eight, I learned that playing and writing music helped settle the tornado of misery swirling in my head all the time. That, and lighting stuff on fire. And throat-punching people.

As a teenager, I found out that getting drunk helps too.

As an adult, I discovered that z-drugs work the best. The higher I get, the less agony I feel. I wish I had some right now, because writing this song isn't helping.

"Fuck!" I smash my guitar against the floor. The wood breaks with a loud *crack!* as the instrument snaps in half.

For the first time since I got the call about Elliott passing away, I burst into tears. Thinking about losing my Deaf mentee kid only makes me sob harder. He meant so much to me, and I only had him for a short amount of time. Sadly, I had Arella for less.

My shoulders are shaking, and I'm wheezing. I don't even understand why I'm crying. Maybe it's because of the way things ended with her. Maybe it's because it happened on the anniversary of the worst day of my life. Either way, my relationship with her was doomed from the start. Whether it was now, like this, or later when the Superiors hauled me off to z-prison for having close relations with an Ordinary, eventually, our relationship would have ended, and I knew that.

So why the hell do I feel this broken? Why, for weeks, did I try to convince myself that we could make it work? Zordinaries and Ordinaries aren't meant to be together. We *can't* be together. Knowing that didn't stop me from falling in love with her, especially when everything with her feels more natural than blinking.

———

MY BODY LURCHES UPRIGHT AS I WAKE. THE SKY OUTSIDE MY window is black. I don't remember falling asleep, especially not on the floor. My eyes are sore, and my neck aches from the way I was lying. Next to me is my shattered guitar in a helpless heap of broken pieces. At least my shorts are dry now . . . mostly.

I flop onto my back and stare at the motionless ceiling fan. I'm not sure how long I stay like that. Maybe it's five minutes. Maybe it's five hours. It doesn't matter.

Eventually, my stomach rumbles. The sky is still black, so it's not time for breakfast. It's been a while since I ate, so I should probably eat *something*.

Inside the fridge, I find salad for two, chicken for two, and pie for two. Disgusted, I slam the fridge shut. Suddenly, I'm not hungry anymore.

The bedroom is worse. My sheets smell like her: sweet lavender and springtime. Groaning, I rip the linens off the bed and hurl them at the wall. The gentle way they slump to the floor pisses me off, so I rip my lamp from the outlet and chuck it across the room. It hits the wall, and the lightbulb shatters to pieces.

What else can I throw?

A book? *Sure.* It lands with the pages open.

Bluetooth speaker? *Definitely.* It leaves a dent in the wall.

Cologne bottle? *Hell yeah.* I thought for sure it would crack, but it merely falls to the carpet, unharmed. *Lame.*

This throwing stuff thing isn't working. *What can I light on fire?*

I glance around for something to burn and find Arella's

dress on the floor. I pick it up and crush it against my nose. As I inhale, every memory I have of holding her in my arms comes rushing back to destroy me.

After I suck up my sorrows, I grab all the sheets and take them, with Arella's dress, to the laundry room. Just before tossing all the linens into the washing machine, I smash her dress against my face again. *Mmm.* It smells so good. Like a mix of happiness and the only sense of peace I've ever had.

I can't do this.

Huffing, I stomp out of the laundry room, leaving her dress on the floor.

With an achy chest, I crawl onto my bare mattress and lie facedown with my arms out wide. I could put another set of sheets on, but why? That sounds like a lot of effort right now.

My bed feels bigger without her on it. Emptier too. I can still picture her here with her back flush against my front. I'd trace my fingertips up and down her arm while kissing her neck. We'd talk about nothing and everything at the same time. I never cared what we talked about as long as I could hear her voice.

"The only stupid thing I did was fall in love with you." Those were some of her last words to me. They keep repeating in my head.

Love. What does that word mean, anyway? Liz once told me that love is a beautiful and fulfilling experience. So far, my experience with love has only been full of pain and regret.

I should have listened to Liz when she told me to stop messing around with Ordinaries. Liz was afraid I'd hurt Arella. Little did we know Arella would be the one to hurt me.

Whatever happened to that "Ari's perfect for you" thing? Those were Liz's words. She said that since I can't sense Arella's emotions, anything I feel for Arella is real and not a reflection of her feelings for me. If Arella is perfect for me, then why do I feel like I've just lost a war?

I want nothing more than to see my girl right now. More

so, I want to see her happy. The image of her that keeps replaying in my mind is the way I last saw her: weepy and angry. I don't want that to be what I picture whenever I think of her. *Hold on. Where's our picture?*

I fly off the mattress and scour my bedroom. It's not here.

I sprint to the living room. I search between the couch cushions, then the kitchen. Nothing.

Where did I—Oh! My music room! I rush in there and find the photo waiting for me next to my notebook, where I wrote that sad guitar ballad about her. It's a song that will never see the studio. The lyrics are too raw. I'd never be able to sing it without choking up.

Thankfully, the rain didn't ruin the photo. It's a little curled at the corners, but it still showcases a happy couple gazing lovingly at each other.

The more I stare at the picture, the more I want to rip it up. I can't bring myself to do it though. I'm weak. Too weak to leave her when I should have. Too weak to throw her dress into the wash. Too weak to destroy the only picture I have of us.

Ripping up this picture will be like admitting it's over.

It's not over.

It *can't* be over.

Back in my bedroom, I search for my wallet. I find it lying open on the carpet. All my cash is gone—all two thousand dollars. *Of course.* Why wouldn't Jess use the time I was outside with Arella to dig through what's not hers? Unfortunately, missing cash is the least of my problems right now.

I'm carefully tucking my precious photo between the fabric of my bifold when I catch a glimpse of some writing on the back. I flip the picture over. The loopy handwriting makes my breath hitch.

I love you, Trey. You are right.
We do belong together.
—Arella

I read it again.

And again.

And again.

The sunrise appears out of nowhere. I haven't slept, I haven't eaten, and I don't feel like doing either. I also haven't let go of this picture since I saw Arella's note.

The absence of her is driving me insane. I need to do the one thing that will completely block her from my mind. Unfortunately, I promised myself—more importantly, Liz— that I would never drink that much or get that high again. Although, back then, I didn't know I'd feel so devastated.

Maybe I can black out for one day. I just won't tell Liz.

No, no, no. I scold myself for even considering it. Nothing good can come from that. Except I could feel better, even if it's just for one night. *That'll be worth it, right?* Probably not. The second I wake up sober, this chest ache will come right back. It always does.

What I truly want is a permanent healing solution, and she's probably in the arms of that other guy right now. The mere thought of it scratches at my throat, leaving it coarse and dry. Instead, I imagine her alone in her bed, sulking like I am. I let out a groan toward the ceiling. Neither image makes me feel good.

Should I call her? Has she tried to call me? Where's my phone? After rubbing my sore eyes, I force myself to go phone hunting.

I don't find it in my bedroom. Or the living room. Or the kitchen. When I still can't find it, I search my music room twice. Nothing.

Huffing, I trudge upstairs to my workout room. Finally, I

find the damn thing sitting next to my Bluetooth speaker. Now that I think about it, this was the last place I used my phone before Jess showed up during my workout yesterday.

Damn. Was that only yesterday?

My phone has five percent battery left. I've got two missed calls. Neither is from Arella. Three texts. None of those are from Arella either. They're all from Liz, dated yesterday.

> You coming to perform tonight or what?

> T?

> Shit. I'm sorry. I didn't realize it's September 5th. Don't worry about coming if you don't feel up for it.

The anniversary of seeing my parents get blown up is not the reason why I skipped out on my band's show last night, but I'll take it.

My phone vibrates in my hand. Liz's name and picture appear on the screen. I let the call go to voicemail, because I'm not in the mood to talk to Liz right now—or anybody. Well, except for one. If Arella called, I wouldn't hesitate to pick up.

A second later, my phone buzzes. It's a text from Liz.

> Are you planning to come tonight?

If I'm not in the mood to talk to people, I'm definitely not in the mood to perform. Especially not on a Saturday, when the Soul House is always packed. But if I skip again, my band manager will have my head. Monique lives for any chance to yell at me. I don't have the energy to deal with her wrath, so I suck it up, grab my leather jacket, strap on my helmet, and head toward downtown Los Angeles.

Riding my motorcycle is lonely without Arella. I can still feel her behind me and her fingers drawing figure eights over my abs. It's not until I've arrived at my destination that I realize I should have stayed home.

Arella usually comes to work with me. Whenever she doesn't, everyone asks about her. Typically, I can tell people she'll be coming when she gets off work. This time, I can't. What will I say instead? I sure as hell am not explaining what actually happened.

I find a parking spot in the back lot, then force myself to dismount my bike. I'd much rather go home, but I drag my feet to the backstage door anyway. On the keypad, I type in the access code.

Beep! The little light turns green, and I step inside.

Marcus is behind his drum set, spinning a drumstick around his fingers when he glances up at me. "Hey, man! Where you—" His face drops. "Damn. Who died?"

I must look like a train wreck. Definitely feel like one. I rub my stubbly cheeks. Maybe if I had trimmed my beard, I wouldn't look so defeated.

"Is Ari comin'?" Kevin, our bass guitarist, asks through a mouthful of chips.

"Marcus! Kev!" Emmy, our pianist, rushes out of the women's bathroom with Liz right behind her.

Liz flashes Marcus and Kevin a stern look, then pretends to zip her lips shut. The room goes silent.

The girls know. I don't know how they know, but they know. I can tell by their distraught emotions whipping me in the face like a chilly gust of wind. Plus, they're staring at me with a sorrowful look in their eyes.

I hate that look. It's the pity look. It's the same look people used to give me when I was known as the little boy whose parents died in a "house fire." *I shouldn't have come.*

Liz whispers something to Emmy, who nods, turns to the boys, and gestures toward the door. Without a word, the guys obey, and they rush outside with Emmy.

When the door clicks shut, Liz approaches me with gentle

steps. The closer she gets, the deeper her sadness bleeds into my head. It mixes with the pain that's been throbbing inside me since yesterday. *I really shouldn't have come.*

"T," she says, all tender and shit.

I hate it. I hate this. I don't want to be treated like I'm wounded. I mean, I am, but I don't want to be treated like it.

"How do you know?" I ask dryly.

"Well, you weren't answering your phone, so I called Ari. She said you broke up with her."

Is that the story she's telling people? Hearing the words *broke up* doesn't help me accept it. I won't accept it. I'm still holding out for the moment someone pops out and tells me this was all just a cruel joke. *The cruelest fucking joke ever.*

I drag a rough hand through my already messy hair. "What else did she say?"

"Not much."

I swallow the hard lump in my throat. "How is she?"

Liz studies me with furrowed brows. "Uh, I'm not sure."

Is she as miserable as I am?

"How are *you*?"

I shrug halfheartedly. "Fine."

"You don't look fine. You look heartbroken."

Is that what I'm feeling? Heartbroken? I guess I wouldn't know. It's never happened to me before. No wonder people say it sucks.

Liz keeps talking to me like I'm a lost puppy. "I thought you were in love with her?"

"I am."

"Then I'm confused as to why you dumped her, but let's talk about this later, okay? We've gotta get ready for our show."

The idea of performing sounds as bad as explaining to Liz what happened. "I don't wanna talk about it."

"I didn't ask if you wanted to. We're gonna talk tonight whether you like it or not."

"Liz . . ." I sigh through her name.

She lifts a gloved hand to my face. "No. Don't argue with me. You won't win."

She's right. With her, I never win.

I guess if there's one person in this world I can talk to about Arella, it's Liz. Liz befriended me even when I was a drunk z-drug addict headed nowhere in life. Liz, of all people, will understand.

I WAS WRONG. LIZ DOESN'T UNDERSTAND, AND I DON'T THINK she cares to.

"What do you mean, you didn't break up with her?" Liz has left her satin gloves lying on the backstage coffee table and has forced me to sit on the couch with her.

The rest of the band and crew left a while ago. I delayed this conversation by taking a long bathroom break. I'd still be in there if Liz hadn't waltzed into the men's room to call me out on my bullshit. Leave it to her to know that I was simply hiding in a stall to avoid this.

"I didn't break up with her. Technically, *she* left me." I can still hear Arella's tires squealing from driving away so fast.

"Why would Ari do such a thing?"

"Because," I groan, "it wasn't working."

"Do you want it to?"

I rub my hands over my face and groan again—louder this time. "Why are you doing this?"

"Because I care about you."

It's ridiculous that Liz cares about me at all. I'm a fuckup. She should start investing her precious energy into someone who actually matters.

I slouch back against the couch. "You've never had to have a therapy session with me about any other girl before. Why do you have to start now?"

"Because Ari's different, and you know it. With her, you're more vibrant and happy. You two have something special most people can't find in a lifetime. It doesn't even make sense, because she's an Ordinary and it's totally illegal and against all biology for you to love her, but I've never seen two people more meant for each other than you and her. I know you believe that too. So why are you acting like you're just gonna let her go?"

Liz is right. Arella *is* meant for me. She's my soul mate— something I didn't even believe in until I felt the *glimmer*. I used to think getting a sickening sense whenever your soul mate was in danger was just some stupid thing Zordinaries made up to put claim on each other—until last month. I was on my way to Arella's apartment when a sudden wave of nausea hit me like bricks to the stomach. My throat went dry and I couldn't stop coughing. Then I found Arella being attacked by spiders.

The week after, when her car was hit by a truck, my body knew something was wrong. I was nowhere near her when it happened, yet sudden nausea hit me again. I got so dizzy, I threw up. Given that Arella's an Ordinary, my sicknesses at those exact times could have been a coincidence, but that's one hell of a coincidence.

"Tell me what you want, T," Liz says. "What would make you happy?"

"I dunno." Happiness seems like a foreign idea right now.

"Do you want her back?"

"I dunno."

"Yes, you do. You either want her or you don't. Which is it?" Liz isn't stupid. We both know the answer. She's just trying to get me to say it out loud.

"Of course I want her back," I grumble.

"Then go get her. Whatever you guys fought about, talk through it."

"It's not that easy."

Liz scoffs. "You're a smart man. Figure it out."

"I can't."

"Why not?"

"I just can't," I snap.

Like always, Liz isn't having my attitude. She snaps right back at me. "Why not?"

I give in. "Because she slept with another man."

"No, she didn't."

I scowl at the conviction in her tone. "How are you so sure?"

"Because Ari would never do that."

That's what I thought too—until she showed me those two lines on a pee stick. "Well, she did."

"How do you know? Did she tell you?"

"No. I know because—" I choke up. "She's . . . She's pregnant."

Liz gasps, covering her mouth with her hand. "No. Maybe the test was wrong." She's going through the denial phase. That was me for the first fifteen minutes after I saw those goddamn pregnancy brochures.

I was cleaning up my house when I accidentally dropped Arella's purse and all her stuff spilled out. As I bent to pick it up, the words *Having a Healthy Pregnancy* caught my attention. I almost fell over.

"She took four store-bought tests and a test at the doctor's office. They all came out positive." I lift a finger. "Which, by the way, does not mean she's positively *not* pregnant."

Liz screws her face up. "Hold on. You thought *positive* on a pregnancy test meant positively *not* pregnant?"

"Well, I fuckin' hoped."

"You know, for a smart man, you're kind of an idiot."

I toss my hands into the air, letting them fall to my thighs. "Thanks for the pep talk, Liz. Really made me feel *loads* better. Same time tomorrow?"

Her hands go up in surrender. "Okay, okay, I'm sorry. I'm

just . . . trying to process all this. If Ari is pregnant, that means she really did sleep with someone else."

"That's what I've been trying to fucking tell you."

Liz slumps back, huffing out a breath. "Damn. That changes everything."

SUNDAY NIGHT USED TO BE *OUR* NIGHT. IT'S THE EVENING I usually have off, and I'd spend those hours just being with Arella. Most of the time, we'd just talk until she fell asleep. Sometimes we'd watch movies or play card games or take walks around my neighborhood.

Sundays are special to me. We had our first date on a Sunday. I took her to my favorite pasta place in Long Beach, where I made her laugh so hard, she wheezed and slapped her knee over and over.

A couple of Sundays later, she taught me how to bake snickerdoodle cookies in my kitchen. That night ended with us throwing flour at each other and sharing our first kiss.

Then there was that one Sunday when we went stargazing at her *thinking spot*, a secluded oak tree at the top of a woodsy hill. There, she explained to me what love is.

"When you love someone, you put their happiness before your own."

Later that night, I told her what really happened to my parents, and she comforted me with a simple touch of her hand to my face.

On a Sunday after that, we made love for the first time, right under that tree. It was the most magical and sensual experience I've ever had.

As I flop onto my still-bare mattress, I mope over the idea that this could be the first of many Sundays I spend alone.

On Monday, everything reminds me of her. Little things like waking up to her side of the bed empty, or walking into the kitchen, where she's not in my T-shirt, pouring herself a glass of apple juice. Or stepping into my shower without a naked beauty smiling back at me.

My shower water ran cold five minutes ago. My body's natural equilibrium is working hard to warm me because I don't care to get out. There's nothing waiting for me beyond these tile walls—the ones that I'm pounding my head against because I'm trying to get her out of my mind.

When I finally gather enough willpower to step out, the mirror is foggy. In the middle of the glass, I swipe a towel in a circle to reveal my face. *Ew.* Bloodshot pupils. Dark eyebags. Facial hair that hasn't been trimmed in who knows how long. I look like a homeless bum.

With a towel around my waist, I drag my feet into my walk-in closet. All her clothes are still hanging up on her side. I debate shoving it all into a box and driving it back to her. It'd be an excuse to see her, but returning her things means she won't be coming back. I'm not ready to admit that yet.

On Tuesday, I don't do anything productive all day. Unless lugging my feet around my empty house and finding things to throw fireballs at counts as productive.

Around noon on Wednesday, Liz FaceTimes me. I almost don't answer, but if I don't, she'll show up here, and that would be worse.

"Hey," I mumble when her face appears on my screen. I take a seat at my kitchen counter.

"Don't even think about skipping tonight. If you don't show up to rehearsal by four, I'll drive over there and throw water balls at you until you beg me to stop."

"Can't I get one pass?" I prop my phone up against my salt shaker. It's too much effort to hold my phone up.

"Hell no. I've given you passes for two days." That's true. I skipped our recording session yesterday and our writing session the day before that. "It's not good for you to be alone, T. I know how you get."

"What's that supposed to mean?"

"Have you been staying sober?"

"Unfortunately," I say with a scoff.

"Good. Now get yourself together and show up tonight."

Let's see . . . Get pounded with water by Liz or leave my house and be forced to talk to other humans? I think I'll take the water balls.

"Come on, T. Please?"

I sigh heavily. "Fine."

"Fabulous. I'll see you later then. And for the love of all things holy, please, trim your beard."

I rub my palm against my long chin hairs. "Is it that bad?"

"You look like the Wish version of Henry Cavill."

On Thursday, only because hunger is clawing a hole through my stomach, I force myself to make some lunch. For the first time in months, I'm cooking for one—that is, if sticking a frozen pizza into the oven counts as cooking.

On Friday, I arrive home from the Soul House mentally exhausted. The fans got a halfhearted performance from me tonight. During the meet and greet, I fake-smiled for all the photos until it was finally over. All of it felt trivial. What's the point when I don't have her?

I can't take it anymore. I need the pain to stop, and I need it to stop now.

I don't register that my feet have moved until I'm already in the kitchen with the cabinet open. From it, I drag down a half bottle of bourbon, some tequila, and a tiny bit of vodka. I don't think about it as I unscrew the vodka cap and chug it all in one breath. It burns on its way down my throat.

The tequila is next. It takes three breaths to finish.

The bourbon takes four.

This isn't enough to get me buzzed, and I need to black out. Years of being a drunk have built up my alcohol tolerance. Couple that with my body filtering it out way faster than the average Ordinary can, and I'm gonna need at least three more bottles—full ones.

My nights used to be filled with popping questionable pills and trying any z-drug I could get my hands on. Hollow sex with women in skimpy outfits. Meaningless fights with big guys in bars. Talking shit to bouncers at clubs, just to get them to drive a hard one into my face. I used to do anything so I could feel something other than the emptiness in my chest.

Two years ago, I cleaned up. Liz made me realize that a pathetic trainwreck isn't what I want to be. Tonight, I don't give a shit what I am.

Through heavy rainfall, I drive to the nearest liquor store, getting there ten minutes before closing. Something makes me go apeshit in the aisles. I toss practically every hard liquor in sight into my basket.

When I arrive back home, I don't waste a second. In my silent living room, on the vacant couch, I rip the seal off a bottle and chug.

The last time I drank with the intent of passing out was after I got the call telling me the cancer had finally taken Elliott. I would have given anything to cure that precious little boy. Right now, I'd give anything to have Arella back.

She would hate me if she saw me drinking like this. The smell of alcohol triggers bad memories of her ex in her head. Because of that, I never drank around her. *And now, she's gone.*

Only once two bottles lie empty beside me do I start to feel something. The blackout is coming, but it's not coming fast enough, so I reach for another bottle. *Bottoms up.*

2

ARELLA

It's been seven days. Seven slow, tormenting days.

I can't eat. I can't sleep. I can't think.

I didn't realize how much time I spent with Trey, until now, when I'm not.

He's ruined me. And he'll continue to ruin me. From now on, every doctor's appointment I'll attend alone, every kick I'll feel from the baby, every time someone comments on my rounded belly, he's all I'll be thinking about.

I've always wanted to be a mom. I've dreamt of this moment since I was a kid, except I imagined this with a ring on my finger and the father-to-be at my side.

I'm terrified to do this alone. What will I tell my grandparents? How will I explain to my future son or daughter why they don't have a father? How does anyone explain to a child that their father thought he was infertile and—

Knock-knock-knock.

I jolt out of bed. *Is it him?* I rush to the door in my pajamas.

"Wipe that disappointment off your face." Javina's wearing a light jacket with the hood up to block the rain from all her black curls. She holds up a carton of ice cream. "Wanna have some rocky road while we plot his murder?"

I roll my eyes, mostly because when she called earlier, I told her not to come. Still, I motion for her to step inside. "We're not going to kill him."

"Of course *we* aren't gonna kill him," she says as she slips her shoes off. "We don't stand a chance against him and those huge arm muscles. We're gonna hire a hit man." Her tone is so serious, I'm no longer sure she's joking.

On the floor of my living room with the ice cream between us, I tell Javina about the blonde chick I saw Trey with. I choke up as I hash out the details of our fight, leaving out any parts that suggest I'm with child. I'm not ready to tell Javina yet. She'll freak out, and I need to be in a place where I'm not also freaking out before I tell her.

"Toward the end, we were fighting quite a bit," I say as I dig my spoon into the now half-gone ice cream.

"About what?"

"Mostly about him keeping secrets from me. For example, he was always up at three in the morning, talking on the phone. I don't think he sleeps."

"Wait." Javina draws her thick eyebrows together. "You don't think he sleeps, like, ever?"

"Ever."

"That's impossible."

"I'll tell you what's impossible. One time, we were at a restaurant, and somehow, he knew there was a teenage boy getting beat up in an alley *blocks* away."

Javina takes a moment to process that before saying, "What?"

"Exactly. Then, there was this whole thing where he kept asking—no, *begging*—me to move to Paris with him. Whenever I asked him why, he kept saying he'd tell me once we got there, otherwise, I'd leave him."

"Again, what?"

"Oh, and let's not forget that on the night he and my ex got into a fist fight, Trey left with gashes in his knuckles. When I saw him three days later, his hand looked brand new. I got so curious that two weeks ago, I asked if he's an alien."

Javina freezes with her spoon halfway to her lips. "And?"

"He claims he's not. Apparently, he's not a superhero or from the future either. Those were my other guesses."

Javina gasps. "What if he's a wizard?"

"Like from Harry Potter?"

"Nah. More like the ones from that show *Charmed*. They have magical powers and shit, and they hide it from society, but they don't need to use any wands."

I go in for another spoonful of ice cream. "I don't think he's a wizard."

"Don't completely rule it out, girl. That's what the wizards want us to do. They live among us and don't want us to know it."

"Do you really believe that?"

"I believe that alternate universes exist, so why not wizards?" She gasps with a hand to her mouth. "What if he's from an alternate universe?"

Alternate universe? *Hmm* . . . Is that the explanation for all of Trey's oddities? Maybe in his universe, never sleeping is normal. I'll have to look into that later.

"I'm still pissed that you waited this long to tell me." Javina waves her spoon in the air. "I warned him not to hurt you. I told him if he did, I'd rip his balls off with my bare hands."

I don't doubt that Javina would try to if given the chance.

She leans back against the front of my couch. "So, do ya think Trey was havin' another woman over *every* time you were at work?"

Pfft. "I didn't . . . until now."

Shaking her head, she says, "I knew pretty boy was trouble."

"What? You were the one who said, 'If you don't marry him, I will.' "

"I still would! We'd have the grandest, most expensive wedding ever. Then, once I was the sole beneficiary of his will, I'd make sure he *accidentally* fell into a mysterious cavern within three years. Can't do it too soon, or it'll be obvious it was me."

Okay, maybe Javina and I watch too many true crime shows.

"Anyway, enough about that asshat." She licks her spoon clean, then tosses it onto my coffee table. "Tell me what's up with you not being on the schedule at the daycare. All your shifts have other people's names on them."

I knew this topic was coming. I've been avoiding it. "Um, I got let go."

Javina lifts an eyebrow like, *No, seriously. What really happened?*

I return her look with a deadpan face.

Finally, she gasps. "What? Why?"

"Remember last month when I was attacked by spiders?"

"How could I forget? After hearing you describe it, I'm *still* having nightmares. You're lucky I'm even sitting inside this arachnid magnet you call an apartment."

Whenever I see a black spot on the wall, I get a flashback of being attacked by thousands of spiders, and it suddenly gets hard to breathe. Thankfully, I haven't found any creepy-crawlies yet, but that moment was so traumatizing that sometimes, everything around here looks like a spider.

I place the lid back over our ice cream. "Since I was gone for a whole week, our director said I needed to provide a doctor's note. Company policy. Trey had one, but he lost it, so he wrote me a new one instead. Our director checked up on it, and apparently, the doctor never said I couldn't go to work."

"Why didn't you tell me? I could have done something."

"I didn't tell you because I didn't want you to start a fight with our director in front of everyone."

Javina scoffs. "That's exactly what I'ma do on Monday."

"No, Javie. Please, don't. She was nice about it. She said she didn't want to fire me but had to because of policies."

"Fuck the policies. You're one of the best we've got."

"It's okay," I say, half meaning it. "I can find another job."

"Have you started lookin' yet?"

"Not yet. I've got some money stashed away, so I'll be fine." *For now.* Soon, I'll need to have enough income to support myself and an expensive newborn.

Javina and I continue talking about life, movies, and her girlfriend until she can't stop yawning. Eventually, the clock hits 1:00 a.m., and Javina leaves.

As I crawl back into bed, the heartache resurfaces like a tsunami. A minute ago, I was laughing at my best friend's jokes. Now I feel like I could burst into tears with the simple thought of him.

Under the covers, I listen to the steady pour of raindrops on my window while I scroll through our old texts. What did I ever say to make him think I'd be capable of sleeping with another man behind his back? The only thing I gain from rereading our messages is a reminder of how in love with him I still am.

The second I finish reading our texts, my YouTube app is up, and I'm typing *Flames in the Night* into the search bar. The first video that pops up is their original song "Fired Up!" I tap it, then shove my earbuds in and turn the volume up as loud as it will go. A familiar drum solo rattles my brain, followed by Trey's guitar riffs. This is the song they use as their upbeat opener for all their shows, so I've heard it plenty. It brings back good memories.

I finish that video, then scroll until I come across their cover of a Justin Timberlake song. I was there for this shoot, like I was for many others. This one stands out to me because in the middle of filming, Trey dropped to his knees in front of me and kissed me like his heart would collapse if he didn't. I'll never forget the intense way he looked at me when he came barreling through that bedroom door and seized my face without a single word.

I can't get through the whole video because it's a bunch of footage of Trey cuddling with some blonde actress playing his love interest. So I skip to the next video.

It's about to play when *Tap! Tap! Tap!*

That can't be the rain. I rip my earbuds out.

"Arella?" someone yells from outside.

The blinds are shut. I know who it is though. No one else ever calls me by my full name.

"Arella, please. I need to see you."

Need? I hop off the bed and yank the blinds up. There he is, sopping-wet hair and all. I unlock the window and crank it open.

"What are you doing here?" I hate that there's a screen between us. My racing heart wants to be near him, and this stupid mesh thing is in the way.

Rain pours over him as he slurs, "I knocked on your door, like, a ba-jillion times. Why didn't you come?"

"I didn't hear it. I was listening to—" I can't admit that I was hopelessly listening to him sing me to sleep. "Music."

"Will you let me in?"

I nod slowly, even though I want him in here so bad, I'm willing to break through this screen. Instead, I rush to the door.

I open it to find Trey more drenched than expected. His black T-shirt clings to his skin, outlining his defined pecs. Raindrops slide down his leather jacket until they hit the concrete. His jeans look like he just crawled out of the ocean.

When we lock eyes, a rush of emotions hits me like heavy sand dumped over my head. It submerges all my other emotions under its weight, replacing them with sadness, anxiety, and heartache. I mean, my heart was already aching, but now it's throbbing.

I don't get a chance to say anything before Trey steps inside and crushes me against him. His arms squeeze me so tight, I lose all the air in my lungs. With a little sigh, he buries his face into my neck. At first, I stiffen, but it's not long before my body softens into him.

The sadness weighing me down is quickly replaced by a warm sense of belonging and hope. A trickle of peace runs from my shoulders to my toes. It's an odd sensation, like an electric current rushing through me, except I think it's coming from him.

We stand in my doorway while the rain drowns my front step behind him. No words. No movement. Just arms wrapped around each other's bodies. I think we both needed this. I, for sure, needed this.

The scent of him is familiar—mostly. Manly cologne, his shampoo, and . . . *alcohol?* Has he been drinking?

"I missss you," he slurs.

I suppose that's my answer.

When I don't respond, he asks, "Do you miss me?"

I've missed you since the moment I drove away. I waited seven days for you to show up, and every minute you didn't felt like years in a dark abyss. What took you so long? Why didn't you come after me? And why are you drunk?

I pull back. "Trey, why are you here?"

He wraps his arms around me tighter, crushing me against his chest again. "I wasn't done yet."

Tears threaten to burst from my eyes. Being held by him makes me feel whole again, so I don't fight it. I'd stay in his embrace forever if I could, but I can't. So I give him another minute before saying into his shirt, "You're soaking wet."

"Sssorry." He lets me go, and I gesture for him to step all the way inside.

After he does, I shut the door, muting the rainfall, then turn to him.

He's gorgeous—a towering muscular frame that was my

safe haven for three months. Light stubble decorates his strong jawline. I used to run my fingertips through that stubble whenever we made out. I used to grip that firm neck whenever he'd scoop me up and carry me into his bedroom. Everything about him is familiar, except for the heavy anguish ingrained between his eyebrows. Selfishly, I'm glad to know I'm not the only one who's miserable.

He places a tender finger under my chin and lifts my head until my eyes meet his. "Were you crying, babe? Your eyes are all puffy."

I draw back from his touch. It's doing things to me. And if he calls me *babe* again, I might let him do *anything* he wants to me. "Why didn't you take your car instead of the bike?"

"I didn't take either."

"Then how did you get here?"

"I walked."

"You walked?" That's at least a two- or three-hour walk.

"Yeah. I'm fucked up. I know better than to drive like this." He runs his fingers through his dark-chocolate hair and shakes the water out. Little droplets sprinkle onto my arms, but I don't care. I'm just relieved he's here, and that the first person he thought to go to while in this drunken state is me.

Does that mean he wants to fix things? Do *I* want that? I think about it for all of two seconds before I almost laugh at myself. Who am I kidding? Of course I want that.

"Why didn't you call an Uber?" I ask.

He scoffs a little. "I did. The dude drove me most of the way before kicking me outta his car."

"Why?"

"He asked me questions like where I was goin' and who I was tryna see. He said somethin' about how taking a drunk man to a woman's apartment meant trouble. So he forced me to get out and drove off."

Mentally, I applaud the Uber driver. Taking a drunk man to a woman's place *can* mean bad news. After surviving an abusive three-year relationship with a drunk, I know just how terrible those situations can get. However, with drunk Trey, I feel completely safe. I have full confidence that he would never hurt me. At least not physically. Emotionally, I'm stupidly wrecked.

"How much did you have to drink?" I ask.

His shoulders slump like I've caught him in a lie. Another invisible bag of heavy sand and sadness dumps over me—from him. "Please, don't be mad."

"How much, Trey?"

He glowers at the carpet. "Maybe, like, two bottles."

"Of?"

"Vodka. Tequila. Bourbon."

I squint at him. "You just named three things."

"All righty then. So I had *three* bottles."

My jaw drops. "You had three bottles of hard liquor? Like, all of it?"

"Probably. I don't really remember . . ."

"How are you still standing?" There's no way he had that much. That would kill him.

"I have a high tolerance."

No one's tolerance is that high.

After kicking off his shoes, he heads to my couch and falls onto it with a plop.

I cringe a little. "Trey, you're wet."

He shoots back up, stumbles over, and leans against me as I steady him. Tingles shoot down my legs from the warm hand he places on the small of my back. I've missed his touch.

"I'm sorry," he slurs. "It's just that I've been walking forever. I really need to sit."

"How about you take off all your wet clothes first? I'll wash them for you."

He complies, first with his jacket, then his shirt. As soon as I see his abs, I realize this is a mistake. I can't see him shirtless. It's my kryptonite.

From his pockets, he drags out his wallet and phone, then drops them onto my coffee table with two light thuds. Then he yanks his jeans and socks off. I grab all his damp clothes and head to the front door to hang his jacket up to dry. When I turn around, he's already got his boxers down.

I shut my eyes and throw my hands up. "Stop!"

"Huh?" A wave of shock rushes through my head.

"Put your boxers back on."

"But you told me to take off all my wet clothes."

"The boxers can stay." I wait a moment before I reopen my eyes.

Trey stands magnificently before me, wearing only a pair of plaid boxers. He gestures toward my couch. "Can I sit now?"

"Sure." With his clothes in hand, I head down the hall.

The world is cruel. Countless times, I've pictured him at my door with flowers, telling me he's come to his senses. He'd say things like "I realized you never would have cheated on me" and "I'm ready to be a father." We'd have the most amazing makeup sex and everything would be okay. Instead, the world drops him off here drunk, looking like a model for men's underwear. What am I supposed to do with this?

In the hallway, I open the pair of closet doors where my washer and dryer hide. I throw Trey's clothes into the washer with some detergent, then start the machine.

Footsteps thump against my carpet as a cloud of gloominess approaches me. I pretend not to notice him as he wraps his arms around me from behind and breathes a shiver down my neck. I have to grip the washing machine just to keep my knees from buckling.

"You're so beautiful," he says with liquor breath.

Instead of melting into him the way I always have, I remain strong and keep still. I need to know what his intentions are before I allow myself to give in to him. The moment I do is the moment I give him permission to break me again.

After a few deep breaths, I gather enough willpower to pry myself out of his grasp, and then I stride into the bathroom. Trey and his cloud of gloominess follow me there.

I open the cabinet above the sink. "How do you feel?"

"Sad." His gaze drops to the floor as he lingers in the doorway. "All the time."

"I meant, how does your head feel?"

"Oh. Um, it's all right. I'll probably be hungover in the morning though."

I shake out two pills from a bottle of ibuprofen and hold them out.

He pushes my hand away. "That's not gonna do anything for me."

I roll my eyes. He sounds like Javina whenever she's had too much to drink. She thinks water doesn't help either, but it totally does. "Just take them."

"I'm serious, babe. Ordinary human pills don't work on me."

Ordinary human pills? What pills *do* work on him then? Superhuman pills? Maybe in the alternate universe he's from, having superpowers is normal. Is that why I can feel his emotions right now? *Oh my god.* Am I carrying a superhuman baby inside me that can sense feelings?

Pushing down the panic in my chest, I stash the pill bottle back into my cabinet. I've still got the two tablets in my palm, though, just in case he wants to take them later.

With gentle hands, Trey pushes the hair from my face and cups my cheeks. My heart thrashes as he presses his lips to my forehead and gives me a light kiss. "I need you, baby."

Oh, how four little words can stir up so much eagerness inside me. The irrational part of me is screaming, *Yes, please!* The rational part of me wants to smack him for trying to claim to be infertile. Maybe in his alternate universe, he is infertile. But in this universe, he's definitely able to make babies.

"Trey, can you please explain why you're here?"

Sighing, he lets me go and steps back. As if he didn't hear my question, he asks, "Can I dry my hair a little? It keeps dripping down my face."

"Sure."

He drags my bath towel off the bar, then freezes. An invisible fist punches me in the gut. "What the fuck happened there?"

It takes me a second to register what his eyes are glued to. It's a gaping hole in the wall below the towel bar—evidence of my ex's lingering presence.

"Nathan," I say, and it's all the explanation he needs.

Trey's face turns sour. "When?"

"A year ago, maybe?"

"I swear, if he ever touches you again, I'll kill him."

I'd think he's just spitting out words, but the conviction in his tone and the anger radiating off him makes me think he's serious.

Trey rubs the towel all over his hair, then hangs it back up. It's not the way I usually do it. I typically spread the towel out to make sure it conceals the hole. Trey's version is messy and hugs the right side too much. I'll fix it later.

"Would you like to sit down now?" I ask.

Trey nods with his hair sticking up in all directions. I open my mouth, about to offer him a comb, then I don't. He looks cute like this.

He gestures for me to walk out first. I do and sense his cloud of despair follow me to the living room.

I set the pills on the coffee table. "I'll leave these here for you to take later."

His gloominess trails me to the kitchen, where I snatch a clean glass from the cabinet and fill it with some filtered water from the fridge.

I offer him the glass. "Drink up."

Without hesitation, he accepts it and finishes it in three gulps. I can't imagine what little time it took him to down that tequila.

"Thanks." He pushes the empty glass toward me.

I fill it again. "Want some more?"

"Maybe later." He stares at me with his captivating blue-gray eyes. If he keeps looking at me so intensely like that, I might fall under his spell again. *Not that I've fallen out of it.*

For the fourth time tonight, I ask, "Why are you here, Trey?"

"I couldn't stop thinking about you."

My heart does a pathetic little happy dance. My head scowls at my heart for being so easily fooled.

Without a word, Trey takes my hand and leads me to the couch. When he sits, he gestures for me to sit as well. I don't, and he doesn't force me either. Instead, he takes my hands into his and kisses the tops of my knuckles. Whatever wizardry spell he's casting on me, it's working.

I plant myself onto the couch next to him. "You can sleep here tonight if you want."

"I don't wanna sleep." He keeps my hands in his so tightly, it leaves no room for me to pull away, which is probably his intent.

"What do you want to do, then?"

"I wanna kiss you."

My lips tingle, as does everything between my legs, betraying me. Thankfully, my brain takes over before my body can. "No kissing. You have to sleep off all that alcohol."

He pouts a little, and it's adorable. "Can we kiss in the morning?"

Finally, I draw my hands back and scowl at him. "Did you forget that we broke up?"

"Not for a second."

I feel a little piece of his soul fall apart somewhere in that dark cloud above his head, and it makes me feel bad for him.

This man has been through a lot. Seeing his parents get murdered. Surviving his abusive uncle. Losing the only child who's ever meant anything to him. They're all reasons as to why he's so guarded, has deep trust issues, and refuses to let people in. And don't even get me started with his lack of self-worth.

I get it. It took me a long time to start healing from my abusive ex, and I'm *still* healing, so if there's anything I can do to help ease Trey's pain right now, I'm going to do it.

I hop to my feet. "Come. I'll let you sleep in my bed."

His eyes light up. "With you?"

Yes, please! "No."

The light in his eyes goes dim. "I'll stay here on the couch then."

"It's okay. You can sleep on the bed, and I can—"

"Arella, what kind of man would I be if I took over a woman's bed and forced her to sleep on these old cushions? The answer is no. I'll sleep right here."

With Trey, I've learned to pick my battles. We're both as stubborn as the other, and I can tell this is a fight I'm not going to win.

I leave him for a moment, then return with the one extra pillow and blanket I own. It's what Javina always uses whenever she stays over. When I hand them to Trey, he takes it, clutching my hand in the process.

"Cuddle with me."

I almost burst into tears. All I've wanted for the last seven days is for him to want me. Here he is, acting like he wants me more than he wants his next breath, and I can't bring myself to let him in. He hurt me—deeply. If we pretend like nothing happened and go back to the way things were, he'll hurt me again. I can't allow that.

Besides, there is no going back to the way things were. I've got his baby growing inside me now. No matter what happens from here, things will never again be the way they were.

"Please?" he begs. "It's been really hard for me to fall asleep without you."

I know how that feels all too well, so I give in.

We lie on the couch with my face pressed against his bare chest. *Oh, the scent of him . . .* He wraps the blanket around us, tucking it under my waist the way he always does. My body relaxes into him as a rush of calmness settles over me. This time, it's not just his feelings. They're mine too.

Trey leans back a little to look at me. "You wanna know something I've noticed?"

"What?"

"You're still wearing the angel wings." He grazes a thumb across the necklace he gave me. The golden wings feature a way-bigger-than-I-can-afford diamond heart in the middle. The tiny engraving on the back reads: *Paris? T.G.*

Maybe that's where the portal to his alternate universe is and he was trying to take me there with him. It would make sense since he said if I knew the reason behind why we had to go to Paris, I wouldn't go—and he's right. I have no desire to leave this universe for an alternate one. Not even for him.

"I guess I forgot to take it off," I lie. I've refused to take off this necklace because doing so feels like disconnecting from him, and I'm not ready for that yet.

He caresses my cheek with his fingertips. "I like that you're still wearing it."

I grab his hand and hold it against my chest. "Why don't you try going to sleep?"

"Do you ever think about me?" he asks as if I didn't say anything.

I clear my throat to give myself time to decide if I should lie or not. "Sometimes." *All the time.*

"I think about you constantly. You're like a never-ending song that keeps replaying in my mind. I can't stop writing lyrics about you either. Every single song I write sounds like a miserable ballad."

Boy, do I want to hear one of those! "Go to sleep, Trey."

He doesn't obey. "I've been thinking a lot about what happened. I want you to know that if the situation was different, I'd ask you to marry me. We'd raise this baby together to be the best little boy or girl the world has ever known. I'd ask you to give me more babies. We'd have a whole bunch of 'em. I'd grow old with you and support you in any dreams you want to make come true."

Tears prick the surface of my eyes. I want that. All of it. *How can I have it?*

Trey's tone goes husky. "The problem is that I can't. Can you understand how much it hurts to know that you're pregnant when I biologically cannot have babies with you? Mental images of you fooling around with another man are tearing me apart from the inside out. I constantly feel like I'm suffocating because my chest aches too much for my lungs to work."

That does it for me. I gasp for air as a cry ripples through me. I can't imagine how much it burns to think you're infertile, then find out your girlfriend is pregnant. If I were him and believed what he believes, I wouldn't be here. To him, it's obvious that I slept with another man.

When I said he should be prepared to pay child support, it probably sounded like I was after his money. I only said that because I was angry. I didn't actually mean it. If I were him, I'd hate me. No wonder he's so broken.

What breaks me, though, is that not once has he stopped to think that maybe, just maybe, this baby is his. How can he be so sure he's infertile? Did a doctor say so? Did he get a vasectomy? Was he born that way? Does he think people from his alternate universe can't have children with the people in this universe?

Suddenly, any hope I had of us getting back together

vanishes. If I were him with all the baggage from his past and the knowledge he has, I wouldn't want anything to do with me.

Trey places a tender kiss against my temple. "Oh, angel, please don't cry."

I can't help it. I've been crying for a week, and feeling his pain mix with mine is only making it worse.

He kisses my temple again. "Remember when we were at your thinking spot under that big oak tree? You told me that when you love someone, you put their happiness before your own. I want you to be happy, baby. It'll kill me, but if you wanna go be with him, go be with him. If that's what makes you happy."

Wait . . . Did he just admit he loves me? He's shown me he loves me, but he's never verbalized it.

I don't have much time to process it, because he keeps going.

"I just want to know what I did wrong, first. What did I do to make you feel like you needed him instead of me? Did I not give you enough? Should I have paid more attention to you? Should I have made you feel more beautiful or bought you more things?"

I've never felt like I needed anything more from Trey than his presence. He's given me everything I've ever wanted and more. He gave me a man who listened to me. A man who truly cared about my hopes and dreams. Someone I felt safe with and protected by. Most of all, he gave me someone who made me feel loved in bed—not used and abused. Trey has made me feel the most loved I've ever felt, without ever saying the words *I love you.* How could he think he didn't give me enough?

"I think I need closure," he says, choking up. "I need a reason to let you go, because obviously, knowing that your heart is with someone else isn't enough. Tell me you're better off without me. Tell me you're happier when you're with him.

Tell me you don't want me anymore. Maybe then I'll be able to move on. I just can't take this pain anymore. I need it to be over."

And there it is—the real reason he's here. Closure. He needs me to give him a reason to let me go. If that's what he came for, I'll give it to him. Maybe then we can both move on. Unfortunately, it'll be separately, but at least we can move on.

Maybe in the future, if we're ever able to mend this rift, we can do a paternity test and things will work themselves out from there. But for now, I just want his heart to stop aching.

3

TREY

The scent of freshly brewed coffee floats through the air. I pry my eyes open to find myself under a blanket I don't recognize. It's fleece, and it smells weird. This isn't my blanket. *Whose the fuck is it then?*

I lurch upward. Something in my neck pinches. It's a kink, probably from sleeping on my couch. *Hold on.* This isn't my couch. It's Arella's couch. *What the hell?*

I shoot up onto my feet. The room spins.

Dizzy.

Wobbly.

I shouldn't have gotten up so fast. I plop back down. Screwing my eyes shut, I rub my temples as a lame attempt to get the hammering in my brain to stop. It doesn't.

When I open my eyes again, I'm still in Arella's apartment. How did I get here? And why am I wearing only boxers?

On Arella's coffee table are a glass of water, my wallet, my phone, and two small pills. *Are the pills meant for me?* They look like Ordinary pills. Well, of course they're Ordinary pills. Arella wouldn't have Zordinary ones. Zordi bodies process Ordinary medicines too quickly for them to work on us.

I down the glass of water within seconds. It refreshes my

dry throat—sort of. I could probably have another glass or two. Maybe it'll get rid of the spinning.

"Morning."

I jerk my head toward the voice. It's Arella, sitting at her small dining table, eyeing me with a hesitant look. *Damn, she's gorgeous.* Her wavy chestnut hair is tied into a braid falling over one shoulder. Her dark purple dress drops to the middle of her thighs. It shows off her slender legs. I have the urge to trail my fingertips up her thighs and lick every part of—*She's still wearing it.* The necklace with the golden angel wings. She's still wearing it.

"How do you feel?" she asks in her usual honeyed tone.

"Shitty." My voice comes out raspy. *Definitely need more water.* "What happened last night?"

"What do you remember?"

The last thing I remember is being a tragic wreck on my couch, guzzling as much forget-her-juice as possible. Judging by the way I woke up half naked in Arella's apartment, I'd say the juice didn't work.

I must take too long to respond, because she says, "You came over late last night. You were a little drunk."

I'm too nauseous to have only been *a little* drunk. Usually when I drink that much, I pass out for hours. I've never driven myself somewhere. I must not have drunk enough to completely shut down my body. Either that or drunk me had a very determined one-track mind.

"Did I talk a lot last night?" I ask, unsure if I want the answer.

"A little."

"What did I say?"

She lifts a shoulder. "Nothing, really."

I can't tell if she's lying or not. With her, I never know. It's one of the many reasons why this woman is still a mystery to me.

"Do you want some coffee?" she asks.

"I thought you don't like coffee?"

"I don't. I bought some a while ago in case you ever wanted some."

That was thoughtful of her. How long ago did she get this coffee for me? Why did she even care to get it? Was it before or after she slept with that other guy?

I sigh heavily and push down the pain. I guess it doesn't matter *when* she got it. What matters is that she made it for me, and it smells delicious. "Yeah, I'll have some, please."

She disappears into her kitchen. After some rustling around, she comes to me and sets a steaming mug on her coffee table.

She's so beautiful. I wish I could have her again. Just one more day. Actually, no. Every day—for the rest of my life. Any less won't be enough.

"Where are my clothes?" *Wait . . . did we have sex last night?* I'll be pissed if we did and I don't remember it.

"In the dryer. They were wet, so I washed them for you. They should be done soon. Your shoes and jacket are by the door. Hopefully, they're dry now."

I lift the coffee to my face and take a whiff. I'm glad she knows I like my coffee black without having to ask. Like how I know she likes her salads with the dressing on the side. Her pasta with white sauces, never red. Her strawberries cut into halves, never quarters, because, apparently, they taste different.

She also likes the toilet paper going over, never under. To her, I do it wrong. Apparently, reloading the toilet paper whatever way it happens to be facing is weird. What else is weird, at least to her, is the way I cover my pancakes with whipped cream until I can't see the pancakes anymore. I don't think that's *that* weird. What's actually weird is that she pours her milk in before the cereal. Like seriously? Who does that?

"How did my clothes get wet?" I want to drink the coffee,

but the side of the mug tells me it's way too hot right now, so I set it back onto the table.

"You really don't remember anything, do you?" She takes a seat on the other side of the couch.

"Not a thing." I groan, mostly because she's never sat so far from me before. The space is maddening.

"You walked here. In the rain."

I raise an eyebrow at her that says, *Come on. Really?* When her deadpan expression doesn't falter, I let out a low chuckle. "I must have been insane."

"I think you just needed someone to talk to."

I hope I didn't say anything stupid. My past drunk experiences tell me I probably did. According to Liz, the saying "A drunk man's words are a sober man's thoughts" rings true for me.

Liz and I are so close that a lot of people think we have romantic feelings for each other. Whenever Liz wants to shut them up, she tells them the story of the time I got so drunk, I booty-called her at two in the morning. Except, it wasn't a booty call at all.

According to her, I begged her to come over because I had something important to tell her that could only be said in person. When she arrived, I spent the next hour lamenting over how much I loved her, as a friend of course, and how if she ever disowned me, I'd jump off a cliff. Not once did I make a move. Liz says that if drunk me wasn't interested in her sexually, then sober me isn't either.

I sure as hell am interested in Arella that way, though, which is why I'm glad I didn't force myself on her last night. *At least, I hope I didn't.*

I don't want to be away from her, but my bladder is killing me. "Can I use your bathroom?"

"Of course."

After a long piss, I wash my hands and examine myself in

the mirror. I look like hell. Messy hair, pale face, and saggy eye bags. *No wonder she left me. Who'd want this?*

I do a quick sniff test to check my breath. *Gross.* It smells like rancid food that's been in a Tupperware for two weeks too long.

I crack the door open. "Arella?"

She answers from the living room. "Yeah?"

"Is my toothbrush still here?"

"Top left drawer."

I pull it open to find a bunch of those free toothbrushes from the dentist, still in the package. Next to those is the one I used the one time I stayed over. I scrub my mouth out with it. Once I'm done, I do another sniff test. *Much better.* It no longer smells like alcohol. The last thing I want is to trigger bad memories for her. *Damn it.* I probably did last night. I'll have to ask her if I did, so I can apologize for it.

I place the toothbrush next to hers, then twist around to dry my hands off. The towel rack is empty. Instead of a towel, what greets me is a giant hole in the wall. *Did I do that?* I can't tell how fresh it is.

I feel around the floor for any debris. Nothing. Maybe she cleaned it up. Maybe that's why there's no towel. Maybe she used the towel to wipe up the mess I made.

I pat my hands off on my boxers, then ball up my punching fist. My heart races as I insert it into the hole. It fits. *Fuck.*

I'm prone to violence when I'm drunk, but *never* have I directed it at a woman. If I tried to have sex with Arella last night and she denied me, would I have hit her? If I did, I'll never forgive myself.

I crack the door open again. "Arella?"

"Yeah?"

"Can you come here?"

Her soft footsteps shuffle across the carpet until she appears in the doorway.

"Did I hurt you last night?" I stare into her eyes, trying to figure out her emotions. I can't allow her to lie to me about this one. Like always, I sense nothing, and her blank expression gives me no answers.

"No," she answers easily.

I scan her face for any bruises, then her arms. *Clear. Clear.* I'm tempted to rip that dress off her body so I can check the rest of her. "Are you sure?"

"Yeah, I'm sure."

"Then where the hell did that come from?" I point a firm finger at the gaping hole.

She hesitates, and it scares me. Maybe she's too afraid to admit I hurt her, like it'll spare my feelings or some shit. *Hell no.* Fuck my feelings. If I hurt her, I need to know so I can make sure it never happens again.

I cup her face and tilt her head up to stare her dead in the eyes. "Babe, if I hurt you, you can tell me. I'll make it right."

"You didn't hurt me, Trey. That was from Nathan a long time ago."

I think she's telling the truth. If so, how have I never seen this hole before? I guess, now that I think about it, I haven't been in her bathroom much. The first time was when I shoved her ex into the bathtub. I was too focused on making sure he knew who was in charge to even look at the walls. The time after that was when I stayed over. She must have kept this hole concealed with a towel.

I let out a breath, then release her from my grasp. "You've gotta tell me if he ever tries to touch you again, okay? It doesn't matter what time, or day, or place I'm at. Call me and I'll come running. Understand?"

She nods with a look in her eyes I don't recognize. All that time spent studying this woman, and here I am, still trying to figure her out.

Together, we make our way back to her living room,

where I dump myself over her couch. My brain rattles inside my skull. I should have sat down slower.

"The dryer has about ten minutes left." Arella sits, still keeping space between us. "Are you hungry? I could make you some breakfast?"

"Why are you being so nice to me? After the way I spoke to you last week, I don't deserve your kindness. I can't even believe you allowed me in last night."

"I wasn't going to leave you out in the rain."

I scoff. "You should have."

She fidgets with the end of her braid, looking anywhere but at me. I can't feel it, but I know she's sad. She's usually pretty smiley around me, and now she's not.

Make her feel better. How? *Apologize.* For what? *For being a worthless piece of shit. For doing whatever it was that made her turn to someone else.*

"Arella . . ." I say softly. "I'm sorry for being such an ass to you."

She nods, pursing her lips. "Yeah, you were an ass."

A tiny smile spreads across my lips. I've never heard her say that word before.

"I'm also sorry for, ya know . . . what you saw." I run a hand through my hair, pulling at it. "I shouldn't have allowed her to—I just wasn't thinking straight because . . . you told me that you're pr—" *Breathe.* "It's impossible for . . ." *Deep breath.* "I felt so . . ." *Crushed.* My hands shake. I fold them together as if it'll stop the shaking. "Sorry. I'm not good at this."

"I get your point."

The room goes quiet. She focuses her attention on the floor while I focus all my attention on her. Little wisps of hair fall from her braid, framing cheeks that I want so badly to kiss. Just last week, I was picking her up, tossing her over my shoulder, and carrying her to my bedroom to kiss every inch of her. Now she's carrying a tiny human inside her that she'll be kissing within nine months. It's crazy how fast things can change—and not in my favor. There's a *very* short list of the things I wouldn't do to make that baby mine.

"Have you told him?" I try to keep my tone impassive as if thinking of her with someone else isn't killing me at all.

She looks up at me. "Huh?"

I glance at her stomach, then back up at her face. "The father. Have you told him?"

Her answer comes too quickly. "Yeah."

I expected her to say something about how *I* am the father. She didn't deny the infidelity this time. Is this it? Is she done denying it? Am I finally going to hear the truth from her lips?

"How did he take it?"

She shrugs nonchalantly. "He wasn't too happy about it."

My voice cracks as I find the courage to ask, "Who is he?"

She doesn't miss a beat. "Some guy I reconnected with from college."

Seriously? She threw away our passionate, sappy romance-movie-worthy relationship for *some guy?* I thought hearing her admit it would make me feel better. It doesn't. The wound has only gotten deeper.

"What's his—never mind. I don't wanna know his name." I'll probably end up in z-prison for crimes even the Enforcers would throw up reading about. "When did it start?"

"A while ago."

"When?" I snap.

She lets out a long sigh. "It—it was before I started living with you."

I guess that makes sense, but . . . "How did you ever find the time to see him once you moved in? We were always together."

"Sometimes I got off work early and didn't tell you."

That makes my throat tighten. How many times did she leave work early to bang him, then came home to me, acting all innocent?

The clock on her wall reads nine thirty. She's usually at work by now.

"Are you off today?" I ask, desperate to change the subject.

"My nanny family is on vacation right now, and I don't work at the daycare anymore."

"Why not?"

She stares at her lap as she picks at her fingernails. "They, um, let me go."

"What for?" Arella works hard, and she's great with kids. I can't imagine why they'd fire her.

"Overstaffed," she says coolly. "I was just one of the many people they chose to cut."

Overstaffed? I thought they were *under*staffed. At least, that's what I gathered from the many conversations I overheard between her and Javina. Either way, if Arella's down a job, that means she needs money.

Wait . . . Is that why she came home early that day? Was that the day they fired her? No wonder she told me to pay child support. She's gonna need it. But what about the father of her child? Shouldn't he be—*Oh no.*

My heart sinks into my stomach. "Is he staying with you . . . and the—um, baby?"

She keeps picking at her fingernails like there's something stuck under there when I know there isn't. Patiently, I wait for an answer. It never comes.

"Arella?"

She still doesn't look at me.

I lean in closer to her. "Arella, please, tell me he's planning to take care of you."

A single teardrop rolls down her cheek as she sucks in a deep breath. She wipes it away with the back of her hand. "No, he's not."

"That son of a bitch." Nothing could ever get me to leave my child. Not money. Not a death threat. Nothing.

Growing up without parents is something I'd never wish on anyone.

I was the kid who got stuck hearing about all the presents the other kids woke up to on Christmas mornings. All I ever woke up to was another day of wishing my parents weren't dead. Other kids had things like family dinners and birthday parties. I had an abusive uncle who banished me to my room just for breathing the wrong way. Other kids spent their childhoods riding bikes and playing video games. I spent mine doing odd jobs so I could make enough money to buy myself new clothes. A hard life is not what I want for this child.

I have to do something. "Go get me your bank account and routing number."

Arella's face crumples. "Why?"

"I'll send you some money." Ten grand should be enough, right? How about fifty? I know nothing about how much it costs to raise a child. A hundred grand? A million?

Last week, in the heat of the moment, I told Arella she wouldn't be getting a dime from me to support another man's child. Now here I am, about to transfer her a million dollars. I guess her scheme worked. Pretend not to want my money, with hopes that I'll hand it over myself. *Genius.* I don't even care. I'll sleep better knowing she's got enough to take care of herself and this baby.

"I don't want your money," she says.

"What?" I expected her to jump up to retrieve those bank numbers for me. "Arella, you're down a job, expecting an infant, and that good-for-nothing girlfriend thief has run away. What the hell are you gonna do?"

"I'll figure it out. I always have."

"Just go get me those numbers." I wave a shooing hand at her, then I grab my phone off the coffee table. I've already got my online bank account username typed in when she crosses her arms over her chest.

"I said I don't want your money."

I swear this woman makes it a point to be difficult. My tone comes out rough. "If you're not gonna accept it for yourself or the baby, then do it for me. I promise you, there are no strings att—"

"I said no."

I groan and chuck my phone back onto the table. "You don't make any sense. Why would you screw around, get pregnant, try to convince me it's mine, then refuse to accept any money? What are you trying to gain?"

"Nothing."

I'm losing my mind. "Is this some kind of sick game to you? Playing with my heart?"

She dips her eyebrows at me like she's offended. "No."

"Do you just enjoy torturing me?"

"Of course not."

I throw my hands into the air. "Then what? Why won't you take my money?"

"Because!" she yells. "I don't want it!"

The room goes silent.

I feel like shit, and it's not from the hangover. I shouldn't have raised my voice at her. I want to apologize, but what ends up coming out is a broken "What was I missing?"

"Huh?"

"You know . . ." I choke up a little. "What does *he* have that I don't?"

She lets out an exasperated groan. "I don't want to talk about this anymore."

My tone goes soft and desperate. "Please, Arella. Just tell me." *And don't try to spare my feelings. I'm already a fucking mess.*

"I don't know, Trey."

"Yes, you do. There was obviously *something* that made you choose him over me. What was it?"

"I don't know. I guess he just . . . he just made me happy."

An invisible dagger stabs me right in the chest. I swallow,

but it does nothing to ease the ache. My gaze falls to my feet. "I . . . I . . . I thought *I* made you happy."

At least, she *seemed* happy. She laughed a lot. I made it a point to get her to smile as much as I could. What could I have done more?

I should stop asking her questions, because every answer she gives only breaks me more. The smart thing to do would be to leave. I got what I wanted: to hear the truth from her. I should be done here. So why don't I want to go?

I've never been known to do the smart thing, so I ask another question. "Do you love him?"

She gets to her feet. "I'm done with this."

I steal her hand, pulling her back down. She comes willingly, and I lift her chin to look her in the eyes. "Arella, please. Tell me. Do you love him?"

"No."

It might be foolish of me, but I believe her. The sincerity in her eyes tells me it's the truth, and I'm relieved. On the back of our photo, she wrote that she loves *me*, not him. As pathetic as it is, I want that to be true.

A loud, mechanic buzzing sound comes from her hallway, startling me.

"That's the dryer." She releases herself from my grasp. I'm left feeling hollow as she disappears from my sight.

She returns with my clothes in hand. They're warm as I dress myself. *I guess this is my cue to leave.*

I shove my phone and wallet into my pockets. "Where are my keys?"

"You walked here, remember?"

"Oh, that's right." I press a hand against the side of the coffee mug I forgot I had. It's cooled down enough for me to drink, so I down it all in one breath.

"Would you like a ride home?" she asks as I rinse the mug out in her kitchen sink.

"No, thanks." I don't deserve anything she's got to offer.

"Can I call you an Uber?" she asks as I slip into my shoes. They're still kinda damp. I shove my feet in anyway.

"I can walk."

"That's a long walk, Trey."

"I'll be fine. Thanks again for the coffee." I open the door, then turn to get one last look at her. She's hugging herself in a way that makes me want to hold her. She only ever hugs herself like that when something's wrong. I don't wanna leave. I also don't have any reason to stay, so I suck it up and step out.

The bright-ass sun scorches my pupils, making my head spin. I only get four steps away from Arella's door before realizing I'm too fucking hungover to be doing this. What makes me think I can walk home when I can barely see straight? Add the heavy burning in my chest, and I'm in no condition to be walking anywhere.

I drag my phone out to call an Uber, then stop. I wanted a reason to keep seeing her, didn't I?

Knock-knock.

She answers the door immediately, as if she was just on the other side, waiting for me to come back. She gazes up at me with wide eyes, looking so adorable, I could pick her up, crash my lips against hers, and never let her go.

Resisting the urge to do all that, I scratch the back of my head. "So, um, on second thought, I'd appreciate a lift."

Without a word, she nods and grabs her purse.

I slouch into her passenger seat as I glare out the window. The blazing sun is still burning my eyes. Arella doesn't turn the radio on as she backs her car out of its parking spot.

I bought her this car three weeks ago. At that time, I would have bought her anything she wanted. Apparently, I'm still willing to do that. If she calls me up tomorrow, next month, or even years from now asking for money, I'll hand it over in a heartbeat, no questions asked.

If for some reason I'm broke, I'll get a fucking job just to be able to send her something. One way or another, I will make sure Arella's baby is taken care of. If she won't accept my money now, she'll be accepting a mountain of diapers on her doorstep in nine months.

The silence between us has never been louder. Typically, when we're in the car, we're holding hands or I've got my palm over her thigh. Right now, we might as well be on separate ends of the earth.

At our first stoplight, Arella breaks the silence. "How would you like me to give you monthly payments for this car?"

"Don't worry 'bout it."

"I told you, Trey, I won't be accepting this car if you don't accept payments for it."

"And I told you it's a gift. No matter what the circumstances are, that hasn't changed."

The traffic light turns green, then she eases onto the gas. "Since I'm assuming you won't be cashing any checks with my name on it, I'll just drop off some cash for you once a month in an envelope."

I shut my eyes and rub my forehead. "I swear, it's like you do everything in your power to be difficult."

"I wouldn't have to be difficult if you didn't make everything so complicated."

I jerk my head back and point at my chest. "Me? *I* make everything complicated?"

"Yes. I never asked you to buy me a car. I mean, who gifts their girlfriend a brand-new car after only knowing them for two months?"

"I didn't buy you this damn car to complicate anything. I bought it to fix a problem. You needed a vehicle, so I got you one."

"Which I want to pay you back for."

I huff. "Arella, if I find any cash on my doorstep, I will take every cent of it plus triple to buy you a crib made of gold and baby clothes imported from a fucking palace. Do you understand?" I expect her to give in. I want her to. Of course, she doesn't.

"Fine. In that case, I'll be leaving this car in your driveway next week with the keys in it after I buy myself a new one."

I shake my head, biting my lip. "You're so goddamn difficult."

She simply stares out the windshield. "So are you."

"We can fight about this all you want, but I'm telling you, if this car is left in my driveway, I'm driving it straight back to your place. We can play that game for as long as it takes for you to get it through your head that this vehicle is yours and I don't want anything for it."

The car goes quiet until Arella chuckles to herself.

Obviously, I've missed the joke. "What's so funny?"

"Whenever we argue, it's always over paying for things. We fought for days when you first bought me this car. We even bickered in the middle of a grocery store at four in the morning over who was buying all those pregnancy tests. Now here we are, *still* fighting because I want to feel independent and you refuse to allow it."

That stings. How many times do I have to explain to her that I don't buy her things to take away her independence? "Arella, I have enough liquid cash to buy you private jets, superyachts, and a mansion the size of a castle. Buying you a car doesn't make even the slightest dent in my bank account. Don't you want to save your hard-earned money for more important things?" *Like, you know . . . a baby?*

"Well, I—" She stops because a vibration comes from my pocket.

I dig my phone out. It's Victor. *Shit.* When I spoke to him three days ago, I promised I'd have more answers to explain Arella's immunity within the week. I haven't told him that she left me, because he's not going to accept that as a valid excuse not to have answers. *What the hell am I gonna do?*

"Is that your uncle?"

I shove the device back into my jeans. "Yep."

"You're not going to answer it?"

"Nope."

"Is it because he's calling during regular-people time?"

That makes the corners of my lips tick up. I like how quippy she can be. I also like that even after we've been arguing, she can still make me smile. "Contrary to what you believe, my uncle and I *can* have conversations during regular-people hours."

"News to me."

Not long ago, Arella questioned me about my late-night phone calls with my uncle. That was also the night she asked me about my tinted windows, how I don't sleep as often as she does, and how my body can heal so fast.

Many Zordi homes have tinted windows so we can use our powers freely without our neighbors spotting it. Zordis only need to sleep every other evening, and our bodies can heal wounds three times faster than the average Ordinary. Couple that with the healing products my parents invented, and we can fix broken limbs within hours.

Arella noticed all of these abnormal-to-Ordinaries things about me. I didn't want to lie, so I never gave her an explanation. I can see why the Superiors forbid us from having close relationships with Ordinaries, because after a while, it gets hard to hide even the littlest things. Like our enhanced eyesight and our natural ability to regulate our body temperature.

The second Arella turns her car into my driveway, my heart races. Our time together is almost over. I don't want it to end yet. "Do you wanna come in and grab your st—"

"No."

I didn't get to finish my sentence, but okay. "Stay here then. I'll get it all for you."

She shakes her head and puts the car into park. "I don't want it. Any of it."

"What about your clothes? Your blanket? Your purple teddy bear?"

"You bought all those things for me."

"Not *all* of it." I unbuckle my seat belt. It makes a *zip* sound as it retracts upward.

"Maybe some clothes are mine, but you bought me that blanket and the bear."

"I bought them *for you*, so they belong to you."

"No," she says sternly. "They belong to you."

I don't think this woman understands how gifts work. News flash: Once it's been gifted, it no longer belongs to the gifter. "I want you to have them."

"Fine, then I want you to have this." She grabs her purse, drags her car key out, and tosses it onto my lap.

I scowl at it before chucking the damn thing behind me. It lands with a light thud against the backseat. "This car is yours, and that's final."

"Fine, then take this." She reaches behind her neck, and before I can stop her, the angel wings are detached from her body. She holds the diamond out to me on a straight arm.

I glance at her, then at the necklace, then back at her. My words come out like a shattered reflection of my heart. "Are you trying to hurt me?"

"Are you trying to hurt *me*?"

"No. I just want you to have your things back." That's not true. Really, I'm looking for any reason to prolong our time together, and apparently, arguing with her is what I went with.

"I want you to have your things back too." She shakes the jewelry. The tiny engraving on the back catches my eye. *Paris?* *T.G.* I envisioned the rest of my life with her in Paris. Right now, that life feels so far away.

I clench my jaw to keep from punching something, then I snatch the necklace from her. Without a word, I lean in to hook it back where it belongs.

She doesn't move as my fingertips graze her soft skin.

Being this close to her is dangerous. I'm about to put my lips all over her neck. Her sweet lavender scent is making me lose control over my thoughts and even my hands. The diamond slips from my grasp and lands on her lap. She remains still as my trembling fingers pluck it back up and I try again.

Not once does she fight me as I take my sweet time getting the clasp to work—surprising, considering she's spent this entire morning doing the opposite of everything I want. Maybe she wants to keep the necklace as much as I want her to keep it. *A man can hope.*

Once the jewelry is back around her neck, I take her hands into mine and gaze deeply into her eyes as a silent plea for her not to rip it off.

When she doesn't, I lower my voice to almost a whisper. "I'll keep your stuff, Arella. Just please, keep the necklace."

4

———————

TREY

I'm fucked. Completely fucked.

Victor has called two more times since Arella dropped me off this morning. I didn't pick up. I can't. Not without something good to tell him.

When he assigned me this mission, one of the first things he said was "Don't fuck this up."

I was determined not to. Back then, my mission seemed simple.

Step one: Get close to this twenty-two-year-old woman to find out the source of her immunity.

Step two: Replicate it, and use it to destroy the people who killed my parents.

Step three: Live out the rest of my life knowing my parents would be proud of me for finishing the research they started before they died.

Thing is, I haven't even completed step one. The moment I found out that whatever tests Victor performed on the last two Immunes killed them, my mission was over. I switched my focus from trying to discover the source of Arella's immunity to protecting it. Maybe Victor's willing to risk innocent lives for a greater cause, but I'm not. Especially not Arella's.

56

Suddenly, it hits me: I've been making a huge mistake.

I've been so down in the dumps over our breakup that I've forgotten the bigger picture: No matter what Arella has done, she still needs my protection. She still needs me to keep Victor away from her. *What the hell am I doing here? I need to get that woman on a plane and fly her as far away from here as possible.*

I launch off the toilet I've been sitting on for the last forty-some minutes, give myself a shake, then pull my pants up. After washing my hands, I check the time on my phone. *Wow, it's late . . . 12:53 a.m. What the fuck did I do all day?* Nothing, that's what. I spent all day sulking over the bullshit I call my life when I should have been working out a plan to get Arella to safety.

Since we're not on the best terms right now, I don't know how I can convince her to run away with me. Maybe that should be the first step of my new plan: Make things right with her. I'll buy her the biggest bouquet of flowers I can find and show up on her doorstep with it first thing in the morning. I'll apologize for everything that happened. I'll confess that I'm in love with her and that I have been for a while. She'll forgive me, right? She has to.

Once I've won her back, I'll convince her to go to Paris with me. If she refuses, I'll try convincing her to help me find my parents' safe house. On a password-protected voice recording hidden in my childhood teddy bear, my parents left me instructions on how to find an underground hideout. The only problem is that I've listened to the recording about a hundred times now, and I still can't figure out where the safe house is.

Maybe this safe house thing isn't the greatest idea. Plus, I don't have time to sit around trying to convince Arella of anything. That woman is too stubborn for her own good.

How about I simply ask her to go on vacation with me? I'll take her somewhere tropical, where she can enjoy a nice view from our resort window. I just won't tell her that we won't be coming back. *Damn.* I'm pretty sure that's called kidnapping. Maybe she won't see it that way if she's sipping mocktails on a beach with her feet in the sand.

All right. That's the plan.

Step one: Win my girl back.

Step two: Take her on vacation.

Step three: Drinks on a beach.

Easy peasy, lemon squeezy.

I'd like to think I can wait until the sun rises to start my new plan, but I'm too impatient for that, so I stand at the kitchen counter with my phone on speaker.

My heart pounds with each ring Arella doesn't pick up. I know it's late, but I had to give it a shot. Maybe she's still up. Maybe she—

"Hello?"

My breath hitches at the sound of her voice. "Arella?"

"Yeah?" She doesn't sound like she's been sleeping. Not that I would have felt bad for waking her up anyway.

"Um, it's me."

"I know. There's a really cool feature on phones nowadays where a person's name pops up whenever they call."

"I wasn't sure if you'd pick up since it's so late." *And because of the way we ended things this morning.*

"You've got a bad habit of making calls outside of regular-people hours, don't you?"

"That's only with my uncle." *And Liz.*

"Is everything okay?" She sounds genuinely concerned. I hate when people give a fuck about me, because I don't deserve anyone's concern. But when it comes to Arella, I want her to give all the fucks in the world.

"Not really." *Nothing's okay when I'm apart from you.*

"What's wrong?"

The words fly out of my mouth before my brain can register that I'm even saying them. "I miss you."

It takes her a few heartbeats to respond. When she does, it sounds tearful. "I miss you too."

I can't hide my shock. "You do?"

"I do."

Those two words give me so much hope. "I want you back, Arella."

A long pause, then she clears her throat. "Are you drunk again?"

"Nope. I'm completely sober."

"You really want me back? Even after I told you that I slept with a guy from college?"

Ouch. I could have gone forever and a day without ever hearing her admit that out loud again. I choke up a little. "Are you done with him?"

She only hesitates for a second. "Yeah."

"Like, completely? You don't plan to ever see him again? Or talk to him?"

"No."

"Ever?"

"Ever."

Maybe it's stupid of me, but I believe her. "Do you think you can forgive me for being a dick to you?"

"I already have." The way she doesn't miss a beat gives me confidence that she means it. "Do you think you'll ever forgive me?"

I don't miss a beat either. "I already have."

I've only been on this call with her for a minute, and hope is already filling me to the brim. Things are going so well. At this rate, we'll be sipping drinks on a beach by tomorrow night.

"Can I come see you in the morning?" I ask, but what I really want to ask is *Can I come over right now?*

There's a long pause before she says, "Trey, I think we have some important things to talk about before we start thinking about getting back together."

She doesn't need to say what for me to know what *things* she's referring to. Little does she know, I was ready to be a father to her baby since the night I found out she was pregnant. We just had a little hump to get over, and now that we are over it, I'm thrilled for this next step.

I want to have a family. More so, I want to have a family with Arella. I picture myself holding a child. I imagine the tiny human calling me *daddy*. If it's a girl, I'll vow to protect her with my life. If it's a boy, can I teach him to be a better man than me? That probably wouldn't be too hard. I've set the bar pretty low.

I sigh and slump my elbows onto the counter. "Do you think I'd make a good father?"

"Why wouldn't you?"

"Because I don't know anything about it. I've never even held a baby. How am I supposed to know how to take care of one?"

"Nobody really knows what they're doing until they do it. Babies are a learning process." The way she says all that gives me faith that I can do this. If it's something I can learn, I'm ready for the challenge.

"Don't they have classes or some shit I can take about parenting?"

The sound of Arella's giggle feels like a warm sunny day after a week of freezing rain. "*You* would take a parenting class?"

"Not alone, but I'd do it with you."

"Trey, I want you to really, *really* think about what you'd be getting yourself into. Having a baby means you can't do whatever you want whenever you want. Life changes when you have a mini human to take care of. It's a lifetime commitment. Are you sure you're ready for that?"

I don't have to think about it. "Yes, baby. I'm ready. I can't guarantee I'll win Best Dad of the Year, but you can bet your ass I'll fight for it."

I'll also fight to keep our relationship off the zovernment's radar. I don't know how yet, but I'll figure it out. All I know, without a doubt, is that I am meant to be with this woman. And nothing is going to stop me.

My phone vibrates. I don't have to look to know who's calling.

"I've gotta go, babe. Is it cool for me to come over in the morning? We can talk about this some more. Maybe look for some parenting classes coming up in the area? I could take you to some bookstores, and we could find some reading material?"

"That sounds wonderful."

I can almost hear the smile spreading across her lips and lifting her cheeks. I feel a thousand pounds lighter already. "Text me the second you wake up, 'kay? I'll come over right away."

After she agrees, I tell her good night, then switch calls just in time.

"Where the fuck have you been, kid?" Victor says through a mouthful of something crunchy. "This is the tenth time I've called today."

It's actually the fourth time, but whatever. "I forgot my phone at home and was out all day." My lie sounds pretty convincing.

"I need you to come to base."

Fuck that. I don't wanna be anywhere near Shadow Ridge right now. "What for?"

"I'm putting you on a new anti-Royals assignment. We need three agents on it, and one of the men I originally assigned to this didn't pass his onboarding tests. You're next on the list."

"What about my current mission?" *The one I've been ignoring for weeks.*

"This new mission is entry-level shit. You can handle both. Besides, you haven't been making any advancements on your current mission. Might as well make yourself useful. The briefing starts in thirty minutes."

The way he says all that means I don't have a choice. He's not *asking* me if I want to accept this new assignment so much as he's *telling* me. "Thirty minutes? I live three hours away."

"Maybe if you had answered your fucking phone, I could have given you more notice. I'll send a Teleporter. Text me your coordinates." *Click.*

Growing up, I begged my uncle to make me a ZIRDA agent. It was my dream to work for the anti-Royals department so I could help bring down the violent organized crime group who blew up my parents.

When I was nine, Victor put me through training where I learned how to throw a proper punch and to control my powers better. He kept saying that once I turned eighteen, he'd assign me my first mission. When that birthday finally came, he told me to get lost.

A few months ago, Victor called me out of the blue to assign me Arella's mission. He said, "It's top secret, typically for level-five agents, but if you think you won't fuck it up, I'll give it to you."

I was ecstatic to be handed such an honor and to be told I could skip the onboarding process. Now I'm being spoon-fed another mission, and I'd rather gouge my eyes out with chopsticks. Can Victor seriously not find any other agent to work this one? I've got more important things to do—like get Arella away from him.

My phone buzzes with a text from Victor.

> We'll be meeting in room 409. Your coordinates?

With a sigh, I Google what my coordinates are and text it to him.

Within seconds, a loud *pop!* bursts into my ears like

someone's cracked a whip right next to me. I wince and cover both ears.

A slender guy who looks barely nineteen appears in my kitchen. The zense in my chest tingles, telling me what I already know.

"Sorry, bro," he says. "I've gotten used to the sound. Barely hear it no more. You must be Big V's nephew."

"Yep."

"You got everything you need on you?"

"Give me a sec to get some shoes on." I head to the garage door where my shoes are, then return to the kitchen to find the dude staring at my living room.

"Where's your TV?"

"Don't have one."

"The fuck do you do all day then?"

I let out an exasperated sigh. "Are you here to judge me for my lack of screen entertainment, or are you here to take me to the Ridge?"

"Right." He holds out his skinny arm to me. "You ever been teleported before?"

"A few times."

"Super. Whatever you do, don't let go."

Reluctantly, I grab onto his arm. Without any warning whatsoever, that loud *pop!* startles me again. It's more painful this time. I'm about to cover my ears until I remember that I can't let go.

My vision blurs, and my ears ring. The sound stops when my feet hit a hard surface.

Icy-cold liquid drenches me from above. The Teleporter tugs me away from the waterfall.

"Sorry, bro. Missed the mark by a few steps."

I spit water out of my mouth, then rub away the wetness on my face. The familiar dark cavern hidden behind the waterfall greets me with a sneering *Why are you back?* I'm wondering the same damn thing. Of all the places I want to be right now, this isn't it. Especially not while wearing cold, drenched clothes. Still, I follow the Teleporter into the black of the cavern.

"You wouldn't happen to be a Pyro, would you?" he asks. "My phone's dead, so I can't use the flashlight."

If he typically uses his phone for light, that means he's either a Hydro, an Aero, or a Terra, who produces rock balls instead of lightning balls. I answer his question by making some flames appear in my palm and throwing them ahead of us.

"Thanks." The guy gestures a hand forward. "After you."

We continue down the cavern with my fireball illuminating the way. The Teleporter doesn't try to make conversation with me, and I'm glad for it. The only sounds are our echoing footsteps and the waterfall fading behind us.

After several minutes, we reach the secret entrance to Shadow Ridge. The door looks like any regular part of the rock wall. I stick my index finger into a little hole and press it against a flat scanning device inside.

Beep! Beep! Beep! A ten-foot section of the wall pushes itself inward, then slides to the left, allowing us inside.

My chest tingles as two security guards approach me, one from either side. One of them is the menacing-looking guy I saw the last time I was here. He's got a scar down his left eyebrow and a scowl that would scare away all children. The other guy, I don't recognize.

Together, they search my body for whatever it is they're told to look for. When they don't find it, they do the same with the Teleporter.

"Clear. You may proceed."

The Teleporter offers the guards a friendly *thanks* before following me to the set of four elevators. We take one of the machines down from floor six to four.

Once the elevator doors slide apart, I step off.

"Do ya know where to go from here?" the Teleporter asks, keeping the elevator open with his arm.

"I got it."

"Super. You were my last pickup for the day, so if ya see Big V, tell him I'll see him later."

"Hold on. How the hell am I gonna get back home?"

The guy shrugs. "All I know is that my shift technically ended at midnight. I just happened to still be around when you needed a lift, so I told Victor I'd do it. If you're still here in the afternoon, I can take ya back then. That's when my next shift starts."

The afternoon? I cannot be here for that long. I have baby-preparation plans with Arella in the morning.

The elevator doors close as I trudge down the hall. With each step I take, my wet shoes squeak over the tile floors and my toes squish against my drenched socks. I fucking hate the feeling of wet socks on my feet.

Following the numbered signs, I make a left, then a right. I arrive at room 409, a small meeting room, to find a young woman in the corner, setting up a zoffee cart. From the back, she doesn't look any older than eighteen. Petite frame. Pale skin. Long brunette hair tied up in a sleek ponytail.

A rectangular table with about ten rolling chairs around it separates me from her. An iPad and some manila folders lie on top of the table. A whiteboard is attached to the back wall, featuring the date Expo-markered in red.

The girl hums to herself as she plugs a coffee machine into the wall.

I knock on the door lightly as an attempt not to scare her. Total fail.

She jumps and flips around, slapping a hand against her chest. "Jesus. You scared me."

I offer her a tiny smile. "Sorry."

"Are you here for the mission briefing?" She's got a soft, mousey voice. It's not irritating to me like most people who talk like that. Hers is more soothing than anything. Like she's teaching a meditation class or trying to relax a baby.

"I am." I step into the room and take a seat in one of the rolling chairs.

"I was told the meeting doesn't start until one thirty." She checks her watch. "It's just past one. You're really early. Would you like some zoffee?"

I haven't had zoffee in forever. It's got enough caffeine in it for Zordis. The Ordinary kind does nothing for us, but it tastes good.

"Black, please."

Steam rises from the mug as she pours a healthy amount of zoffee for me. As she sets the mug down in front of me, my zense activates.

"I've never seen you before," she says with a bright smile that feels more friendly than flirty. I appreciate her for it. "You must be new or a field agent."

"Field agent." I hold my hand out for a shake. "Trey."

"Katie." She accepts my palm with her little hand. As we shake, her eyes go wide and blank. I know that look. It's the same look Liz used to get whenever she touched my hand and my most painful memory invaded her mind.

A rush of anxiety radiates off Katie as she draws her hand back. As if practiced, she erases any evidence from her face that she just used her powers on me and is nervous about it. I'm not in pain, so I'm gonna assume she's got an ability like Liz's that allows her to see into my head. I wonder what she just saw. I'm tempted to ask, but I'm not in the mood to discuss whatever glimpse into my life she just got. None of it is good.

Instead, I feign ignorance. "What's your role here?"

"I'd like to say I'm a field agent too, but for now, I'm just Victor's assistant."

"What do you do for him?"

"Whatever he wants. I run errands around base, deliver

messages, do paperwork here and there." Katie sits in a seat two away from mine and gestures toward my steaming mug. "And I make zoffee. Ya know, the important stuff."

I lift my mug to take a sip. It burns my tongue a little. "Zoffee is important. It takes a skilled person to brew it well."

"Victor says I'm the best at it. He assigned me my first on-base mission today—not because I make good zoffee. I've been asking for a mission for months. I'm super excited about it."

I know she is by her excitement rushing through my head. "What is it?"

She narrows her eyes at me. "You're a field agent. You should know the rules. We don't go into details about missions amongst each other."

"Right. I was just testing you."

"Surrre you were." Katie gestures toward my damp clothing, with her eyebrows pressed together. "So did ya swim here?"

"The Teleporter ported me here right under the waterfall."

She giggles. "Sorry, I don't mean to laugh. That's just kinda funny. You don't seem to mind that you're wet though."

"It's whatever." I do mind, but what can I do about it? It's not like I possess a gift that can make my clothes instantly dry.

Victor appears in the doorway, wearing a dark brown suit. "Katie, the folders, please."

Katie jumps to her feet and grabs the manila folders from the end of the table. She hands them to Victor with a mousey "Here you go, sir."

"Thank you." Victor makes his way around the table to the head seat. Two of his bodyguards station themselves on opposite sides of the room. A third one stands outside the door. "Katie, can you text me updates on your mission as you go today?"

"Yes, sir." She takes her iPad from the table and hugs it against her chest.

"Thanks. Nothing else for now. Feel free to take a break before your assignment arrives. Shouldn't be too long."

I'll never understand how Victor can talk to people so nicely when he always addresses me with revulsion. When I was a young child, Uncle V was my best friend. He'd take me out for pie at two in the morning. We'd ride around the neighborhood on roller skates. We'd have sleepovers at his house and spend hours building blanket forts together.

After Aunt Jodi left him for her soul mate, leaving behind only an apology note, he transformed into the angry man he is today. Now he acts as if looking at me is detrimental to his health. The day he lost her was the day I lost my Uncle V.

Sometimes, I still hold out for the day he returns to that loving uncle I made all those good memories with. Deep under all that bitterness somewhere, way, *way* deep, I'm confident there's that same man who used to treat me like his own son. I'd be lying if I said that when I accepted Arella's mission, I didn't hope my success would bring that man back.

The room is silent after Katie leaves. Neither Victor nor his bodyguards acknowledge my existence, so I take a sip of my zoffee and pretend they don't exist either.

A few awkward minutes later, two field agents join us. They take the chairs across the table from me. One is a stocky short man. The other is a tall blonde woman with tattoos running up and down each arm. Victor chitchats with them for a while with a smile on his face that's never directed at me.

It's just before one thirty when Victor says, "All right. Let's get started."

Good. The faster we start, the faster I can get outta here. I want to be at Arella's apartment as soon as she wakes up.

"The Royals have been getting their hands on powerful weapons," Victor says. "By that, I don't mean guns or tanks. They're collecting Tickers. Anyone know what that is?"

When the other agents shake their heads, I raise my hand. Quickly, I realize it's a mistake.

"What is this? A fucking middle school? Put your goddamn hand down and answer the question."

Resisting the urge to snap back at my uncle, I lower my arm. "It's a Pyro with an illness called smother. Unlike Dormants where their powers just aren't active, Zordis with smother still have active flames. The flames are simply *smothered* as if their skin's a containment system. They can't produce fire outside of their bodies, but inside, those flames and energy build until they eventually explode like a bomb."

Victor nods, the most approval I've gotten from him in years. "The range of a Ticker's explosion is anywhere between five feet to five miles. It incinerates everything in its path."

"Sounds like a bad day for anyone nearby," tattoo lady says.

"Correct, and word on the street is that the Royals have found a way to control when those explosions happen. They've been kidnapping Tickers and using them to attack Ordinary government officials. Did you hear about that bombing in Lisbon six months ago? Authorities never found any traces of explosives. Can you guess why?"

"So," I say, dreading my next words, "the Royals are using unwilling suicide bombers?"

"Exactly." Victor slides a manila folder down the table to each person.

In mine is a blurry picture of an Asian woman standing outside a grocery store. The photo is paperclipped to a single sheet of paper with the name *Kim Nguyen* on it. Under that are the words *somewhere in Nevada*. There's no home address, no other names, not even a clue as to where or when the picture was taken. *What the fuck?*

When I received Arella's manila folder, it was loaded with hours' worth of reading material. I wouldn't be so pissed about this folder if the other agents didn't clearly have multiple photos to work with, paperclipped to stacks and stacks of information.

Victor continues, "Ever since word got out that the Royals are kidnapping Tickers, the Tickers have gone into hiding. Unfortunately, that makes it harder for us to track them down and protect them. Each of you has been assigned a different Ticker. Your job is to find them before the Royals do and bring them here for safety."

"What if they don't want to come?" I ask.

"Then you force them."

My face twists into hard lines. "So you want us to kidnap them?"

Victor shoots me a lethal glare. "Would you rather the Royals do so first? Better us than them, right?"

I mean, he has a point, but I still don't like the idea of taking someone by force. It's always bothered me that ZIRDA is willing to end ten lives to save ten thousand. When I was a kid, I thought I'd understand it when I grew up. Here I am at twenty-six, and I still don't understand it.

For the next two hours, the four of us brainstorm tactics we can use to find these Tickers and bring them to base. I'm not sure how Victor thinks I can find someone when all I've got is a blurry photo and a common name for a Vietnamese woman. The other agents have things like places of employment and names of relatives. I'm pretty sure Victor assigned the hardest Ticker to me with hopes that I'll fail.

Wait . . . What if that's why he assigned Arella's mission to me? What if he knew that finding an explanation to her immunity was a wild goose chase from the start? If so, what's his game? Why would he want me to get close to Arella if discovering the source of her immunity is impossible?

The meeting finally ends around seven in the morning. Six hours. Six whole fucking hours of pretending to be interested in a mission I have no intention of even starting. By tonight, I'll be on a beach, sipping out of pineapples with my girl.

After tossing the manila folder into the trash, I fold up the photo of Kim Nguyen with her single sheet of useless information and stick it into my back pocket. Then I rush out of the meeting room without saying a word to anyone.

Somehow, I need to find a way back home. First things first though; I gotta find a bathroom. We weren't given a single break throughout that entire meeting, and I consumed four cups of zoffee.

I find a bathroom down the hall and stumble into it. My head spins as I unzip my semi-dry jeans. When I finish peeing, I'm woozy as hell. I have to slap my palm against a wall just to steady myself on my way to the sinks. Nausea rises up my stomach as I wash my hands. I'm about to dry them off when vomit races up my throat.

I half run, half stagger past the urinals and back into the first stall. My knees hit the floor just as I throw myself over the toilet bowl and cough. Nothing comes out. I cough again, gagging as my body convulses like it wants to puke, but it doesn't. I wish *something* would come up, because at least then, I'd feel a little better.

For who knows how long, I gag into the toilet bowl, trying to cough up my intestines. After a while, my chest hurts from heaving and my throat's dry as fuck. *I need water, stat!* The cafeteria is two floors down. I could get water from there if my body would stop shaking.

I feel like I've been on a plane for an hour while the pilot does flips in the air. *What the hell is going on?* Was it something I ate? I haven't eaten much lately because of my lack of appetite. For dinner, I had a granola bar. Beyond that, all I've had is zoffee. Was there something in that? The other agents and Victor had zoffee from the same brew I did. Are any of them sick? Whatever this is, it's almost as bad as—I gasp. *The glimmer!* It's Arella. Something's wrong.

I push myself off the floor and stumble out of the bathroom like I would stumble out of a bar at three in the morning. When I reach the elevators, I stab the *up* button almost fifteen times, even though it lit up the first time I pressed it. A *ding!* sounds, then the doors slide open.

In my haste to rush into the machine, I run into Katie on her way out. Her face smacks right into my chest.

"Ow!" She rubs her forehead with her hand not hugging her iPad.

"Sorry." I grab her shoulders to steady her—or am I steadying myself? Either way, neither of us falls.

She offers me a warm smile as she steps back into the elevator with me. "You're just the person I came to find."

"What for?"

In her sweet little voice, she says, "I'm here to take you to the second floor. Victor needs you."

Fuck no. "Whatever it is, tell him he's gonna have to wait. I've gotta go." I'm putting my foot down this time. He didn't give me a choice earlier, and I didn't fight him on it. I'll fight him now because this time, Arella's in trouble.

"Where do you gotta go in such a rush?"

"Home. Something came up." I'm about to press the 6 button when Katie grabs my arm.

"I'm sorry. Unfortunately, I can't allow you to leave." Even though she says it in her mousey little voice, it triggers a pang of fear inside me.

"What're you gonna do to stop me?"

"Um, let's just say you don't wanna find out." Whatever gift she has that makes her confident she can overpower me must be good.

Without hesitation, she presses the 2 button, and the doors close. Then she offers me another of her sweet smiles. They're beginning to irk me.

Katie eyes me as the elevator takes us downward. "Are you okay? You're lookin' a bit red."

"I'm fine," I say as my arms go numb, my head throbs, and my legs feel like they're about to give out, and—

Ding!

I follow Katie out toward the community room, even though I want to run straight back into the elevator. Behind the glass walls, a group of four agents are on their laptops, working together. Opposite them is the cafeteria. The rest of this floor is a bunch of sleeping accommodations. Some bedrooms are better than others. The higher-level agents have rooms that are more like luxury apartments complete with their own kitchens and walk-in closets.

When I lived here, my bedroom was basically a square space where the twin-size bed took up half the floor. It included a little closet and a teeny bathroom, where the toilet always broke down. I'm pretty sure Victor assigned me that room because it's the shittiest and farthest away from everyone else.

As we pass the cafeteria, I spot a woman in her late thirties, who I've never seen before. She's reading a book floating in front of her face while she cuts into a plate of pancakes. A group of men in their forties or fifties sit at a table two away from the woman. I don't recognize any of the men either.

As soon as Katie takes two rights then a left, I know exactly where she's going. I'll bet the burn marks are still on the door from all the times I accidentally set my bedroom on fire. Whenever I got too upset, which was quite often, I'd lose control of my powers. My stuff would fly around the ceiling and bang against the walls. If my emotions were really bad, everything would catch on fire. After the fifth time that happened, Victor assigned a Hydro to live in the room across from mine. That lady's job was to extinguish my fires before they spread too far.

I follow Katie down the last hallway. At the end of it are all three of Victor's guards standing outside the closed door of my old bedroom. I was right. The burn marks are still there.

"Why are we here?" I ask.

Instead of answering my question, Katie types a four-digit code into the keypad. I doubt it's the same code from when I lived here. After releasing the chain lock that was never there before, she opens the door and steps aside for me to head in first.

My heart drops at the sight of the woman sitting on my old bed. She's wearing a white T-shirt she doesn't own. I know because it's four sizes too big. The shorts she's wearing aren't hers either. I know because they're orange, and Arella never wears orange.

I glare at my uncle across the room. "What the fuck is this?"

5

———

ARELLA

EARLIER

I WAKE UP FEELING GROGGY WITH A SLIGHT HEADACHE. I'M about to get up to grab some medicine when the handcuffs stop me. *What?*

I jerk upright. I'm on a twin-size bed with yellowed sheets. The walls around me are charred from the floor to the ceiling. The clock on the wall is warped like it's been melted at one point. Parts of the carpet are blackened too. *Where am I? And has someone been burned alive here?*

"Good morning." A young woman stationed on a folding chair in the corner smiles sweetly at me. She looks about eighteen or nineteen. If she's the reason I woke up in a strange place wearing handcuffs, that wholesome look on her face is very deceiving.

"Where am I? Who are you?"

"I'm sure you have a lot of questions," she says calmly as if she wasn't watching me sleep a minute ago. "I'll answer as many questions as I can. My name's Katie."

"Where am I?"

"You're in Shadow Ridge."

Why does she say that as if it's the same as saying "Welcome to New York" or "This is Miami"? I've never heard of a town called Shadow Ridge. "Where is that?"

She places the iPad onto the floor under her chair. "Sorry. I'm not allowed to share that information."

"Not allowed by who?"

"My boss. Oh, that reminds me. He asked me to text him when you woke up." From the inner pocket of her blazer, she pulls out a phone with a pastel pink case. After she types out a quick message, she slips it back into the same pocket.

"Who's your boss?" My breaths are short, and my chest feels tight. I'd like to think this is a dream, but it feels too real.

"You'll meet him soon."

Call it a gut instinct, but something tells me I don't want to meet her boss. "How did I get here?"

"Two of our agents escorted you in. They sedated you in your sleep with a harmless injection. You're waking up around the hour you're supposed to, so that's good."

The tranquil way this girl says all that does nothing to silence the danger alarm blaring in my head. Also, how can she tell me so casually that I've been "sedated"? Is knocking people out and dragging them out of their home against their will a normal occurrence around here?

The baby growing inside me tells me Katie is anxious. It's not the same anxiousness I feel. Mine is laced with a pounding fear while Katie's is more like what I feel when I'm running a few minutes late for work.

I wish I knew how this baby is sensing other people's emotions. It happened the other night with Trey and now Katie. I'd like to say it's a pregnancy thing, but I'm pretty sure it has more to do with Trey being from an alternate universe. I'd be a little more freaked out by it if I hadn't woken up in a bed that doesn't belong to me.

"Why was I kidnapped?"

"Whoa, hold on there," Katie says with a hand out, palm forward. "Let's not use such harsh words. We prefer to say that we're borrowing you."

Borrowing? She can't be serious. "Borrowing usually means you have intentions to give it back."

"Then yes, to your definition, you've been borrowed."

I suppose that means they're not planning to kill me. That's good, right? "When do you people plan to return me?"

"That, I'm unsure of. It probably depends on how long it takes to figure you out. Anyway, I think that's enough questions for now. My boss will be here soon, and I've gotta get you cleaned up. Your pajamas are dirty."

I glance down, and she's right. There's literal dirt, all brown and crusty, across the bottoms of my pajama pants. I was not wearing these when I went to bed last night, which means someone dug through my drawers and dressed me before stealing me from my apartment. *How did I get so dirty?*

"I've picked out a new outfit for you. It's on the counter next to a pair of flats." Katie points toward the bathroom. The door sits ajar, giving me a view of the toilet. From the pocket of her dress pants, Katie produces a small metal key. "I'm going to uncuff you, but only if you promise not to hurt me. It's my first day working an on-base mission, and I'd prefer it if everything goes smoothly."

She's slightly smaller than me, so I think I can take her, but I don't know what or who lies beyond these bedroom walls. Also, I think her innocent face is just to fool people. I bet she knows karate or something.

"What if I don't want to change my clothes?"

Katie shrugs. "You're welcome to stay in your dirty pajamas, but I think you'll be more comfortable not. If you really want your current outfit back, I'm happy to launder it for you first."

It boggles my mind how she's speaking to me so friendly.

This isn't how I imagine most kidnappers talk to the people they've kidnapped. "I'll change my clothes."

"Great, and you promise not to hurt me if I release you?"

Only if you promise not to hurt me. "Sure."

Katie uncuffs me from the bars of the bed frame. "I'll give you a few minutes to get cleaned up. Feel free to shower too. I'm not sure when you'll get a chance to next."

That doesn't sound promising.

From the bathroom, I sense Katie's anxiety growing. I can't see her, but I know she's pacing the bedroom. Somehow, this baby knows every emotion running through Katie. From how weak or strong it's coming to me, I know her distance from me too. Since she's the only person I can sense right now, I'm going to assume there's no one else nearby. Either that, or this baby can only sense one person at a time.

I'm in the middle of showering the mysterious dirt off my feet when Katie knocks on the bathroom door, which does not have a lock. I checked.

"You almost done?"

"Almost." I turn the shower off and step out to examine myself in the mirror. There's no evidence that I've been hurt in any way. I suppose that's a positive.

I come out wearing black flats, a white T-shirt that dwarfs me, and a pair of ugly orange shorts. I return to the bed where Katie, if that's her real name, cuffs me back to the bed frame. I go willingly because I don't know what else to do.

From watching true crime shows with Javina, I've learned that the victims who comply with their kidnappers' demands are the ones with the highest percentage of making it out alive. So far, it doesn't seem like Katie wants to harm me. I'm sure her boss does though.

Whatever happens, I have to get through this alive—for the baby. The first chance I see of a possible escape, I'm taking it.

"You've got really long hair." Katie stands in front of me,

stroking my hair. I lean backward, but she cups the back of my neck and forces me toward her. In one swift movement, she unhooks my necklace and tucks it into her bra.

"Hey, what are you—"

"I'm just tying your hair up for you," she says, giving me a firm *shut up* look.

I don't know why, but I do. With the hair tie around her wrist, she pulls all of my long waves into a ponytail. As she finishes, she gently tugs on my hair, forcing my head back. My attention lands on a small security camera bolted to the ceiling behind her. Is she trying to tell me we're being watched? *Maybe she's here against her will too.*

"There!" Katie says, stepping back to admire her work. "Now you won't have to worry about getting that long mane of yours tangled up during your stay."

"My stay? What is this? A hotel?"

"It's no five-star resort, but it's not a crappy side-of-the-road Motel 6 either."

"Then what is it?"

She doesn't answer. Instead, she plants herself back onto the folding chair and returns her iPad to her lap. For a few minutes, she does stuff on the tablet in silence. I don't say anything because I'm too busy scanning the room for possible exits.

No windows. No vents big enough for a person to climb through. There are two doors: the one to the bathroom, which I've already inspected for exits, and the other that Katie is so obviously guarding.

"There's no way out," she says, not looking up from the iPad. "You might as well stop searching. Despite what it looks like from inside this little bedroom, you're not in a house. You're in an underground facility surrounded by about two hundred trained agents. Beyond that is a forest that stretches as far as your eyes can see."

That's all great information to note to the police once I get out of here. *If* I ever get out of here. If what Katie's saying is true, I don't think I'll see my home again until they want me to.

A steady vibration comes from Katie's pocket. She pulls out her phone to read the screen. *Wait.* That's not her phone. It's mine!

"Your *Grammy* is calling. Is she expecting you or something?"

Last night, I called my grandma with the intention of telling her about the baby, but she was already asleep. Instead, I left her a voicemail saying I had something important to talk to her about. It must be morning now—not that I could peek out a window to be sure.

My phone stops vibrating. Seconds later, it buzzes with a text.

"What did she say?" I ask as Katie reads my phone screen.

"She said, 'Hi, sweetie. Sorry, I was sleeping last night. You said you had something important to tell me? I'll call again in a bit.' " Katie returns my device to her pocket. "Are you pretty close to your grandma?"

"Yeah."

"So she'll find it weird if you don't call her back?"

"Definitely."

With a long sigh, Katie drags out her pink phone again. She types something on it, then waits for a reply. It comes a few seconds later. "My boss says you need to call your grandma back and talk to her as if you weren't here."

"You mean, as if I'm not being held captive?"

"Exactly."

"And if I refuse?"

She folds her hands together in her lap. "I think my boss would prefer it if you called."

"Look, I don't know who your boss is, but I'm assuming he's the reason I was kidnapped, so I'm not going to do anything he wants me to. If he's saying he wants me to call my grandma and tell her that nothing's wrong, I'd rather jump into a pit of flesh-eating snakes."

Katie blinks at me before returning her thumbs to her phone. After a moment, she straightens her back. "He's almost here."

Less than thirty seconds later, the door opens and in walks a tall man wearing a brown suit. The big gray mustache above his lips barely hides the scowl on his face and the emotions to match.

Three other men accompany him. Two step into the room and stand on opposite corners. The third guy stations himself outside the door as Katie shuts it.

I can sense them. Every single one of them. Katie, Mustache Man, his two bodyguards, and the one out in the hall. Turns out this baby *can* sense more than one person at a time. They just have to be close enough.

"You need to call your grandma back now." As Mustache Man speaks, the long horizontal scar on the front of his neck moves up and down. Either he had surgery or someone tried to slit his throat. My bets are on the latter.

Something about his face makes me squint at him. He looks familiar. Like an actor I've seen in a movie. I can't place him though.

I don't respond to Mustache Man with words—only glares. He glares back with his piercing eyes. I want to know his name and everything about him so that when I leave here, I'll have everything the police need to put him behind bars.

"Are you going to call your grandma back or not?"

Again, I remain silent. I'm not going to comply with his demands that easily. *So much for everything I've learned from those true crime shows.*

"Katie!" he shouts so loudly, she jumps. "Proceed with Plan B. He's in the bathroom on the fourth floor. I'll work on trying to convince her by the time you return with him."

"Yes, sir." With her iPad in hand, Katie retreats out of the room.

I almost shout at her to not leave me alone with this scary man, but she's already gone. Strangely, without her, I feel more vulnerable.

Mustache Man approaches me. The closer he gets, the more his irritation twists into curiosity. He wants something from me. I can see it in the way his eyes are staring straight into my soul. What does he want?

"Leave us," he says. Almost instantly, his two guards exit the room. They don't go far though. I still feel their presence right outside the closed door.

Now that it's just me and Mustache Man, he closes the distance between us in two strides. As he does, his blue eyes turn black like he's being possessed by a demon. I crawl backward on the bed, screaming at the top of my lungs.

"Get away from me!"

"Hold still," he says and reaches for my neck.

I swat him away with my free arm. "Don't touch me."

"I said hold still." He grabs me by the neck and forces me to meet eyes with him. His eye color has returned to blue, but it's not long before a cloud of black takes over his pupils again. It's like something out of a horror movie.

"Let me go!" My words come out stifled from how solid his grip is around my throat. I claw at his fingers.

Surprisingly, he releases me and takes a step back. I cough and gasp for air as he runs a hand through the top of his salt-and-pepper hair.

His frustration radiates toward me from where he stands. "I don't even know why I'm trying. Of course it won't work."

Whatever he was trying to do to me, I'm glad it didn't work. Above all else, I'm glad he wasn't trying to sexually assault me—although I have a feeling that whatever he was trying to do is much worse.

Something about him isn't right, and it's not just because

his eyes can turn completely black. There's something oddly familiar about him.

Minutes later, when someone bursts through the door shouting, "What the fuck is this?" it hits me.

This man looks like an older version of Trey Grant.

6

———

ARELLA

For a second, I'm relieved to see someone I know. However, when Trey doesn't immediately punch Mustache Man and carry me out of here . . .

"The girl's grandmother is expecting her to call," Mustache Man says. "I've asked her to call the old lady back and act normal, but she's refusing. Think you can persuade her?"

Trey's body goes stiff. Anger radiates off him so strongly, I can't sense Mustache Man anymore, or Katie, who has returned herself to the folding chair in the corner.

Trey barely moves as he glares at his older look-alike. "What the hell is she doing here?"

Mustache Man speaks calmly yet firmly. "I figured that since you're gonna be busy working your new mission, we could go ahead and accelerate your first one."

I've got to be dreaming. There's no way that Trey, *my* Trey, is a part of this.

Trey doesn't stop glaring at Mustache Man. "Why wasn't I consulted first?"

Mustache Man narrows his eyes at Trey. "What makes you think I need to consult *you* before making any decisions? Now, do you think you can convince her to call her grandma or not? If the answer's no, get the hell out and go be useless somewhere else."

Finally, Trey turns his attention to me. His chest rises and falls like he's not getting enough air. I hold back tears as we lock eyes and I silently plead with him to stop whatever's happening.

He must not hear my plea, because he clears his throat and says, "I'll convince her to call."

I burst into tears, covering my mouth with my free hand. *This can't be happening.* My breaths are sharp as Katie hands my phone to Trey, and he accepts it.

Mustache Man heads toward the door. "Katie, send me a full report when it's done, then return her phone to me. I'll be in my office."

"Yes, sir." Katie stands to open the door for him.

Mustache Man points to the bulkiest of his three bodyguards. "I want round-the-clock security on this Ordinary. You're first."

"Yes, sir," the man replies.

Even with the door shut, my baby senses Mustache Man and his two guards as they head down the hall. After several footsteps, I don't sense them anymore. I'll assume that's because they're out of my baby's range, not because they disappeared off the face of the planet.

Now I'm left alone in a silent bedroom with Katie and this master of deception I used to call my boyfriend.

Suddenly, everything starts to come together: Trey's late-night phone calls, his irregular sleeping habits, the mysterious air about him. He's been living a double life this whole time. He's a criminal. I think I prefer him being from an alternate universe over this.

"Could you give us a few minutes?" Trey asks, slipping my phone into his back pocket.

Katie nods. "Sure thing."

Trey waits until the door clicks shut behind her before he eyes the charred walls. At first, I think he's looking for an escape route like I did, but once his eyes land on the camera behind him, he turns back to me.

For a moment, he just stares. It's nothing I'm not used to. He's always had a habit of staring at me, except this time, it's not in admiration. He's looking for something. I'm not sure what.

I jolt back a little when he drops to his knees at my feet. Silent tears roll down my cheeks as he continues to scan my body up and down.

"Did anyone hurt you?" His question comes out in barely a whisper.

I can't respond, because if I do, I'll burst into tears again.

"Arella . . ." My name comes out like a plea. "Did anyone hurt you?"

There's no evidence of it on his face, but the baby senses relief from him when I shake my head. I want to tell him that, technically, no one's hurt me. Not as much as it hurts to see him here and to know that he's involved in this.

"How did you get here?" His voice is still a whisper.

My words come out through choked tears. "I woke up here."

He grits his teeth together. "So they fucking kidnapped you?"

It's nice to hear someone call it what it is. I want to say, *Of course they kidnapped me. Do you think I willingly drove here myself?* What I actually say is "Who's *they*?"

He ignores my question. "Why are you handcuffed to the bed?"

I glower at him and wipe my damp face off with the bottom of the gigantic T-shirt I'm wearing. "You're asking me like *I* should know? When I woke up, I was already cuffed to this stupid bed, and that Katie girl was sitting on that chair, watching me sleep. Do you think I have any clue what's going on? I don't even know where I am."

"You're in Three Rivers."

"Your hometown?"

A nod.

"Why am I here?"

My question is met with silence. Trey springs back onto his feet and groans while running a hand through his hair the same way Mustache Man did. They've got to be related. Mustache Man is probably his dad. Trey's story about how his parents were killed was just a cover-up for his parents being criminals or to gain my sympathy. I can't believe I trusted anything he ever said to me.

In a regular tone, Trey asks, "Can you call your grandma back?"

"No."

"Arella, you have to."

"Says who? Mustache Man? The guy who a minute ago was choking me by the neck and—"

"He did what?" Trey's entire body goes rigid.

I shoot dagger eyes at him. "Don't be so surprised. If he's willing to sedate and kidnap me, he's probably willing to do much worse."

"You were sedated?" To himself, he says, "That explains why I didn't feel it right away."

Feel what?

Trey's hands clench into fists as he sucks in a deep breath. When he lets it out, his fists relax. "Did he do anything else to you?"

How can I explain that Mustache Man probably tried to melt me with his black eyeballs without sounding like I'm crazy? Does Trey know he can do that?

"Who is he?" My tears are starting to let up because I'm more angry than shocked now. I want to know what's going on, how Trey is involved, and most of all, I want to go home.

"His name is Victor. He's the CEO of ZIRDA California, which is a secret organization that, um . . ." Trey's gaze falls to a burn spot on the carpet. "It's complicated."

A secret organization? That, along with some words Katie said earlier, like *mission* and *underground facility surrounded by about two hundred trained agents*, makes me feel like I've been sucked into some messed-up spy movie.

"Better question," I say. "How do *you* know Victor?"

"He's, um . . . my uncle."

I knew they were related. Maybe that means Trey wasn't lying about his parents getting blown up. Victor is probably the abusive uncle who took him in after the explosion. "Did you help your uncle kidnap me?"

"No. Fuck no. If it wasn't obvious, Arella, I'm just as shocked to see you here as you are to see me."

"He's your uncle!" I shout. "You really want me to believe you had nothing to do with this?"

"I didn't!" he shouts back.

I must be dumb, because I actually believe him. Mostly because my baby senses how angry he is about this. Correction: *our* baby. Oh my god, I'm pregnant with a baby who belongs to a man with a PhD in lying. *How is this my life?*

Trey paces the room, pulling at his hair before finally turning to me. "Could you please call your grandma?"

Does he really think saying *please* will change my mind? "I said no."

"Look, I know you're probably scared right now, but trust me, everything's gonna be okay." The way he says all that makes me think he's trying to convince himself, not me.

"Why should I trust *you*? You're one of them!"

How could I not have known? This should have been the first question I asked him on our first date: *Hey, is your uncle a crazy dude running a secret organization in an underground facility crawling with secret agents?* My second question should have been *Are you one of those secret agents?* The next guy I meet, I'll make sure I know the professions of *all* his uncles before even considering having dinner with him.

I glare at Trey with the most venomous look I can muster. "You've been one of them this whole time, haven't you?"

His silence is all the answer I need to lose any hope I had left in him.

7

ARELLA

I'm firm in my refusal to call my grandma. Eventually, Trey and Katie give up asking. Trey simply hands my phone back to Katie, and then she tells him to leave. At first, he hesitates, but eventually, he shuffles toward the door.

On his way out, I catch a glimpse of the big guy guarding my exit. He looks like the white version of Dwayne "The Rock" Johnson. I don't know how I'm going to escape with that man around. I can't take him on. He's triple my size.

When the door shuts, Katie flashes me a gentle smile. "Are you allergic to anything?"

My response is automatic. "Liars and people who don't use their blinker."

She giggles, covering her mouth with a hand. "I'm glad you can still make jokes, given how scared you must be, but I was asking if you have any food allergies."

She's wrong. I'm not scared. I'm terrified. I'm making jokes because it's keeping me centered. Otherwise, I might be hyperventilating in the fetal position right now.

"No allergies," I say.

"Excellent. I'll be right back."

She leaves and returns a few minutes later with a food tray

in hand. On it is a bowl of cereal, some milk in a glass, an apple, and a granola bar.

She sets it onto my lap. "Eat up."

"No."

She frowns at the food. "Do you not care for Cheerios?"

"I don't care to eat any offerings from criminals."

This girl has the *audacity* to look offended. "I haven't committed any crimes. You don't have to eat if you don't want to, but for your information, lunch doesn't start in the cafeteria for another three hours. Judging by what's on your schedule today, I think you're gonna want all the energy you can get."

I don't like the sound of that. "What's going to happen to me?"

Katie doesn't answer with her mouth, but the pity in her eyes tells me all I need to know.

I glance at the food, then back up at her. I'm about to ask if it's poisoned but figure if it is, at least I won't have to endure whatever it is they've got planned for me, so I pick up the apple and take a bite.

My breakfast is long gone by the time Katie's iPad chimes. She leaps off her chair and plucks that precious metal key out of her pocket. "It's time."

"For what?" I have a good feeling that whatever she's got to say next won't be good.

"To take you downstairs. Before I uncuff you, I wanna tell you that your stay here will be more comfortable if you don't try to run. The last person tried and was put into a straitjacket. Those things are uncomfortably heavy. I don't think you want that."

The last person? That means I'm not the first. If that's the case, what happened to the others? Do I even want to know?

Katie continues, "I was the one who suggested not restraining you at all. I told Victor it would help you be more agreeable. He wasn't fond of that idea, so we compromised with restraining only one of your arms instead. I know you don't have any reason to trust me, but I sure hope you won't purposely ruin my chances of proving to my boss that I can have good ideas. So, do you think you can be agreeable?"

"I'll be agreeable if you give me back my necklace."

For the second time, Katie shoots me a firm *shut up* look. It quickly disappears and fades into a warm smile. "Glad you're promising to behave. Now let's get you downstairs."

This girl is either a psychopath or she's up to something. Maybe she's both. She'd better not think I'm going to simply brush off that she stole my necklace. It doesn't matter that the man who gifted it to me is a . . . well, I'm not sure what he is. A spy? A secret agent from another universe? Whatever he is, I still want my necklace back.

Katie leads me down the hallways, passing a plethora of numbered rooms like in an apartment complex. The big guy who was guarding my door follows closely behind me. After a few turns, we pass what looks like a community area across from a cafeteria. A few people are scattered around the tables, typing on laptops.

In the elevator, I make a mental note that there are six floors. I also note that they're keeping me captive on the second one. Katie presses the 1 button, and then the doors slide together.

Katie cuddles her iPad close to her chest as the machine takes us down. I'll bet there are lots of important things on that device. Like incriminating notes, names of all the secret agents here, and a way for me to send for help. I've got to get that iPad from her.

Ding! The elevator opens to a new floor.

I follow Katie down the wide hallways while the big guy tramps behind me in his heavy boots. I log as many details of this place into my brain as possible. White walls, gray doors, cream tiled floors. Behind a glass wall is a group of six rowdy men. Two are wrestling each other on padded mats while the other four cheer them on.

In a fitness room, two men and three women are running on treadmills or lifting weights. I don't get a long enough glance to memorize any of their faces. I'm not even sure how any of this information is going to help me later, but I continue to memorize things anyway.

We pass a few more rooms, but they don't have windows for me to see through. The signs on the outside say things like *Fireball Throwing Practice*, *Terra Training*, and *Artificial Sunlight*. I don't know what any of that means.

Through a set of double doors, we enter a giant auditorium with a square boxing ring in the center. Empty rows of seats stretch from the boxing ring all the way up to the back walls. In the ring are a group of people having a conversation. One of them is Mustache Man, otherwise known as Victor, Trey's uncle and the man who organized my kidnapping. The baby senses excitement from him instead of the frustration that was simmering in his gut earlier. Whatever he's excited about can't be good for me.

Katie stops at the bottom of the stairs leading into the boxing ring. She gestures for me to step up.

I don't.

"Get in," Victor orders.

Three. Besides Victor, there's three of them in the boxing ring, and they're all ready to do whatever it is they do to their captives in there. *No thank you. Hard pass for me.*

Victor snaps his fingers. "Craig, assist the girl, will you?"

I yelp when the big guard scoops me off my feet. Then he stomps up the stairs in his boots and drops me into the center of the boxing ring.

I don't move a muscle as Victor throws a leg over the ropes to stand on the other side of the ring. Then he draws a circle in the air with his finger. "Surround her. One of you at each corner."

As if they're robots—maybe they are—all three people plus Craig migrate to separate corners of the box. I stare at each one, memorizing anything about them that can help the police identify them later.

Craig, if that's his real name, is a forty-something white male with neck tattoos that seem to run all the way down to his fingertips.

Guy two is another white male, maybe late thirties, with muscles practically bursting out of his shirt. Short brown hair. No visible tattoos.

The other two are women. The first one is Asian—maybe Korean. She's the shortest of them all. She also looks the youngest, maybe nineteen or twenty. She has a pixie haircut with blue highlights, plus floral tattoos running down her upper arm, and she's chewing on a piece of gum.

Female two looks in her mid-twenties. Slender figure, long curly red hair, and lots of freckles.

Okay, now all I have to do is remember all that . . .

"Let's try one at a time first," Victor says from the sidelines. His deep voice echoes throughout the emptiness of the auditorium. "Derek, you first."

The muscular guy steps forward and snaps his fingers in my direction. I glance around, looking for something coming at me, or something to fall onto me from the ceiling. When nothing does, he snaps again.

"Maybe I need to touch her." Derek comes to my side. I think about running, but his stern gaze makes me stay in place. Besides, there's nowhere for me to go.

I flinch when he grabs my arm and holds it. His grip gets tighter as I try to jerk away from him.

"Let go." I yank my arm back until he releases me.

"What the . . . ?" He gapes at me. "Pixie, come here for a sec."

The Asian woman pops up from her squat. In mid-stand, Derek snaps his fingers, and she stills like she's been paused in a movie. She doesn't blink. She doesn't chew on her gum. I'm not even sure if she's breathing. My mouth pops open as my eyes go wide.

"So my powers *do* work." Derek snaps his fingers again.

Pixie finishes her stand like the movie's been unpaused. She must know what happened, because she narrows her eyes at Derek. With two fingers, she points at her eyes, then at him. "I'm watchin' you, jackass."

Victor waves a hand at the big guard. "Let's keep this movin'. You're next, Craig."

As Derek returns to his corner, Craig points a firm tattooed finger at me. His strides are long as he closes the distance between us. The closer he gets, the more I back away.

"Don't come any closer." My voice betrays me. It comes out weaker than I wanted it to.

Craig backs me into the ropes, pinning me there. I punch his chest, but it's as effective as punching a statue. He doesn't even flinch. He continues pointing a finger at me, even pressing it against my forehead—hard.

"How are you doing that?" His shock flashes through my mind.

Doing what?

"Sorry, Derek." Craig unpins me, then points a finger at the muscular guy. With the sound of a balloon releasing air, Derek shrinks to the size of a small dog. I scream, but I'm the only one who does. None of the other people look slightly surprised—not even Katie, who's typing away on her iPad from the front row of the auditorium seats. Is seeing people shrink like that normal around here?

In a tiny, high-pitched voice, Derek shouts, "Hey! Unshrink me!"

Pixie draws her arm back like she's about to pitch a baseball. In the palm of her hand, a ball of water appears. She tosses it at mini Derek, and it lands right over his little head, drenching him.

"That's fucking rude!" Derek shouts in his high-pitched voice. "Craig, unshrink me, you bastard!"

Craig points his finger at Derek. With the sound of air being blown into a balloon, Derek returns to his normal size. He leans against the ropes for support. "Damn. That shit hurts," he says as he wrings out the bottom of his drenched shirt.

"The shrinking or the water ball?" the Asian woman asks.

"The shrinking, bitch. Yours, I barely felt."

I don't even see the water ball grow in her hand before it's launched across the room. Derek ducks, and the water splashes all over the floor.

"Missed me, bitch," Derek says, grinning.

A third water ball appears in the woman's hand. She raises it into the air as it doubles in size. "Call me a bitch one more time."

"Enough!" Victor shouts. "Pixie, since you're so eager to use your powers, why don't you go next?"

"Gladly." Pixie's water ball evaporates in a cloud of steam in her hand, then she marches toward me and stops barely a half step from my face. I log more of her features into my brain: nose ring, sharp eyebrows, plump lips. How am I going to remember all this?

Her minty breath wafts over my nose as she puckers her lips into an O shape. She blows air at me. I wait for something to happen, maybe for my face to melt or my eyeballs to pop out. Nothing happens.

Pixie steps back as her genuine confusion races through my head. "No fucking way." She takes the gum out of her mouth and blows air at me again.

Then she blows a third time.

Finally, she twists on a heel, puckers her lips, and blows air in Derek's direction.

He slaps his hands over his ears. "Ow! Stop!"

Pixie does and returns her gum to her mouth. She smirks at me as if we're good friends. "I just love fuckin' with him."

"Ruby," Victor says, "how 'bout you try?"

The redhead doesn't move from her spot. Instead, she simply raises her open palm out to me and hisses through her teeth. When nothing happens, she advances toward me. Her black booties click with each step she takes until she's right in my face.

"Is it workin'?" Derek asks.

"Do you hear her screaming in pain?" Ruby says.

Screaming in pain? What is she trying to do to me?

"If you touch her, will it work?" Victor asks.

Ruby places her hand on my arm and hisses again. When nothing happens, she releases me. Then she directs her hisses at Derek. He drops to his knees and screams like he's being attacked by giant cobras. When Ruby puts her arm down, the screaming stops.

"What the fuck?" Derek is still on his knees, clutching his stomach. "Going through an incinerator would be less painful than that."

Ruby shrugs, smirking a little. "I had to make sure my powers still worked."

Who are these people? Better question: *What* are they? They seem to have abilities of some kind and are testing them out on me. For some reason I don't know and am deeply grateful for, their powers don't work on me. *Why?*

Maybe Javina was right about Trey being from an alternate universe. Except, it wasn't him who was sucked into my universe; I've been sucked into his. It's the only explanation I have for everything I'm witnessing.

"Gather 'round her," Victor orders. "Let's try all four of you at the same time."

Derek, Craig, Pixie, and Ruby trap me against the ropes as they fix their gazes on me. I don't pause. My body doesn't shrink. I don't hear anything that makes me want to cover my ears. I don't collapse to my knees with pain either.

"Pixie, give her a splash," Victor says. "Everyone focus!"

Pixie raises both arms as a giant water ball forms in her hands. I raise my arms to try to block her, but she wins. Icy-cold liquid drenches me.

I spit out the water and wipe at my face.

"Well, she ain't immune to elemental powers," Pixie says.

There's that word again. *Powers.* How did these people get their powers? If they are *people* at all.

"Do it again," Victor orders.

The second water ball is even colder.

I shiver as the four of them continue trying to accomplish whatever it is they want to accomplish. The longer nothing happens, the more the cloud of irritation above Victor grows.

"How are you doing that?" Victor asks.

I wish they would stop asking me that as if I know the answer. My jaw quivers as I push the wet hair from my face.

"All right, let's be done," Victor says. "Pixie, help the girl out."

The other three step back as Pixie waves her hands in circles. In slow steam clouds rising to the ceiling, all the water soaking my body disappears. My shirt that was soaking wet a second ago feels like it just came out of the dryer. *What kind of magic is this?*

"Katie!" Victor shouts, and it makes her pop out of her seat. I think she's been typing notes on her iPad this whole time. "Take the girl back to her room. Give her the questionnaire."

In her mousey little voice, Katie says, "Yes, sir."

Together, Katie and Craig escort me back to the elevators. I think about running, but now that I've discovered they're wizards, I don't stand a chance.

Back on the second floor, we take a few turns down the hallways before we reach my corner jail cell disguised as a bedroom. On the doorframe is a chain lock that disheartens me. I didn't think I had any chance of escaping before. Now it seems impossible.

Katie types a few numbers into a keypad on the door. When it beeps, she gestures for me to step inside. I do, because what else can I do?

While Craig stations himself outside my door, Katie clicks it shut. The sound of the chain lock sliding into place makes me choke up.

"Take a seat," Katie says, pointing at the bed. She plops onto her folding chair and offers me a smile. "I'll leave you uncuffed if you promise not to attack me."

I stay standing where I am. "Why do you have to cuff me at all? I don't have magic powers to fight you with. There's no way I can get out of here. Although, if I did attack you, it doesn't seem like your powers work on me, so maybe I *could* win in a fight."

"First off, the cuffs aren't really to keep you from attacking me or to keep you from leaving. It's more to keep someone from taking you. We've been having a problem with double agents lately, so you can never have too much security on your assets."

She's calling me an asset like I'm something they own. *Am I their slave now?*

Katie continues, "Secondly, it's not magic, and please, don't say that word out loud around here. Most Zordis get really offended when our gifts are referred to as *magic*. Third, some of our powers *do* work on you. It's only the internal ones that seem to have no effect. And lastly, I don't need my powers to subdue you. I grew up learning karate."

I totally called that. "Zordis? That's what you call yourselves?"

"We don't just *call* ourselves that. It's what we are. The technical term is *Zordinary*, but we shorten it to Zordi."

"And you're what? Aliens? Mutants? Lab experiments gone wrong?"

Katie lets out a little laugh. "You have quite the imagination, don't you? We're humans, just like you, except we have gifts. Now how about you sit down? It's my turn to ask the questions."

Sighing, I do as I'm told and plant my butt onto the mattress.

Katie taps around on her iPad, then says, "I've got a pretty long list of questions. All you've gotta do is answer them honestly. Think you can do that?"

The questions start off normal enough: Where did you grow up? Do you have any siblings? What did you study in college?

Once the questions are about my family, it gets weird: Did your mom or dad have a sexually transmitted disease at the time of your conception? Was your mother on any drugs or prescriptions while she was pregnant with you? Have you or your parents ever been bitten by an exotic spider?

I don't understand how these questions are relevant. How would I know if my parents had an STD at the time of my conception or if my mother was on drugs? That's not a typical dinner conversation. Even if it was, I never got the chance to ask.

"I told you already," I say exasperated. The warped clock on the wall reads eleven thirty. It's been almost two hours since we began this stupid interrogation. "My parents died in a car accident when I was three. I don't even remember them."

"Do you think there's a chance your parents were Immunes too? Like, maybe it runs in the family?"

"No! No! No!" Normally, I don't like to shout. Right now, I want to shout so loudly, the sky can hear me. I haven't seen the sky yet today, so I'm questioning if it still exists. "I don't know the answers to your dumb questions! I didn't even know I was immune to anything until today!"

Katie's expressionless as I chuck a pillow at her. She doesn't even flinch as it hits her shoulder and flops onto the floor. I let out a scream toward the ceiling, then burst into tears.

It's quiet for a moment while I cry into my hands, letting out all the emotions I've been bottling in since I woke up. I feel Katie's gaze on me as she waits for me to stop sobbing.

When I don't, she slaps her thighs and stands from her chair. "Welp, I think it's time for lunch. I'll be back in a bit. We can finish the questionnaire after you eat."

There's more? How can there be more?

Five minutes later, Katie returns with two food trays. My sobbing has subsided and turned into occasional hiccups. I'm regretting every decision I've ever made that landed me here, and all I want is to crawl into my nice comfy bed at home and never come out.

"Do you prefer turkey or ham? I made one of each. I'll have whatever you don't want."

"Turkey," I say somberly.

She hands me one of the trays. "I made it myself. If you want, I'll take the first bite, so you know it's not poisoned."

"Don't bother. If it is poisoned, at least it'll end this misery."

Katie puckers her bottom lip out into a little pout. "Oh, come on. Am I really *that* bad to hang out with? I think you'd prefer me over the last guy. He was kinda mean. He also had a gut that hung over his belt and a beard so long, you could braid it. Honestly, he looked like an ogre. And that's saying something, because Zordis are naturally pretty fit. We have higher metabolisms than Ordis, so that guy had to really let himself go to get all that flub."

That explains how Trey has such perfectly toned abs. All this time, I thought he just put a lot of effort into his exercise.

Turns out, he's got a mutant body that makes it easy for him to look fit.

"Can I sit with you?" Katie eyes the other side of the twin bed. "This chair is aching my bum."

"Sure."

We rest our food trays between us, then take a bite into our sandwiches. If someone snapped a photo of this moment, it'd look like Katie and I are best buddies, having a friendly bedroom picnic. In reality, I met this girl this morning and I know nothing about her, except that she works for a man who organizes federal crimes. Oh, and that she's a thief. *Is my necklace still in her bra?*

"You asked me a million questions earlier," I say. "Can I ask you some now?"

"You can ask, but I can't promise I'll give you the answer, even if I know it."

"I'll take all the answers you can give me. First, I want to know what your *mission* is."

Katie swallows her food, then says, "Victor assigned me to be your overseer. I'm in charge of making sure you're fed, dressed, and arrive on time to your appointments. Honestly, I think *overseer* is just code for *glorified babysitter*. This wouldn't have been my first pick from the pool of on-base assignments, but it's a stepping-stone."

"What would have been your first pick?" I open my bag of chips.

"My dream is to be a field agent, doing stuff out in the world where I can make a big difference. That's not to say the people who work on base aren't making a difference. Of course the janitors, the cooks, the maids, and even me, as Victor's assistant, are important. We're the oil for the gears to function properly—the gears being the field agents.

"But this type of work doesn't light my soul on fire, ya know? It's hard to feel like I'm making an impact when I'm confined down here all day and night. I guess if I had to pick something on base, I'd like to be in project management. I could help write up mission plans for the field agents and make sure they're getting done."

By the way Katie talks about this place, it sounds like a well-functioning establishment—not a place that houses kidnapping criminals.

I finish the bite I'm eating, then say, "So, this is just a job to you? Like, you're getting paid for this?"

"Yes, technically this is a job. Just like anyone else, I get paychecks, and I have days off where I'll go see my family and stuff. But to me, working for ZIRDA is much more than that. I want to build a career here. When I'm old and retired, I want people to say my name and think, *Wow. She saved a lot of lives.*"

How can Katie talk about saving lives when I feel like mine is at risk? "What does ZIRDA stand for?"

"Zordinary Innovations Research and Development Agency. We began as an organization who designs and improves inventions that progress the lives of Zordis. For example, our agents are the ones who created the z-net, which is an Internet that only Zordis can access. It was also our agents who invented z-ink, which is the ink our kind uses to print books that only our eyes can see. Over the decades, ZIRDA has become more than just inventors. Now we also work to fight off the Royals, who are the biggest organized Zordi crime group in history."

I take a sip of water and ask the question that's been on my mind since this morning. "What's Trey's role here?"

"Field agent."

That's not the answer I was looking for, so I try again. "What's his mission?"

"I'm not sure exactly. Agents aren't allowed to speak in detail about our missions with each other, but it's only right to assume that his mission is to get you to give Victor what he wants."

A little piece of my heart breaks as I flashback to meeting

Trey on the side of a busy highway. It's hitting me now that maybe my flat tire wasn't an accident. I choke back some tears and say, "I'm going to assume that Trey's mission is to figure out how I'm immune to your people's powers, but what happens after that?"

"I'd assume that ZIRDA will try to replicate your immunity so we can use it to take down the Royals."

"What makes them so bad?"

"Everything. While most Zordis believe that living in peace with Ordinaries is optimal, the Royals believe that because Zordis have powers, we're the superior humans. They think Zordis should be the ones running the show, and they hate that we are the ones who have to hide our true selves. Some Royals even go to the extreme and believe that all Ordinaries should be eradicated. They've gone as far as mass genocides and biochemical weapons that cause worldwide viruses killing off only Ordinaries. The Black Plague, the Spanish flu, SARS—all started by the Royals."

I have no idea if she's feeding me lies or not, but for now, I'll assume she's telling the truth. What reason does she have to lie about where the Black Plague came from? "And Ordinaries are . . . ?"

"People like you."

"Is that like muggles in Harry Potter? Non-magic folk?"

Katie scolds me. "Again, it's not magic. It's called gifts or powers."

"How did you get them?"

"We're born with 'em," she says, like it's common knowledge. "It's passed down by genetics. Which reminds me, would you mind if I held your hand for a moment? I'm curious to see if my powers will work."

I respond by holding my arm out to her with full confidence that she won't hurt me.

After setting her half-eaten sandwich down and wiping her

fingers off on a napkin, she takes my hand and closes her eyes. A few seconds later, she lets me go and picks up her sandwich.

"Did it work?" I ask.

"No. I can't control when my body power works, anyway, but it's safe to assume that no matter how hard I try, it won't work."

I don't have a clue as to what *body power* means, and I don't care to ask. My brain is too overloaded with all this information. Secret agents with magic powers fighting the bad guys who apparently caused the Black Plague? And they want to use *me* and my strange immunity to their magic to defeat them?

I never signed up for this.

8

———

TREY

"*Son, your mama and I wanted to make sure that you'd be safe and taken care of. That's why everything we have is now yours, including a safe house by our secret rock.*" My father's words replay from the button-size device I found in my old teddy bear. I don't know why I'm listening to this. I've played the recording so many times now that I have it memorized.

My mother's voice comes next. "*When you get to the rock, take a hundred steps away from Cheesy. There, you'll find the safe house. You're the only one who can get into it. Remember that Trackers can't sense you once you're inside and underground.*"

No matter how many times I play this recording and scour the woods, I can't find the safe house. Before, I searched for it out of curiosity. I wanted to see what my parents left behind for me. Now it's the only way I can keep Arella safe. I *need* to find it.

The sun beats down on me as I comb the same wooded area in Julian, California, as I have multiple times before. *Inside and underground.* I understand the underground part— hence all the holes surrounding me that I dug and refilled. It's the *inside* part I'm having trouble with. *Inside what?* All that's around me are trees, trees, and more trees.

As I continue searching, I play the recording again. The one line that keeps sticking out to me is *"Aunt Debbie is the only person you should trust, and the only person you should take with you."*

Why is my mother's sister on the trustworthy list but my father's brother is not? Did my parents know something about Victor that I don't? If they didn't trust him, does that mean I shouldn't either? Not that I do anyway.

Even while I was actively working my mission, any time I discovered anything about Arella that seemed out of place, I never told Victor about it: her parents dying on the same night as mine. How that news article stated that three-year-old Arella—I mean *Hannah Calder*—died too. How whenever I made her orgasm, I was able to break through her immunity walls. Something in the back of my mind kept me from telling Victor any of that, and I'm glad for it.

For weeks, Victor was adamant that I bring Arella to him for a bunch of bullshit tests. I had a feeling that if I didn't do it, he would send someone who would. I never thought he'd go as far as kidnapping her. *Is he fucking serious?* That's not how ZIRDA ever handles things with Ordinaries. Usually, ZIRDA is more discreet and causes no harm. I thought he'd simply send another guy to get Arella to fall for and start the process over. Now that I know he's willing to kidnap innocent Ordinaries, I'm starting to question all of his decisions.

Victor has been the CEO of one of the largest ZIRDA bases in the United States for the last nineteen years. During that time, I've witnessed him shut down Royals operations before they even began. I've seen him personally train the new agents and help them draw up missions to keep Ordinaries safe. Throughout the years, he's accomplished a lot of good. That's why I usually give him passes for treating me like dirt.

Without ZIRDA working to develop and distribute the necessary life-saving vaccines to save Ordinaries from all those bioweapons the Royals have unleashed, there might not be many Ordinaries left. Without ZIRDA, the Royals would have a higher kill count. Without ZIRDA, the Royals probably would have won by now.

I fully support ZIRDA's purpose. I even commend Victor for running ZIRDA California for all these years. It's not a job for the weak. But being the CEO of a ZIRDA base doesn't mean he can do no wrong. And with Arella, he's wrong. Sedating her? Kidnapping her? Handcuffing her to a bed? Is this what he did with the last two Immunes instead of asking them to be part of a secret medical study the way ZIRDA usually does? Are his crazy methods the reason why the other two Immunes are dead?

On my way out of the Ridge earlier, it hit me why Victor didn't give me a choice to come to the base: He needed me preoccupied while he sent some agents out to kidnap my girl. I'll bet anything that Kim Nguyen isn't even a real person. I'll bet he simply stole that picture off the Internet and purposely prolonged that briefing meeting to keep me busy.

My parents would have never stood for this. Maybe this is why they stopped trusting Victor. Maybe the three of them disagreed on how ZIRDA should handle missions, and this is what drove them apart. Whatever happened, I need to stop dwelling on the past. Instead, I need to focus on getting Arella out of Shadow Ridge.

The base is completely guarded and crawling with other agents. If I had to guess, I'd say there are at least a hundred people there. Maybe two hundred. I won't make it three feet into the hallway with Arella in tow without someone stopping me. Whether it's Katie or that guard Victor has stationed outside, or the security guards, *someone* will stop me.

I slump onto the dirty ground with a huff. This plan is impossible, especially because I'm doing it alone. I could recruit help, but who? The only other Zordis I've had contact with recently are Liz and Jess.

Liz doesn't even know that I'm a ZIRDA agent. Even if she did, I refuse to bring her into this. I'm not willing to risk her life, and I think that's what it'll come down to in order to get Arella outta there—risking lives.

I'd be willing to risk Jess's life, but there's no way in hell she'd help me. Especially not after the way I kicked her out of my house. Besides, the thought of having to see her again is more unappealing than seeing a dog get run over.

So, it's up to me and only me. Whatever I'm planning to do, I have to do it quick. I have no idea how many days the previous Immunes lasted in the Ridge before their innocent lives were stolen. Arella's already been in there for half a day. The sooner I can get her out, the better.

I play the recording again.

"When you get to the rock, take a hundred steps away from Cheesy."

Back on my feet, I return to the rock my parents used to bring me to all the time. We used to camp here and lie down on blankets, stargazing. I know now that it was their way of helping me remember this place.

Cheesy is the name I gave a tree off in the distance. It's covered in holes. When I was a kid, I thought the holes were from birds and other animals. Now I'm pretty sure my parents put those holes there on purpose to give me a sense of direction. Telling a young child to take a hundred steps north or south isn't as effective as "take a hundred steps away from Cheesy."

For the gazillionth time, I start at the big rock, then turn my back to the holey tree and walk forward while I count my steps. *One, two, three . . .*

One hundred steps later, I'm back in the general area I've been scouring every time I try looking for this damn safe house. There's nothing here. No house. No sign that there ever was one. No bunker entry. Not even a trapdoor.

I hike around for a while, trying to see if there's anything I missed. Eventually, I give up. I'm pretty certain there's no safe house here.

With a heavy heart, I climb back onto my Harley and

begin the long ride back to Shadow Ridge. Ideally, I'd have a safe place to take Arella to once I get her outta there, but she can't wait until after I find my parents' invisible safe house. For now, I just need to rescue her. I'll figure the rest out later.

Shit plan, I know, but what else can I do?

9

TREY

At the entrance to Shadow Ridge, I stick my finger into the fingerprint scanner hole. *Beep! Beep! Beep!* The large door slides open. Two security guards are waiting for me on the other side.

I expect them to ask me why I'm here without being summoned, but they don't. *Odd.* Typically, field agents aren't allowed to enter the Ridge unless they have an appointment. I'm not gonna question it though. If they're slacking on their duties, I won't complain.

Carlos, the guard I used to pull pranks on as a kid, greets me with a grunt. "You again?"

I'm not in the mood to give him shit, so I keep my mouth shut.

"What?" he says. "No smart-ass comment? No rude remarks about my gray hair or my big-ass nose? Are you goin' soft now?"

"Just pat me down so I can get going."

"Sheesh. Someone's got their balls caught in a zipper."

As Carlos frisks me, I scan the security room. Multiple screens of all sizes show footage of people walking down hallways and gathered in the community room. The more screens I see, the more I think my already impossible rescue mission seems more impossible. They've got their eyes on everything, and there are people everywhere.

The other security guard stares me down from his rolling chair with a look on his face like he wants to strangle me. He's the guy with the eyebrow scar, who I wouldn't have even considered pulling pranks on as a kid. It's not normal for Zordis to have scars. With our ability to heal quickly and the healing products my parents invented, a Zordi has to *want* a scar to have one, or the injury had to have been pretty severe.

"Clear," Carlos says and steps back.

Without a word, I head toward the elevators.

I press the *down* button as my heart sprints like I'm running from a bear. I thought once I got in here, I'd know what to do. Not only was I wrong, but I'm starting to think this is a suicide mission.

The base has been having an issue with double agents lately. People might assume I'm one of them, which, technically, I am. No, I'm not working for the Royals, but I'm working for myself. If an agent sees me trying to walk outta here with Arella, they won't know that, and they won't hesitate to kill me. I doubt Victor would stop them either. I definitely should have thought this through more.

Ding!

One of the four elevators arrives and invites me in. I wait for two women to step out before jumping inside and pressing the 2 button. I don't know if I have permission to see Arella, but I'm going to. I need to make sure she's okay and assess the situation before I formulate the rest of my get-her-the-fuck-out plan.

When the elevator doors reopen, my breath hitches. It's her. She's still in that giant white T-shirt and those tattered orange shorts. We lock eyes, and it takes everything in me to not throw her over my shoulder and run. I'll throw fireballs at anyone who tries to stop me if that's what it takes. The only reason I don't do exactly that is because Katie and Victor's hulk-size security guard are standing right next to her.

"Oh, hey!" Katie says in a cheery tone. "That was quick."

"What was?"

The three of them join me in the elevator as Katie says, "I left you a voicemail, like, thirty seconds ago. Victor wants to see you immediately."

I had shut off my phone on the way here. I didn't want it to make any noise while I was in the middle of sneaking Arella out. "What's he want?"

"We're about to find out." With her hand not holding the iPad, Katie presses the 1 button.

"You mean you don't know?"

"He didn't tell me. I was just told to bring the Immune down to the battle box again."

I narrow my eyes at Katie because, surely, I didn't hear her right. "Again? As in . . . she's already been there?"

I scan Arella for any signs of cuts or bruises. She looks normal enough—if I ignore her puffy red eyes and that bleak expression.

"Not to worry," Katie says. "Unlike what the battle box is normally used for, that's not what happened this morning."

My memories of being in the battle box consist of fists and lightning balls hurling at my face. The battle box is where agents train in hand-to-hand combat and test their powers on each other. Arella belongs nowhere near that thing.

"Then what *did* happen this morning?" I try not to sound as enraged as I feel but fail.

"Victor asked three of our most powerful field agents to come in to test their powers on her. They tried a few methods to see if it would work."

"What kinds of methods?" I'm still failing at keeping my voice in the chill zone.

"The kinds that didn't work. Maybe that's why Victor wants you here. You've spent the most time with her. Maybe he thinks you can provide some insight on how we can crack her secret."

I've already cracked Arella's secret. *Well, sort of.* I know that I can break through her immunity walls by making her orgasm, but that's it. If anyone asks for more answers beyond that, I don't have them. I don't know how or why it's then and only then that I can sense her, and I don't care to know. The only thing I care about is keeping her safe.

Ding!

Arella doesn't look at me as the four of us step off the elevator. She still doesn't spare me a glance as we make our way down the wide halls. I'm aware that I deserve her cold shoulder, but it still stings. I wish there was a way for me to silently tell her that I'm working on getting her out. *Just hang in there, baby.*

As I follow Katie, I count how many agents we pass. Twelve. Some in the fitness center. Some heading into the pool room. One janitor mopping the floors. One security guard patrolling.

I can't see an exit route from here. Especially not when we're on the first floor, and the only exit to the surface is on floor six. At least, that's the only exit I know of. As a kid, I heard rumors of secret passageways in and out of Shadow Ridge, but I never found them. I'm sure Victor knows them all, but I doubt he'll share that precious information with me.

Katie leads us through a set of double doors and into an auditorium. In the battle box is Victor with two young women. One has long red curls and is wearing black leather pants. The other has short blueish-black hair and is chewing on some gum. Both women have eager energy shooting at me. *What the hell are they so eager about?*

"Look at that!" Victor says. "He's here already. I guess we can go straight into the second part of tonight's plan. Join us in the box, kid."

Something tells me I don't want to. Something also tells me I don't have a choice.

"Ordinary, are you gonna come up willingly this time, or will I have to ask Craig to assist again?"

Craig must be the name of Victor's security guard, because he's about to lift Arella when she throws a hand up.

"Don't touch me. I'll do it myself."

I trail her up the stairs and through the ropes, resisting the urge to ask if she's okay. Meanwhile, Katie and Craig take seats on the sidelines.

"What's going on?" Sparks flicker between my fingertips—a reflex I've developed from being in the battle box so often before. Also, I'm not liking the smug way those two women are looking at me.

Victor ignores my question as he nods at the Asian woman. "Go ahead, Pixie."

The woman puckers her lips. Before I can produce a single flame, an agonizing high-pitched sound shoots into my ears. I slam my palms against the sides of my head. It does nothing to block the pain. It hurts like hell. There are no other words to describe it. Just hell.

I drop to my knees. "Stop! Stop!"

It doesn't stop. If anything, it gets louder and stings more. In the corner of my eye, I see Pixie glance at Victor. He nods, then she stops blowing. The pain subsides, leaving a ringing in my ears.

"Goddammit!" I shout. At least, I *think* I shouted. I can barely hear myself. "What the fuck was that?"

Victor acts like he didn't hear me. He turns to Arella. "Use your immunity to shield him from Pixie's gift."

Arella draws her eyebrows together. "I . . . . I don't know how to do that."

"Try."

Out of nowhere, tiny invisible pitchforks attack my ears again. This time, it's louder and more excruciating. I wouldn't be surprised if my eardrums were bleeding. No matter how hard I press my palms to my ears, the agony stays the same.

Arella yells something. I can't hear what though. Her mouth looks like she's screaming "Stop! Stop!" The terrorized expression on her face makes me want to hold her and tell her I'll protect her, but I can't get off my knees long enough to get to her.

When Pixie closes her mouth, the sound stops. More importantly, so does the piercing pain. I fall onto my hands, gasping for air as the ringing returns.

"Fuckin' warn a guy!" My shouting sounds muffled.

Arella rushes to my side, dropping to her knees, with her hands cupping my face. Her touch feels like drinking an ice-cold bottle of Healing Water—therapeutic and refreshing.

Her lips move, but I can't make out the words. *Is she asking me something?* She yells at Victor, but I can't hear that either. They shout at each other for a moment before the ringing fades and my hearing slowly returns.

"We'll stop once you do what you're told," Victor says.

"I told you already! I don't know how!" Arella turns back to me with tears pooling in her eyes. "Trey, please tell me you're okay."

I offer her a weak grunt as I get to my feet. Arella holds me steady as I use her shoulder to keep me upright.

I scowl at the pathetic excuse for the only relative I have left. "Whatever you're trying to get her to do, it won't work."

"It will," Victor says. "She just needs the right motivation."

"No!" I slash my hand through the air. "You're treating her immunity as if it's a gift like ours. Like it's something she can use and control. For all we know, it's not possible for her to control it at all, let alone project it."

"It *is* possible. We got the last Immune to project his immunity onto someone else, which means she can too. She just needs to focus."

What? Victor never mentioned he got that far in this research. Why didn't he tell me? What else hasn't he told me?

"Ruby! Your turn!"

The redhead takes one look at me and hisses through her teeth. I collapse to my hands and knees again. The feeling of a hundred—no, a *thousand*—snakes biting into my skin takes over my entire body. I scream out as my muscles clench and burn. My arms give out, and I fall face first onto the floor.

"Stop!" Arella launches herself at Ruby. Pixie holds Arella back as Ruby keeps her eyes trained in my direction.

My body convulses like I'm being tasered from all sides. I lied earlier. Pixie's eardrum-stabbing power isn't hell. This is. Pure, unfiltered hell.

"Project your immunity onto him!" Victor orders.

"I can't! Just stop! Please!"

Victor slices a hand through the air. Finally, Ruby drops her arm. The agony on my skin fades. My body is left with a lingering burn.

I turn onto my back, panting as my vision goes blurry. I can't feel my thighs or anything below them. I would have taken Pixie's ear pain over whatever the hell that bullshit was.

"Let me go!" Arella shouts. A second later, she kneels at my side.

I can't see her because I can't get my eyes to reopen. I only feel her warm palm press against my stubbly cheek.

"Trey!" She says my name through a broken sob. "I'm so sorry. I don't know how to make them stop."

"I told you already," Victor says from across the battle box, "you just need to focus. Imagine yourself protecting him with metal shields or maybe some armor. If you don't save him, he will die. Ruby, hit him again."

I brace myself for the pain. It doesn't come.

"You sure, Big V?" Ruby says. "I went pretty hard on him. He might need a break."

"He can handle it."

No, I can't! I don't get a chance to say that out loud because the stinging ache in my limbs returns. I lose all control over my convulsing body. Someone could be throwing knives into an open wound in the middle of my chest and it would feel like butterfly kisses compared to this.

My limbs tremble against the floor.

Nausea.

Throbbing.

Vomit rises in the back of my throat.

Arella drapes her body over mine as if it'll shield me from the stinging pain. It doesn't. Not even a little bit.

"Stop!" She sobs into my chest. "Stop hurting him!"

"Project your immunity onto him!" Victor shouts.

"I can't! Stop! Please!"

"Ruby, go harder!"

Seriously? There's a setting above this one? The torture increases. It's like snake venom, and bee stings, and being mauled by a jaguar, and—

Arella pulls me into her lap, clutching me against her front. She rocks back and forth as my body trembles in her arms. Tears pour down her cheeks as she screams, "Stop hurting him! Stop hurting him! Stop hurting him!"

Somehow, I find the strength to get some words out. "Arella, please, make it stop."

She takes my face into her hands and gives me a squeeze. "I don't know how."

"Please," I beg because she's my only hope. "Make it stop."

My vision's blurry again. I can't feel my legs. *Are they still attached to my body?*

Arella breathes deeply as she mutters inaudible words to herself and rocks me in her grasp. If this is my end, I won't be too mad about it. I'm in the arms of the woman I love. What could be better?

Suddenly, the burning stops. My body goes limp. I don't

gasp for air this time. My lungs are too tired for that. Instead, my breaths come out short and ragged. Arella's tears roll down her face and onto my cheeks. I want to wipe her tears away, but I can't feel my arms.

"I never told you to stop!" Victor shouts.

"I didn't," Ruby says through hisses. "I'm still going."

Victor gasps at the same time Pixie does.

"She did it," Pixie says. "She actually did it."

10

TREY

"You monsters!" Arella keeps me tight against her body, and I'm grateful for it. "How could you do this to him? He's barely breathing."

"The kid knows it's for the greater good." Victor stomps toward her and stops only to yank her up by her arm.

I tumble out of her grasp and onto the battle box's floor, too weak to catch myself. I still can't feel my limbs.

"Ruby! Do your thing."

I cry out as the invisible snakes sink their teeth into my skin again.

"Stop!" Arella collapses next to me. She cups my face and shuts her eyes. It takes a moment before the agony disappears and my body stops shaking.

"Are you stinging him?" Victor asks.

"Yes," Ruby hisses.

"Outstanding! That's twice in a row."

I can't open my eyes enough to see it, but I know Victor's grinning. I'll bet this is one of the happiest days of his life. He gets to see me suffer while he performs tests on an Immune. Win-win for him.

"Pixie, how 'bout you give it a shot?" Victor says.

"No!" Arella cups my face tighter. She presses her forehead against mine, whispering something I can't make out. I wait for the ear pain to come. It never does.

"She's blocking it," Pixie says.

I pry my eyes open just enough to see my girl with tears streaming down her cheeks. With a quivering hand, I wipe one away.

I've always been amazed by this woman. At first because she was immune. Then because of her inner strength. Then because of how she got me to fall in love with her so effortlessly. Now she's projecting her immunity onto me. She's absolutely incredible.

For the second time, Victor pulls Arella up by her arm, snatching her away from me.

Arella punches him in the chest. "Let me go!"

Panting, I twist onto my side, then hoist myself onto my elbows. It takes a few breaths before I'm able to push myself onto my knees.

"Quit manhandling her!" My voice comes out coarse, like I've smoked a pack a day for fifty years.

Victor ignores me as he shoves Arella toward the Asian woman.

The flames between my fingers flicker.

"Hold hands with Pixie," Victor orders.

Pixie grabs Arella's hand and keeps her there.

"Ruby, do your thing on Pixie."

Screaming, Pixie falls to her knees. The stings mirror onto my body for a second before I draw back my Empath power to avoid it.

"Stop!" Pixie shouts.

Ruby drops her hand immediately.

Pixie lets go of Arella's hand and pants. "Jesus fucking Christ! Couldn't you have gone easy on me?"

Ruby grits her teeth together apologetically. "Sorry, Pix. That was on my lowest power."

Victor points at Ruby. "Go hold the Ordinary's hand."

With a few clicks of her heels, Ruby does what she's told. Once her hand is joined with Arella's, Pixie is ordered to blow at her. Ruby shrieks toward the ceiling, clutching one of her ears, until the pain stops.

"Sorry, Roobs," Pixie mimics. "That was on my lowest power."

Victor crosses his arms over his chest. "Ordinary, do whatever you did on Trey on the girls."

Arella shakes her head. "I don't even know what I'm doing."

"Go hold Trey's hand again."

Arella doesn't waste any time obeying that request. She stands at my side and grips my arm like it's a lifeline. I think about running and dragging her with me, but I doubt I can make it out of here without one of us getting hurt. For once, I'm glad I can't sense her emotions. The expression on her face is enough for me to know that she's scared to death. *I'm scared too, baby.*

"Both of you," Victor says. "Hit him with all you've got."

A piercing sound stabs my ears as my body burns like it's on fire. Arella squeezes my hand harder, closing her eyes. I fall to my knees, counting at least ten seconds of pure agony before it finally stops. Arella kneels at my side, gripping onto my hand so tight, it hurts. I plant my other hand against the floor to keep myself from collapsing over. My breaths come out in heavy pants.

"Let go of him," Victor says.

"No!" Arella squeezes my hand harder.

Victor wrenches her up by her hair. Hearing her scream hurts me more than what those women have been doing to me. I don't think about it as I shoot up onto my feet, grip Arella by her waist, and yank her behind me. Flames appear in my palm, and I chuck them at the back of my uncle's head. My fireball misses and falls to the floor before disappearing into a cloud of smoke. Stupid, because I rarely miss. My trembling fingers are throwing me off.

Victor twists on his heel and shoots me a death glare. "Did you just throw a fireball at me?"

"I told you to quit manhandling her!"

The auditorium goes silent. The look in Victor's eyes screams murder. The anger radiating off him says he'll do it. I wouldn't put it past him.

Surprisingly, Victor relaxes his shoulders and turns to the women. "Thanks for your time, ladies. You're dismissed."

Without a word, Pixie and Ruby exit through the double doors. The second they're gone, Victor comes at me with a fist up. I push Arella out of the way and duck. She stumbles to the side as I back the other way. As I hoped, Victor follows me, hurling another fist at my face. This time, it lands. My head snaps to the side as pain explodes up my jaw.

"How dare you attack me!" He aims a kick at my chest. I manage to get out of the way, only to get sucked into a tornado. Spinning, it carries me toward the ceiling. Victor circles his wrist in the air as his tornado whips me from side to side, round and round. "I should have gotten rid of you after the police dropped you off on my goddamn doorstep! If I wasn't the only living relative you had left, I would have unloaded your dumb ass with someone else. You've been nothing but a fucking nuisance, you worthless piece of shit!"

I kick, and swim, and jump. I even try using my telekinesis. Nothing works to get me out of his spiraling tornado. I'm trapped, and I'm dizzy.

"I should kill you right now for throwing that fireball at me. Teach you a fucking lesson!"

The air is sucked from my lungs as the tornado disappears. From the ceiling, I fall straight back into the battle box and land on my front. My head bounces back from the impact as agony flares up my cheek. Wheezing, I force myself onto my knees only to find Victor pointing a finger at Arella.

"Quit that shit!" he says.

My girl shoots a dirty look at him. "You've spent all day trying to get me to do this, and *now* you want me to stop?"

The auditorium goes silent again.

From the stands, a deep voice says, "She's got a point, boss."

Victor directs a glare at Craig. "Nobody asked you."

I get to my feet and march across the battle box to stand in front of Arella protectively. "This is over. You have no right to treat her like this. No right to be yelling out orders to her or manhandling her like she's a fucking ragdoll. She's an Ordinary. A person that we, as ZIRDA agents, have sworn to protect."

"Well, aren't you Mr. Righteous tonight?" Victor scoffs and even has the nerve to chuckle. "You don't get it, kid. Within the last day, this Ordinary has gone from being unable to tap into her immunity to activating it while making skin-to-skin contact with you. Then, just now, she projected it onto you while you were near the ceiling. That's way more progress than the last Immune.

"Don't you see? She's it! She's the key we've been looking for. The ultimate win against the Royals. Once we can get her to fully control and project her immunity, she can help us wipe them out of existence. And once we can replicate her immunity to make the rest of us immune too, this could be the end for the Royals. It all begins here—with her."

Having the right intention doesn't justify purposely hurting innocent people. Clearly, Victor has no boundaries when it comes to completing his life's mission of eliminating all the Royals. I'm certain that he'll kill off as many Immunes as it takes to finish the job. Yes, the Royals tried to kill him and they succeeded in killing his younger brother—my father. We both lost people we loved at the hands of the Royals, but at some point, we need to say enough is enough.

When Victor first assigned me to Arella, he said the goal

was simply to find out the source of her immunity. No one was supposed to get hurt or kidnapped. Somewhere between here and there, he has justified doing whatever it takes to get what he wants. We can find another way to bring down the Royals. A way that aligns with ZIRDA's values of protecting Ordinaries.

I wish I could say all that to Victor, but it won't change his mind. He's so blinded by his need for vengeance that he's drifted too far off the path of what's right. He thinks it's okay to kill one to save a thousand, but if that one is Arella, he'll have to get through me first.

"Craig, get your ass up here and make yourself useful," Victor says.

In an instant, Craig is in the battle box with us. I keep Arella close behind me.

"Craig has the ability to shrink anything down to the size of a grain of rice," Victor says to Arella. "Unless you want Trey to be squashed under my shoe, you'll project your immunity onto him."

Without a single warning, Craig points at me, and I'm falling. Except, I'm not. The room has gotten bigger. Every passing second makes everything sound louder and echoey.

My already aching body doubles over as I clutch my stomach. Vomit sprays out of my mouth onto the floor, and then I cough as another wave of vomit rises inside me. Arella's shriek vibrates through the air as a giant shoe appears above me.

———

SOMEONE SHAKES MY ARM. MY EYES POP OPEN.

Katie leans back into a chair and stares at me with a honeyed smile. *How is this girl always so happy?* If I wasn't an Empath, I'd think it's fake, but the energy I sense from her is light and content.

"Good morning," she says and holds out a bottle of Healing Water to me. She glances at the iPad in her lap. "Actually, no. Good afternoon! How ya feelin'?"

I sit up and glance around. Sterile white cabinets. A sink in the corner. A beeping sound coming from a machine. An IV is taped to my arm, connected to a bag of fluids. I'm on a hospital bed with crisp white sheets. I've been here before. Many times. This is the infirmary on the third floor of Shadow Ridge.

I accept the Healing Water and unscrew the cap. It's hard to move. My arms are sore, and my fingers have lost some dexterity. Still, I put my lips against the opening of the bottle and chug. It's the berry-flavored kind—my least favorite. I didn't even check the label before consuming it. Still, I drink it all in one breath.

"Wow," Katie says. "That's one hell of a party trick."

I press a button on the side of the bed. The top half of the mattress folds upward until it's in a comfortable position for me to lean against. My hazy head has a pounding migraine, and I swear I can still hear Pixie's ringing in my ears.

"Where is she?" My voice comes out scratchy.

"In her room."

The fuck she is. If Arella was in "her room," she'd be in her apartment. "Why aren't you there with her?"

"Victor told me to check on you. He wanted me to make sure you were okay."

I scoff, and it hurts my throat to do so. "He hasn't cared about my well-being since I was a kid. Why start now?"

Last night, Victor almost killed me. I'll bet if no one was around, he would have. When I was trapped in his tornado, I sensed his rage and need to bang me against the ceiling until every bone in my body was in pieces.

"Victor has to care about you somewhat," Katie says. "He's asked me to check on you at least five times a day since that night in the battle box."

That night in the battle box? Instantly, the haze clears from my head. "Say again?"

"I said that Victor's gotta care about—"

"No, no. Not that. What was the last part?"

"Um, that he's asked me to check on you multiple times since that night in the battle box?"

My body stills. "And how many nights ago was that?"

"Three."

"Three?" *She's gotta be kidding me.*

"Being shrunk does a lot of trauma to a person's body. Not to mention you were shrunk and reshrunk almost ten times in a matter of five minutes."

I don't remember that. I must have passed out by that point. I point to the IV sticking out of my arm. "What the hell is this for?"

"Fluids and pain medication, according to the nurse. She said you'd need at least another two days to fully heal, but Victor insisted on getting you back into the battle box today."

I let out a *fuck that* chuckle. "What makes him think I'm gonna willingly allow people to torment me like that?"

"I don't think you have a choice. Victor won't stop this research just because it causes you a little pain."

"A little? I was knocked out cold for three days! I'd rather be a lion's chew toy than ever get volun-told to participate in that bullshit again."

"While you've been out, other people have been volunteering. Victor's tried countless methods to get the Immune to project onto someone other than you. So far, every test has been unsuccessful." Katie straightens her back and smiles. "Now do you think you can get up? We don't want to keep Victor waiting."

11

____

ARELLA

Two days ago, I woke up to Katie strolling into my prison room, carrying a food tray.

"Wakey wakey!" she said in her overly cheery voice. I wasn't sure if she did that because she's naturally cheerful or if she thinks it would make me less anxious about being held captive against my will. "I wasn't sure what you'd want, so I grabbed one of everything." She placed the tray onto the nightstand. It was covered with an assortment of baked breakfast goods and a glass of milk. Then she drew out a metal key from her pocket to uncuff my ankle from the bedframe.

Before going to sleep the night before, I had convinced Katie to cuff my ankle instead of my wrist. It was hard to sleep with my arm like that.

"Last night was a big night for you," Katie said. "You made the first step to controlling your immunity. Victor's so thrilled, he added four new meetings to your calendar to try it again."

I hated how she said all that like I was an employee here. I sat up and rubbed the crust from my eyes. "Where's Trey?"

Katie scooted her folding chair closer to the bed. Her

128

energy, all anxious and apprehensive, wafted toward me. "He's still in the infirmary."

"Is he okay?"

"He's not dead, if that's what you're wondering." Between Katie's uneasy emotions shooting at me and the troubled look on her face, I assumed Trey wasn't doing too hot.

When Craig the Hulk shrunk him over and over, Trey threw up four times and coughed up blood. No matter how much I begged, Victor refused to let me hold him. That heartless man kept pinning me down and screaming at me to project my immunity onto Trey from across the battle box. Projecting onto Trey while he was in the tornado had felt like a one-off chance. I didn't know how I had done it or how to do it again.

I cried hysterically while Victor kept shouting, "Focus! Focus!" into my ear. Because, you know, shouting at people like that is helpful. When Trey, the size of a cat, slumped onto the floor and didn't look like he was breathing, I lost it.

I screamed at the ceiling, and somehow, I did something to make Trey return to his normal size. After that, no matter how hard Craig tried, he couldn't shrink Trey again.

Then and only then did Victor call for someone to drag poor, unconscious Trey to the infirmary. In the meantime, Katie and Craig escorted me back to my prison room. With my ankle cuffed to the bed, I cried myself to sleep, wondering if I'd ever see Trey again.

Hearing that Trey was still alive gave me a tiny bit of relief—assuming Katie was telling the truth.

When I finished eating breakfast, Katie directed me to the shower and handed me a new set of clothes. I could already tell this outfit would fit me better.

"It's from my own closet," Katie said. "We're about the same size, so I figured why not? Your current outfit was plucked from the lost and found. If you want your pajamas instead, they're clean now."

"I appreciate you sharing your clothes with me."

Twenty minutes later, I stepped out of the bathroom, wearing a plain black V-neck and some gray leggings.

For the rest of the day, they kept me in the "battle box"—a fancy name for their torture station disguised as a boxing ring. I held hands with countless *volunteers*, as Victor called them, while Pixie and Ruby tormented each person with their powers. I tried everything I could to protect them but failed.

Around nightfall—not that I knew for sure, because I hadn't seen a single window in this place—Katie dropped me off in a small lab room with a lady wearing a white lab coat.

Throughout the night, White Coat Lady performed a series of tests on me—Everything from checking my reflexes to drawing blood samples to taking my handprint. She examined every part of my mouth, eyes, ears, and vagina. I had never been so violated in my life, and that was saying a lot after spending three years with a man who used to force himself on me. What was she looking for?

White Coat Lady spent another eternity asking me health-related questions, some of which Katie had already asked me. Some of my answers made her ask follow-up questions. Other times, she just nodded and moved on.

Once the interrogation was over, the White Coat Lady secured me to a medical bed. The leather straps were so tight against my wrists and ankles, they pinched my skin.

"Shield yourself from the shock," she said as a sizzling lightning ball appeared in her palms.

"No!"

The lady dropped the orb onto me. A surge of electricity rippled through my veins. I screamed out, and my body convulsed, tugging against the restraints.

"Picture something around your body." Another sizzling ball appeared in her hand. "Armor, a box, a glass tank, anything that will protect you."

The glowing ball landed on my chest again. I yelled toward the ceiling as brutal torture tore through my limbs.

She did it again.

And again.

And again.

Every time, I was unable to protect myself, no matter how badly I wanted to. From the content emotions I sensed from her, she didn't feel bad for hurting me.

I heaved for air when the electrocution finally stopped. *Is it over?* Something pinched the side of my neck, then White Coat Lady placed a syringe onto a metal tray.

My words came out between short breaths. "What did you just do to me?"

"It's a z-drug called perrizophine," the lady said, like she drugged people all the time without their consent. She probably did. "This small dose will deactivate your immunity for a few hours. At least, we're going to see if it does."

I didn't know if it deactivated my immunity, but it had definitely deactivated my baby's ability to sense people. All of a sudden, I couldn't sense White Coat Lady's emotions anymore.

The door opened, then Victor sauntered in. The sight of him disgusted me. "Any progress?"

"Not much," White Coat Lady said.

"Did you hit her with the perrizo yet?"

"Just did."

"Great. Lemme take a look at her."

White Coat Lady stepped back to give Victor some space. With both hands, he held my head still. As he stared into my eyes, I balled up some saliva in my mouth. The second a black cloud smoked up in his pupils, I spat at him.

Victor bounced back with a groan. "You nasty little bitch."

I'd been called worse by my ex, so I didn't care what he called me.

White Coat Lady held out a towel to Victor. "Sir."

Victor wiped his face off, then tossed the towel behind him. "Got any duct tape?"

From a drawer, the lady pulled out a roll of silver tape and ripped off a piece. Victor took it from her. I squirmed as he tried to seal it over my mouth. Since I could only move so much, he won our battle. I panted through my nose as he ripped a second piece of tape off the roll.

"For good measure," Victor said as he stuck it over my mouth.

Within seconds, that black cloud took over the whites of his eyes again. What was he trying to do? Burn a hole through my face? Read my mind? Or maybe—I internally gasped. Was it mind control? That was how all these people worked for him so willingly, wasn't it? He was trying to turn me into one of his minions. Maybe it worked on the other people, but it wouldn't work on me. Well, they weren't *people*, exactly. They had to be aliens. Aliens who could take the form of humans.

If not that, maybe they were X-men. Katie claimed they were simply humans who were born with powers. Were X-men born with powers? I couldn't remember. I'd only seen one X-men movie, and it was a long time ago.

With a huff, Victor stepped back, and his pupils returned to normal. "It's no use. Not even the perrizo is lowering her immunity walls. I suppose since the z-drug didn't work, we can rule out that she's part Zordi and that immunity is her gift."

White Coat Lady crinkled her face. "How could she be part Zordi? It's impossible for us to reproduce with Ordis."

Ahh. That explained why Trey said he was infertile. It wasn't that he couldn't make babies. He just couldn't make babies with regular humans. It all made sense. Except, not. If it was "impossible" for these aliens to reproduce with humans, then how did I get pregnant?

Victor scoffed loudly. "It's also impossible for someone to be immune to our powers, yet here she is. I'm not saying I had bets on her being part Zordi. That was just one of the many theories I came up with to explain this freak of nature."

Me? A freak of nature? Of all people to be calling someone a freak of nature, why was it the man who could turn his eyeballs completely black?

The two of them continued talking, but I couldn't make out their words anymore. Suddenly, my eyelids felt heavy . . .

YESTERDAY, I WOKE UP FROM A NIGHTMARE, DRIPPING WITH sweat. I gasped for air as I sprung upright.

Katie's chair was empty. The only light was coming from the crack under the door. It was too dark to read the wall clock. It must have been early if Katie wasn't around yet.

I had to use the bathroom, but I couldn't get in there with my ankle handcuffed to the bed. As far as I knew, Katie was the only person with a key, and I had no way to contact her.

After a while of tossing and turning, I concluded that I couldn't fall back asleep while my bladder was that full. The thought of wetting the bed was too embarrassing for me to consider. Maybe I could ask that guard to get Katie for me.

Wait . . . Where's the guard? Normally, I could sense his presence out there, even if he was only feeling content. I didn't sense anyone outside the door. I sat up again to see if I could spot his shadow through the bottom crack. No shadow.

Why would Victor leave me unguarded? Maybe something happened and everyone left. That terrified me. They wouldn't ditch me here all alone, restrained to a bed, would they? Why was the idea of that worse than the idea of them taking me back to the battle box?

A while later, the door crept open, then Katie tiptoed in. She used the flashlight on her phone to see her way to her chair. Quietly, she sat and did something on her iPad as the sound of that dreaded chain lock slid into place.

So there is *someone out there.* Why couldn't I sense them? Why couldn't I sense Katie either? That drug the White Coat Lady injected into me had to have worn off by now.

Oh no. I glanced at my belly and gave it a rub. *Please be okay.*

Katie glanced up from her iPad and found me staring at her. She jolted back and slapped a hand over her chest. "Ah! You scared me."

"Sorry." I half meant it.

"I didn't realize you were awake." She stood to flip the light on.

I squinted from the brightness.

Katie returned to her chair, scooting it closer to me before settling back onto it. "How did you sleep?"

"I had a bad dream."

"What was your dream about?"

Victor holding me back while those two women torture Trey until he takes his last breath. What else? "Um, I'll just say that you people aren't only scary in real life."

"I'm sorry." She offered me a sympathetic look. I couldn't tell if she meant it or not. Her emotions weren't coming to me. "What's that like?"

"Being surrounded by scary people?"

"No, dreaming."

I tilted my head to the side. "You've never had a dream?"

"Zordis don't dream. For some reason, we can't. There's no study that explains why, but there are theories. The one I believe the most is that because we only need to sleep every two days, our brain completely shuts down during that time. Therefore, no dreams."

"Weird." But not as weird as how they could go two days without sleeping. That explained why Trey was up all night so often.

"Sooo," Katie said, "what's it like?"

"Um, I guess it's like living real life, but it's in your head and crazy things can happen."

She nodded slowly with her mouth partly open, like she was trying really hard to understand the concept of a dream. "Fascinating. I've heard that sometimes it feels like a hallucination or like you're watching a movie."

"I guess so."

"I'd like to experience a dream one day. It sounds fun."

A long silence sat between us. It felt partly awkward and partly calming. Most of my time here had been chaotic. That was the most normal conversation I'd had since being kidnapped.

Katie cleared her throat. "He's still in the infirmary, in case you're wondering."

I was wondering, so I was glad she told me without me having to ask. "Is he okay?"

"The nurse said his vitals look better than yesterday. He still hasn't woken up though."

"Like at all?"

"At all."

The poor guy. Trey must have been in really bad shape if he couldn't wake up. *Wait . . .* I narrowed my eyes at Katie. "How do I know he's still alive? What if you people have already killed him, and you're lying to me about it?"

"I guess you'll just have to trust me. If you don't, you can trust that Victor won't get rid of the only person you've successfully projected your immunity onto. Anyway"—Katie slapped her thighs with her palms—"are ya hungry? Should I go get you some breakfast?"

"Actually, could you let me into the bathroom first? I've had to go for a while."

"Sure thing." She released my ankle, and I practically ran to the toilet.

After I did my business, I checked the water. Only yellow, no red. I leaned down to inspect it a little closer, just in case I missed a speck. Still no red. I was sure of it though. I'd been sure since the moment Katie walked into this room and I couldn't sense her. Maybe I wasn't bleeding now, but I would eventually.

I braced myself against the sink as the reality of what had happened sunk in. I was sad. Why was I so sad? It was an unplanned pregnancy with a man who turned out to be a mutant with superpowers. Two nights ago, I saw fire come out of his hand. His *hand.* Who knew what else he could do?

His baby had the power to sense other people's emotions. If a Zordi fetus could do that from inside the womb, what else could it do? Would it have thrown fireballs inside me? Would I have had the power to make fire come out of my hands too? How insane! I should have been relieved that the baby was gone, but I wasn't.

Before I was kidnapped, Trey and I talked over the phone about raising this child together. Stupidly, I believed with all my heart that it was something he wanted. Especially since he still wanted me after I lied about sleeping with "some guy from college." I figured that once we had patched things up, I could confess that I'd lied and prove he was the father, then everything would be okay.

I didn't realize how much I wanted to be a mother—until the opportunity was stolen from me. I collapsed to the tile floor and cried into my hands. It wasn't a silent cry either. It was one of those ugly cries with my mouth fully open as I wailed.

The bathroom door jerked open and hit me. Katie popped her head in. "You okay?"

I shook my head, unable to answer with words.

She gestured for me to move over. I did, scooting closer to the toilet so she could get in. Once she was through the door, she clicked it shut.

Katie sat on the floor with me and rubbed a tender hand over my shoulder. "What's wrong?"

I didn't have it in me to explain. The only thing I had the strength for was to cry. Katie didn't force me to speak. She simply circled her arms around me and hugged me tight. I let her because something about her made me feel at ease. Plus, I was willing to take any form of comfort.

We stayed like that until my sobbing subsided. I wasn't sure how long it was.

Through hiccups, I asked, "What happens to you people when you die?"

She pressed her eyebrows together. "What do you mean?"

"Like what happens to your bodies?"

"Um, we just . . . die. Obviously, we lose our powers, and everything about our bodies become like Ordinaries. Well, except for Shifters. If they die in another form, whether it's an animal, an object, or another person, they'll stay that way."

Shifters? Apparently, that wasn't just a thing in books and movies. "Does anything special happen when a Zordi dies *before* they're born?"

At first, Katie's face scrunched together, then her eyes went wide and she whispered, "Are you pregnant?"

"Was." That single word almost made me burst into tears again.

Still hushed, she said, "Are you saying you were pregnant with . . . a Zordi?"

I nodded.

That mousey voice of hers disappeared as she continued whispering, "That can't be. Our biological makeups are too different for fertilization to happen. The Ordinary egg isn't strong enough to hold the nature of a Zordi sperm."

I stared at the bathroom floor. "Maybe whatever makes me immune to your powers also makes me immune to all that."

Katie thought for a moment, then shook her head. "Nope. It's impossible. Your immunity has nothing to do with your reproductive organs. For you to have conceived a child with a Zordi, you'd have to be a Zordi with Zordi eggs in your ovaries. It's impossible for you to be one of us because you don't have any gifts. And if immunity was your gift, it would have been turned off by the perrizophine. Last night, your body was affected by only the sedative part of the perrizo, and you took to it faster than the average Zordi, which further confirms that you're an Ordi. Also, our zense doesn't activate around you."

"Zense? What's that?"

"It's a little tingle we get in our chests whenever we're within an arm's length of each other."

"Interesting." By the look on Katie's face, I could tell she was about to ask, so I beat her to it. "No, my chest doesn't tingle around you guys."

"Immune *and* a Mind Reader. You really are something special." She leaned in to me again, lowering her voice. "How are you so sure you were pregnant with a Zordi baby?"

"I've only slept with one man recently. And for the last few days, up until last night, I was sensing everyone's emotions."

Katie gasped, then lowered her voice so much, I could barely hear her. "Your baby was an Empath. You must have been at least seven or eight weeks along. That's when our mind powers begin developing in the womb."

That timing was right. "Mind powers?"

"All Zordis are born with three gifts. Our mind power is the most powerful because it begins developing the earliest. Our body and elemental powers are determined before birth, but those don't develop until we're about a year old. Then, it's not until puberty when our powers become fully developed."

It was nice to know that my baby couldn't have thrown fireballs or made tornados inside my uterus.

Katie went back to whispering. "Does he know?"

I match her tone. "Does who know what?"

"The father. Trey." She points at my stomach with her eyes. "Does he know?"

"Yeah, I told him."

"He didn't think the baby was his, did he?"

I shook my head as a single tear rolled down my cheek. "No, he didn't."

"I wouldn't have believed you either. Even now, knowing that your baby was sensing emotions in the womb, it's *still* hard to believe." Katie leaned in to my ear, then said softly yet firmly, "Victor cannot find out about this."

I whisper back. "Why?"

"Think about it. He's already doing whatever he can to find out the source of your immunity and to get you to control it. Imagine what he'd do if he knew you could carry a Zordi child."

I pictured myself restrained to a bed as a bunch of Zordi men violated me while Victor sat on the sidelines, taking notes. It would go on for months to years before I was pregnant again. Assuming it was possible for me to carry a half-human, half-wizard baby to term, Victor would have his hands on the world's first half-and-half baby. I didn't even want to think about what he'd do with that child.

Katie stood and offered me her hand. "Come on. We've gotta get outta here before they find it suspicious that I'm in the bathroom with you for this long."

Sighing, I took her hand and allowed her to help me off the floor.

12

ARELLA

It's been three days since I've seen Trey alive. I trust that Katie's telling me the truth, but I won't fully believe her until I actually see him. She's been giving me updates on his condition after she checks on him every few hours. So far, he still hasn't woken up. Knowing he's been out cold for this long worries me.

"Welcome back," Victor says as I step into the boxing ring. I do it willingly because I don't want Craig touching me again.

I can't sense Victor or Craig's energy. I can't sense Pixie, Ruby, or Derek either. Suddenly, I feel the most alone since being kidnapped. Before, I had the presence of my unborn baby. Now I have no one. I don't even have Katie. After she fed me breakfast, she left, and I haven't seen her since. It was Craig who brought me lunch and escorted me down here.

While I hug myself in the corner, Victor speaks to his four minions in a low voice. I can't make out anything he's saying. Judging by the head nods coming from the others, it looks like Victor's giving them instructions.

Behind me, the double doors open with a squeak. Katie strolls in with Trey at her side. He looks rough: messy hair, dark beard lining his jaw, and grayish skin. His gaze never leaves me as he climbs up the stairs and into the battle box. Meanwhile, Katie finds a seat in the front row of the auditorium.

"Now that everyone's here," Victor says, "let's start. Ordinary, go hold Trey's hand."

I don't need to move because in an instant, Trey is at my side. A troubled storm brews in his eyes as he intertwines his fingers with mine. I hate how normal it feels to hold his hand and to feel the warmth his touch sends up my arm. He's the very reason I'm here, and I shouldn't be comforted by him. Still, I'm relieved to see him alive. No matter what he's done or how we got here, he doesn't deserve to be tortured.

Victor takes a few steps back until he's leaning against the ropes. "Today's objective is to see how versatile the Ordinary's immunity can be. Once we get an idea of that, we'll take more time in the upcoming days to explore each of her skills to strengthen them."

Days? That's how long they plan to torture Trey in front of me? One second is already too long.

"Ordinary, your first goal is to see if you can project your immunity onto Trey without us hurting him first. Think you can do that?"

"She has a name," Trey growls.

Victor points a stern finger at him. I squeeze Trey's hand to protect him from whatever powers Victor is about to use on him. Nothing happens. Instead, Victor shouts, "Don't speak unless you're spoken to."

Trey squeezes my hand back as if to say he'll protect me; however, *he's* the one who needs protection. "Stop referring to her as *Ordinary*. She has a name."

"I will call her whatever the fuck I please. Now, are you gonna shut your goddamn mouth, or do you wanna keep being a nuisance?"

Trey grits his teeth together. "I never signed up to be your test puppet."

"You signed up for this when you accepted this mission."

"No. I signed up to find out the source of her immunity. This"—Trey gestures around the room—"is not what I—"

"Shut your fuckin' mouth!" Victor crosses his arms over his chest. "If you delay this session one more time, I'm releasing you from this mission. Actually, I'll be releasing you from all of ZIRDA. Speak another word without my permission. I dare you. Craig can escort you straight out to the waterfall, and you'll never be allowed back for any reason. Is that what you want?"

Trey clenches his jaw together as he sucks in a breath and slowly lets it out. I can't sense the anger radiating off him, but I can definitely see it. Keeping his job must be important to him, because he doesn't say another word.

"Anyway," Victor says, "Ordinary, project your immunity onto him. When you're ready, Pixie will blow his ears. Again, your goal is to prevent him from feeling any pain before it comes. Got it?"

I glance up at Trey, who looks back at me with a *you can do it* confidence in his eyes. It makes me believe I can.

"Take a moment to prepare yourself," Victor says. "Let Pixie know when you're ready."

I close my eyes and replay the things they did to Trey three nights ago. I hear him screaming. I see his body shaking against the floor. I picture him throwing up blood. Then I open my eyes, squeeze Trey's hand, and give Pixie a nod.

She closes the distance between us until she's three steps away. Then she puckers her lips and blows.

"Fuck!" Trey tries to cover his ears as I squeeze his hand with all my might. Barely a second later, he puts his arms down and breathes normally again.

"Did she do it?" Victor asks.

"I'm blowing," Pixie says. "He seems to be okay."

"Good." Victor claps as if we're part of a show. He should get a refund for his ticket because I never auditioned for this play, and I don't want to keep performing in it. "Immune, let's try that again. This time, *really* focus."

I squeeze Trey's hand with both of mine. Pixie blows again. The same thing happens. Trey screams in agony as he uses his free hand to cover an ear. *Does that even do anything?*

"Try again," Victor says.

And this goes on for the next half hour. No matter how much I beg, Victor keeps ordering Pixie to hurt Trey, who's on his knees, gasping for air. I kneel in front of him and cup his face. His cheeks are red, and the whites of his eyes are too.

"I'm so sorry," I plead in a low voice, hoping he'll forgive me. "I want to shield you from the pain, but I don't know how."

"Don't apologize," he whispers as he wipes the tears from my face with his thumb. "None of this is your fault."

My body hiccups from all the sobbing I've been doing. Trey knits his eyebrows together and presses his lips into a hard line. He looks like he's a second away from putting me over his shoulder and making a run for it. A part of me hopes that's why he's still here and is just waiting for the right time. I'm not the only one who needs escaping anymore.

"Stand up," Victor orders. "Let's raise the stakes a little. Ruby, how 'bout you try?"

Oh no. Not her. Whatever power Ruby has seems to feel like death crawling through the bloodstream.

Trey helps me to my feet, and I seize his hand. He closes his eyes, bracing himself for the pain. I shut my eyes too, just as Ruby raises her arm and hisses. *Don't hurt him. Don't hurt him.* I wait for Trey to scream, but he doesn't.

"She's blocking it," Ruby says.

I don't dare open my eyes because I can't lose concentration. I don't know if she's still stinging him or not.

"Pixie, you give it a shot."

A moment later, Pixie says, "She's blocking mine too."

"Excellent!" Victor says, clapping. "What progress! Let's

move on. Immune, your next goal is to protect Trey from an ice ball. Derek?"

On cue, Derek stands from his squat and draws an arm back. A sparkling ice sphere flies through the air, straight at Trey's head.

"Fuck that." Trey ducks and drags me down with him. The ice ball lands behind us and shatters against the floor. I don't get a chance to take another breath before a second ice ball soars through the air and hits Trey right in the stomach. He coughs and falls to his knees as another ice ball whizzes through the air. It hits him again, right in the face. That's going to leave a mark.

"Stop!" I shout. "I don't know how to shield him from stuff like that."

"And three days ago, you didn't know how to shield him at all," Victor says. "So try harder!"

Derek readies another ice ball and launches it at Trey. I rush in front of Trey and brace myself for the impact. It never comes. Instead, I'm tackled to the floor as the ice ball flies past me and shatters into pieces.

"What are you doing?" Trey shouts as he does a push-up over me.

"What do you think I was doing?" I yell back as I shove him off me. "I was trying to save you!"

"By using yourself as a barrier? Are you fucking crazy?"

"Obviously, my immunity isn't working. What else do you expect me to do?"

We get to our feet as the auditorium goes quiet and I ignore the pain in my tailbone.

Trey shakes his head at me as he says in a low voice, "Don't ever do that again. Ever."

Victor taps his chin. "Maybe testing with elementals is rushing things a little. Let's go back to internal powers, shall we? Immune, your next goal is to project onto Trey without touching him and to do it before Ruby has a chance to bite him with her powers. Let her know when you're ready."

A part of me wants to tell Victor he can go shove a stick up his ass. The other part of me is realistic and knows I don't have a choice. So I close my eyes and concentrate. The auditorium remains quiet for almost a minute. No one dares to interrupt my process. Finally, I keep my eyes shut as I raise up a thumb.

No one says anything for a moment.

Victor is the first to break the silence. "Are you attacking him?"

"I am," Ruby says through hisses. "She's blocking it."

"Excellent! What an improvement!"

I reopen my eyes, then Trey falls to his knees, shrieking. *Oh no!* I rush to cup his face. At an instant, he stops screaming.

In the corner of my eye, I see Ruby lower her hand. "She must have stopped projecting while I was still biting him."

"Interesting," Victor says. "Let's try this. Immune, come to me."

I don't. Not that I can anyway, because Trey rushes off the floor and stands in front of me.

"No," Trey says.

"What?" Victor snarls.

"I said no! Arella doesn't want to be a part of this. She never did. We're done."

"We'll be done when I say so." Victor strides over and takes me by the hand, tearing me away from the only person here who cares about my well-being. "Pixie, Ruby, Craig, you three hit Trey with your mind powers at the same time. Derek, I'll hold her down while you throw ice balls at her."

"What?" Trey shouts. "Hell no! You've gotta be crazy if—"

"Go!"

Trey drops to the floor as he covers his ears and screams. Slowly, his body shrinks until he's the size of a cat.

"Stop!" I rush toward him, but Victor yanks me back by my hair. An ice ball zooms at me and hits my arm. I cry out as the pain shoots up my shoulder.

"Project your immunity onto him," Victor orders.

Another ice ball soars toward my face. I duck while Trey's high-pitched wails echo throughout the auditorium. Victor sidesteps to dodge the ball, and it shatters against the floor.

"Stop!" I shout, but another ice ball is already whizzing through the air. It hits my stomach. I clutch my front as I fall to my knees and burst into a sob. "I can't save him! Not while I'm being attacked!"

"That's the point. You need to learn how to project your immunity, even when you're distracted and under pressure. Derek will stop hurting you once Trey stops screaming."

I punch at Victor's hands that are still gripping my hair. "Let me go!"

A spiky ice ball rockets straight at me. I duck to the side. The spikes glisten under the light as it flies past my arm so close, it tears the sleeve of my shirt. Victor releases my hair to dodge the ball.

Free now, I race to save Trey. I'm halfway across the boxing ring when my feet are lifted off the ground in a tornado. The air leaves my lungs as I spin in circles. Then I collapse to the ground, back at Victor's feet.

He jerks me up by my arm and pins my back against the ropes. "That worthless piece of shit is going to die if you don't help him."

Trey's screams echo from across the boxing ring.

"Project your immunity onto him. Focus. Picture yourself projecting a shield around him. What color is it? What shape is it? What is it made out of? Center your mind around those concepts." Victor steps aside and gives Derek a nod.

Derek doesn't waste a second producing another spiky ice ball in his hand and chucking it at me.

"I'm imagining the shield," I say through tears as I dodge the sharp sphere. "It's not working."

"Try something else. Bubble wrap. A brick wall. Couch cushions. A house. Pick something. Imagine every little detail of it and focus!"

I close my eyes and center all my energy in Trey's direction. I imagine the bubble wrap. He keeps screaming. I imagine the brick wall. Then the couch cushions. Then the house. He's still screaming as Victor continues shouting at me. I don't know why he thinks that's helpful. It's making me lose all my concentration.

With deep breaths, I tune Victor out. Then I imagine a wave of ocean water rushing toward Trey, drowning him with my immunity. While he's under that water, no one can touch him. No one can hurt him. The water circles around him, while still giving him pockets of air to breathe in. He's safe under my water. He's protected. They can't hurt him.

Finally, the screaming stops. I open my eyes. The sound of a balloon being blown into resonates through the auditorium as Trey's body expands back to normal size. Craig is still pointing at him, Ruby is still hissing, and Pixie is still puckering her lips, but the screaming has stopped.

Victor grins and claps. "Good job."

I rush across the floor and drop to my knees. Trey's body is limp as I cradle him against my chest. He pants heavily as tears stream down both our faces.

"How could you do this to him?" I shout at all of them because I don't blame only Victor. He may be their leader, but the rest of them are all choosing to do this too. And for what? A stupid paycheck? Is torturing people really worth a few dollars?

Suddenly, Trey lurches upward. He raises an arm into the air with his fingers outstretched. A small garbage bin whizzes through the air from across the room. He catches it in midair and heaves into it. I stand and step back as the smell of vomit fills my nostrils.

Any other time, I'd be reeling over just witnessing Trey move an object by merely summoning it with his hand, but it's the least weird thing I've seen all week.

"Anyone got a theory as to how this Ordi is immune to our powers?" Derek asks.

"She's probably an alien," Pixie says.

Funny, I've been thinking the same thing about them.

"She's gotta have a gene defect," Ruby says.

Trey's coughs echo throughout the auditorium as he vomits into the garbage bin some more.

"We've done thorough DNA testing on her," Victor says. "We've also cross-referenced her results with the other Immunes. There's no DNA pattern to link them. Not a single one."

"What's your theory, Big V?" Derek asks.

"Oh, I dunno. I have a few. Everything from radioactive spiders to sorcery. No matter what we do, we can't figure it out."

They're all having this conversation as if the man they just tortured isn't puking his guts up right in front of them. Doesn't anyone care about Trey?

"I've gotta give him some credit," Ruby says, staring at Trey with an *ick* face. "Most people throw up within the first minute."

"Ladies," Victor says, "why don't you two take Trey up to the infirmary? Derek, you are dismissed."

I feel helpless as Pixie and Ruby slump Trey's arms over their shoulders and drag him out of the box. I'm about to follow them when Victor seizes my arm. He holds me tight and waits until the women have left with Trey before he speaks.

"What did you picture in your head?"

I yank my arm back and shoot him a nasty look. "Don't touch me."

Victor slaps me across the face, and my head snaps to the side. I've had worse, so I simply cup a palm against my burning cheek and continue glaring at him like he's more disgusting than a maggot in my sandwich.

"Answer my question. What did you picture?"

"I'm not telling."

I expect him to smack me again. I even brace myself for it. Instead, Victor narrows his eyes at me before turning to his security guard.

"Hey, Craig. Don't you think Katie will look just as cute when she's the size of a button?"

From the stands, Katie's eyes go wide. The second Craig takes one giant step toward her, I blurt, "A brick wall."

Victor raises a hand, making Craig stop in his tracks. "Come again?"

"I imagined a brick wall."

"What color?"

"Red and brown."

"How tall?"

"I don't know? Pretty tall? It surrounded him in a circle. Kind of like he was at the bottom of a well." I can't believe how convincing I sound.

Victor takes a moment to process what I told him, then says, "Interesting."

13

―――――

TREY

"How long was I out for?" I ask Katie when I wake up in the infirmary again. She's on a chair at my bedside, typing something on her iPad.

In her sweet little voice, she says, "It's been about seven hours."

I drop my head back onto the pillow and let out a breath of relief. I swear, if she would have said I'd been out for another three days, I would have waltzed up to my uncle with the biggest fireball I can make and hold it against his face until his skin melted off.

I rub my face with my palms. "What time is it?"

"You just missed dinner. It's almost nine."

Dinner? That sounds good. The emptiness in my stomach is beginning to get excruciatingly painful. I can't remember the last time I ate.

"Want some Healing Water?" Katie holds out a bottle of heaven to me.

This time, I read the label first. Lemon-lime, my favorite. When I finish drinking it, I toss the empty bottle into the air and point at it as it flies across the room and lands in the trash.

I'm surprised my powers are working. Last night after I

climbed into this medical bed, I pointed at the blanket to pull it up, and it barely hovered. Poor thing fell limply to the floor. No matter how many times I pointed at it, it wouldn't rise.

Technically, I don't need a blanket, since my body will regulate my internal temperature during my sleep, but I like having a blanket for the comfort it provides. I was too weak to bend over to pick it up, so I figured I'd ask the nurse to do it whenever she came in to check my vitals. I fell asleep before she arrived. It was either her or Katie who must have picked up the blanket and draped it over me.

Katie crosses one leg over the other, then places her hands over the iPad in her lap. "So, you're a Kinetic?"

"Yeah." I press a button on the bed. With a mechanical buzzing sound, the mattress folds upward.

"You like it?"

A little *eh* grunt comes out as I exhale. "I like it more than my mind power."

"Do you wanna share what that is?"

Usually, Zordis don't openly discuss what their mind powers are. Many powers are seen as intrusive or dangerous, so it's cultural to keep that information private. Mine is a power that falls into the intrusive category. I'm not a person who'll tell people what my mind power is unprompted, but when asked, I don't mind sharing. "I'm an Empath."

A rush of adrenaline races through Katie. She's good at hiding her emotions. If I wasn't an Empath, I wouldn't have a clue that her anxiety just spiked, because she shows no signs of it on her face. If knowing I can read emotions makes her nervous, that means she's hiding something. Now I want to know: What's she hiding?

"I'm a PMT," Katie says as she works to regulate her nerves. I'm pretty impressed. Within seconds, she's back to feeling content.

I rack my brain, trying to figure out what PMT means.

"Premonitioner," she says.

"So, you're a Seer?"

"Not exactly. Seers can control what they see and get their visions on demand. PMTs can't control either. We see whatever decides to come to us, and our visions come randomly. Mine only come when I touch someone's hands, and it doesn't happen every time I touch someone. My visions can last up to ten seconds, but typically, it's just a two-second flash, and it's always from that person's point of view. Because I rarely have context, I rarely understand them."

"You had a vision the first time we met, didn't you? When we shook hands."

She nods slightly.

"What did you see?"

A tiny smirk creeps over her lips. "I saw you punch me."

"What?"

"Yeah. Right here in the face." She points at her left cheek.

"Well, shit. I'm sorry." I've never hit a woman before. I'm not sure why I'd start now or why Katie. The girl looks as fragile as a carton of eggs. If I punch her, she'll be down for the count. "Do your visions always come true?"

"Not always. If they're bad, I'll do things to prevent them. Like once, I went to lunch with a friend and I got a vision of her falling off a boat to her death. She hasn't been on a boat since."

"Do you know why I hit you?"

She shakes her head. "That's the thing, my visions only show me *what* happens, never *why*."

"I can relate. My powers only tell me *what* people feel, never *why*."

"Speaking of which, how are you feeling? Better enough to get back into the battle box tonight?"

I let out a deep *you've gotta be fucking kidding* laugh. "Hell no."

"Victor won't like that answer, so I'll just tell him you need a few more minutes to rest before we head down there." Katie picks up her iPad and begins typing, except the device is backward. The screen faces me. I'm about to say something until my name catches my eye.

Trey, read carefully. Camera behind me. On the way to the elevators, we'll pass a supply closet on the right. It's unlocked. Put your hand over my mouth and drag me into it. I'll explain there. Ask me for more Healing Water when you're done reading this and you're ready to go.

My heart rate kicks up. I do everything I can not to show it on my face. What does she need to explain to me in private? Is this a trap? Should I do it anyway?

Only one way to find out. "Could I get some more Healing Water?"

Katie shines one of her many smiles my way. "Of course."

After she discreetly flips her iPad back over and clicks a few buttons, probably deleting all evidence of that note, she heads to the mini fridge in the corner. When she comes back, she has another bottle of Healing Water in her hands. This time, it's the plain water flavor.

I drink it in its entirety with a good feeling that I'm gonna need all the healing I can get.

"Welp," Katie says with a slap of her thighs, "we should get going. Don't wanna keep Victor waiting."

I let out a bitter grunt as I slide my aching body off the bed. Katie plucks my leather jacket off a hook by the door and hands it to me. I slip into it, then follow her out of the infirmary.

The hallway is silent as I trail behind her. We pass a security guard patrolling the area. He barely looks up from his phone as we cross paths. Every echo of our footsteps makes my heart pound harder. The anxious energy simmering in Katie's gut makes me anxious too. I read the signs outside each door as we pass them.

My heart skips a beat when I spot a door coming up marked SUPPLY CLOSET. I expand my powers to check if anyone's around. The closest emotions I sense are from four people in a room around the corner. I don't waste a second. I snatch Katie into my arms with a hand over her mouth. She pretends to struggle as I drag her into the closet with me.

Once inside, I let her go and she turns the lock. A tiny fireball appears in my palm, illuminating the many mops and spray bottles around us.

"We don't have much time," Katie says in a low voice. My flames dance across her sweet and innocent facial features, but gone is her mousey voice and that ever-present smile. Replacing it is a firm tone coupled with a frown that means business. "There aren't cameras in here, but there are out there. If someone up in security saw you nab me, we have about one minute before they're here, so listen carefully."

"Wait." I put my hand up, then magnify my mind power toward the security room. In that general area, I sense energy from two people. Neither seem alarmed. "We're good."

"How are you so sure?"

"Do you really want me to explain, or are you gonna tell me why you told me to kidnap you into a supply closet?"

"Right. Okay, Victor is planning to get rid of you the second the Immune projects her immunity onto someone besides you. He's pretty confident she can do it. I overheard him giving orders to Craig to shrink you, then play off your death like it was an accident during testing. You need to get outta here. Tonight. And take the Immune with you."

Why doesn't it surprise me that my uncle has plans to off me?

"There's a tech lab down the hall." Katie points in that direction. "Go past the elevators, take the first left, then two doors down is room 317. In the far back right cabinet are perrizo guns—the sedative kind, not the normal kind that Enforcers use to subdue people's powers in z-prison. I've preloaded two guns for you. Each one carries thirty shots. Aim well. One shot will subdue your target's powers and make them drowsy. Two doses should knock 'em out within seconds. Do not—I repeat—do *not* kill anyone on your way out. Half of these agents are *real* ZIRDA agents."

My face screws together. "What do you mean, half?"

"I don't know if I have time to explain. Are you sure we're good? Check again."

I do, even though I know we're okay. "My empathy power has been stretched throughout this entire floor and up to the security room this whole time. I'll let you know if anyone's coming."

"Excellent. I'll try to make this quick. Basically, this ZIRDA base has been compromised."

"Compromised? By who?" As soon as those words leave my mouth, I know the answer.

"The Royals, duh. More specifically, Victor. Over the years, he's been slowly getting rid of the real ZIRDA agents and replacing them with Royals. He's done it so discreetly that it took this long for anyone to notice."

Victor? A Royal? It doesn't make any sense. How could he work for the same people who murdered his younger brother? Plus, they tried to kill him too. Katie's gotta be lying.

I eye her through slits. "How do you know this?"

"ZIRDA Toronto was the first to recognize that there was something fishy going on here. Every time they collaborated with ZIRDA California to defuse one of the Royals' schemes, somehow, the Royals were always two steps ahead.

"A few months ago, Toronto sent two agents here to do some snooping on the pretense that those agents needed more-intense training. They were never heard from again. I was sent here from ZIRDA Minnesota to find out what happened to them and try to uncover what's going on here. Victor thinks I was sent here because I want to be a field agent and my CEO thought I needed more experience at a larger base first. Thanks to my submissive-girl act, Victor took me in as his assistant.

"Through some snooping, I found out Craig shrunk and crushed those two Toronto agents under Victor's orders. But that's not all I've uncovered. There's heavy shit going on here. Everything from human trafficking to suicide bombing, and they're creating another bioweapon."

Suicide bombing? It hits me. Those Tickers—the ones Victor sent those two agents out to find—Victor doesn't want to protect the Tickers. He's the goddamn Royal who's been kidnapping them to use as unwilling suicide bombers. *Fuuuck. I think I'm gonna be sick.*

Katie continues, "I send weekly notes to my CEO about my progress here. Victor thinks I do that because she's monitoring my experience to determine when I'm ready for field work. Really, I'm just encoding secret messages to her about what I find here. Since Victor reads and approves all my notes to her before I send them out, I can only give her so much info. She's building a case against him and trying to get some other ZIRDA bases involved to take him down."

I let out a scoff. "You've been here for how long now? Why is Victor still in charge? What the fuck is taking so long?"

"These things take time, okay? We've gathered the evidence, and my CEO has been in contact with some of the other bases, but a proper takedown can't happen overnight. If it makes you feel any better, after this last Immune arrived, I asked for reinforcements. I'm determined to keep her alive."

A little hope sparks in my chest. "That's great. When are your people coming?"

"Um, I dunno. It could be days. Could be weeks. That's if they're sending anyone at all. They'll only come if they think it's safe to."

"What if your life was in danger? Shouldn't they make saving you a priority?"

"I knew the risks when I took this field assignment. My CEO told me up front that she'd rather let me die than risk more lives. I told her I wouldn't want it any other way."

Kill ten to save ten thousand. Seems like the other ZIRDA bases believe in that mentality too. Except, this base isn't ZIRDA anymore. At least, fifty percent of it isn't.

Wait . . . "How do you know that half of this base is still ZIRDA and the other half isn't?"

Katie shrugs nonchalantly. "I don't know—not for sure, at least. In my time here, I've only *theorized* that it's fifty-fifty. I've only been able to confirm that seventeen people here are good."

I whisper yell. "Seventeen? That's it?"

"Well, you can't expect me to run around asking people what side they're on. I have to be discreet about it. Including you, that's eighteen."

"How are you so sure I'm not a Royal?"

Katie gives me a *come on* look. "Victor wouldn't try to kill you if you were. Also, I did my research. Back in May, Victor assigned a field mission to some guy in the LA area who had no prior record of being a ZIRDA agent. I thought for sure you were another Royal that Victor recruited to test out his *infatuation theory.*

"When I researched you, I discovered that your parents died under mysterious circumstances. All of ZIRDA knows that's code for 'The Royals did it.' That was my first sign you weren't one of them. Once I met you, I was one hundred percent sure. The agents before you personally brought in their Immunes for testing. Your Immune was taken in by other agents, and you seemed genuinely livid to find her here."

Because I fucking was.

Katie's words are making my knees weak. I'm not sure if I should believe her or demand proof. We don't have time for that though. Also, something she said is rubbing me the wrong way.

"What do you mean by 'Victor's infatuation theory'?"

"You really haven't figured it out yet?" Katie pauses to look at me. I make my fireball bigger just so she can see my *I don't have a clue* look. She rolls her eyes at me like I'm an idiot. I feel like one. "Many, many years ago, ZIRDA discovered that some rare Ordinaries are immune to our gifts. As a research and development agency, naturally, they brought in these Immunes to analyze. The Immunes were told they were part of a top-secret medical study led by the government, and they were even paid for their services. Ya know, normal ZIRDA stuff."

This is information I've known. I let Katie continue anyway.

"Eventually, the Royals found out about the Immunes too. They began kidnapping the Immunes from ZIRDA to try to weaponize them. I've estimated that at least five have died from Victor's brutal tests over the last nineteen years. With the last three Immunes he found, yours included, he's been trying out his *love* or *infatuation* theory. He thinks with the right stakes on the line, he can get an Immune to project their immunity onto someone else.

"Since kidnapping Immunes and torturing their families in front of them would give away his cover, he came up with this plan to plant a Royal into the Immunes' lives. The Royal would get the Immune to fall in love with them. Then Victor would arrange their kidnappings to make the Immune think they were both in danger.

"Once here, he'd have some agents torture the Royals the way he did with you. The rest of ZIRDA wouldn't think it's suspicious because it's one of our agents getting hurt. Because you know, it's okay to torture our own people if it's for the greater good." Katie rolls her eyes and huffs.

"Anyway, Victor's plan failed. The two previous Immunes he tried the love theory on never developed strong enough feelings. The last Immune got close, but once he found out the woman he loved never loved him back, he could no longer project his immunity onto her.

"So, Victor needed someone to play the lover part who

didn't know his end game. He needed someone who could take on this mission and develop the feelings back to make the infatuation stronger."

I blow out a breath as the weight of the world comes crashing onto my shoulders. "And that's where I come in."

"Yep. You were the perfect guy for Victor to use. Single, good-looking, around the same age as the Immune, and you even live in the same area. Over the last few weeks, he's been running tests on you to see if you've developed the infatuation he wanted you to. I process most of the mission notes that Victor receives from our field agents. One of the notes came from an agent Victor has stationed at a hospital in LA named David Jordan."

That's the zoctor I spoke to after Arella was in the car accident Victor caused. Is that doctor actually a ZIRDA agent or is he a Royal?

Katie continues, "David Jordan's note included some MRI results and a paragraph about your reaction to finding out that she'd been hurt. Once Victor knew that you were 'visibly distraught,' he was ready to move on to the next phase of his plan: getting you here with her. That's when Victor assigned me my first on-base mission. He said that she'd arrive within the week, but she never did.

"For the next month, Victor had plans to send agents out to nab her three times. Each time, you must have said something to make him put it off, which only excited him more. It further confirmed that you had real feelings for her. I think he allowed you to put it off because he wanted you to continue falling for her, with hopes that a deeper connection would yield better results. Something must have happened between you and the Immune last week, because all of a sudden, Victor wrote up mission plans to get you here immediately."

I know exactly what happened. Victor must have found out that Arella and I broke up, and decided he needed to get us here before our feelings faded. But how did he know? Did he have someone watching us?

"I hate to say it," Katie says, "but Victor's infatuation theory worked. He's had the most success getting your Immune to project onto—"

I slap a hand over Katie's mouth, then I squeeze my fireball out. She doesn't protest. A few seconds later, the two people I sensed coming down the hall stroll past our supply closet.

"You wanna join me in the Artificial Sunlight room tonight?" a woman asks.

"Ya know," a man says, "I've worked here for almost ten years, and I've never been in that room. What's it like?"

"Seriously, Mark? It's like a beach vacation in there. And if you've got the room to yourself, it's like you're on your own private island where the sun is always shining."

The rest of their conversation trails off as they turn the corner toward the elevators. I take my hand off Katie's mouth, and she breathes again. My fireball returns to my hand with a burst of heat and light.

I speak first. "How can I get Arella outta here safely?"

"You must have had some type of plan already cooking in your head. What was it?"

I scratch the back of my neck. "Um, I was just gonna sneak her out of her room."

"How were you going to unlock her handcuffs?"

"Easy. I'm a Kinetic. I can wave at almost any lock to open it."

"Okay. How were you going to get past the Hulk?"

"Um, I dunno. Maybe I'd tell him that Victor sent me to take her down to the battle box alone."

Katie narrows her eyes at me and cocks her head to the side. "What if I was in the room?"

I shrug my shoulders with another *I dunno* look. "Maybe I would have told you the same thing?"

"But I'm assigned as her overseer. I'd know if Victor wanted her there or not. What kind of dumb plan is that?"

"Listen, I never said it was any good."

"It's shit, is what it is."

I think I prefer the mousey version of Katie. This one is mean. "All right," I huff, even though she's right, "you come up with something better."

"I already have. That's why those perrizo guns are preloaded for you. Again, room 317. Far back right cabinet. Once you get those guns, aim at whoever you see. Once everyone's gifts are subdued, you'll have a better chance of getting outta here with the Immune—alive.

"Now, before you go, remember that vision I had when we first met? I lied about what I saw." Katie reaches down her shirt and pulls out a shiny object from her bra.

I move my fireball closer to it, then gasp. It's Arella's angel-wings necklace. But why does Katie have it?

"In my real vision, you were outside an apartment building, asking a woman where her angel-wings necklace was. You said something about it being proof. Later, when I saw the Immune for the first time, I realized she was the woman from my vision. And there she was, wearing an angel-wings necklace. I thought maybe she didn't have it in the future because Victor stole it. I took it off her to give to you. Hopefully, I just prevented my vision from happening."

"Thank you, Katie. You have no idea how much this necklace means to me." I accept the jewelry. As our hands touch, Katie's breath hitches and her eyes go blank. Seconds later, she blinks and returns to the present.

I place the necklace into my front jeans pocket for safekeeping until I can hook it back where it belongs. "Did you just get another vision?"

"Yes. I—I think I just saw your death."

My lungs stop working. "What?"

"And I think it's soon."

Shit. "Describe your vision to me. What did you see?"

Katie shuts her eyes and thinks. "Um, you were running from some men. Probably Royals. Three of 'em. They catch up. One is a Slasher. He stabs you. Left side of your stomach. You collapse to the ground as the other two drag the Immune into a van. You get stabbed again, and that's it. Everything goes black. My visions never black out like that unless . . . well, you know."

I gulp as the trauma of seeing my parents' mutilated faces whips through my mind. Is the Slasher who attacked them the same one who's going to kill me?

"On the bright side," Katie says, "this vision means you manage to get the Immune outta here alive."

Her words give me no reassurance. "Where am I when this happens?"

"I'm not sure. I saw shops. One had cats in it. Lots of 'em. Toy cats. Golden with one arm waving."

Golden toy cats waving? What the fuck? What kind of shop sells those? "What time of day was it?"

"Maybe late afternoon? The sun was out for sure. God, they're going to kill you in broad daylight. The bastards."

Hell no, they're not. "I'll make sure to avoid any shops with waving cats while the sun is up from now on."

"Good." From the inner pocket of her jacket, Katie pulls out an ID card with her name and face on it. "Take this. You'll need it to access room 317."

I shove the card into my back pocket. "Thanks."

"Oh, and you'll need the code for her door. It's 5634."

Goddammit. How am I supposed to remember all this? I repeat the numbers in my head a few times. "Okay. Got it."

"All right. You ready for the most important part?"

"There's more?"

She tilts her head back to look me square in the eyes. "You need to punch me."

"What?"

She points at her cheek. "Right here in the face. And do it hard."

"No way."

"Trey, you have to. I can't blow my cover. Why do you think I told you to drag me in here? When they review the camera feed, it needs to look like you attacked me, interrogated me in this closet, then stole my ID card."

"There has to be another way."

"There isn't. And if you wanna continue dinking around in this closet forever, we can, but we've already spent a lot of precious time in here."

"Goddammit," I groan because she's right.

"Look, Trey, my parents were killed by the Royals too. I was ten, and I've wanted to be a field agent ever since. I've been training since I was eleven, so I've gone through much worse than one punch." She braces herself against the shelves, then closes her eyes. "Don't hold back, okay?"

I can't believe I'm about to do this. Sighing, I form a fist, draw back, then release.

Katie's head snaps back as she moans. "Jesus, fuck. You couldn't have held back just a little?"

"But you said—"

"Kidding, kidding. Kind of." She rubs her cheek with her palm as she slumps onto the floor. "Now go."

14

TREY

The sign reads 317 Weapons Technology Lab.

On the black device near the door handle, I wave Katie's ID card. It beeps, and a little light flashes green. I let myself in and shut the door behind me.

The room is dark. Instead of turning the lights on, I toss a fireball into the air. My flames hover beside me as I pin my back against the door. My hands shake as my breaths turn ragged.

Can I really pull this off? Me against a hundred? Maybe two hundred? *Fuck.* The idea of that many people coming at me at once is gruesome. I won't stand a chance. I can't do this. This is crazy. *Why the hell am I doing this?*

An image of Arella pops into my head. She's probably handcuffed to my old bed right now, scared out of her mind. She's probably more freaked out than I am. Trapped in a place with people she doesn't know? That's frightening. I can't imagine what went through her head when she saw everyone using their powers.

I have to do this. I have to save her. And if I die in the process, at least I died trying.

I expand my empathy outward. The closest emotions are

from several rooms down the hall. It's two people, and they're . . . well, they're having a good time, that's for damn sure. I don't think I'll have to worry about them getting in my way.

Up in the security room, everything seems normal. Two people. Both are content. They've got too many screens to keep an eye on for them to have noticed me casually strolling into this room. The rest of the base seems clear too. No one feels alarmed or is running toward me. For the moment, I'm good, so I rush to the back cabinets.

Hold on . . . Did Katie say left or right? *Shit!*

I think she said right. I pull the door of the top cabinet. It clicks against the lock. I wave a hand at the keyhole and try again.

The cabinet opens. Inside are a bunch of small throwing knives lined up in four neat rows. Knowing ZIRDA, they're probably much more than simple throwing knives. They could be laced with something. Either way, they aren't perrizo guns.

Just in case, I take two knives and shove them blade-down into my back pockets. They're fucking huge, though, so they stick out like Excalibur in the stone. With these things in my jeans, I won't be able to walk around casually anymore.

I drag the leg of my jeans up. I'm about to stick one knife into my sock when I stop. Whatever this knife is laced with probably shouldn't touch my skin. How can I—*oh, I know!* I kick my shoes off and take one sock off. Then I drag the sock over my other foot. I put one knife back where I found it, then stick the second knife between the two socks until it's secure. When I shove my feet back into my shoes, it feels weird. One foot is bare while the other is double-socked. It'll have to do though.

With a thunk, I shut the top cabinet, then unlock and open the bottom one. Three rows of handguns stare back at me. *Which ones are the preloaded ones?* I bring my fireball closer to them. On the bottom row, two of the weapons are facing the opposite way of the others. I pick one up. It feels heavy. I pick up one of the firearms from the top row. It's definitely got less weight to it. *Thank you, Katie!* She definitely made this idiot-proof.

I shove the preloaded guns into the front of my jeans, then hide them behind my unzipped jacket. It's been years since I've shot a gun, but with the help of my telekinesis, I'll be able to make every shot count. I'll have to, because what I have is enough shots to knock out thirty agents, which isn't even close to what I need.

I leave room 317, acting as nonchalant as possible. Then I freeze. Down the hall, that security guard who was on his phone earlier steps out of a dark room with a short blonde girl. They both have guilty, satisfied smiles on their faces that drop the moment they see me.

Without a word, I make my way toward the elevators as if to say *I didn't see nothing.* I sense them stay where they are while I press the *down* button. My heart thrashes against my ribs because if those two weren't busy worrying about getting caught in their own dirty affairs, they might question why a field agent was in the weapons room.

Ding! The elevator arrives, and I rush into it.

When my ride lets me off at the living quarters, I step out with a dry lump in my throat.

In the community room, half the tables are occupied by agents playing poker. It must be tournament night, which explains why it's so empty on the third floor. As a kid, I used to stand outside those glass windows and watch them play, knowing exactly who was bluffing and who wasn't. *Couldn't poker night be any other night but this one?* Why couldn't they all be in their rooms, where they can't see me?

A few of the agents glance up as I pass by. I keep my face impassive, even though my heart is pounding like I've been running laps around a football field. One guy stares a little longer than he should. *Is he an Empath too? Can he sense me freaking out?* Eventually, his head drops back to his cards and he goes back to playing the game.

The closer I get to my old bedroom, the shorter my breaths get. What am I gonna say to that hulk-like Shrinker who's always guarding Arella's door? The same story I was gonna sell him before? But Katie said my idea was dumb. I should come up with something else, and I'd better do it fast because I've got less than thirty seconds.

I turn the corner. *Fuuuck.* Craig eyes me as I saunter down the hall. I hope I look casual enough. The man's energy swings at me, all alert and defensive. I brace myself for the burn that rips through my body whenever he shrinks me, just in case he decides to.

When I reach him in my normal size, I offer him a tiny smile. Not too big, where he'll think I'm up to something, and not too small, where it looks super fake.

"What are you doing here?" Craig says like it's peasant-minded of me to even think I belong in his breathing space.

"I'm here to take the Immune to Victor."

"What for?"

I begin to think of a lie until the truth hits me. If Victor had actually told me to bring Arella to him, he wouldn't have told me why. He would have simply said, "Just do it," so I shrug nonchalantly. "Dunno. He didn't tell me. Just ordered me to come pick her up."

Craig steps aside to allow me access to the keypad.

Suddenly, my brain freezes up. *What was the code again?*

A heartbeat passes. Then another. And another.

"You ain't got the code?" Craig's wariness spikes inside me.

"Nah, I got it." I type in some numbers as I silently pray to the keypad code gods. *Please be correct.*

When the light blinks green, it takes everything in me not to let out a sigh of relief.

I open the door and step into the dark room. I'm about to close the door when a hand slams against it.

Craig peeks his head in. "Where's Victor's assistant? Wasn't she at the infirmary with you?"

The lie comes out easily. "She was. She's already with Victor. She said something about getting there before me so she could have him approve some notes."

"I see." The door shuts.

This time, I do let out a sigh of relief.

"Arella?" I flip the light on.

She sits up and squints with a hand cupping her forehead. "Trey?"

The sound of my name coming from her lips is like hearing my old favorite song for the first time in years. It's familiar. It's soothing. It's everything I've been living for.

I wave a hand over the handcuff around her ankle. It falls to the floor with a clank.

She rubs her ankle. "What's going on?"

"Just follow me and stay close, okay?"

Like the stubborn person she always is, she crosses her arms over her chest. "Tell me where you're taking me first."

It hurts that she doesn't immediately shoot off the bed and into my arms. She doesn't trust me anymore. I understand why, but it still stings. It takes me a second to recover internally. When I do, I whisper, "I'm busting you outta here."

Her eyes go wide as she springs off the bed and slips her feet into a pair of flats. *That's more like it.*

I open the door to find Craig standing there with his phone held up. "You son of a bitch. Almost had me there. I just heard from Victor. He's not even on base."

I'm about to reach into my jeans for a perrizo gun when a searing burn takes over my body. The room grows bigger and bigger with each sharp breath I suck in. I clutch my stomach. Vomit is coming.

Arella's screams echo above me as a giant Craig squats

over me. His enormous hand is about to grab me as I snatch one of the guns from my jeans. I'm not sure what damage a tiny perrizo gun will do to him, but it's all I've got.

Suddenly, the burning stops. I fly into the air as the room returns to normal.

"What the hell?" Craig stumbles backward, hitting his back against the wall. Shock, then anger, courses through my head as he glares at me, then at Arella.

It hits me what she just did. I can't believe she did it so fast.

"You bitch." Craig balls his hand, draws back, aims at her, and—

Ssspt! My shot misses. It hits the wall behind him. Craig freezes and glances back at the little needle sticking out of a burnt area in the wall. He shoots me a venomous look as a lightning ball grows in his hand.

"You bastard!" He launches his sizzling ball at me.

I duck. The ball hisses as it zips past me and scorches the wall.

Another glowing orb soars toward my chest. As I step aside to dodge it, another one flies straight at my face. I wince as it stops barely a fingertip from my nose, then falls to the floor and disappears. Another lightning ball flies through the air. This time, it stops a fist away from my face and also drops to the floor.

"What the fuck?" Craig shouts, then points at Arella. "It's you again, isn't it? You're blocking my powers from—"

Ssspt!

"Ow!" The needle hits his shoulder. He plucks it off, then flicks it to the carpet.

I still have the gun up, aimed at him. The look on his face tells me I'm in for it. He opens his palm. This time, no sparks appear. Shock consumes him as he closes, then opens his hand again. No sizzling. No glowing light. Nothing.

Before he can make another move, I pull the trigger. *Ssspt!*

The shot hits him right in the chest. This time, he doesn't pluck it off. Instead, he wavers, then falls face-forward with a heavy thud.

I'm about to let out a sigh of relief when a siren blares. *Brehh! Brehh! Brehh!* "Intruder alert! Intruder alert!"

In the hallway, red lights flash from the ceiling. Next comes a man's deep voice over the speakers. "Floor two. Royal spy. White male. Leather jacket. Blue jeans. Pyro. Kinetic. Empath. Kill on sight. I repeat, kill on sight."

Fucking great.

I expect Arella to look as terrified as I feel. Instead, she glances up at me with a firm confidence in her eyes. She grabs my hand and slips her fingers between mine.

With the most conviction I've ever heard her speak with, she says, "I'll make sure they can't hurt you, Trey. Just get me out of here."

15

TREY

Brehh! Brehh! Brehh!

The siren is maddening. At least the words *intruder alert* have stopped repeating. The red lights are still flashing though.

I sense a mass of people racing toward us. There's so many, I can't count them all. They're running from the community room and jumping down the stairs with a *ready to kill* energy that erases all the assurance Arella just instilled in me.

I grip her hand tighter in mine. "Don't let go, 'kay?"

She nods, then we step over Craig's unmoving body and sprint out of the room. The red lights are brighter out here, making it hard for me to see. Halfway down the hall, I stop and turn around, jerking Arella with me.

"What are you doing?" she shouts over the siren.

I tug her with me back toward the bedroom. Then I point a finger at the one shot of perrizo sticking out of the wall. It flies toward me and stops a breath away from my nose. The tiny cylinder is still full of green liquid. *Perfect!* I pluck it from the air and shove it into my pocket. I'm gonna need every dose I can get.

171

Hand in hand, we run again. I pull one of the perrizo guns out of my jeans and throw it into the air. It hovers in front of us while I pull out the other gun and hold it up. We're about to turn the corner when I get an idea. Arella's body slams into mine as I stop.

"Ow!" She rubs her forehead.

"Sorry." Never letting go of her hand, I kneel and slide a gun down the hall. The weapon skates across the floor past a few closed bedroom doors before coming to a halt. I snatch the weapon hovering in the air and slide it down the hallway too. Then I pin my back against the wall and close my eyes.

The crowd of people darting toward us is turning the corner.

Now they're halfway down the hall. Suddenly, the lead person stops.

"Where'd these guns come from?" a woman asks.

I peek one eye around the corner and lift my hand. The guns swoop into the air. As I pull an imaginary trigger with my finger, the guns go *Ssspt! Ssspt! Ssspt!*

One by one, the agents' lightning balls fizzle out and the flames in their hands turn into smoke. The agents grip their necks and shout profanities.

"It's a perrizo gun!"

"Who's controlling it?"

A man punches the air behind the gun. "Not a Vanisher."

A woman toward the back points at me. "There! It's him! The spy!"

Fuck. I keep pulling the imaginary trigger. The lead woman goes down first. Then the guy behind her. Then the guy behind him. One after another, they fall with thuds, until everyone's lying on the floor.

I feel bad. It's likely that half these people are the good guys. I don't have time to dwell on it, though, because more people ready to kill me are on their way.

I tug on Arella's arm. "Come on!"

We rush over the sea of limp bodies, trying our hardest not to step on anyone. There's between twelve to fifteen of them, which means I don't have many perrizo shots left.

"Are they dead?" Arella asks.

"No, just sedated." It amazes me how she can be so concerned about these people after what's happened to her.

I wave a hand at the floating guns. They fly ahead of us as I scan the walls for any shots that missed. *One, two, three.* I point at each spot of green sticking out of the wall. They flutter down the hall, after the guns. I pluck the dose out of my pocket and toss it into the air. With a *zip!* it goes flying too.

Arella and I freeze mid-step when a man dashes around the corner. He aims a rock ball at us and releases. I aim one of my floating doses of perrizo at him.

Ssspt!

Halfway to me, the rock ball explodes, and the debris falls to the floor. The man plucks the tiny green cylinder off his arm.

Ssspt! He collapses to his knees.

One of the bedroom doors opens. A young woman in pajamas comes stumbling out. The red lights flash across her sleepy features. "What's with all the noise?"

You shoulda stayed in bed, lady. I point at two floating doses, then point at her. *Ssspt! Ssspt!* She collapses too.

From around the corner, a fireball rockets toward my face. The floating guns clank against the floor as I grab Arella and drag her down with me, covering her with my body. The fireball whizzes over my head. Heat singes the top of my hair, and I pat my head to put out the sparks.

Another burst of red-hot flames shoot at us. I open my palm. A fireball appears in it, and I toss it at the one threatening to burn us. The flames collide in the air with a blistering explosion. Arella screams as I cover her with my body again. The sparks land all over my jacket, and some on the back of my neck.

"Ow." I rub the speckles of pain away, then hoist Arella onto her feet. "You okay?"

Instead of answering me, she screams and tackles me to the floor. I wrap my arms around her as we fall onto my back, and she lands on my chest. Pain erupts up my spine as a glint of green flies through the air where I was just standing.

"Another!" Arella shouts.

I spot it coming at us and close my fist. The needle pauses in midair, then darts back toward the woman who shot at me —with my own damn gun. She tries to avoid it, but I swerve the needle to follow her. The needle lands in her collarbone. She groans as she plucks it off and flicks it to the floor.

Arella pushes herself off me. We get back onto our feet just as the woman with both my guns in her hands points them at me and fires. I close my fists again, forcing the needles to stop and drop to the ground. Then I wave my hand at the guns and they soar out of the woman's grasp, then twist to face her.

Ssspt! She falls onto her side.

Heavy footsteps thunder around the corner. A group of agents appears with their hands armed with element balls. Flames, lightning, rocks, and spiky ice fly through the air. I wiggle my fingers at both guns.

Ssspt! Ssspt! Ssspt! The element balls tumble to the floor in midair.

A female agent stares at her empty hands. "It's perrizo! Avoid the shots!"

Yelling, the agents charge at us. There's too many of them. I can't shoot fast enough. Arella and I retreat backward as we dodge fireballs. The flames land around us, then smoke out on the floor.

Ssspt! Ssspt! Two men in the front tumble to the floor,

tripping the others. I keep my focus on my floating guns and continue pulling the triggers. One by one, the agents fall down, except one guy who ducks and aims a fireball at my guns. It hits one gun, which explodes with a deafening *BOOM!*

Pieces of metal firework through the air. I throw my hands up just in time. Barely a finger from my cheeks, the shrapnel stops. As I drop my hands, the pieces tumble to the floor. Arella gapes at me, wide-eyed.

I pull her behind me as I spot a perrizo dose on the floor. It's still green. As I wave my hand at it, it flies into the air and straight into the neck of the guy who blew up my gun. He grunts as he plucks it out. I aim my remaining gun at him.

Ssspt! He face-plants against the floor.

A middle-age woman appears from around the corner and points at me. I let out a wail as my skin burns with searing heat. The woman keeps her fingers aimed at me as I fall to my knees.

"No!" Arella slaps her palms against my face, holding them there.

Within seconds, the pain stops. *Thank fuck.*

Brehh! Brehh! Brehh! The siren seems to have gotten louder. I push back onto my feet and take Arella's hand in mine.

A flash of green whizzes toward me. I sidestep it just in time. Skin Burning Lady has my last gun in her hands. She pulls the trigger again. I clench my fist. The needle stops in the air, turns, then flies right back at her. She dodges it and shoots at me again. Twice. I halt both needles in the air and spin them around.

Ssspt! Ssspt! They hit her at the same time. She plummets, landing over the guy at her feet. I point a finger at my gun. It flies out of her grasp, toward the ceiling, and hovers there.

I scan the walls and spot several perrizo shots sticking out, still green. I point at them, then they zip down the hall at the five agents sprinting at us. Four of the doses hit, making the two biggest guys collapse to the floor. The other three agents open their hands. I wave a hand, making the last of my floating perrizo shots rocket toward them. Their shock consumes me when their element balls disappear in their grasps. With deep frowns, they charge at us.

I point a hand at my gun hovering near the ceiling. The weapon clicks, but nothing shoots out. *Fuck.* The gun drops to the floor as I drag Arella behind me, then arm my hands with fireballs. I launch them into the air. The first one hits the female agent right in the head. She wails at the top of her lungs as the smell of burnt hair stings my nose.

The two men behind her dodge my other fireballs, so I throw more. And I keep throwing them until both men are on fire. I'm about to tell Arella we'll run past them when a woman appears from around the corner and gasps. She raises her arms into the air. A giant water ball bubbles over the three agents' heads. Then another and another. More keep coming until the agents are drenched and their clothes aren't flaming anymore. Wet and angrier than before, they put their fists up and sprint toward me.

"Arella, get back!"

She races down the hall behind me as one of the drenched men smashes his fist against my face. Miserable pain explodes through my cheek. The man aims his fist again. This time, I duck and hurl a punch right back. I make contact with his nose with a loud *crunch!*

"Fuck!" He clutches his face as he collapses to the floor.

Someone jerks me back by the collar of my jacket. A large fist slams right into my temple. My vision goes blurry as the man slugs me in the gut. I bend over, clutching myself as I cough.

"Grab the girl!" the man shouts.

The woman with pieces of hair sticking out of her almost-bald head darts toward Arella. Screaming, Arella runs back the way we came. I throw a fireball at the woman, but it misses and hits the wall, then smokes out.

The man's fist thumps against the side of my head again. Two more men rush out from down the hall and join him. I block a punch. They land a kick. I throw a fireball at one. He ducks it. From down the hall, another woman appears and aims a lightning ball at me. It lands on my chest, and my body convulses.

The men punch me again.

And again.

And again.

A second lightning ball hits my arm, sending burning waves of hell through my bones. Another kick in the face. Another punch in the stomach.

One of them drags me up by the front of my shirt. Somehow, I find the strength to put my hands on his head. Flames come rushing out of my palms. The man stumbles back, grasping his face.

Another lightning ball whirls at me. I duck just in time. More fire lights up my palms, and I launch it into the air. One after another, flames blast out of my hands until I can hear every single agent screaming. I keep chucking fireballs as I run backward toward Arella.

Brehh! Brehh! Brehh!

When I turn the corner, I find my girl on the other end of the hallway, being dragged across the floor.

"Let me go!" Arella shouts as she punches at the almost-bald lady.

The lady keeps her grip on Arella's hair, then stops at a door and stabs the keypad with her finger. She gets the door open just as a fireball lights up my palm. I'm about to throw it when I stop. What if I miss and hit Arella? I can't risk it. Instead, I wave a hand at the door. It shuts in the lady's face.

"What the—"

"Let her go!" I yell.

The lady shoves Arella down, then sprints toward me. Big mistake. I have a clear shot now, and I take it. My fireball spins through the air until it lands on her, but she doesn't catch on fire. My fireball simply rolls off her wet clothes and falls to the floor.

"You traitor!" The lady heaves a fist at my face. I duck and trip her with my leg. She falls, and I climb on top of her, straddling her hips. My fists collide with her face, one after another. Once her head falls limply to the side, I stop.

Shooting back up, I rush to Arella. She's already back on her feet and meets me halfway.

"Did she hurt you?" I ask, scanning her body for any blood.

Arella clutches her cheek. "She punched me a few times, but I'll be okay."

I'll take a better look at her later. For now, I grip her hand, and we run back down the hall. As we go, I scan the walls for any last doses of that precious green liquid. I find none.

After we get past the sea of unconscious bodies on the floor, we turn the corner.

"Give me a fucking break," I mutter as three men from the other end dash toward us.

The biggest guy points his fingers at the floor, making it vibrate beneath my shoes. I lose my balance and fall backward into the hard wall. Arella is torn from me as she falls onto her knees. Over the trembling floor, I crawl toward her.

"Are you o—" I don't get to finish my sentence because I catch a glimpse of red-hot flames flying toward us.

Arella shrieks as she throws her hands up over her head. I crouch over her and brace myself for the fiery impact, but it never comes. The fireball stops just before hitting my cheek. It tumbles to the floor, then smokes out.

A second fireball whirls through the air. Arella screams again with her hands up. This time, the flames stop an arm's length away.

My mouth falls open. "How are you doing that?"

Her arms tremble. "I have no idea."

I help her onto her feet. "Well, keep doing it, 'cause it's working!"

Brehh! Brehh! Brehh!

I grab Arella's hand as we dash toward the three men coming at us. With my free hand, I throw fireballs at them. One after another, after another. The men do the same at me, but none of their fireballs reach me. Each one hits the invisible wall that's always two steps ahead of me. Their balls roll to the floor and disappear in puffs of smoke. I've never been more impressed by Arella. She's doing the impossible.

Feeling safe behind Arella's immunity shield, I pull the leg of my jeans up and grab the knife from my sock. I aim it at the biggest dude, then throw. It's about to hit the guy's chest when he throws his arms up and the knife stops in midair. The man twists his wrists, then the knife comes rocketing back toward us.

I raise a hand to stop it, but it doesn't stop. And it's aimed straight at Arella. Just as the metal slices through her invisible wall, I jerk her toward me, but it's too late.

Her scream pierces my ears as the knife slashes the side of her arm. The blade somersaults onto the floor with a few clanks, leaving a trail of blood in its path.

All the air leaves my lungs as Arella rips her hand out of mine to cover the fresh wound on her upper arm. She falls to her knees, screwing her face together in misery.

I've barely got a second to catch my breath before the knife zips off the floor, straight at me. I clench my fist. The knife stops just in time. With a twist of my wrist, it flies back the other way.

"Fuck!" The big guy stumbles backward, clutching the weapon sticking out of his chest until he collapses onto the floor and goes limp.

I point at the knife again. It shoots out of his body and

straight at the next guy. He swerves away, but I twist the knife around, and it hits him in the back. With a wail, he falls onto his front. The wailing stops as his head droops to the side.

"Mark!" The last guy stares at his friend in devastation before shooting me a killer glare. "You piece-of-shit Royal spy!" His fireballs whiz toward me, one after another.

"No!" Arella shouts as she raises a bloody hand into the air.

The flaming balls stop so close to my cheeks, their heat prickles my skin before they roll onto the floor and vanish.

"How the hell are you doing that?" the guy shouts.

The blaring siren suddenly stops, then everything goes quiet. A second later, the red lights stop flashing too. Why did they—two women with high energy sprint from around the corner. One has short black-and-blue hair. The other has long red curls.

"Oh, come on," I say through a groan. "Anyone but them." I brace myself for the stabbing in my ears and the bites on my skin, but they never come. I glance behind me. "You're doing great!"

Arella, still kneeling and clutching her bloody arm, shakes her head. "I'm not doing anything."

"Ah!" The guy with fireballs in his palms falls to the floor. His hands are smoky as he clutches his ears. He screams as his body jerks and shudders. It's only seconds before he bends over and vomits. I almost feel bad for him because I know the feeling all too well.

Pixie stops blowing, then hooks her thumb at him. "I think he's one of us."

"How do you know?" Ruby asks.

"Look at him. You really think the Royals are gonna recruit someone as scrawny as this dude?"

"I'm not the Royal!" the guy shouts and shakes a finger at me. "He is!"

Two fireballs appear in my palms.

"Nah," Ruby says. "Trey's one of the good guys."

My jaw drops. *Whhhaaat?*

"Sorry it took us so long," Ruby says. "We got a little held up on the way down here."

Pixie saunters past me and peers down the hall. A sharp whistle leaves her lips. "Damn. Homeboy was busy. You gotta see this, Roobs."

Ruby dashes past me to glance down the hall. "Holy moo maker! Are they all dead?"

"No," I say as my fireballs disappear into smoke between my fingers. "They're all sedated, I think."

"How did you do that?"

"Perrizo guns."

The women glance at each other, then back at me.

"You got any more?"

I shake my head. "I used every shot."

"Dammit," Pixie says, snapping her fingers. "We might need—"

"Trey?"

The little hairs on the back of my neck stand up as Arella's frail voice calls my name. I hurry to her as she tips backward, and I catch her just before her head hits the floor.

"Arella?" I can't breathe. "What's wrong?"

Through half-closed eyes, she says, "I—I feel weak, and sleepy, and . . ."

Ruby steps up behind me in her clacky black boots. "What happened to her arm?"

"She was hurt by that knife." Because my hands are busy holding Arella up, I nod my head toward the two guys lying limply on the floor. I swallow hard. That could have been Arella.

Pixie marches toward the guy with the knife sticking out of his back. She pulls it out and holds it up as blood drips from it. "I can't tell for sure, but I think it's laced with perrizo. There's a bunch of these in the Weapons Tech lab on level three."

After wiping the knife off on the guy's shirt, she sticks it into her back pocket.

"Got anything to tie her arm with?" Ruby asks me.

I shrug my jacket off, then drag my shirt over my head. Ruby helps me tie it around Arella's limp arm, then I slip my jacket back on and zip it up.

"Okay," Ruby says, "let's get her outta here."

16

TREY

ARMED WITH MY TWO NEW BODYGUARDS, I CRADLE ARELLA and carry her down the hall. She's struggling to keep her eyes open.

The smell of ripe vomit attacks my nostrils as we approach the cafeteria. When we turn the corner, countless bodies are draped over the floors. There's puke everywhere.

"They're not dead," Ruby says. "At least not *all* of them."

"Don't feel too bad," Pixie says. "Most of the dead ones are Royals. We think."

"You think?" I say.

"Well, there ain't no way to be sure, is there? We took guesses. Educated guesses. Sometimes you can tell just by lookin' at 'em. Like that scrawny dude back there—totally not a Royal.

"Victor knew the other ZIRDA bases have been investigating him, so lately, he's been bringing in *real* ZIRDA agents as a lame attempt to get people off his case. But he only keeps the weak and pathetic ones on base—like that Katie girl. The powerful ones, like us, he sends out on useless missions as field agents to keep us away from here."

I adjust Arella in my arms as I continue following the women. "How did you guys know Victor's a Royal?"

"We were transferred here from ZIRDA New York," Ruby says. "We work closely with ZIRDA Toronto. They were the first to smell something fishy here."

"Speaking of which," Pixie says, "Victor disappeared tonight. When we heard the siren and your name over the intercom, we figured you was tryna save the Immune and got caught. The first thing we did was rush to find Victor. One of his guards told us he was off base."

"Where is he?" I ask.

"We dunno," Ruby says. "We didn't get a chance to find out before his guards attacked us. They must have figured we were using the alert as our chance to kill Victor—which, I suppose they weren't wrong."

Pixie rubs the side of her head. "That one guard punched me so hard, I swear I saw stars like they do in the cartoons."

"What happened after you guys got away from Victor's guards?" I ask.

"We rushed down to help you, duh! On the way, we ran into a bunch of agents rushing down from all the other levels. Since we didn't know which side people were on and we had already blown our cover, we screamed out, 'Victor's a Royal!' Anyone who didn't look surprised and tried to shut us up, we aimed to kill."

My arms are getting achy from carrying Arella like this. She's still slumped against me as we pass more bodies lying on the floor.

"This guy is dead. I made sure of it." Pixie gestures toward a buff guy lying facedown in a pool of his own blood. I think his name was Derek. "I knew he was a Royal from the moment I met him. When I looked him up later, I found out he's the guy who arranged that school shooting at a Zordi elementary school in Texas last year. Many agents' kids went to that school. Not a single child came out alive."

God, I fucking hate the Royals.

When we finally arrive at the elevators, Ruby presses the *up* button as Arella's head droops backward. My heart collapses into my stomach. I can't tell if she's breathing. *Oh, baby, please be breathing!*

Pixie must read my mind, because she places two fingers against Arella's neck. "She's alive. Just knocked out."

I let out a breath of relief.

Ding!

As we step into the elevator, I expand my empathy up and out. "There's a group of people in the security room. I can't fight them off with my arms full."

"It's the other ZIRDA agents," Ruby says as the elevator closes then rises. "After the battle down here, we told the ones who were still alive to guard the entrance. Don't let anyone in or out, and detain Victor on sight—those were their orders."

The elevator reopens, and we're greeted by three men armed with lightning balls. They close their hands the moment they see Pixie and Ruby.

"Is this the guy?" one of them asks.

"Yeah," Pixie says, "and we've gotta help him protect this Ordinary at all costs."

At an instant, the men surround me like they're the Secret Service and I'm the president—or, more specifically, Arella is.

The women lead me into the security room, where a group of bloodied-up men and women are gathered around the monitors. Sadly, there's no more than twenty of them. *Is this really all who's left?*

Lifelessly leaning against the corner is that security guard with the eyebrow scar. He's bleeding out from a deep wound in his chest.

Pixie hooks a thumb toward the guy. "Did y'all make sure he was a Royal before ya offed him?"

"He was definitely a Royal," a familiar voice says from

behind me. "He was one of the men who kidnapped the Ordinary and brought her here."

I spin around to face Katie. She's got a bright red mark on her cheek where I punched her. I still feel bad about that.

"What if the dude only kidnapped the Ordinary under Victor's orders?" Pixie asks. "Victor could have fed him some bullshit to get him to do it."

Katie arches a brow at her. "If anyone from ZIRDA gave you orders to drug and kidnap an innocent Ordinary to bring here, would you have done it?"

"Hmm. Point made. Now what about this guy?" Pixie points at the other security guard duct-taped to a chair. It's Carlos—with some duct tape around his mouth too.

"We weren't sure about him," Katie says. "That's why we detained him instead."

The gray-haired man shakes his head and mumbles something under the tape. His emotions tell me he's scared shitless. Is he scared because we suspect he's a Royal and might kill him, or is he scared because he *is* a Royal and we'll kill him? Hard to tell.

"Listen up, guys!" Pixie shouts. "We've gotta help Trey get this Ordinary outta here. Ruby and I will leave with him to help keep her safe. We could use at least two more while the rest of you stay here and guard the base. Who's got the best gifts to come with us?"

A slender Black man in the back raises his hand. "I have enhanced speed."

Pixie flashes him a thumbs-up. "Thanks, Dash. Anyone else?"

"I want to come," Katie says. "I have the power to—"

Errr! Errr! Errr! A high-pitched alarm goes off.

"Incoming!" a blonde woman shouts with her attention on the monitors. "Looks like ten. Maybe fifteen. They're being ported in next to the waterfall."

The group shouts over each other at the same time.

"They're running through the cavern!"

"What do we do?"

"What if they're on our side?"

"They're not! Victor's with them!"

I catch a glimpse of Victor on a screen, barking orders to people. I hug Arella tighter against me. Is that why Victor left the base? He went to recruit more of his fellow Royal buddies? *Fucking traitor.*

"Secure the entrance!" someone shouts.

The blonde searches around, then slams her hand against a red button labeled EMERGENCY LOCKDOWN.

Ruby turns to Pixie. "How are we gonna get this Ordinary out now?"

Pixie's voice booms over everyone else's. "Does anyone know another way outta here?"

"There are secret passageways," I say, "but I don't know where they are."

Ruby scoffs. "Well, that's helpful."

From his chair, Carlos mumbles and wiggles his body.

Pixie rips the tape off his mouth so fast, it looks painful. "Here's your chance to prove you're one of us, old man. Do you know another way out?"

"There's a tunnel," Carlos says, "in the Artificial Sunlight room."

"Where in that room?"

"Untie me, and I'll show you."

Pixie glances up at Ruby. "Think we can trust him?"

Ruby shrugs. "Do we have a choice?"

"Tell 'em, Trey," Carlos says. "You've known me since you were a kid. I let you play all those damn tricks on me over the years, and I never once ratted you out to Victor. You know I'm good!"

The women turn their attention to me, waiting for an answer. I wish I could say for certain that we can trust Carlos, but I can't. How can I know what side anyone's on, when my own uncle has been on the dark side this whole time?

"I don't know if I can vouch for him," I say and sense Carlos's stomach drop.

"Whatever you're gonna do," the blonde says, "do it fast! They're trying to blast through this door with their powers!"

Pixie slides the knife out of her back pocket and uses it to cut apart the duct tape restraining Carlos to the chair. "Try anything funny and I'll blow those little ears off your head. Got it?"

Carlos nods, then hops to his feet. "Follow me!"

With Arella still in my arms, I trail Carlos to the elevators with Pixie, Ruby, Katie, and the Speeder at my side. Together, we climb into the machine as Ruby stabs the *close doors* button repeatedly until the doors shut.

Katie turns to Carlos. "How do you know about this tunnel?"

"I used to patrol before I got assigned to entrance duty. When you patrol for almost twenty years, you tend to know things."

"What if he's leading us straight into a trap?" the Speeder asks.

Pixie pats his shoulder. "Good thing you're here, Dash. Once we get to the tunnel, you can run through it first to make sure it's good before we all go."

The Speeder nods. "Sounds like a plan."

"If it counts for anything," Carlos says, "I was with ZIRDA for many years before Victor took over."

I wish that counted for something, but if the Royals can turn Victor, they can probably turn anyone.

Ding!

"Let me go first," Pixie says.

Without anyone having to say it, they all shift to stand in front of me as the elevator opens. Ruby even prepares her hands with fireballs. I appreciate the effort, but I already know we're good. I don't sense anyone on the other side.

Pixie steps out and peeks around the corners before calling out, "Clear!" Only then do the rest of the group step off the elevator and Ruby's hands smoke out.

Carlos leads us to the Artificial Sunlight room, where he holds the door open for everyone else. I step inside with Pixie and Ruby protecting my front while Katie and the Speeder guard my back. I stare at Arella's chest to make sure it's still rising and falling. Slowly and slightly, it is.

Carlos shuts the door behind him. "Follow me."

A fake sky stretches above us with an artificial sun so bright, it stings my eyes. I wait a second for my vision to adjust and return to normal. Blazing heat attacks my skin. On cue, my body's natural equilibrium kicks in.

Since Victor made up a rule that this room was for agents only, I've never been in here. Seeing it for the first time makes me feel like I've been transported onto a deserted island. A sandy beach covers the floor as far as I can see. Glistening blue water sweeps over the shoreline in calm waves. Some blue tables are stationed around the beach with padded lounge chairs under giant white umbrellas. If someone showed me a picture of this room, I wouldn't think it was indoors.

Carlos points toward the rocky, tree-covered cliffs in the distance. "The tunnel is just on the other side of that."

As we hike across the beach, Pixie presses her fingers against Arella's neck again. "She's good."

"Thanks for checking."

"Aren't your arms tired, bro? She's, like, all deadweight."

I let out an exhausted grunt. "My arms are so numb that I can't feel them anymore."

"How about one of us carry her for a bit?"

I'm about to accept her offer until I realize it means I'd have to let Arella go. It's not that I don't trust them to keep her safe. Pixie, Ruby, and Katie have more than proven that they're willing to take risks to help save Arella. Carlos and this Dash guy are still in yellow status, but for now, I'm choosing to allow them near my girl. Either way, none of these people will protect Arella to the extent that I will. If it comes down to it, I'll take a fireball for her. I'm not sure if any of them would do the same. For that reason, she's staying as close to me as possible, even if it makes my arms fall off.

"Never mind," Pixie says. "That was a stupid question."

"I'm sorry," I say. "It's not that I don't trust you. It's—"

She puts a hand up. "Say no more. If it was my baby sister, I wouldn't give her to someone else to carry even if my arms were broken."

I'm glad she understands.

A sudden burst of panic rushes through my head as double the emotions invade my mind. It's all coming from the sixth floor above us. "Fuck."

Everyone turns to me. "What?"

"I think the Royals just got through the main entrance."

"Shit," Ruby says. "Maybe we should have secured the door to this room in case they—"

Dash disappears with a *whoosh!* and a gust of air that blows Ruby's curls into her face. The ground rumbles for a moment, then a few seconds later, Dash returns with another *whoosh!* "We're good now."

"What did you do?" I ask.

He smirks and nods his head toward the door. "Take a peek."

We all turn.

Katie gasps with a hand to her mouth. "I can't even see the door anymore."

I can't see the beach behind us either. A forest of dark green trees now stands between us and the door.

"I'll keep working my Earth powers," Dash says. "Just keep going."

As we close the distance between us and the other side of

the cliff, Dash remains a few steps behind. The ground rumbles with each tree that pops out of the sand. From the branches, he grows thick thorny vines, making it almost impossible to see through his forest.

When we finally make it to the other side of the cliff, Carlos stops to examine a large crack running up the rocky wall.

"There's a hidden keypad here somewhere." Carlos sticks his hand between the crack and feels up and down. We all wait a moment before he sighs. "I—I can't find it. Maybe I'm looking in the wrong crack."

Pixie whips the knife out of her back pocket and points it at the old man's face. "Or maybe you're just purposely wasting our goddamn time. Is there even a tunnel here?"

Carlos throws his arms up in surrender. "I swear there is!"

"Point to where the entrance is," Katie says. "I'll get it open."

With Pixie still pointing her knife at him, Carlos gestures toward a part of the cliff that looks the same as all the other parts of the cliff. "It's around there."

"How big is it?" Katie asks.

"I dunno. Maybe big enough for a small car to fit through?"

"Okay. Everyone, stand back."

I take about three steps backward. So does everyone else.

Katie shakes her head at us. "Um, no. You're gonna want to have a lot more space than that, I promise you."

Without a word, everyone takes another ten big steps back until our feet almost touch the waterline. It must be far enough because Katie twists around to aim her stare at the cliff.

Suddenly, a square part of the cliff glows red, then *BOOM!* Debris fireworks through the air. Rocks the size of watermelons land in the sand with hard thuds. A cloud of dirt and sand makes me cough. In the corner of my eye, I see

Carlos lift his hand and circle it above his head. A gust of wind blows the debris away. Once the air clears, it reveals a dark tunnel and a grinning Katie.

Carlos lowers his arm, then the wind stops. "Told ya there's a tunnel."

Pixie shoves her knife back into her pocket, then pats Carlos on the shoulder. "You did good, old man."

"Where does this tunnel let out?" Ruby asks.

"The forest, I assume," Carlos says. "I haven't actually walked through it. I just knew it was here."

"Dash?"

"On it." With a *whoosh!* the Speeder disappears.

This time, he's gone for almost ten seconds. The whole time, I expand my powers upward to sense how things are going upstairs. From what I can tell, a lot of people have died. The number of people I can sense has almost halved. Thankfully, I don't sense anyone on their way down here—yet.

Whoosh! "The tunnel is about a half mile long. It lets out into the forest. I even surveyed the area up top. It's clear."

Ruby lights up her palms with fireballs, then throws them into the tunnel to light the way. "All righty, peeps. Let's get this Ordinary outta here."

I'm so overwhelmed with gratitude, I'm speechless. This is the ZIRDA I know: a team who works together to do good things, to save Ordinaries, and to keep the Royals from causing harm. This is what I thought I was working for this whole time. This is what I've wanted to be a part of my entire life.

17

TREY

Ruby leads the group with her fireballs flickering against the tunnel walls. I've got Pixie on my left and Katie on my right. Carlos and Dash are at my heels. I think I trust the men now—not enough to ask one of them to carry Arella, but I trust them enough to let them walk behind me without wondering if they'll try something. Even if they do, the women will stop them. I'm sure of it.

"Is Pixie your real name?" I ask as our footsteps echo with each step. The silence was killing me.

"Nah. I go by Pixie here because my real name is Anna Jung. It's kinda lame and plain for how badass I am, huh?"

"That's not as lame as *my* real name," Ruby says. "My family's been calling me Ruby since I was born, and I've been going by it ever since. Barely anyone even knows what my real name is."

"*I* don't even know what your real name is," Pixie says. "And we're besties."

"Tell us," Carlos says, grinning.

Ruby shakes her head with a chuckle. "Hell no."

"Helga?" Pixie asks.

"Ew!"

"Olga?"

"No."

"Gertrude," I say because that name just sounds funny.

"Definitely not."

"Bertha?"

"Okay, stop." Ruby rolls her eyes. "It's Agatha, after my great-grandmother."

Pixie spits out a laugh. "Agatha? No fucking way."

A baseball-size fireball appears in Ruby's palm, and she holds it close to Pixie's face. "If you ever call me that, I'll burn you alive."

Pixie throws her arms up in surrender, still laughing. "Noted."

"What's your real name?" Carlos asks Dash.

"Henry," Dash says simply. "But everyone's called me Dash since I was toddler."

"And you, Katie?"

"My name is actually Katie," she says. "Not short for Katherine either. It's just Katie."

"I take back what I said about you, girl," Pixie says, keeping a steady pace at my side. "I called you weak earlier, but apparently, you're not. That timid voice and submissive personality fooled me good."

Katie lets out an adorable chuckle. "Where's my Oscar?"

"That's one hell of a mind power too," I say, ignoring the burning ache in my arms. I don't know how much longer I can carry Arella like this. "Now I know why you were so confident you could overpower me when I tried to leave."

"I only said that to scare you. I can't blow *people* up—just things."

"I see. I guess if you could blow people up, you probably wouldn't exist."

Even before Zordinaries went into hiding, the zovernment controlled what powers remained in our genetic existence. Whenever a gift is classified as too dangerous or deadly, the zovernment puts it on the Extinction List. Then anyone with that power is sterilized to prevent others from being born with that gift.

There used to be people who could control minds, swap minds, and some even had a death touch. Now that those people haven't reproduced for almost thirty generations, those powers don't exist anymore.

"Deadly people slip through the cracks all the time," Ruby says. "Especially if they're a child of a Superior. My sister is living proof of that."

"What do you mean?" I ask.

Ruby twists around and walks backward as she raises a brow at me. "Think about it. Once our powers come in around the age of one, our parents are required to register our gifts with the zovernment, right?"

"Right?" I say like a question because I don't know where she's going with this.

"My sister's body power is one that skipped a few generations in our line, so there isn't a record of this gift being in our genetics. She can make your blood literally boil until it kills you from the inside out. Do you really think my parents were going to register her as a blood-boiling killer? That's instant extermination, my dude."

"What? I thought the zovernment just sterilizes those babies."

"Mm-hmm." Ruby turns around to face the front. "That's what the zovernment says they do because that's what they want you to *think*. In reality, they just take those babies away and pop them into an incinerator."

Katie slaps a hand over her heart. "Oh god."

"Sorry for the visual, but that's exactly what happens. It's easier, faster, and it's the most effective way of preventing that baby from ever being a danger to people in the future."

Kill one to save the others. Seems like the zovernment has

adopted that ideal too. Am I the only one who doesn't think that's okay? Isn't there another way?

Ruby continues, "Now, let's say you work for the zovernment and you know that's where those babies end up. No zovernment official in their right mind would ever register their own child with a gift on the Extinction List, knowing it's a death sentence for their baby, so people lie. They cover it up. They go into hiding. Whatever it takes to save their kid. According to the zovernment, my sister can look at any animal to hear its thoughts—you know, something completely harmless and not life-threatening at all, and most importantly, hard to prove."

"Honestly," Dash says from behind me, "if it was my kid, I'd do the same."

"Me too," Carlos says.

Me three. I'd kill a hundred people before I let anyone take my child away from me. I guess that doesn't make me any better than the zovernment.

I glance at the woman in my arms with my shirt still tied around her knife wound. The man who threw that knife at her is now lying either sedated or lifeless in a pool of his own blood, and I have no regrets. I'd do it again if it meant saving her, and I feel the same for the unborn child growing inside her belly. This baby isn't mine, but it's Arella's. That means it's a part of her, which means I'll stop at nothing to make sure it's safe too.

"Does anyone know of a good place I can take Arella once we get outta here?" I ask.

"Our ZIRDA base in New York might take you in," Ruby says. "And I promise, our CEO is *not* an undercover Royal."

"I dunno," Pixie says. "The boss would need some convincing. You know how she is about bringing in outsiders."

"But Trey's not an outsider. He's a fellow ZIRDA agent."

"Who is related to Victor. She won't trust him. She might

think it's a trick Victor came up with to get him into our base."

Being associated with that monster by blood disgusts me. What would my dad say if he knew his older brother ended up joining the group of criminals who ended his life? Suddenly, it hits me: What if Victor's the one behind the murder of my parents? His neck was slashed on the same night that my parents were blown to bits. What if that was just a cover-up to make it seem like he wasn't involved?

The story Victor told me was that the Royals showed up at his house, demanding he take them to Shadow Ridge, and when he refused, they slashed his neck and left him for dead. If the Royals had really wanted him dead, wouldn't they have slashed him enough to make sure he couldn't survive?

"I can take you to ZIRDA Minnesota," Katie says. "My CEO will take care of you two in a heartbeat."

That sounds amazing. "How are we gonna get there?"

"Any way we can. Walk. Steal a car. Ride a bus. Stow away on a plane. Whatever it takes."

The idea of having an entire ZIRDA base, a *real* one, protecting Arella makes my heart swell. With them, no Royal will be able to get within twenty steps of my girl.

Eventually, we arrive at a long set of narrow wooden stairs leading upward.

"This is the end of the tunnel," Dash says. "It's just up these stairs, then we come out of a tree. Let me go first again to make sure it's all clear." With a *whoosh!* and a slight gust of air, Dash disappears. At the top of the stairs, some moonlight shines through a small door. The rest of us climb the stairs in silence.

When Dash doesn't come back right away, I stop and project my empath power upward. Like how Trackers can't trace people who are underground, my empath powers can't sense anyone above ground while I'm under it, so I get nothing.

Pixie pauses a few stairs ahead of me. "You okay?"

"Something's not right." My heart rate kicks up a notch. "It's been at least ten seconds, and Dash isn't back yet."

"Roobs?"

"On it." In an instant, Ruby runs up the stairs.

The rest of us stay where we are while she heads to the surface. Just as she exits the top, she screams. Then come the wails of a bunch of men.

"Help!" Ruby shouts. "I can't fight them all myself!"

Without wasting a second, Pixie, Katie, and Carlos race up the stairs.

"Stay here!" Pixie shouts to me.

Stay here? And do what? Wait for them to either win or die before I can get Arella to safety? *No fucking way.* If they're being attacked up there, they're gonna need all the help they can get.

I scurry back down the steps and gently lay my unconscious Arella over the tunnel floor. My arms gain a tiny sense of relief from letting her go.

"I'll be right back, baby. I promise." Then I sprint up the stairs two at a time, shaking the ache out of my arms.

The second I step out of the hollowed tree, madness swarms my head. Shock, anger, and fear shoot at me from all around. Lightning balls whizz through the air. The forest catches on fire with each fireball that misses its human target. A rock ball the size of a basketball flies straight at my face. I duck just in time, and it hits the base of the tree behind me.

Everyone is screaming and shouting. It's too dark, and there's too much commotion for me to make out who is who. All I know is that there are more of them than there are of us.

A large man wails as he drops to his knees and covers his ears. Behind Pixie, another large man charges at her with his arm transformed into the shape of a machete.

"Pixie! Behind you!" I run to help her until I trip over

something soft on the ground and fall on my face. When I turn to look back, I gasp.

At my feet, Dash's lifeless body stares back at me. He's bleeding out of a deep gash in his neck. They must have killed him the second he got up here. I guess that proves he really was on ZIRDA's side.

"I'm sorry," I whisper to him as I hoist myself onto my feet. Just as I do, a loud *pop!* pinches my eardrums. A slender man appears in front of me. It's the Teleporter who brought me here.

He hurls a fist straight into my nose. I stumble backward as pain explodes up my face and something wet trickles into my mouth. Blood. Salty and metallic. I wipe at it with my hand, then launch my bloody fist back at him. He disappears with another *pop!* as I stumble forward, and my fist catches nothing but air.

Pop! The man kicks me from behind. I face-plant into the ground, then turn and aim a fireball at him.

Pop! My fireball hits a tree, setting it ablaze.

Pop! The Teleporter appears on top of me. He straddles me and punches my face. Then he does it again. And again. And again. He grabs my neck and chokes me as a punishing jolt of lightning races down my legs. I scream out in pain, clawing at his fingers digging into my throat.

This isn't my end. It can't be. Arella needs me.

I draw my arms back as some flames flicker between my fingertips, but I can't gather enough strength to produce a fireball.

Suddenly, the lightning stops and the man groans in agony. His body convulses as he falls onto his side. I kick him away from me.

"Stop! Stop!" he shouts.

A hissing sound comes from behind me.

"St—" The guy vomits in his own mouth, then coughs as he chokes on it. Seconds later, his body goes still.

Ruby offers me a hand and helps me off the ground. "Grab the Ordinary and get outta here!"

"What about you guys?"

"We'll hold them back! Just go!"

I don't need to be told twice. I climb back into the hollowed tree and race down the steps. Arella is exactly where I left her, unmoved and unharmed. I heave her limp body into my still-aching arms, then sprint back up the stairs.

When I step out, the women and Carlos are guarding the entrance. Ruby has two men shaking on the ground, wailing like dying cats. Pixie has another three people on their knees, with their hands clasped against their ears. A few guys are swirling around in Carlos's giant tornado. Katie is throwing ice balls at two women as a tree behind them glows red.

BOOM! The tree explodes. The women attacking Katie go flying through the air. When they land on the hard ground, the emotions of one of them leaves my head.

"Run!" Katie shouts. "We'll cover you!"

Since I don't know where in the forest I am, I don't know which way to go. But anywhere is better than here, so I pick a direction and sprint.

I'm barely five steps away when Katie screams from behind me. "No! Carlos!"

Instinctively, I turn just as Carlos's emotions disappear from my head. A giant tree root sticks out from the ground, piercing him right in the chest. Three people scream as Carlos's tornado vanishes and they fall to the ground. It only takes them a second to get onto their feet. One of them punches Katie in the stomach as the other two run toward me.

I drop Arella's feet to the ground to free a hand, then chuck fireballs at the men. Clumsily, I hug Arella's upper body against mine, dragging her with me as I stumble backward and dodge the fireballs flying toward us.

"Arella!" I shout as I shake her. "Wake up! I need you!"

Her immunity would be so fucking helpful right now.

Fighting people off is a hell of a lot harder without her invisible wall of protection.

The men are gaining on me. Another fireball rockets through the air and grazes my arm. The heat sears my skin before the fireball lands in the grass behind me, setting it on fire. The ground rumbles beneath my feet as two tree roots pop out of the ground. Their sharp ends fly straight toward my chest. I fall backward and land on my back just as the roots swipe the air where I was just standing. I lose my grip on Arella, who rolls away from me and lands on her side.

The Terra attacking me points his fingers at the ground again. The dirt rumbles beneath me until another tree root shoots out of the ground and circles my legs.

"No!" I shout as the roots drag me away from Arella.

In the corner of my eye, I see the Terra lift his hands into the air. His roots whip me upward, then slam me back onto the ground. Searing pain tears through my ribs. I clutch my side as I'm lifted into the air again, then my face crashes against the hard ground. More agony fires throughout my ribs. I cry out as the tree roots fling me toward the sky a third time. I'm bracing myself for the impact when suddenly, the roots stop. I dangle above a tree as the man below me cries out in pain.

"You little bitch!" Ruby says through hisses.

The tree roots around my legs glow red. They're warm against my jeans until they slowly break apart and release me. I fall to the ground, landing face first—on my ribs again. The agony burns like hell.

"Sorry," Katie says. "I didn't know how else to get you down."

I push onto my knees and clutch my side. I taste blood again, and it's so hard to breathe.

"Get up, Trey!" Katie shouts as she tosses ice balls at someone behind me.

What the hell does she think I'm trying to do, have a tea party? "Give me a fucking second, will ya?"

"We don't have seconds. You need to get her away from here."

I'm barely back onto my feet when Pixie shouts, "No!" Then she puckers her lips and blows toward the large man hoisting Arella over his shoulder.

Katie and I race toward the man as he drops Arella onto the ground and clutches his ears. My girl limply rolls onto the ground.

With a grunt, Katie hurls her fist into the man's face. Then she draws back and does it again. The petite woman sure hits hard. The man's pain mirrors onto my own face, but it's nothing compared to the agony in my torso.

"Go, Trey!" Katie shouts. "Get her outta here and hide!"

Aching, I pick up Arella off the ground and cradle her against my burning chest. Then I run.

18

ARELLA

A RUSTLING SOUND MAKES MY EYES FLUTTER OPEN. I'M LYING on my right side with my head against a hard floor—a dirty floor. It's covered in mud, dry leaves, and who knows what else.

It's dark. Some slivers of moonlight shine through the cracks of . . . tires? I'm lying under a large table pushed against a corner with tires stacked around it. *Where am I? How did I get here?*

Wherever I am, it smells like rotten wood and stale dung that's been rained on. *Gross.* At least I'm out of that evil lair now. *Well, I think I am.* Why else would there be moonlight?

Someone's lying behind me with their arm limp beneath my neck. Their other arm rests over my ribs. It's Trey. I don't need to turn around to see his face for confirmation. I know it's him by the sound of his steady breaths and the familiar way his muscular body feels against mine.

My left arm is throbbing. There's something wrapped around it. I reach up to feel it. It's a shirt. *When did a shirt get tied around my arm?* The last thing I remember is that knife slashing me. Everything beyond that is a blur.

I have to get out of here. I have to get away from Trey and

anyone else with magical powers. They're trouble. Every last one of them. Once I get away, the first thing I'm doing is contacting the police. They'll keep me safe for sure. After that, I'm going to find a baked potato and some bacon. I'm so hungry, I could probably eat the whole pig right now.

With the gentlest of fingers, I pick up Trey's arm draped over me and slowly rest it over the nasty floor. His breathing remains steady. Dry leaves crunch and crackle beneath me as I move to sit upright. I go slow, careful not to wake him up. *So far, so good.*

Once I'm upright, I take a closer look at the tires barricaded around me. They're stacked in rows, three high. I only need to move one row to give me enough room to get out. *Maybe if I go slow enough . . .*

More leaves crunch beneath me as I maneuver into a kneeling position. Trey moans softly as his head slumps against the floor. I hold my breath and wait for him to move again. When he doesn't, I exhale.

At the row of tires farthest from Trey's ears, I give the bottom tire a gentle push. It doesn't budge. I push again, harder this time. With a light dragging sound, the tires shift forward a tiny bit. I stop and eye Trey. Thankfully, his eyes are still shut.

I'm about to push the tires again when a rustling sound makes me freeze. I think it's coming from the other side of the wall. It might be a small animal outside or the wind blowing leaves around. When the rustling stops, I resume my escape.

The tires make another small noise against the floor as I push them again. Trey doesn't move. I give them another shove. This time, I feel resistance. Something on the other side is blocking the tires from moving any farther. *Dang it!*

I peer out the small opening I've made. It looks like I'm in a barn. Straight ahead is a rusty car—or what's left of it. Next to that are a couple of old tractors with missing wheels. More rubber tires lie in a pile near the wall. A line of old, broken shovels leans up against some shelves. Everything is covered in dirt.

Trey lets out another tiny moan, making me stop and stare at him. A beam of moonlight shines through my small opening, hitting him just right. I let out a little gasp. Trails of dried blood drip from his temples, all the way down his neck. The bruises on his cheeks are a bright shade of red and purple. A cut on the side of his lip is crusted over in blood. *How did he get so banged up?* It must have happened after I passed out.

Even with all the gore covering his face, he looks peaceful. I don't think I've ever seen him asleep before. Correction, I've *never* seen him asleep before. I almost feel bad for leaving him like this. Not bad enough to stick around though. I want nothing to do with him and his supernatural friends. Not unless one of them has the power to turn back time to before I was kidnapped.

Since the opening isn't big enough for me to crawl through, I'll have to move the row of tires next to it. It takes me a few pushes, but eventually, my opening becomes big enough. I'm about to crawl out when another rustling sound stops me. I yelp as a huge rat scurries across my legs, making me jerk backward, straight into Trey.

"Ah!" His arms flail around as the rat climbs up the tires and weasels its way out the other side.

All the tires fly across the barn as Trey shoots out from under the table and onto his feet. Two fireballs magically burst into his hands, one in each palm. They're so big and bright, they illuminate everything around us.

"Stay down!" He takes a firm stance in front of me as his head swivels from side to side. "Where are they?"

"Who?"

"The bad guys!"

"Not here."

He turns to me, still holding the flames. "Then why did you scream?"

"It was a rat."

Finally, his fire goes out, drowning the barn in darkness again. He slaps a palm against his forehead. "Fuck."

He dashes across the barn toward the pile of tires and seizes one off the top. It must have belonged to a tractor because I've never seen a car with a tire that big before.

"What are you doing?" I ask as he rolls the tire to me and flops it at my feet. "You know we'll need the rest of the vehicle for this to be of any use, right?"

A little smile tugs at the corners of his lips. "Only you can make me laugh when we're being hunted by people who won't hesitate to drive tree roots through my heart."

The mental image of that makes my throat tighten.

Trey points at the large tire. "Do you think you can work your magic on me?"

Funny that he calls *me* magic when *he's* the one who can make flames come out of his hands. "Why?"

"Because all they need is my DNA to give to a Tracker, and they'll know my exact location by sensing the use of my powers. If they were tracking us when I used my powers just now, it probably won't take 'em more than a few minutes to know we're here. Then all they need is a Teleporter, and they'll be here within seconds. I need you to make me immune so I can fly us outta here before they arrive."

And *this* is why I need to get away from him. *He's* the one they're tracking. Not me. Still, my current choices are to get out of here faster *with* Trey or slower *without* him, so I offer him a firm nod. "I can do it."

"Great." He sits in the hole of the tire, then spreads his legs apart and pats the space between them.

I accept the invitation by leaning my back against his front. He hisses through his teeth, and I stiffen up. "Are you okay?"

He groans and winces. "I'm fine."

My heart pounds uncontrollably as he wraps his arm around my waist like a seat belt. Internally, I scowl at my heart for betraying me. My body can't react this way around him anymore. *Not allowed.*

My stomach betrays me with butterflies when Trey slips his fingers between mine. Everything in my body tells me I'm safe—except for my head, which is shouting, *He's dangerous! Get away from him!*

I flashback to the night I questioned Trey about his abnormalities. After he refused to tell me his secret—one I didn't realize could be this insane—I asked, "Are you dangerous?"

Without hesitation, he said, "No. Not to you."

"Who are you dangerous to?"

"Anyone who tries to hurt you."

I think he knew at that time. He knew people were going to kidnap me, and he did nothing to prevent it. Maybe he's not dangerous to me directly, but he's dangerous by association. The second I'm able to, I'm getting away from him. Far, far away.

"You ready?" Trey's breath on the back of my neck sends warm tingles down my spine.

Stop! I mentally shout at myself. Screw my body for loving the feel of him on me. Actually, screw the world for putting me in this situation. Why give me a man I feel safe with, only to make being with him the most life-threatening situation I've ever encountered? It doesn't make any sense.

"Arella?"

I pull myself out of my swirling thoughts and imagine my waves of water crashing around him. I visualize the water soaking him from head to toe, drenching him with my immunity. "Okay, I'm ready. Just don't let go of my hand."

By now, I'm pretty confident in my ability to project my immunity onto Trey without having to touch him. The hand holding is simply for assurance. At least that's what I'm telling myself.

"I'll start slow, then I'm gonna go fast, 'kay?" Trey lifts his free hand, then the tire carries us into the air and we soar through the giant hole in the barn's ceiling.

It blows my mind how he's doing this. Seeing him move a trash bin from one side of the room to another is one thing, but this? The fireballs, the skilled fighting, the being a member of a secret underground spy ring thing. What else don't I know about him?

We zoom over a quiet house, then above some woods and a small lake.

More woods.

Another house.

More woods.

Then it's just woods for a while.

"Arella, I think you're cutting off the circulation in my leg."

I release the death grip I didn't realize I had on his calf. "Sorry."

"It's okay. I won't let you fall, babe. Just relax."

Relax? He wants me to relax? I haven't been able to relax for what feels like weeks. Now he's telling me to relax while I'm jetting across the sky on a smelly tire to get away from my abductors? *Yeah, right.*

"Don't call me *babe*," I say with a little bite to it.

His hands droop a little. Then he clears his throat and says somberly, "Sorry."

How can so much pain come out in one little word? If I could still sense other people's emotions, I'm sure I would have felt his heart shatter in his chest. Suddenly, I feel bad. Not bad enough to take it back though. This man has no right to be calling me *babe* anymore.

He clears his throat again. "Are you ready to go faster?"

"Sure." My head jerks backward into his shoulder as we

speed through the air like we're on a roller coaster. "Can I turn around to face you? The wind is making it hard for me to breathe."

"Of course. Do you wanna land first?"

"I think I can flip around up here." Slowly, I rotate, sticking one leg into the air over his head, then dropping it at his side. The entire time, he holds me tight around my waist and never lets me go. I wish he didn't make me feel so safe, yet so terrified at the same time. It's not that I'm terrified of him; it's the people who are after me *because of him*.

I lock my ankles together behind him while my hands find the back of his neck for support. He winces and lets out a pained grunt.

I release my grip a little. "Am I hurting you?"

He forces a tiny smile. "I'm just a little sore."

He's totally lying, but that's nothing new. Either way, I'll try to stay still so I don't hurt him anymore.

Now that we're out of the darkness of the barn, I'm able to get a better look at his bloody face. It's worse than I thought. I think he's bleeding from the side of his head. But that's just a guess, because there's so much blood covering him, it's hard to know where it's all coming from.

I feel the need to take a wet rag to his face and an urge to kiss the pain in his eyes away. It's the same pain I saw in him the first time he saw me handcuffed to that bed—and all the other times he looked at me while I was in the evil lair.

I believe him when he says he had nothing to do with physically abducting me. If he did, he wouldn't have been so genuinely shocked to see me there. I know he cares about me, too. Why else would he have attacked his uncle for manhandling me? Why else would he have risked his life to save me? Even though he's part of the reason why I needed saving in the first place, I won't discredit that he's the one who got me out of there.

"Thank you, Trey," I say in a sweet whisper. "That was brave of you."

Trey's face crinkles as more anguish swims across his face. He bites down on his bloody lip and shakes his head. I wait for him to say something, but he just keeps staring at me with that broken look in his eyes.

It takes a while for him to whisper back, "That wasn't bravery."

"What was it then?"

"I dunno, but I don't feel brave." He lets out a ragged breath like he's about to cry. It makes me tear up too. I want to cry whenever I think about how they tortured him until he went unconscious for three days. And then they tortured him *again*. No matter what he's done, he didn't deserve that.

"Arella, I'm so sorry." He chokes on his words. "None of this was supposed to happen."

I glance over the edge of our flying tire, unable to look him in the eyes. If I do, I might burst into a sob.

The forest is dark and quiet. The treetops seem to wave goodbye at us as we pass them. I feel Trey's gaze on me as I swallow the dry lump in my throat.

His apology feels sincere. I wish I could tell him that it's okay. I wish I could tell him that what happened to me wasn't his fault. But it's not okay, and some of this *is* his fault, and I'm ready to know how much.

19

ARELLA

I STARE OVER THE EDGE OF THE TIRE AS THE WIND BLOWS against my back. "If I ask you some questions, will you answer them honestly?"

"Yes," Trey says with a firm nod.

"What planet are you from?"

He scrunches his eyebrows together. "Earth. I'm not an alien."

Pfft. "You could have fooled me."

"Do you see antennas coming out of my head?"

I run my fingers through the top of his hair to check and my hand gets caught in the dried blood matting up his dark strands. "They could be coming out of your butt or something. I've seen a lot of wild stuff recently. Nothing can surprise me now."

"You've seen me naked. Many times. Don't you think you would have noticed if I had antennas sticking out of my ass?"

You'd think so, but then again, I didn't know he could make fire come out of his bare hands. How am I supposed to trust my ability to notice things—ever? "If you're not an alien, then what are you?"

"Human . . ." He scowls hard and has the audacity to look offended.

"You said you'd be honest, remember?"

"I *am* human, Arella, just like you. Except I was born with powers—and I guess I have a few bodily differences."

I pull my long hair to one side and hold it there to keep it from flying into Trey's face. He hasn't complained about it, but I can't imagine he likes being continually whacked by my waves. "I didn't know there could be humans born with powers."

"That's because you're not supposed to know. The entire world used to know about Zordis. Our kinds used to live cohesively. Eventually, we were forced to go into hiding because Ordinaries began mass-murdering us."

"How did that happen when you guys can overpower us with your superpowers?"

"First off, superpowers is a term only used when referring to superheroes, like the ones in comics and movies. Our gifts are simply passed down by genetics. Think of it like getting your nose from your dad or your hair from your mom. There's nothing super about that."

I wonder who in Trey's line of genetics had the power to sense emotions like my baby did.

Trey continues, "Secondly, there are more of you than there are of us. Back in the early 1300s, Ordinaries created a poison and distributed it through alcohol. While it did nothing to an Ordinary, it was deadly to Zordis. Two million people dropped dead over the span of a year, and no one knew how it was happening.

"Once the drug was discovered, the zovernment decided we couldn't live in harmony with Ordinaries anymore, so a bunch of Scrubbers came together to wipe the memories of all Ordinaries and erased any evidence of our existence."

A secret society of people with powers that the entire world used to know about, who then erased everyone's memories because they were being murdered by poisoned alcohol? This is getting crazier by the minute. "And the zovernment is?"

"The Zordi government. Also called the Superiors. Casually, we call them the Supes. It's made up of Keepers and Enforcers. Keepers are the head honchos who make the rules. Enforcers are like the police."

"And Scrubbers—are those like people who go around with that thing from *Men in Black*, zapping people's memories away?"

Trey lets out a light chuckle. "No, they don't need a zapping thing, just their powers. One of my Zordi schoolteachers said that eighty-nine of the most powerful Scrubbers in the world came together to erase and alter all Ordinaries' memories at once. Sorta like how you project your immunity onto me, they did the same onto everyone in the world."

I tilt my head to the side. "Zordi school?"

"Yeah. From the age of one, when our body and elemental powers come in, to eighteen, in addition to Ordinary school, all Zordis go to Zordi school at night. We learn things like our people's history, our biology, and the way our powers and bodies work. It's like Ordinary school, except without math since that's universal."

"Hmm. It sounds like there's way more to this Zordi thing than simply having"—I almost call them *superpowers* again—"gifts."

"There is. We have our own culture, lifestyles, holidays, and festivals. There are a few islands around the world that are only inhabited by Zordis for those who refuse to acknowledge that Ordinaries exist. Everyone there gets to use their powers freely."

"Liz is a Zordi, isn't she?"

At first, he hesitates, then nods and says, "Yes, she is, but how could you tell?"

"Because she looks like one. You all have this impossible beauty about you. Everyone's so healthy-looking, with perfect skin and straight teeth. Katie said you guys have higher metabolisms too. Liz has the same beauty you and Katie do. Also, I can't imagine you could be as close to her as you are and be able to keep this big of a secret from her."

He purses his lips and nods. "You're right. I wouldn't. It's actually against Zordi laws to have close personal relationships with Ordinaries. My relationship with Liz would probably cross that line."

"Where is the line?"

"Dating, for sure. Kissing and sex are definitely off the table. Basically, we just need to keep as much of a distance as it takes to prevent Ordinaries from noticing that we're different."

Trey broke all those rules with me. We dated, we kissed, and we had lots of sex. I noticed he was different the first time we went out for dinner. I should have questioned it more back then. I should have demanded that he tell me how he knew that teenage boy was getting beat up in an alley from all the way at the restaurant. Instead, I ignored it because I was charmed by his beauty, his humor, and the way he made me feel so protected.

"What happens if the zovernment ever finds out that an Ordinary knows about Zordis?"

Trey swallows hard. "It means a scrub for the Ordinary and z-prison for the Zordi who caused the exposure. Depending on intent, it could mean death."

This is a lot for me to process. It's as if I've recently discovered that math exists and I'm trying to understand all of its elements from simple addition to calculus in one day. It feels impossible, yet I'm curious and I want to know it all. I suppose that's a little counterproductive when I'm also trying to forget that any of this ever happened.

However, it's not the existence of Zordis I want to

forget. I mean, not all Zordis are bad. I wouldn't say Trey's a bad person, and neither is Liz. I never got the feeling that Katie was bad either. It's not having powers that makes them bad. It's how they use them, and that's the part I want to forget.

I want to forget that Victor had Trey spinning in a tornado while he threatened to kill him. I want to forget hearing Trey's screams while they caused him so much pain, he could barely breathe. I want to forget that Derek threw spiky ice balls at me while Trey fought for his life only a few steps away. Just like those spiders in my apartment, I've got a good feeling these moments will haunt me in my sleep.

With a light finger, Trey tucks some of my stray hairs behind an ear. That entire side of my body tingles, betraying me again. "I know you probably have more questions, but I have some I wanna ask you."

My voice comes out breathy. "Okay . . ."

"First, you're still making me immune, right?"

"Mm-hmm."

"Great. Second question: What do you think about when you're doing it?"

"Water," I say easily. "A wave surrounding you, protecting you with an impenetrable liquid shield."

"Wow." He chuckles under his breath. "That's ironic."

"How so?"

"Water is my weakness. It's ironic that you, my only other weakness, would imagine it drenching me as protection."

"*I'm* your weakness?"

His expression falters like he's baffled over how I didn't already know that. "Of course. I'd do anything for you."

No one's ever said those words to me before—and with such conviction. A light fluttery tingle fills my belly. I push it away because I can't let his charm put me under his spell again.

"Where are we?" I ask as an attempt to change the

subject. All I've seen for the last however long we've been airborne is trees. Not a single house or road in sight.

"We're currently flying over the Sequoia National Forest."

"Where are we going?"

Trey lifts a hand, making our tire fly higher into the air. "We're gonna do this until the sun rises. Then we'll have to find a different mode of transportation."

"You mean, like, the *Ordinary* kind?"

"Yeah, that."

My stomach twists into knots as the question I've been wanting to ask him for days slithers into my head. I swallow hard as I gather the courage to make the words leave my mouth. "Was it all a lie?"

Trey's gaze locks with mine as his lips part. Something in his eyes dies a little as he sucks in a pained breath. "Arella, I—"

"Was my flat tire an accident?"

The way his face drops makes me wish I wouldn't have asked. For a while there, through that brokenness in his eyes and the sorrow in his voice, I wanted to give him the benefit of the doubt. I wanted to pretend like he merely got caught up in this mess too, like he wasn't part of a grander scheme from the start. Like it was only *after* we started dating that his uncle saw an opportunity and took it.

Trey hangs his head low. "No, it wasn't an accident."

My heart shatters to pieces. How could I be with a man for three whole months and not realize he was pretending the entire time? I'm impressed. His acting skills are top-notch. He should win an award for those amazing performances he put on. Everything from prancing around the grass with that invisible woman to making me think he was in love with me too. He even had Javina fooled, and barely anything gets past that woman.

How long did he know of me before pursuing me to find out the source of my immunity? How did he even know I was immune in the first place? Was he stalking me? If so, for how long? And why did he have to pop my tire? Was he trying to make me feel helpless so he could swoop in and play the hero? I almost laugh. It worked, so I guess it wasn't that terrible of a plan.

God, I feel so stupid! I allowed him to spin a web of lies right in front of me, and I walked straight into it—willingly. He made me believe he actually wanted me. I should have known that a man as rich and as gorgeous as him wouldn't pursue me of his own accord. Of course he had an ulterior motive.

Oh, god . . . and I slept with him! Worse, I was going to have his baby. I saw the rest of my life with this guy. I wanted him there when I opened my first bakery. I wanted to be with him as he toured the world with his band. I can't believe I thought all those things could happen when, this whole time, he was just using me.

My nose stings as I hold back tears. I want to slap him and curl into him at the same time. I hate that he's the one who hurt me but is also the only person I want to hold me until the pain goes away. *Was any of it real?*

Trey scowls at me. "Stop that."

"Stop what?"

"You look like you're questioning everything I've ever done or said to you. Arella, I need you to know that it may have started off as a way to get information from you, but that's not how it ended. I realized halfway through that I'd fallen in—"

"Tell me," I say, cutting him off because I don't want to hear him finish the rest of that lie. I fold my arms over my chest. My hand hits the T-shirt tied around my left arm, and it irritates my wound, but I don't care. The pain that shoots up my shoulder and down my arm is nothing compared to the agony throbbing in my chest. "Tell me everything, and don't leave anything out."

"Okay," he says so calmly, it only pisses me off more. "Where would you like me to start?"

"From the beginning! Where else?"

"Well, there's the beginning from when I met you and the beginning from when my parents died."

I squint at him. "What do your parents have to do with you manipulating your way into my life?"

"Okay, okay. It sounds like I'm gonna need to start from when my parents died."

After a deep breath, he tells me all about the night he witnessed his parents' murder. Everything from when the Royals burst through the front door and attacked him, to seeing his mother get beat up by a man twice her size, to when his dad threw him on the couch and kinetically tossed him out the window just before the house exploded into a mushroom of fire.

"I didn't have any other relatives, so I was forced to live with Victor. After he became the CEO of ZIRDA California, he moved to Shadow Ridge, so that's where I grew up. You already know that Victor was abusive to me. He liked to beat me up and call me things like *worthless kid* and *piece of shit*. He hid the fact that my parents left me money until the day I turned eighteen, when he finally told me about my inheritance, then told me to get lost.

"After I left, I didn't hear from Victor until he called me in early May, out of the blue. He said there was an Ordinary in the LA area who was immune to Zordi powers and if we could find out the source of her immunity, we could work to replicate it and have the upper hand against the Royals. He explained that he needed someone to get her to tell them everything about herself and the best way to do that was to pretend to date her. I've wanted the Royals gone since I was seven, so I didn't hesitate to say yes."

I think back to all those times Trey asked me about my

grandparents and my parents. Yes, I found his questions odd, but not odd enough to come to the conclusion that he was on a secret mission to learn everything about me to relay back to his devil of an uncle.

Trey drags a hand through his matted hair as he sighs. "Tonight, I found out from Katie that Victor's actually a Royal. His real plan was to get us to fall for each other so he could torture me in front of you until you learned to control your immunity.

"Once you did, his plan was to get rid of me, then who knows what he wanted to do from there. If I had to guess, he probably would have kept you locked up in the Ridge for as long as it took to find a way to replicate your immunity. If not that, he'd probably torture you into projecting onto his Royal buddies while they carried out their missions of destruction."

The idea of spending my entire life locked up in that underground hideout scares me. What scares me more is knowing that my grandparents and Javina would have spent the rest of their lives wondering what happened to me. I doubt *kidnapped by her ex-boyfriend's uncle* would have been at the top of their list.

Trey continues, "Since I thought Victor was operating under ZIRDA, I never thought he'd go as far as kidnapping you. I was under the impression that this was just about getting information. No one was supposed to get hurt, Arella, especially not you.

"ZIRDA is an organization of good people who do good things. They started as a research and development agency that ended up also being the people who fought to protect Ordinaries from the Royals. Because, ya know, the fucking zovernment wasn't doing anything about the Royals' bioweapons, nor were they stopping the Royals from going around murdering innocent people for no goddamn reason.

"After Victor told me he planted those spiders and caused

your car accident, I should have known he wasn't with ZIRDA. A *real* ZIRDA leader would never purposely risk an Ordinary's life. It doesn't make any sense why he'd work for the very people who murdered his little brother, so the possibility that he switched sides never even occurred to me. Even now, knowing what I know, it *still* doesn't make any sense. What reason does he have to work for the Royals? What did they say to him to get him to turn?"

I gather all my loose hairs to one shoulder again. "You've said that Victor used to be like a second father to you, then, like flipping a switch, he treated you like trash. What if he's under someone's mind control? Is that a thing in the Zordi world?"

Trey gives me an *I dunno* shrug. "It's a gift that's on the Extinction List, but I just found out today that some people still slip through the cracks, so who knows? Victor being under mind control makes a hell of a lot more sense than him willingly joining the criminals who believe that Zordi humans deserve more than Ordi humans just because we were born with powers."

He lets out a long sigh. "Fuck, Arella. If I had known about Victor earlier, I woulda kidnapped you myself—in a heartbeat. I wouldn't have wasted all that time trying to convince you to move to Paris. Within minutes, I woulda had you duct-taped to a seat on a private jet on the way to Europe."

I was wrong when I thought Trey had done nothing to prevent my abduction. Turns out, he had tried, although his plan was stupid. *Move to Paris? Seriously?* Couldn't he have come up with something better? Something with a higher chance of my cooperation? I don't know what that would be, but anything would have been better than *let's move to another country forever.*

I shake my head at him, but mostly, I shake my head at myself. I fell in love with a man from a world of people with powers who live in secret among those without powers. And the only reason we met was because his manipulative uncle sent him on a mission to find out if I had a gene defect or if I had ever been bitten by a radioactive spider. Nothing Trey and I had was real.

Now here we are on a floating tire after I was kidnapped and he was brutally tortured and we almost died trying to get away. And for what? Even after dodging all those fireballs, we *still* don't know what makes me immune. What did anyone gain from all that?

"Arella." Trey says my name like a plea. "Please tell me what's going through your head because that look on your face is scaring me."

"What look?" I snap.

"Um, you look sorta mad."

"Because I *am*. Wouldn't you be if the one and only man you decided to let into your heart after being in an abusive relationship turned out to be a fake? What was your plan after you got the information you wanted? Were you just going to break up with me and move on like the moments we shared never happened? Like it didn't mean anything?"

He lets out a pained breath. "At first, yes. But once I fell in—"

"You pretended to like me and got me to fall for you knowing what my history was like with Nathan. You knew that I felt like I'd never find someone who could treat me right, yet you kept going on with your deceitful mission anyway."

He softens his tone as if it'll calm me. "The goal was to casually date you for a few weeks. Things between us weren't supposed to go as far as they did. Real feelings were never supposed to get in the way."

"How do you think I would have felt when you suddenly ended things between us once you finally got the information you wanted?"

He gestures toward the forest below us. "Should I land so we can talk this through?"

"No," I shout with my hands in fists. "I want answers, and I want them now."

He lets out a long sigh. "My plan wasn't to break up with you. It was to get you to break up with me."

I force back the tears threatening to stream from my eyes. "Right, like that makes it any better? Either way, you would have conned me into falling for you, only to disappear from my life. Do you really think I wouldn't have been hurt by that? How am I ever supposed to trust another man ever again?"

"You're right, Arella. You're one hundred percent right. That's one of the reasons why I couldn't leave you. The idea of hurting you hurt me."

I throw my arms up and let them flop back into my lap. "Well, look at us now, Trey. I'm hurt—emotionally and physically. If you wanted to keep me from getting hurt, you failed. Just like how you failed your mission to find out what makes me immune. I hope it was worth it, because I swear to you, the second this nightmare is over, I never want to see your face again."

Trey's breath hitches. He stares at me with his mouth slightly open like he can't believe what he just heard. I mean what I said though. The second this is over, I never want to see him again. I don't even want to think about him. I want to move on with my life as if he never existed and none of this ever happened.

With a hard swallow, Trey breaks his gaze from mine and stares down at the trees with a somber look on his face.

Neither of us says anything for a while. I said all I wanted to say, so I just keep my eyes on the forest as I try not to cry.

Occasionally, I steal a glance at Trey. Every time I do, I wish I hadn't, because with each glance, the light in his eyes is dimmer. They're glossed over with a pain in him I've never seen before. Seeing it makes the large crack running through the middle of my heart break deeper.

After a long time, Trey clears his throat and looks up at me. "Arella?"

My heart skips a beat at the sound of my name on his lips, but I'm still mad, so I huff out a breath. "What?"

His Adam's apple moves up and down as he swallows hard. His voice comes out low and husky like it's taking all his energy just to speak. "At your thinking spot, you told me that when you love someone, you put their happiness before your own. If you're saying that once this is over, you never want to see me again . . ." He lets out a ragged sigh, looking anywhere but at me. "Then okay. If that's what makes you happy, then when this is over, I'll force myself to walk away."

Hearing him say it out loud makes it more real, and suddenly, it terrifies me. Never see Trey again? *Is that really what I want?* I think about it for a moment, only to come to the conclusion that I don't know. What I do know is that being with him is dangerous and it's detrimental to my life. That should be reason enough to never want to see him again.

"But before I do that," Trey says, still avoiding my eyes, "I want you to know that I never pretended to like you. I've always liked you. From the moment I saw you, I was completely and utterly captivated by you. Then, the more time I spent with you, the more I fell in love with you."

I try to convince myself he's feeding me a spoonful of lies, but he sounds so genuine.

"You hooked me in with your kindness and your sense of humor. I fell in love with your laugh and the way you made me feel whole. I fell in love with the way you were fixing me without ever making me feel like I was broken. You made me feel like I had a purpose, and you still do. My purpose is to keep you safe and to make you happy.

"So, once you're safe, I'll do whatever it takes to make you happy. And if that means I never get to see you again, then . . ." He shakes his head at himself, biting his bottom lip. After letting out what sounds like a painful breath, he finally looks up at me, and the light in his eyes completely disappears. "I'll do it, Arella. I'll walk away."

I'm not sure who he's trying to convince that he *can* do such a thing—me or himself?

20

TREY

THERE'S A GAPING HOLE IN MY CHEST WHERE MY HEART USED to be. My lungs feel tight, and I can't really feel my arms anymore. I've always known that emotional hurt can also make a person physically hurt. I found that out when I was seven.

The pain I feel now is different from the pain I felt when I lost my parents. It's not that one pain aches more than the other; it's just a different type of ache. It's been nineteen years since my parents died, and I still feel the gut-wrenching agony in my chest from that. How many years will it take before I stop feeling the agony of losing Arella?

It took me a while to come to the conclusion that walking away is what's best for her. It'll kill me to do it, but I'm going to do it. I love this woman with my entire soul, and if never seeing my face again is what she wants, then okay. I just hope I'll be able to function after walking away, because the mere thought of having to do it makes me want to leap over the edge of this tire.

Eventually, the trees below us aren't as dense and we fly over a house. A light-blue Subaru sits in the gravel driveway, parked behind a rusty white pickup truck.

With a soft thud, I land the tire next to the driver's side of the Subaru. Up the long driveway stands a house with a ton of windows. Inside, it's dark. The five emotions I sense coming from the house are all muted, which means they're sleeping.

Arella wastes no time hopping off my lap as if she can't get away from me fast enough. The last twenty-ish minutes up in the air felt like hours. Neither of us spoke, and she barely even looked at me. I wish I could say it's just her pregnancy hormones making her give me the cold shoulder, but I'm pretty sure Arella would be acting this way, pregnant or not. I know I deserve it, but it still hurts.

"What are we doing here?" she asks in a low voice.

I reply in an equally low voice, "We're getting the *ordinary kind* of transportation."

Her mouth pops open. "You mean we're going to steal a car?"

"What did you think I meant when I said we were gonna get a different mode of transportation?"

"I thought you meant we were going to take a bus or something."

I throw my arms up and spin around. "Do you see any bus stations 'round here?"

She glares daggers at me. Maybe I should tone my attitude down a bit. Yes, I'm emotionally damaged and my ribs are screaming at me with every breath I take, but that doesn't mean I should take it out on her.

"Relax." I almost call her *babe*, then stop myself. "We're just gonna *borrow* a car."

"Like how your uncle *borrowed* me?"

Ouch. She might as well have shanked me with a serrated knife straight through my chest. It probably would have hurt less.

I'm ashamed to call Victor my uncle. Before, I excused his cruelty toward me because I thought he was doing good things for the world. Now that I know he's just a piece-of-shit double agent, I have no excuses for him. I want nothing to do with him, and I'd appreciate it if Arella would stop calling him my uncle. That man is not family to me, and he hasn't been for a long fucking time.

Arella crosses her arms over her front. "We're not stealing a car."

I wave a *don't worry about it* hand through the air. "I'll pay 'em back later."

"How?"

"When this is all over, I'll come back and leave them cash on their front step for whatever this car is worth, plus triple." I pause and wait for her to give in. When she doesn't, I sigh exasperatedly.

We don't have any other options, and she knows it. She's just so mad at me that she's being difficult on purpose. Unfortunately, we're running out of darkness and I can't keep talking nicey-nice to her anymore, so my tone comes out firm. "Look, Arella. The sun's about to come up, so we can't fly on this tire for much longer. We need a car so we can go find a Healer who can fix your arm. The closest Healer isn't for at least another few hours—by car. I'd suggest we walk, but that'll take us days, and I can't wait that long because I'm pretty sure I've got a broken rib, and this shit fucking hurts." I point to my right side, where my throbbing pain is coming from.

Ignoring the misery, I continue my rant. "I'm exhausted from using my powers, both from flying us over a whole-ass forest and from fighting off all those dickheads trying to kill me. Now, can we *please* steal this car so we can get the hell outta here before the family that lives inside that house wakes up and calls the police?"

Arella softens her defensive stance and gapes at me. "You have a broken rib?"

"I think so. Maybe a few."

Her jaw drops. "A few? Trey, why didn't you tell me?"

"It's not important."

"Not important? Not even when I was using you as a chair earlier? You winced every time I moved even a little bit, and you didn't think it was important to tell me you have broken ribs?"

I shrug, and it feels like fire in my ribs to do so. "I'm fine."

"You're *not* fine. We need to get you to a hospital."

It's my turn to gape at her. "Are you serious? We're not going to a fucking hospital. That's like putting a beacon on our heads to tell the Royals exactly where we are. We're gonna go find a Healer who can fix me up faster than any hospital can. Now, as much as I enjoy standing around arguing with you, we've gotta get going." I hook a thumb toward the Subaru. "You gonna let me steal this car or not?"

She ponders it for a moment, then says, "Fine, but we're not stealing *this* car."

"You got somethin' against Subarus?"

"No. I have something against stealing from a family with small children." She points through the back window.

My eyes follow her finger to two car seats strapped into the back. "What's your point?"

"It's expensive to have babies. This family is off-limits."

Our lives are in danger, and of course Arella still cares more about some children she's never met than she does herself. She's been pregnant for, what, a few weeks? And she's already thinking like a mother. I wish I could say I'm bothered by this, but it only adds to the many reasons why I love this woman.

Reluctantly, I grunt and return my ass to the tire. My side burns the entire time I bend and adjust to sit comfortably— well, as comfortably as I can get.

I spread my legs, then gesture for her to join me.

Arella hesitates. "How should I sit so I won't hurt you?"

"The way you were before, facing me. Much better than when you leaned your back against me."

Once she's back on top of me, I offer her my hand to put hers in. She understands why without me having to say it. After she tells me she's ready, I fly us over the treetops again.

Two empty roads over, we approach another house.

I'm about to land when Arella says, "We can't steal from these people either."

"Why not?"

"They only have one car. What if someone needs to go to work in the morning?"

The third house we find has four vehicles parked along the gravel driveway. The one at the end is a rusty tan Nissan Altima. I almost drop my jaw when Arella doesn't pick a fight with me about swiping it.

With her hand in mine, I wiggle my fingers at the locks. They pop up with a click, then we climb in.

The car smells like toe jam and expired yogurt. The backseat is covered in fast-food wrappers that have been collecting there for who knows how long. Dripping down the steering wheel is a questionable crusty white spot. I can't imagine what it looks like under a microscope. I'm so fucking grossed out, I'd rather be back on that tire, but the sun's peeking up. We can't risk being seen anymore.

Behind the wheel, I take Arella's hand again, then point at the empty keyhole. The engine sputters to life, then I ease us away from the house.

"How did you do that?" Arella asks from the passenger seat. She keeps her hand in mine, even though I don't need her immunity anymore. Now that the car is started, I won't need my powers for a while. Still, I won't draw my hand back, nor will I say anything about it. I'll only have Arella for as long as she needs me to keep her safe. I don't know how much longer that'll be, so for now, I'm going to selfishly take as much of her as I can get.

The headlights on this car suck ass. They're so dim, I can barely see what's ahead of me. "How did I do what?"

"Unlock the car and start it without the key?"

"Do you know how locks work?"

She cocks her head to the side. "Sort of."

"You know how keys have those ridges that go up and down? All it does when you stick those ridges into a lock is push the mechanisms up a specific way to unlock it. I simply use my Telekinesis to do the same."

"But how do you know how far to push up those mechanisms?"

"I just feel it, I guess. Like it just clicks in my brain when I've got all the right ones up. Kinda like pushing a button and stopping once you feel resistance."

She nods with her lips pursed. "Interesting."

With one hand on the wheel, I make a right turn. Then I glance at the dashboard and groan. "We're gonna have to stop for gas soon."

"How soon?"

"We've got a quarter tank-ish. There's no way in hell we'll make it to Las Vegas on that."

She twists at the hip to face me. "Why are we going to Vegas?"

"To find a Healer." Has she already forgotten that I told her that's what we're trying to do?

"And the closest one is in Vegas?"

"No, the closest one is in LA, but we can't go to that one. The Royals know I'm injured. I'd be surprised if they weren't waiting for us outside the Healer's shop in LA right now." And outside my house, Arella's apartment, our friends' houses, the Soul House, and any other place we're connected to.

"Wait. If they're expecting you to go to a Healer, then why are we going to one? Shouldn't we do the opposite of what they think we'll do?"

She's right, but I don't know any other options for us. "Can your immunity fix broken bones?"

"No."

"Then we're going to Vegas and hoping for our lives that Victor doesn't already have people waiting for us there too." I don't know what I'll do if Victor ever gets his hands on Arella again. Actually, I do know. It's violent and inhumane. I'll make sure he can never touch another innocent woman ever again, and I won't even feel guilty about it.

"How can a Healer heal me if I'm immune to their powers?"

I slow the car and stop at a stop sign. After checking both ways, I ease back on the gas and keep heading straight. "They can't, but they'll have Healing Goo that'll work on you."

"Okay. What happens after we visit the Healer?"

"We'll go into hiding."

"Where?"

I wait until we pass a dark blue pickup truck driving on the other side of the road before I answer. "Ideally, I'd take you to the safe house my parents left for me, but I can't find it. So, we're going with Plan B."

"Which is?"

I run a hand through my hair until my fingers get caught in some dried blood. "Um, I haven't figured that part out yet."

Her jaw drops. "What?"

"Hey," I say defensively, "my only plan was to get you away from Victor. I haven't been able to strategize beyond that."

"So you expect me to just blindly go along with this nonexistent plan of yours? I thought you had more than this."

"I do. My plan exists. It just exists . . . in the future."

She laughs—a really condescending laugh. "The *future*? That's wonderful. That's just wonderful."

"All right, Miss Sarcastic-and-judgy, I'm open to ideas if you've got 'em. Do you know of a place we can stay where they can't find us? Preferably underground."

"Why underground?"

"Trackers can't sense people while they're underground. I

mean, I could go without using my powers forever, but there are Trackers out there who can sense people without waiting for them to use a gift. They're rare, but they exist. It's better to be safe than sorry. Plus, in general, if we're underground, it'll be harder for them to find us."

Our car reaches another intersection. I turn left, hoping it'll take us toward Nevada. If Arella asks if I know where I'm going, I'll lie because there's no way in hell I'm admitting to her that I'm driving off of *gut feelings*.

I'd use my GPS if I still had a phone. Earlier, after I hoverlogged through the forest with Arella slumped over my shoulder, I climbed onto my motorcycle that was hiding behind some trees, then placed Arella over my lap, straddling my front and rode off. I kept her secure against me with one arm while I controlled my bike with the other. We rode away from Shadow Ridge until my damn motorcycle ran out of gas. That's when I stashed my bike out of sight and continued on foot.

At one point, I stopped to give my arms a break from carrying Arella. When I pulled my phone out of my pocket, it came out in two pieces. I don't know why I was surprised, because if my ribs got smashed, it's likely my phone did too, so I ditched the broken device on the side of the road and kept carrying Arella until I found a place for us to hide.

A smelly barn wouldn't have been my first choice, but at that point, I would have settled for any type of shelter. I was exhausted, everything ached, and I needed to sleep so my body could heal. Unfortunately, the little nap I had did nothing for me. I still feel like I've been hit by a train— multiple times.

Now that I think about it, even if I had my phone, I probably wouldn't turn it on anyway. What if Victor was tracking me on it?

"Is your parents' safe house underground?" Arella asks.

"Yes, but like I said, I don't know where it is. I know the general location, but that's it."

"How do you know the general location?"

"My parents left me a message—sorry, a *riddle*, in my childhood teddy bear telling me about it."

Her eyes go wide as she gasps. "That's the bear that kept asking you for a password!"

"Correct."

She perks up in her seat. "What's the password and riddle? Maybe I can help."

I don't want to, but I have to let go of her hand to be able to dig into my pocket. Otherwise, I'd have to drive with my knees, and my body is way too fucking sore for that.

After shifting Arella's diamond necklace to the side, I find the button-shaped device. I haven't pressed it since I was whacked against the ground, so I hope it still works.

I press the button.

Nothing happens. No robotic voice saying, "Password?" Not even a sign that it's *trying* to work.

I press the device again.

Still nothing.

I flip the device over and find a small crack down the center. *Great.* With a sigh, I toss it into the sea of trash behind me. "Good thing I've got it all memorized. The password to unlock the message was a song my mother wrote for me to encourage me to keep moving forward in life."

"Can you sing it?" Arella asks.

So I do. "When you're lost without me, you'll always have Andy. When you feel you don't belong, hug this bear and sing this song. Look to the sky when you feel down. Know that things will turn around. Work twice as hard to the finish line. Now it's your time to shine."

"That's some password," Arella says.

"Yeah, I know." After a deep breath, I recite the recorded

message from my parents, word for word, and try not to choke up at the end. Speaking the message to someone is like admitting out loud that my parents knew whatever mission they were working on could kill them, and they still chose their job over me. I hate having to verbalize that my parents abandoned me on purpose.

"Are you sure that's it?" Arella asks when I finish. "Did they leave you a map or something? A follow-up message in a second bear?"

"Maybe they did and it got blown up when the house exploded. I dunno. Either way, that's all I've got."

Arella bends forward and opens the glove compartment. She's pretty brave to poke through it with her bare hands. I wouldn't be touching anything inside this biohazard of a car if I didn't have to.

"What're you looking for?"

"Something to write on. Aha!" She holds up a crumpled receipt like she's won a prize. "Now I just need . . . aha!" She holds up a pen with the most adorable *I did it* face. "Sing that song and tell me that message again. I'm gonna write both down."

"Why?"

"Because maybe once it's transcribed, we'll be able to see a secret message."

I raise a skeptical eyebrow. "You think my parents left me a cypher?"

"They could have."

"They died when I was seven. I wasn't smart enough to decode a cypher at that age. My theory is that they gave my Aunt Debbie information that was supposed to help me decode this but that information died with her."

"Come on, Trey," she says, slumping her shoulders. "At least let me *try*."

"Fine." Slowly, I tell her the lyrics to my mother's song. Arella scribbles each word down until it fills the entire backside of the receipt. When she's done, she sits back to admire her work.

"This is wonderful! Now tell me the message."

I say every single word exactly as my parents said it, until Arella's got a backside of another receipt covered in her loopy handwriting.

As we continue down our route, Arella reads the words to herself over and over. I remain quiet while she thinks, admiring her determination to solve this puzzle. If I thought my parents had left me a cypher, I would have done this already. I won't tell Arella she's wasting her time though. The more she's thinking about this, the less she's thinking about how mad she is at me.

I'm going to make this up to her. I don't know when, and I don't know how, but someday, someway, I'm going to make up for my mistakes.

21

TREY

THIS STARVING CAR HAS BEEN BEGGING FOR ME TO FEED IT with gas for the last fifteen minutes. Every minute or so, it yells at me with an annoying *Ding! Ding!* and a flashing gas-tank icon.

If we run out of fuel, I'll have to use my powers to hover this car down the road as if I was driving it, because the goddamn sun is up. I'm not confident I can do that. Arella and I on a rubber tire is one thing, but a whole-ass car? And for how long?

I'm so exhausted, I could close my eyes and fall asleep within seconds. I'm so hungry, my body is withering away. My head's pounding, and I can barely breathe without my ribs throbbing. Using my powers will only weaken me more, and if I get so weak to the point that my powers shit out again, then what? I can't imagine Arella will let me steal another—

I gasp when I see it. It's like a light at the end of the longest and darkest tunnel, right there on the corner of an intersection, next to a Subway. A sandwich sounds amazing right now. I doubt it's open at—I check the clock on the dashboard—seven in the morning.

Arella peers up from the two receipts she's written on. "Oh, goodie! A gas station. It's about time."

She has no idea.

"You gettin' anywhere with that?" I pull the car up to the closest gas pump and shift the gear into park. I sense one person inside the general store. A maroon Hyundai Elantra is parked at the side of the building. It must belong to the employee inside.

Carefully, Arella folds the receipts in half, then half again, and slides them into the side pocket of her leggings. "I think I have to be at your secret rock for any of this to make sense. I have some theories though."

"Like what?"

"What if when your mom asked you to take one hundred steps, she was thinking they were kid-size steps?"

"Tried that. I took kid steps and adult steps." I unbuckle my seat belt and feel something sticky on my fingertips. *This car is so fucking nasty.*

"Could the song be a clue? Like the part that says, *work twice as hard to the finish line.* Maybe that means you need to take two hundred steps, not one hundred."

Now that's an idea! If that works, this woman is a genius. "I've never thought of that. How 'bout we take a trip there after we see the Healer?"

"Sounds good."

"Great. Now could you help me shut this car off?"

She places her palm into mine, takes a deep breath, then nods. "I'm ready."

I point at the ignition, and the engine stops rumbling. Arella's about to open her door when I stop her with a hand over her thigh. "What are you doing?"

She gives me a *what do you think I'm doing?* look. "Going to the bathroom?"

"Can you wait 'til I'm done pumping?"

"Why?"

"Because I need you at an arm's length at all times."

"I'll be fine." She rolls her eyes, and I can't understand why. Does she not realize how much danger we're in? Or how much it'll kill me if something happens to her again? She reaches for the door handle a second time.

I grab her arm. "Arella, please. Don't make this harder for me than it already is. How can I protect you in there if I'm all the way out here?"

"I wouldn't need your protection if you hadn't put my life in danger in the first place."

Ouch. I never meant for her to get hurt. Once I realized she could be, I did what I could, short of kidnapping her myself, to try to get her out of Victor's reach. And that was back when I thought he had good intentions. If I had known he was a double agent, I one hundred percent would have tied her up and flown her to a deserted island—save her first, answer questions later.

"Arella . . ." My voice cracks at the end of her name. "I am so s—"

She throws a hand up to silence me. "Whatever. I don't want to fight about this. Just go pump the gas. I'll hold it in."

I stare at her as I debate whether or not to continue what I was gonna say. What good will an apology do anyway? No words can ever erase what's happened to her.

My chest feels like it's weighed down by a grand piano as I exit the vehicle. I barely read the machine's screen as I press buttons. I can't remove the way she just glared at me out of my head. As I stick the nozzle into the car, I clench my jaw to hold back from breaking down.

While the gas pumps, I glower into the distance with my back facing the car. I can't let her see the bullshit falling from my eyes. I blink it away as I force my body to suck in a deep breath. Slowly, I let it out. Then I suck in another. I should do it again, but it's hurting my ribs, so I quit.

When I'm done with the gas, Arella doesn't speak to me as

we head toward the general store. She barely even looks my way when I hold the door open for her. I know I deserve the silent treatment. That doesn't make it hurt any less.

A bell above the door rings as the door shuts behind me. Bright lights shine above the many aisles of candies, snacks, and trucker hats. No one is at the counter. One person's blah energy wafts toward me from behind a door marked OFFICE. EMPLOYEES ONLY.

I'm like a puppy with separation anxiety as Arella and I head into separate bathrooms. It's the first time she'll be out of my sight since I got her away from Shadow Ridge. I'm hesitant to leave her, but if the Royals suddenly appear here, I'll know it the second I sense more than one person.

After I do my business, I scrub my bloody hands off with soap and water at the sink. In the mirror, a gory version of myself stares back. Dark untrimmed beard. Bruised cheeks. Gashes in my lips. Lines of crusty red drip down my face. I look like a victim in a horror film.

I stick my head under the faucet to wash off my face and hair. It hurts like hell to bend into the sink like this. Still, I do it until the water runs clear. When I glance back up at the mirror, the blood is all gone—mostly.

I hiss through my teeth as I unzip my leather jacket. Spots of black and blue cover my torso. The area where my ribs are on fire has the worst discoloration. With a light finger, I press on it. Big mistake. It stings so much, it sends the pain all the way down to my calves. *We've gotta get to that Healer—stat.*

Carefully, I zip my jacket back up, then exit the bathroom. Since I took so long, I thought Arella would already be out here waiting for me, but she's not. A quick glance around the general store shows no signs of her either.

I knock on the women's bathroom door. "Arella?"

No answer.

I knock again, harder this time. "Arella?"

I curse that I can't sense her. I turn the knob, expecting it to be locked, but it opens. The bathroom is empty. My stomach plummets.

I sprint across the aisles. "Arella!"

She's nowhere in sight. *Did she return to the car?*

I bolt out of the store. At the car, I peer through the windows. She's not here. *Where the fuck is she? Did they find us? But how?* I would have sensed them arrive. Arella would have screamed, and I definitely would have heard that.

A spike of anxiety comes from inside the store. I still only sense one person. Why are they suddenly—it hits me. *She's asking for help.*

I rush back toward the store with so much adrenaline that I almost forget about the agony in my torso. The bell above the door rings as I sprint inside. Exactly like before, no one's at the counter. Not missing a beat, I jump over the counter and burst through the office door.

At least, that's what I was *trying* to do.

Instead, my body slams into the locked door, and it ignites a fire throughout my rib cage. I brace myself against the wall and groan as I press a hand against my side. It takes me a few seconds to recover. Once I do, I wave a hand at the doorknob and stumble in.

A thick man wearing glasses sits in a rolling chair behind a messy desk, with a cell phone pressed to his ear. He takes one glance at me, then his fear whips me in the face.

"Could you explain that again, sir?" a woman says from the phone.

I march up to the pudgy guy with the DENNIS name tag pinned to his polo shirt. I snatch the device from his hands and glare at the screen. The numbers 9-1-1 flash back at me. I press the big red End Call button, then chuck the phone onto his desk. "What did you tell them?"

Dennis puts his hands up in surrender. "I—I told them that some people appeared out of nowhere and kidnapped a young woman out of the store."

"What?"

"I—I saw it happen on the security cameras." He points to a computer monitor showing a bunch of empty aisles.

"What do you mean, some people appeared out of nowhere?"

"Like they j—just appeared. Like out of thin air. Then they disappeared."

I pull at the ends of my hair. *You've gotta be fucking kidding me.* I just went through hell getting her away from them, and they stole her back within mere seconds with a goddamn Teleporter?

How did they even track us here? Arella assured me she was making me immune the whole time and—*Wait* . . . How did the Teleporter pop Arella out of here when she's immune? There's no way. Also, why did this man's anxiety only spike now and not while I was in the bathroom when he would have seen it on the cameras? He's lying, and I bet I know who told him to.

I grit my teeth together as I grab Dennis by his polo and yank him toward me. "Where is she?"

"I—I told you! They took her!"

"No, they didn't." I shake him. "Where. Is. She?"

The man shrinks into himself. "Please! Don't hurt me! She just told me to call the police and to tell you that some guys appeared like magic and took her. I just did what I was told. She looked like she was bleeding. I thought I was helping her!"

"No! *I'm* the one trying to help her! Do you realize what you just did by calling the police? Now *they* know exactly where she is. They're probably on their way right now."

Some rustling comes from the other side of a door marked SUPPLIES. I drop Dennis back into his chair and run to the supply closet as the door swings open.

Arella slams into my chest on her way out. My ribs light on fire again. I take a moment to gasp for air, then I lay it on her.

"What the hell are you doing?" I grab her by her shoulders and shake her. I'm not trying to stay calm anymore. I can't. I've never been so angry with her. "Why did you tell him to call the police?"

She shoves me off her. "Because I want someone I can trust to come get me."

Ouch. She'd rather trust a bunch of strangers in uniforms than me. Add that to the growing list of things she's said that will tear me apart at night. "Arella, the Royals have people planted all over the system. We can't trust anyone! Now come on. We've gotta go before they get here." Seizing her unwounded arm, I tug her toward the exit.

She jerks her arm back and stands her ground. "No. I'm not going anywhere with you."

I press the heels of my palms against my temples. "Please, please, tell me you're joking right now."

"I'm not. Staying around you is dangerous. *You're* the one they're tracking. Not me. Wouldn't it make the most sense for me to get as far away from the thing they're tracking as possible?"

I toss my arms up and let them flop to my thighs. "Fine. Let's say we do that. Where are you gonna go? It's not like you can run back to your apartment, or Javina, or your grandparents. They'll find you there. And once they do, who's going to protect you?"

"They won't find me. I'll hide."

I scoff. "Where?"

"I can't tell you! What if they capture you and torture you for that information?"

I screw my eyes shut and pinch the bridge of my nose. She's being difficult on purpose, and the only thing it's accomplishing is wasting time. "You're not telling me where because you don't know of a place to go."

"Okay, maybe that's true. If it is, it's not much different from your nonexistent plan, except my plan is better because mine doesn't involve sticking around the thing they're tracking!"

I hate that she's mostly right. The only thing she's got wrong is that, while I might be dangerous by association, I'm also the only person in this world who's willing to die to keep her alive. She's safer with me than she is without.

I debate throwing her over my shoulder, chucking her into the car, and driving away. Save her first, answer questions later. She can be mad at me all she wants. At least then she'll be safe. The Royals could be here any—

Pop!

From right outside the gas station, three people's emotions enter my head.

22

―――――――

ARELLA

Trey may be trying to protect me, but I wouldn't need his protection if I hid somewhere by myself, then got help from someone the Royals weren't tracking.

I thought once Trey realized I was missing, he'd drive away to look for me, and then once the police got here, I could be safe with them. Not once did I think the cops were Royals too. Is the entire government system infested with bad guys?

Pop!

Trey's eyes go wide. He grabs my hand and drags me back toward the supply closet I was just hiding in.

"Arella, I swear to fucking god if they get their hands on you again, I will lose any sanity I have left. So please just do what I say, get to the back of this closet, and don't come out for any reason. Got it?" Without waiting for a response, Trey shoves me into the closet and shuts the door.

I'm drowned in darkness. The only light coming in is from the tiny crack under the door.

From the other side, Trey whispers, "Get under that desk and hide, or they'll kill you too."

Earlier, I got a glimpse of the inside of this tiny supply closet. It's full of boxes, mops, and a vacuum. None of it

244

looked organized, and there's no way I can get to the back without making noise. Besides, I can't see anything. So I stay exactly where I am.

It's silent for a few seconds, then that bell above the door rings.

"You check the bathrooms," a woman says off in the distance. "Bruce and I will go this way."

"Yes, ma'am," a man says.

Seconds later, the office door handle clicks.

"Locked," a deep voice says. I picture the voice belonging to a seven-foot man with huge arm muscles and a thick chest.

The woman scoffs. "Seriously, Bruce? You're a Porter. Since when has a locked door ever stopped you?"

"Right." *Pop!*

What comes next sounds like utter chaos: people shouting, things toppling over, and a shriek that would leave a man's mouth only if he was kicked in the balls or stabbed in the chest.

"What the fuck?" Dennis shouts. "Fire just came out of—"

"Get down!" Trey yells.

Someone screams at the top of their lungs. It's not Trey's screams. It didn't sound like deep-voiced Bruce or the woman either, so it must have been Dennis.

"Find the girl!" Bruce says. "I've got him!"

A loud yelp grabs a hold of my heart like someone is reaching into my chest and sinking their sharp nails into it. I'd know that sound anywhere because it's the same sound I heard for days as they tortured him in front of me.

I'm about to leap out of the supply closet to save him when a thought hits me: Whatever I can do out there is the same thing I can do from right here. Closing my eyes, I picture Trey in my head and imagine shoving him into an ocean. Waves of water surround him like a liquid shield. Within seconds, his screaming stops, then a man grunts with pain.

"What the hell?" Bruce shouts.

I keep imagining my waves surrounding Trey as someone kicks against the locked office door. It must be the other guy trying to get in. He kicks again. Then again. And again, until the door crashes against the floor.

"You help Bruce!" the woman says. "I'll find the girl."

Instinctively, I grab the closet's door handle and pull it back. I feel for a lock, but there isn't one. From the other side, the woman attempts to turn the handle. My heart races as I put all my weight into keeping the door shut. The woman tries turning the knob again and yanks. This time, the door opens a crack, and I catch a glimpse of her before I yank on the doorknob and brace my feet against the doorframe to secure my precious barrier.

"Get away from there!" Dennis yells.

Bang! Bang! Bang!

I jolt with each loud gunshot that echoes through the air. Just outside the closet, someone's body thumps against the floor, blocking all light coming through the door's bottom crack.

"Lisa!" a man shouts. "You worthless Ordinary! You fucking killed her!"

"Get away from me!" Dennis shouts.

"Ow! You'll pay for that."

"I said, get away!"

Bang! The door rattles as someone's body thumps against it.

"And I said you'd pay for that," a man says from right outside my door.

Dennis cries out in a half squeal, half yelp. He gurgles, then his screaming stops. His thick body thumping onto the floor makes me gasp.

With a grunt, the man picks up the woman's body and moves her away from the closet. I pull on the door handle with everything I've got, but it's not enough. The man twists the handle, and the door is yanked open.

Trey lets out a gut-wrenching wail. If he's wailing, that means he's alive, but that also means I've lost concentration.

A bald man grabs me by the front of my shirt. "I've got her, Bruce!"

I punch and kick at my captor as I picture waves of water surrounding Trey again. A second later, his wailing stops.

"How are you doing that?" Bruce asks, and it's the first time someone's asked that question and I've been happy about it.

"Hurry up and kill him!" my captor says as he blocks my punches.

"What the fuck do you think I'm trying to do?" Bruce chucks an ice ball at Trey's head.

Trey dodges the spikes, then runs the other way as he tosses a fireball at Bruce. The flames miss, hitting a stack of cardboard boxes instead. The boxes catch on fire with flames crackling toward the ceiling.

A flash of flying dark gray metal catches my eye. I yelp as my captor releases my shirt just as a large filing cabinet hits him. The metal bangs against his head with a bone-crushing *clank!* I'll never be able to unhear.

The man falls to the floor with the heavy metal cabinet landing on top of him. I expect him to get right back up, but he doesn't even stir.

"You bastard!" Bruce shouts as he punches Trey in the face. Trey stumbles backward, clutching his cheek. Bruce, who's almost twice the size of Trey, kicks him in the stomach. Trey falls backward with a grunt, then Bruce climbs on top of him.

"Arella, run!"

Bruce wraps his hands around Trey's neck. Trey claws at the man's hands as I glance around for something I can hit the guy with, something heavy, like a fire extinguisher, or a large—
I gasp. A handgun! It's lying on the floor inches from Dennis's limp body.

I dive toward the weapon as if someone else was going for it too. It's heavier than I thought it would be. I've never held a gun before. *Are they always this heavy?* My hands shake as I hold it up and aim it at the man straddling Trey. *Oh no.* What if I miss? What if I hit Trey? How do I do this? Do I just pull the trigger?

Suddenly, an ear-piercing alarm blares from the ceiling. Seconds later, the sprinklers activate and rain onto everything.

Trey wails as Bruce beats his large fists into Trey's ribs. I keep imagining my ocean waves surrounding Trey as I aim my weapon. I can't get a good shot though. Bruce keeps moving, and my hands keep shaking. I command my feet to get closer, but they don't listen. They're frozen where they are.

"Run!" Trey shouts as he grabs the man's face. A burst of red flames appears in his hands. Bruce screams over the blaring alarm and falls backward, clutching his head.

Now that he's away from Trey, I aim the gun and pull the trigger. *Bang!*

I miss. I pull it again. *Bang!*

And again. *Bang! Bang!*

The man's body jolts twice, then he stops moving altogether.

My ears ring as the gun slips from my shaky grasp. Water drips down my forehead and into my eyes.

Trey's propped up on his elbows, gaping at the dead man, then loses his strength and slumps onto his back.

I rush over to him. "Trey!"

His breaths are sharp as I take his face into my hands. The side of his head is bloody again. So are his nose and his lips and, well, everything.

"Arella . . ." My name comes out in a scratchy broken tone. I barely hear it over the high-pitched beeping of the fire alarm. He points. "My leg."

I slap a hand over my chest and gasp. Something has

sliced through his jeans and cut into his left thigh so deep, I could stick my fingertip into it. His blood has already soaked through his jeans, all the way to his calves.

Trey pushes himself back onto his elbows to get a better look. "It's pretty deep, huh? Those fucking ice balls. I tell ya, they can be sharp as hell."

I take another glance at his thigh, and it makes me queasy. It's one thing to see this stuff on TV; it's another to see it in real life.

After I suck in a deep breath of courage, I get to my feet and dash to the supply closet. It takes me a bit of rummaging to find a first aid kit on the top shelf.

When I return to Trey's side, he's lying on his back with his eyes closed, breathing heavily. I set the first aid kit down next to me, then work on getting his belt unbuckled.

Trey grabs my hands. His voice comes out coarse and weak like it's taking all his strength just to speak. "Arella, listen to me. They could be sending more people. You need to go."

"Okay. Let's stop the bleeding first." I reach for the button on his jeans.

He grabs my hands again. "No, Arella. The wound is too deep. I'm . . ." He lets out a painful exhale. "I'll only slow you down. I'll probably bleed out anyway. Just forget about me and get outta here."

Tears well into the corners of my eyes. I shouldn't have asked Dennis to call the police. All I wanted was for this nightmare to be over. I never meant for anyone to get hurt. Now Dennis is lying lifeless on the floor from whatever Baldy did to him as revenge for the woman who is now bleeding out from the holes Dennis put into her. Baldy is still unmoving under that heavy filing cabinet and barely a step from where I'm kneeling is the large man I shot. All of that didn't happen just for me to leave Trey behind to bleed to death. No way.

"You'll be okay," I choke out. "We just have to stop the

bleeding until we can get you to a Healer." I get the button of his jeans undone, then I slide the zipper down.

Trey grabs my hands a third time. "Arella, this is not the time to be difficult. More of them could be here any second. A fire department is probably on their way too. Go look through that employee's pockets for his car keys. Then—"

"No!" I shout as tears fall from my eyes. "You're going to be okay. Just let me wrap you up."

"We don't have time for that. Just leave me. You were right earlier. *I'm* the one they're tracking, not you. So you need to get into that guy's car and—"

"No!" I shout over the constant beeping. My body trembles with a sob as I grab his hand and pin it against the floor. "I'm *not* leaving you! No matter what you say, I'm not! So you can either keep fighting with me and waste time, or you can just let me stop the bleeding!"

He stares at me with his mouth slightly open and his eyes dazed. Once he realizes this is a fight he won't win, he gives me a curt nod. Then he flops onto his back and sucks in a sharp breath. "Be quick."

I'm still crying as I cut the jeans off his body with scissors from the first aid kit. Once they're off, I toss the denim aside. His entire leg is dripping with blood. Some of the red has soaked his boxers too. Ignoring the queasy feeling in my belly, I pour an entire bottle of hydrogen peroxide over his wound.

"Fuck!" Trey chomps on his bottom lip as he groans through his teeth.

"I'm sorry," I say as I clean off as much red from his leg as I can with antiseptic wipes. Honestly, I don't even know if this is what I should be doing. I'm a professional with Band-Aids over the knee on children, but this?

A few minutes later, I have Trey's thigh wrapped in gauze and medical tape as tight as I can get it. Hopefully, the pressure will keep the bleeding at bay for now. Once I've got him on his feet and leaned against the wall for support, I go dig through Dennis's pockets. In the first pocket I shove my hand into, I find a set of keys.

When I turn back around, Trey has hobbled over to his jeans and is emptying the pockets, shoving all his stuff into his jacket pockets. Then he tosses the bloody jeans aside and throws a fireball at them. "Okay, let's go."

23

ARELLA

WE'RE PARKED AT THE SIDE OF A WALMART. THE SUN BLAZES high in the sky, making Dennis's car hot. We're almost out of gas, so I don't want to waste it on air conditioning. I'd roll the windows down, but I can't risk someone looking in and seeing that I've got a bloody man sleeping in the front seat.

A while later, I'm halfway through eating a banana when Trey finally stirs and blinks his eyes open.

"Morning," I say.

He sits up, adjusting the seat with him as he squints out the bright window. "Where are we?"

"Walmart." I swallow down the rest of my banana, then toss the peel into a plastic bag with my sandwich and granola bar wrappers already in it.

"Where exactly is this Walmart?"

"Barstow, California—according to the signs I passed on the way in." When we left the burning gas station, my only goal was to get as far away from it as possible, so I drove without knowing where I was going. As far as I can tell, I took us in the general direction of Las Vegas . . . *I hope.*

"Barstow," Trey repeats. "I think that's still another two or three hours from Vegas."

I tear a banana off the bunch and hold it out to him. "Want one?"

He accepts the fruit from me, then peels it open and takes a small bite.

"Does your body naturally heal faster than an Ordinary's?" I ask.

"Yep. Zordis heal during sleep, just like Ordinaries, but much faster."

"I see that. The bruises on your face are almost gone. I can tell where they were, but it looks like what my bruises look like after a week. Is your special healing thing powerful enough to fix broken ribs or a deep thigh wound?"

He groans as he takes another bite of the banana. "I fucking wish."

"Are you hungry for anything else?" I reach back to grab the other three grocery bags from the backseat. I dig through one as I say, "I've got a sandwich, granola bars, chips, apples, and water. If there's anything else you'd like, I can run back in to grab it."

"I'll take a water, please."

I pull out a bottle and hand it over.

Trey chugs it all in one breath, then scarfs down the rest of his banana. He tosses the peel into the same bag I tossed mine in.

I pluck an apple from the food bag. "Here."

He shakes his head. "I should take it slow. I haven't eaten much for days."

I drop the apple back into the bag. "Oh, right."

Now that I think about it, that makes sense. Ever since I was kidnapped, he's been in the infirmary for most of that time. Any time he wasn't in there, he was getting used as a test dummy for people's powers.

I dig through the second bag and drag out a pair of black sweatpants. "I figured this would be more comfortable for you than jeans. I also got you a new shirt, socks, boxers, and some clothes for me too. We can change after I redress your wound."

From the third bag, I pull out some first aid supplies. While in the store, I almost bought some ibuprofen until I remembered it wouldn't do anything for him. Do Zordis have special pain medications they can take? If so, where can we get some?

"Thanks, Arella. All of this is great."

"Thank yourself," I say, gesturing toward his wallet sitting in the cup holder. "You paid for it."

"With cash?"

"Of course. I've seen movies."

When I made it to this Walmart, Trey was still out cold, so I dug through his jacket pockets for his wallet. That's when I caught a glimpse of his bare chest and realized the shirt tied around my arm is probably his. Up until that point, I hadn't thought about where this shirt had come from.

Knowing this man literally took the clothing off his back to give to me makes me feel even worse for trying to ditch him. At the time, getting away from him seemed like a good idea. Now, knowing the Royals have people everywhere, I'm positive the safest place I can be is with Trey.

"Fuck." Trey hisses through his teeth as I clean around his wound with baby wipes. His thigh isn't bleeding as much as it was before, but it still looks gnarly.

After I rewrap his wound with clean gauze and fresh medical tape, I use more baby wipes to clean off his bloody face. The whole time, he lies still and stares at me with an admiration in his eyes that gets my stomach to flutter with love-sick butterflies. This time, I don't try to fight the feeling. For me, there's no resisting this guy.

I unzip his jacket to reveal a red and purple discoloration over his right rib cage. I can't imagine how painful it is. The rest of his torso doesn't look any better. He groans while I help him get into his new shirt—a plain black one, of course. After that, I help get the rest of him into fresh clothes.

"Do you want to put your jacket back on?" I ask, holding it up.

He pants heavily as he slumps back into his seat. "Not right now. That requires more moving."

I set his jacket onto the backseat, then get dressed in my own pair of black sweats and shirt.

"Matching outfits," Trey says. "I likey."

"I don't think I've ever worn all black before. I feel like a ninja."

"You sure shoot like one." He places a gentle hand over my knee. "Thank you for saving me."

I can't look at him as I say, "I wish we could have saved Dennis."

Trey keeps his hand over my knee. "That man was so brave. When that lady ran toward the closet, he didn't hesitate to shoot her. He helped save you."

"And I'll never be able to repay him for it."

"I'll never be able to repay *you* for saving me."

I offer him a warm smile. "I suppose we're even now."

He scoffs. "Not even close. You only needed saving *because* of me."

"Technically, I put you in danger too. I was the one who told Dennis to call the police."

His gaze falls to his lap. "I'll admit that even though it makes me sad, I understand why you did that. You also didn't know the Royals have connections with the police."

"And you didn't know your uncle is a psychotic evil maniac with henchmen."

He scoffs again, shaking his head. "Don't remind me."

I place my hand over his on my knee. "Like I said, we're even now."

"It doesn't feel that way, but I'll take it." He turns his hand over to intertwine his fingers with mine. A warm tingle spreads up my arm, all the way to my shoulders.

It's always felt natural for us to hold hands. Like the way it's always felt natural for us to kiss and make love. If Ordinaries aren't meant to be with people like him, then why does being with him feel so right to me?

"Arella?"

It's official: No matter what happens, I'll always love the sound of my name on his lips. I flick my eyes up to meet his. "Yeah?"

He gives my hand a little squeeze. "Thanks again for not leaving me behind."

I roll my eyes at him. "I can't even believe you asked me to do that."

"I didn't ask. I was telling, but I shoulda known you'd be difficult."

Pfft. "If I wasn't difficult, you'd be bleeding out right now."

"Actually, someone would have found me by now. And if it was the Royals, I'd be dead."

I shake my head at him. "I can't believe you were so ready to accept that fate."

"Well, I thought I was gonna die like, fifteen different times recently, so yeah, I was ready."

"I'm glad you're alive. Now let's get you to a Healer."

GIVEN HOW WE LEFT THE GAS STATION IN A CHAOTIC, GORY, fiery mess, Trey and I conclude it's best if we aren't anywhere near Dennis's car. The Royals or the cops are probably looking for it, so we ditch the car at the Walmart and head a few blocks down to a Greyhound station. Over my shoulders is a newly bought backpack filled with food, water, first aid supplies, and Trey's jacket.

The sound of buses releasing air surrounds us as Trey and I step up to the Greyhound station. Correction: I step up. Trey is limping.

I'm glad I cleaned his face, because even without all the blood covering it, people are staring at us. More specifically, the *women* are staring at Trey.

I almost forgot what it's like to be out in public with the YouTube-famous, gorgeous musician Trey Grant. In LA, we couldn't walk into a single restaurant without someone approaching him for a picture. Thankfully, no one stops us as we make our way past all the people waiting on benches for their buses.

"How can I help y'all?" a lady says from behind the ticket counter. The name tag on her shirt reads LATOYA.

Trey flashes her a sweet smile. "Could I get ten tickets, please?"

The lady barely looks up at him from her computer. "Where to, sir?"

"I'll take one-way tickets for the next buses to Los Angeles, San Diego, Las Vegas, New York, and Houston. Two each."

Finally, the lady looks up at him. From behind her glasses, she knits her eyebrows together. "Is you sayin' you want one bus that will take you to all dem places?"

"No. I'd like tickets for five different buses to all of those places. Two each."

The lady skeptically eyes Trey, then me, then him again.

Trey doesn't miss a beat. From his wallet, he holds out two hundred-dollar bills. "Please?"

Latoya doesn't hesitate to seize the cash and stuff it down her bra. Sighing, she turns back to her computer. Then her long sparkly nails clack against the keyboard. "Don't ask questions, Latoya. Don't ask questions. Just mind ya damn business," she mutters to herself.

A few minutes later, Latoya tells us our total. Trey pays all twelve hundred of it in cash, which only makes her shake her head at us more.

As she hands us five sets of tickets, she says, "Whatever y'all is up to, I ain't want nothin' to do with it. If anyone asks, I was just doin' my damn job."

"And if anyone asks," Trey says, "we were never here."

She flashes him a thumbs-up. "Deal. Now get outta here before y'all get my ass fired."

We exit the ticket booth as Trey slips the tickets into his sweatpants pocket. Then he smiles down at me. "You still hungry?"

I hike our backpack higher up my shoulders. "Starving."

"Me too. Our bus won't leave for another twenty minutes. Let's get something to eat."

The building next to the ticket office is a mini food court. Square tables are scattered around the center area and blissful-looking food stands are lined up around the exterior. The options range from burgers to pizza to Chinese and more. At the end sits a little shop filled with candies, bottled drinks, and souvenirs.

It doesn't take us long to decide on something. We're so hungry, everything sounds good. Together, we join the short line for Panda Express. Not long later, we have two Styrofoam containers of Chinese takeout in hand. We pick the closest table and sit on opposite ends to devour our meal.

"Mmm," I moan as I have my first bite. "This is the most amazing Chinese food in the world."

Trey stuffs his face as he nods. "Heaven is what this is."

I'm halfway done with my lo mein when I ask, "Did you buy all those tickets to throw them off our trail, or are we going somewhere other than Vegas?"

"Still Vegas."

"How did you know which cities to buy tickets for?"

Trey scoops up a spoonful of his fried rice. "I picked cities that have Chinatowns, because every Chinatown has a Healer.

Hopefully, if they're tracking us, and I'll bet they are, they'll have a good time trying to figure out which Chinatown we—"

Something behind me catches Trey's attention. His eyes go wide as he drops his plastic fork. Under his breath, he mutters, "Fuck."

I freeze and resist the urge to glance behind me. "Are they here?"

"No," he whispers. "Look."

My chair squeaks against the floor as I spin around. I follow Trey's gaze to a small TV hanging from the wall. I gasp as a female news anchor stares into the camera, saying words I can't hear, while a picture of me is shown beside her head.

The closed captions read, " . . .twenty-two-year-old, Arella 'Ari' Rance, who was reported missing by a friend yesterday. The friend says Rance hasn't answered her phone for a few days, which is unlike the missing woman. When the friend stopped by Rance's apartment, the place had been broken into and Rance was nowhere to be found."

The captions continue as a photo of Trey replaces mine. "Police say their number-one suspect is Rance's most recent ex-boyfriend, Trey Grant. Grant has not been seen or heard from since around the same time Rance went missing. Grant has a violent criminal record, including two counts of disorderly conduct and one misdemeanor."

The news anchor continues as Trey's photo slides off screen. "This morning, we had the opportunity to interview one of Grant's ex-girlfriends. This is what she had to say."

My already racing heart thumps faster as the screen changes to video footage of a blonde woman being interviewed outside a red house. I recognize her right away.

Someone holds a microphone up to Jess's moving lips as the captions read, "Trey and I have been on and off for the past few years. Whenever he gets too angry, he pops me in the face, and I leave. Weeks later, he'll beg for me to come back with promises that he'll change. But you know men like him; they never do."

The screen returns to the news anchor with another picture of Trey. "We've asked close friends of Grant for comments. None have agreed. If you have any information that can help the police locate twenty-two-year-old Ari Rance, please call this tip line."

I turn back to Trey, who drops his head into his hands. I reach over the table to rub his shoulder. "It's okay. When this is all over, I'll clear your name."

"I hate her," he says under his breath. "I fucking hate her. I've never laid a goddamn hand on her like that, and she's gonna go tell a news station that I abused her for years? Is she fucking serious?"

I draw my hand back and rest it over the table. "Are you really more mad about that than the world thinking you've kidnapped me?"

"Kind of." He huffs out a frustrated breath. "I have it in me to kidnap you, but I would *never* abuse a woman like that."

"Okay, *I* understand what you mean when you say you've got it in you to kidnap me. I know you'd do it if it meant protecting me, but please, if anyone else asks, especially the police, don't say that out loud."

Trey offers me a tender smile as he puts his hand over mine on the table and squeezes it. "Thank you for understanding me. That is *exactly* what I mean. Now let's finish eating. Once we're done, we're going shopping."

24

ARELLA

"You look good in a hat," I say as we claim the farthest seat in the back of the bus. We're some of the first people to board. I slide in next to the window, then set our backpack at my feet.

Trey settles down next to me. "You do too."

I wince when he accidentally rubs against the shirt tied around my arm.

"Oops. I'm sorry, babe—I mean, Arella."

I almost forgot I had told him to stop calling me *babe*. I'm fine with him calling me that. I only told him not to because I was angry.

I press against my arm to ease the ache. "It's okay. It doesn't hurt much unless it's bumped. I'm more worried about your ribs and thigh than my arm."

"Funny. I'm more worried about your arm." Trey stands and gestures for me to stand as well. "Let's switch spots so I don't bump your arm anymore."

After we switch, Trey glowers out the window from behind a pair of black sunglasses—another purchase from the souvenir shop. I've got a matching pair covering my eyes. I think he's trying to see if anyone out there is a Royal. Can he know that someone's a Royal just by looking at them?

Katie said Zordis feel a special tingle in their chests whenever they get close to each other. Does Trey's tingle work from a farther distance?

Katie also explained that every Zordi has three powers. Trey's elemental power is Fire, and his body power is telekinesis. I don't know what his mind power is, nor will I ask right now because I don't want him to lose concentration on whatever he's doing. Whatever his mind power is, it was able to tell him that a teenage boy was getting roughed up in an alleyway, and it's able to tell him if someone's a Royal just by looking at them.

The bus is about half full when the bus driver finally shuts the door, and we roll away from the Greyhound station. Only then does the tension in Trey's shoulders relax.

Since the closest people to us are three seats away with headphones on, I turn to Trey and ask in a low voice, "Are there a lot of your kind in the world?"

"Lots. Most live in Europe and Asia."

"And is everyone either a ZIRDA agent or a Royal?"

"No. Most are just regular people. Think of ZIRDA like a secret organization that does research, develops products, and also works to stop the Royals. Then think of the Royals as violent gang members."

I tilt my head to the side. "Why is it up to a research facility to stop violent criminals? Didn't you say you guys have a special government?"

"The zovernment is useless when it comes to getting rid of the Royals. A part of me thinks the Royals pay them off. It wasn't until after the Royals caused the Black Plague that ZIRDA started their anti-Royals department, and only because at the time, the zovernment was too busy still trying to clean up the mess from the mass genocide and worldwide scrub job. Considering that was over six hundred years ago and the Royals are still around, I think it'll take more than the zovernment and ZIRDA to get rid of them."

I take a moment to process all that before asking, "Why don't the zovernment and ZIRDA work together to fight off the Royals?"

"Because that's not how things work. That's like saying, why don't the cops team up with regular civilians to stop crime? To the zovernment, ZIRDA is just a bunch of researchers who *think* they're vigilantes. To ZIRDA, the zovernment is nothing more than some elites in uniforms who only care about keeping Ordinaries from finding out about us."

"Interesting." There is still so much I want to learn about Trey's world, but my eyelids are getting heavy. I fall asleep within minutes.

When I wake up to our bus pulling into the Greyhound station in Vegas, Trey is wide awake.

"Why didn't you take a nap?" I ask as I lift my head off his shoulder.

"How can I protect you if I'm sleeping?"

My heart does a little backflip in my chest. It's endearing how much he cares about me and isn't afraid to show it.

"Besides," Trey says, "I was enjoying watching you sleep. Whenever you stayed over and it wasn't my night to sleep, I used to spend those hours just holding you and trying to sync my breaths with yours."

With anyone else, that statement would be creepy. With Trey, it's wholesome. He told me once that he used to hate cuddling until he cuddled with me. I'm happy to know he likes cuddling with me enough to do it for hours upon hours without getting bored.

I tilt my head back so he can see my smirk. "When this is over, I'll be sure to tell the media that watching women sleep is one of your favorite hobbies."

Trey lets out a light laugh. "They'll love that."

We're the last to leave the bus. When our feet are back on the ground, Trey spends a moment scanning the crowd.

"I think we're good." He takes my hand, then leads me toward a row of taxis waiting for passengers.

We pick a taxi toward the front of the line and climb into the backseat.

"Gold Coast Hotel and Casino, please," Trey says.

Fifteen minutes later, the driver drops us off outside a large white building with wide arches in the front. Some gold letters at the top of the building read CASINO.

I wait until the taxi is gone before saying, "I thought we were going to Chinatown."

"We are."

I glance around us because I must be missing something, but even after a second look, I confirm that there's nothing here that remotely resembles a Chinatown. No Chinese characters on buildings. No pagodas. No dragons with open mouths scaring off the evil.

"In case anyone asked him, I didn't want the driver dropping us off *inside* Chinatown," Trey says as he begins half walking, half limping down the sidewalk. "We're only a few blocks away."

"How many is a few?" One block already sounds like too much. This backpack is heavy, my body is sore, and these flats I'm wearing are almost paper thin. I might as well be barefoot.

"Would you like me to carry you?"

"Are you serious? You have broken ribs, and you can barely walk on your own."

He shrugs nonchalantly. "I carried you with my broken ribs before. And I did it for miles."

"What? When?"

"How do you think I got us to that barn after my motorcycle ran out of gas?"

My mouth drops. "You had me on a motorcycle while I was passed out?"

"Yep."

"Where is it now?"

He shrugs again. "On the side of a road somewhere."

"But you love that thing."

"Not as much as I love you."

My heart skips a beat as I gaze up at him. His eyes meet mine with a look that says, *I mean those words with every fiber of my soul.*

Earlier, when we were on the flying tire and he confessed his love to me, I didn't know how to feel. At the time, I was trying to process the idea that we didn't meet by accident and that he spent weeks fake-dating me solely to gather information for his uncle. Hearing him say the L-word again now, I *still* don't know how to feel.

I keep putting one foot in front of the other. "Didn't you say that besides your memory box, your motorcycle is your most sentimental possession?"

Trey told me once that I'm the first woman he's ever taken on a motorcycle ride. He said his motorcycle is special to him because it's what he rode while he traveled the states, searching for his *place in the world*. He said he had never wanted to share that experience with anyone else until he met me.

"You remember me saying that?" Trey says.

"Of course. You don't open up a lot. Whenever you do, I take notes."

He keeps his attention on the sidewalk. "I've opened up more with you than I have with anyone else."

"That's not true. Don't you tell Liz everything?"

"Nah. She has to force it out of me. And trust me, I make her work for it."

Liz has told me on more than one occasion that Trey is like a puzzle box: *"No matter how hard you twist and turn him, he won't open. However, if you're patient and keep working on him, you'll be rewarded with bits and pieces, but it's still never the full picture."*

At the time, I wasn't sure if I agreed with Liz's description of Trey. I thought after he had shared with me that his parents hadn't actually died in a house fire that I had unlocked everything I needed to know. Turns out, Liz was right.

I play with the straps of our backpack as I ask, "Have you ever told Liz that you love her?"

Trey's answer comes easily. "No. Not soberly, anyway. She claims I said it once when I was wasted, but I don't remember it, which means it doesn't count."

"It probably counts for her. I actually think it counts more because it was unfiltered."

"I don't love Liz the way I love you, if that's what you're wondering."

"I'm not. I've seen how you two are together. The kind of relationship you guys have is pretty exceptional, but not romantic."

He lets out a little scoff. "You should say that to the media. Maybe they'll stop making up stories about me leading her on."

"Okay, to review, the list goes: Trey Grant did not kidnap me, he does not abuse women, he likes to watch women sleep, and he does not want to bang Liz Hart."

A bright smile lights up his face, and it's the brightest one I've seen on him in what feels like weeks. "Yes. In that order."

I miss these moments between us when we're just talking, all light and playful. I miss the way things were when simply being with him was enough. I miss feeling like as long as I had Trey by my side, everything else would fall into place. Can we ever be like that again?

I don't know how that can happen, considering that law forbidding Zordis from being with Ordinaries. If the zovernment is afraid that I'll find out about their world, that ship has sailed. Maybe now I can be an exception. Is that a thing? Can they make exceptions?

I can't be the first Ordinary who has found out about Zordis. Trey mentioned that they erase the memories of those people, but since they can't do that with me, what would happen instead? I'm not sure if I want to find out.

I know we've made it to Chinatown when some reddish-orange pagoda roofs with curved edges appear in the distance. The signs say things like THAI FOOD, PHO, and SUSHI. Still no dragon statues warding off bad people, but there is a golden statue of an Asian man riding a horse.

Trey leads me past a bunch of shops. Most of them look slow and empty. The parking lot is pretty vacant too.

We're walking past more shops when Trey stops and his body goes rigid. I follow his gaze to a storefront window, where a bunch of miniature golden cat statues are waving at us with one arm. Trey stares at them like they're about to spring alive and attack him.

Suddenly, he grabs my hand. Then he flips around and scans the parking lot.

I give him a moment before asking, "Is everything okay?"

"Uh, yeah." With a tug on my arm, we continue walking. Not even for a second does Trey release his firm grip on me. I don't mind. It's giving me a sense of comfort and safety.

His mind power must be some type of danger alarm. That's how he knew that teenage boy was getting hurt. That's how he can know if a Royal is close. If his danger alarm went off just now, why aren't we trying to hide?

My feet are achy by the time we stop outside a store with a turned-off neon sign that says GINSENG. The inside is dark and messy. Cardboard boxes are scattered all over the floor.

A handwritten note on a blank sheet of paper is taped to the inside of the door.

Closed for remodeling. Reopen Oct 1.

"You've gotta be fucking kidding me," Trey grumbles.

"Is there another Healer nearby?"

Trey responds to my question by banging on the glass door. "Hello?"

I seize his arm. "Stop! Didn't you read the sign? They're closed."

He ignores me and slams his other palm against the glass. "We need help! Please!"

"Trey!" I try shoving him from the store, but it's like trying to move a house. He barely budges. "Stop it. No one's here."

"Yes, there is. Two people are inside this shop, and they heard me. They're just refusing to come out."

"How do you know? Can you see through walls?"

He knocks again. "Please! It's urgent!" He bangs some more until his fist stops in midair. "Thank fuck. Someone's coming."

A short Asian man in his early sixties glares at Trey and me as he unlocks the door. He opens it a crack just so he can yell at us in his thick Chinese accent. "Can you read duh sign? Open October one! Right now, not October one!"

"We need your help," Trey says.

"Come back October one." The man is about to shut the door when Trey sticks his arm through the opening.

"Please, I'm begging you. She's hurt. All she needs is a little Healing Goo."

I'm not the one who needs the most healing; Trey is.

The gray-haired man wiggles a finger in the air. "You know duh law. No healing foh her."

"She already knows about us."

The Asian man scolds Trey like a father would a son for swearing when he shouldn't have. "You should be in z-prison then. Now go away before I report you to duh Enforcers."

"Please! She's sliced badly." Trey points at the bloodstained T-shirt wrapped around my arm.

The Asian man is still unfazed. "Maybe next time you don't play with sharp tings."

"She was kidnapped by the Royals. They're the ones who hurt her. Please? I'll pay whatever you want."

"Royals?" The Asian man's eyes go wide as he shoves, or attempts to shove, Trey from the door. "No, no, no! Go away! Do not bring dem here. I don't want trouble."

Trey opens his mouth, probably about to beg again, when a woman yelling from inside the store stops him. She's yelling in Chinese, and she doesn't sound happy. The Asian man responds in the same language in an equally yelly tone. The woman shouts back, then appears from around a shadowy corner. She looks a few years younger than the man— probably his wife.

With a hand to her chest, she gasps. Slowly, she approaches the door. The whole time, she stares at Trey with her mouth wide open. It's not the same astonishment he usually gets from the young women who recognize him off social media. This lady's shock feels different. Maybe she recognizes him from the news. If that's the case, why is she not running to call the police? Instead, she's . . . tearing up? *Huh?*

"Are you . . ." She takes a step closer. "Are you Trey Grant?"

Trey grips my arm. He looks like he's about to run away and drag me with. "Who wants to know?"

"Wow. You are not a kid anymore, but it's definitely you. You look so much like your father." The lady turns to her husband, scolding him. "Trey Grant shows up at our door, and you want to kick him away? How ungrateful!"

The Asian man throws his arms up. "How was I supposed to know who he is? He is not wearing a name tag."

"Please excuse my husband's cluelessness." With a beaming smile, the lady shoves her husband aside and waves for us to enter their shop. "Come in, come in. Let me get a better look at you."

I glance at Trey, who looks back at me with a weary look. Still, he grips my hand tightly, and we enter the store.

While the Asian man locks the door behind us, the lady gapes up at Trey. He's almost two heads taller than her.

"Wow. You're so big, and tall, and very handsome. Look at your arms." She takes the liberty of squeezing his muscular bicep. "I can't believe it's really you. And who's your friend? She's so beautiful. Very long hair and—" The lady with no boundaries is about to touch my waves when Trey extends a protective arm in front of me and pulls me behind him.

"Don't touch her. Tell me who you are. How do you know me?"

The lady is unbothered by Trey's *ready to attack* stance. She slaps a hand against her forehead. "Oh, right! I apologize. I'm being rude. Of course you don't remember. My name is Li-Fong. Most people call me Li. You used to call me Auntie Li-Li. This is my husband, Tao. Your parents were our best friends. Come, come. I'll show you."

Trey gives me a look like, *should we follow this lady?* I respond with a shrug. Curiosity must take him over, because he grabs my hand again. Then we follow the eager woman through her dimly lit store that smells of herbs, spices, and dry earth.

"Watch your step," Li says. "We're remodeling. There's stuff everywhere."

She's not exaggerating. The shelves are covered with giant glass jars filled with dehydrated things. I can't even begin to guess what they are. Boxes are stacked on top of each other so high, I'd need a ladder to reach the top. I can barely see any of the wood flooring through this chaos.

Li takes us down a long flight of stairs, flipping lights on along the way. The steps creak under our feet. When we reach the bottom, she flips more lights on. The basement is one big room that's dim, cool, and has equally as much stuff everywhere.

One half of the basement is a little kitchen featuring cluttered countertops and a dining table for two. Opposite of that is a small living room with a loveseat and some end tables covered with old books.

The other side of the basement looks like a giant office, with an array of desks, chairs, and storage shelves along the walls. Every surface is littered with big books, glass jars, and tattered boxes.

On a desk in the corner is a bunch of papers with Chinese characters written on them. From the bottom drawer, Li drags out a photo album and flips some pages until she finds what she's looking for. She removes one of the 4x6 prints from the book and hands it to Trey. He accepts it with the hand that's not holding mine.

"This picture was taken when you were only a year old," Li says.

Trey gapes at the photo with his mouth slightly open. I steal a glance too. The picture features five people standing outside this shop with a banner above them that says GRAND OPENING!

Younger versions of Li and Tao are standing next to Trey's mom, who's holding baby Trey over her hip. On the other side of Trey's mom is a younger version of Victor. In the picture, he's smiling so brightly, I barely recognize him. I've only ever seen Victor scowling. It's weird to see him look so happy.

"Your parents came to visit on opening week to help us kick off this shop," Li says. "For many years, they visited almost every month. They always brought you to play with our kids, who are slightly older than you. I doubt you remember them either."

"I don't," Trey says with his attention still glued to the photo.

"My husband is the original Healer who provided the teardrops for your parents to research and develop the formula for healing products. Our cut of the royalties allows us to live a pretty good life."

"Uh . . ." Trey points to the picture. "This is definitely me, and that's definitely my mom, but that's not my dad. That's my uncle, Victor. My dad and Victor were born only fourteen months apart, and they looked a lot alike, so a lot of people got them confused."

Li stares at Trey for a lingering second before she turns to Tao, who's leaned against a table behind us. She says something to him in Chinese. Tao responds in Chinese with a half shrug. Li says something while gesturing at Trey, and Tao responds in more Chinese. They do this back and forth for a moment before Li's attention returns to Trey.

"All right," Li says. "We decided you should know the truth."

Trey's shoulders go taut. "What truth?"

"Victor is not your uncle. He's your father."

25

TREY

I'm not breathing. I—I don't think I know how to anymore.

"Maybe you should sit down." Li snaps her fingers. "Tao, hurry. Bring him a chair. One for the girl too."

The world seems to blur as Tao appears behind me with two clanky folding chairs. I don't register anything he says as he puts a hand on my shoulder, gently shoving me into a chair. My ribs ache as I sit.

Tao says more stuff to me. I know because his mouth is moving, but his words aren't making it to my brain.

The knot in my chest tightens as my fingers tremble. My breaths are short. My mouth feels dry. I feel like I'm going to fall over. *Breathe*, I command myself. I shut my eyes and try to take in a breath, but my lungs don't obey. If I can't get myself under control, this entire place will go up in flames.

A warm pair of hands cups my face, jump-starting my lungs. Finally, I can breathe again. I know whose hands these are because they're the same hands that have always centered me before.

I open my eyes to find Arella's brown ones staring back at me. She's kneeling in front of me with concern etched into her furrowed brows. Behind her, Li and Tao are whispering to each other in Chinese.

"I'm sorry," I choke out, staring at my shoes. I can't look anyone in the eyes.

Arella doesn't take her hands off me. "You're okay, honey. Just breathe."

I suck in a deep breath through my nose, then let it out through my mouth. She just called me *honey*. She hasn't called me that in too long. Hearing it offers me a tiny sense of peace.

"Tao asked you if you'd like some water," Arella says.

I keep my focus on her, hoping she'll continue to calm me. "Water sounds great."

Tao's legs leave my sight. On the other side of the basement, a fridge door opens, then closes. Then Tao returns with two bottles of water. He hands one to Arella, then one to me. I place mine in my lap while I continue trying to pull myself together.

Li grabs another folding chair from the other side of the room and sets it in front of me to sit on. Tao does the same, then Arella climbs into her own chair until the four of us make a square. As if reading my mind, Arella scoots closer to me, placing her hand over my thigh. It's exactly what I need.

Li folds her hands together in her lap. "I can tell you as much or as little as you'd like, Trey. Just tell me when you're ready."

"I'm ready," I lie.

"How much do you want to know?"

"Everything," I say breathlessly. "I want to know everything."

"All right. Um, how about I start from the beginning? Your mom, Suzie, and I met during our first year at California State University in Fresno. We became instant best friends and did everything together. That's the year she met Andy too. They began dating right away. He proposed the next year and they got married the next."

Li leaves our talking square and returns with the photo album she had earlier. She pulls out a 4x6 print and hands it to me. In the photo, my mom is wearing a lacey white dress. Two ladies stand on each side of her. One is Aunt Debbie. The other is a younger version of Li. They're wearing matching burgundy dresses and holding bouquets of flowers.

"I was a bridesmaid. Suzie's sister was the maid of honor. Small wedding. Close friends and family only. Victor flew in from New York just to attend. Over the years that Suzie and Andy were together, she and Victor didn't have many interactions. Victor was super focused on finishing his engineering degree, and he spent a lot of time with his fiancée, Jodi, in New York. After he finished his degree, Victor and Jodi moved to Three Rivers, where Victor started working at ZIRDA. Shortly after, they were married as well.

"Suzie and Andy had already been ZIRDA agents for about a year. They were researching how to transfer the healing ability from a Healer's tears into a usable product. It was Andy who theorized that it *could* happen and the both of them who put in the years of research to *make* it happen.

"In the end, it was Suzie who made the groundbreaking discovery of which chemical component of a Healer's teardrop gave it its healing abilities. She named it *Chemical T*, after Tao."

I've never heard the history behind Chemical T's name before. As a kid, I thought my mother named it after me. Now I'm realizing it couldn't have been named after me. She discovered the chemical before I was born.

Li continues, "Once Suzie and Andy knew which chemical component had the healing ability, they needed a way to extract it from the teardrops. That's where Victor comes in. He was the engineer who designed the machine that could remove Chemical T. Smart man, that one. He designed, built, and modified hundreds of machines before it worked.

"Anyway, through long nights working in the lab together,

Suzie and Victor fell in love. You should have seen them, Trey. Your parents were made for each other. From the way they looked at each other to the way they could communicate without saying a single word. There's no doubt in my heart they were soul mates."

I know the feeling. That's exactly how I feel about Arella. There's not a single doubt in my heart that she's meant for me.

Li continues again, "The night Suzie found out she was pregnant was the night I found out about the affair. Tao and I had already moved here to Vegas, so Suzie and I didn't get to see each other much. We were still best friends though. We spoke on the phone every day. I thought we didn't keep secrets from each other until she called to tell me she was pregnant with her husband's brother's baby.

"That weekend, she and Victor drove out here so we could talk. That's when Tao and I got the whole story. They told us that the affair had been going on for a while and that no matter how many times they tried to end it, it felt like torture to be away from each other. They cried over how much they already loved their unborn baby. Getting pregnant only reinforced their love for each other and confirmed how badly they wanted to be together. I told them they should be together, until they explained why they wouldn't divorce their partners. It was a wholesome reason, really. Very selfless. Those two always had the good of Zordi people in mind."

"What was the reason?" I ask, desperate to know. "Why couldn't they be together?"

"At the time, Andy was in the midst of creating a liquid solution that could preserve Chemical T. You see, the chemical doesn't survive outside of a Healer's body for more than five minutes. That's why it took so long for Suzie and Andy to discover the chemical in the first place. Can you imagine putting something under the microscope to study for over a year, not realizing that the chemical component you're looking for had died off within five minutes of it leaving its source? The time they wasted . . ." Li shakes her head with a sigh.

"Because Andy was in the middle of creating the preservation solution and was near completion, your parents decided they couldn't tell him they were in love. They were concerned that if Suzie left Andy, he would quit working on the project and they would never see it finished, so your parents made the tough and heartbreaking decision to raise you as if Andy was your father.

"In the end, it took Andy another year to finish the preservation solution. Then it took them all another three years of research to create healing products in the forms of a beverage, an ointment, and a mist.

"For all those years, Tao and I watched how much it killed Victor to have to say he was your uncle. The only times he ever got to freely be your dad was when they came here to visit us. Here, Victor didn't have to hide how much his spirit brightened every time you sat in his lap. He could barely take his eyes off you as you ran around and played with our kids. The way he looked at you was the same way he looked at your mother—with pure love and happiness."

I think I'm in shock. I can't move. I can't do anything but blink. Everyone's staring at me, waiting for me to react. I don't know how to, mostly because I don't believe it.

Does this lady really expect me to believe that the cruel and abusive man I grew up with is my father? The man who allowed adults to beat on me until I bled—when I was a kid? The man who refuses to call me by name and opts for demeaning terms? The man who used me in his Royal-based schemes, who just days ago almost murdered me? That man? My *father*? No way in hell.

"How did my mother know for sure that Victor was my father?" I ask. "If she was having sex with both of them, it could have been either of them."

"I asked the same thing," Li says. "Turns out, when Suzie

found out she was pregnant, she and Andy hadn't been intimate for months. Once the decision was made to raise you as Andy's son, Suzie went home and seduced him that night. Two weeks later, she made a show of being shocked by a positive test. When you were born, she told everyone you were early. Since Andy and Victor look so much alike, no one questioned it when you grew up looking like Victor, because you looked like Andy too. Tao and I were the only ones who knew the truth."

"No!" I burst out of my chair. It falls behind me with a *clank!* The unopened bottle of water in my lap tumbles to the floor and rolls away. My ribs burn from the sudden movement. "You're lying! Victor can't be my father."

Tao, who has barely spoken a word this whole time, calmly says, "Ask yourself, Trey, what reason do we have to lie?"

I think about that for a moment, then sigh. He's right. They have nothing to gain from lying to me.

"Here," Li says as she hands me the entire photo album. She points to one of the pictures on the page. It features a toddler me sitting in Victor's lap. He's hugging me tight as he kisses my cheek with a light in his face I've never seen in him before.

I flip the page to find more pictures of me with my mom and Victor. Most of the photos look like they were taken somewhere in this shop. Some are of me learning to walk while Victor holds my hands. There are a few photos where he's got me sitting on his shoulders with my little fingers gripping his dark hair.

In one picture, my mom stands with me on her hip, feeding me a blue popsicle. The colorful evidence is all over my face. In the background, Victor stares lovingly at my mother the same way I always stare at Arella.

I flip the page again, and my heart drops. These images were shot so early that my mom is still pregnant. Victor has his hand splayed across her rounded belly as he kisses her temple.

In another photo, they kiss each other's lips as he hugs her from behind and cradles her belly like it's his entire world.

The more pages I flip, the more I get a glimpse into a past that seems impossible. My mom and Victor look genuinely and hopelessly in love with each other.

"We assumed you already knew," Li says. "After Suzie and Andy were killed, didn't you go live with Victor? Why didn't he tell you the truth? By that time, Jodi was long gone, and without Andy around, he had no reason to keep it a secret anymore. We figured he would have told you right away."

"I thought you guys were *best friends*?" I sneer. "Wouldn't he have told you if he had told me?"

"Actually, as soon as Jodi left him, Victor broke things off with your mother. She was devastated. None of us could understand it. One day, he was completely in love with her. The next, he didn't want anything to do with her. It was like if he couldn't have Jodi *and* Suzie, he didn't want either of them at all. Around that time, he also stopped speaking to us. No matter how many times we've reached out over the years, we never heard back. Years of friendship right down the drain."

Now *that's* the coldhearted Victor I know. Selfishly, it makes me feel slightly better that I wasn't the only one he pushed away. But why my mother? If he was as in love with her as these pictures depict, what changed?

The room goes silent as I gather my thoughts. I feel sick, and disoriented, and confused, and *fuck* . . . my ribs are killing me.

As if reading my mind, Tao stands and points toward a padded medical chair in the corner. "You came here for some healing, right? Let's do duh lady first."

"Actually," I say, snapping out of my bewildered state, "you won't be able to heal her. She's immune to Zordi powers. You can use healing products on her though."

Tao glances at Li with a look that says, *What's duh boy talking about?*

Li responds with a *hell if I know* shrug.

I don't blame them. It's as strange for me to say that someone's immune to Zordi powers as it is for them to hear it.

"What do you mean, she is *immune?*" Tao asks.

"See for yourself."

Tao gestures toward my T-shirt wrapped around Arella's arm. "Can I heal foh you?"

Arella nods. Tao kneels by her chair, then carefully peels the bloody fabric off her skin. She winces a little.

"Just sit still." Tao closes his eyes, then hovers his hand over Arella's knife wound. A moment later, when nothing happens, his mouth pops open. "How?"

I'll never get tired of seeing the shock on people's faces when Arella amazes them with her—what can only be described as—magic. "Told ya."

"Let me try," Li says, perking up. "Tell me a lie."

"Um, I hate bacon," Arella says, and it makes me smile. This woman loves bacon. Whenever she eats it, she moans like I'm eating her out.

"Hmm," Li says. "My inner alarm didn't go off. I can't see through your body either." Li aims her gaze at me. "I can see through Trey's body though." She turns back to Arella. "Tell me another lie."

Arella thinks for a moment. Then her eyes flick up to me. "I'm not in love with Trey."

It takes my shattered heart a second to realize she means the opposite. I haven't forgotten that each time I've confessed my love to her, she's never said it back. I didn't tell her I love her with hopes that she'd return the words, but I'd be lying if I said I wasn't *hoping* she'd say it back. In a way, she just admitted that she loves me. It's not the same as actually hearing her say *I love you*, but it's close enough.

"Hmm," Li says. "Try another one. Something obvious, like one plus one is five."

"Um," Arella says, "the grass outside is blue."

Li gasps with a hand to her chest. "Wow. She really is immune."

While Li grabs the healing products for Arella, Tao asks me to climb into the medical chair. I don't hesitate to obey. With a few cranks of a lever, the back of the chair reclines, and suddenly, I'm staring into a blinding chicken lamp clamped above me.

"The ceiling lights down here are kinda dim, huh?" I say.

Tao scoffs as he examines my face. "Landlord said to install good lights down here, it be over three thousand dollah and I am responsible for pay. I said no thank you, went to duh store, and got three lamps for less den thirty bucks. Do same job, but cheaper."

"Didn't Li say you guys get royalties from healing products?"

"Yes. One percent."

I do the quick math in my head. "That's still six figures a year."

Tao wiggles a finger at me. *Tsk. Tsk.* "Having money does not mean you should spend it on three-thousand-dollah lights when thirty-dollah ones do duh same job."

I feel that. I collect fifteen percent on my parents' inventions and still buy plain shirts online that come in a three pack for twenty bucks.

Tao lifts my shirt up, then gasps. "Aiyah! What duh hell happened?"

"Royals," I say, and it's all the explanation he needs.

Closing his eyes, Tao hovers his open palms above my torso. "Three broken ribs and a lot of bruising. How long ago did dis happen?"

"Twelve hours, maybe?"

He slaps the side of my head. "Why you not come sooner?"

"Ow!" I rub the spot he hit. "We got here as fast as we could."

"Not fast enough. Now be quiet so I can work."

Tao's warm palms press against my aching ribs. The light pressure he applies makes me wince until, gradually, the pain fades away. Several seconds later, the pain is completely gone.

Next, Tao places his hands on either side of my face. Soon after, my cheek isn't throbbing anymore and my headache has vanished. The soreness at the back of my head disappears too.

When he drags my sweatpants down and tears the gauze off my thigh, he makes some more *tsk-tsk* sounds. He places his hands over my thigh, and I hiss when he applies some pressure. This time, it takes at least a minute before the pain disappears. Once it does, I take a look at my thigh. Minus the remaining blood on my skin, it looks normal again. Not even a scar to show for it.

Tao leaves me for a second, then comes back with clean hands and a wet towel. After he wipes off the blood from my leg, he does one more pass on my body. Everywhere he hovers his hands, the aches diminish until they're gone.

"Done."

I sit up and press a finger against my ribs. No tenderness. No agony. I don't even flinch. Why didn't we start with this instead of Li's crazy story?

Arella is in the middle of getting her arm wrapped with gauze when I kneel at her side.

"Wow." Her eyes go wide. "You look brand new."

"I feel it too."

Tao taps my shoulder and hands me a bottle of Healing Water. "Foh her face bruises."

"I'm almost done," Li says as she finishes taping the gauze around Arella's arm. "Although, I'm confused as to how the Healing Goo will work if she's immune to our powers."

I unscrew the cap off the lemon-lime Healing Water and hand it to Arella. She accepts it with her free hand and chugs.

"For some reason," I say, "Arella's not immune to healing products. I've used them on her before, and she takes to it. I think it has to do with the power coming at her from *outside* her body. She can get burned by a fireball, but if someone's got the power to incinerate her from the inside out, she'd be immune to that."

"Interesting," Li says, then taps Arella's shoulder. "All done, beautiful girl."

"Thank you." Arella finishes the Healing Water, then tilts her head back to look at me with crumpled eyebrows. "When did you ever use healing products on me?"

"How do you think you recovered from that car accident so quickly? That Sprite I kept giving you wasn't Sprite."

She stares at the empty bottle in her hands. "Huh. I never would have—"

Thud! Thud! Thud! Someone pounds against the front door upstairs. Instinctively, I seize Arella's hand. She jolts out of her chair and squeezes mine back. By the concentration in her eyes, I'm certain she's projecting her immunity onto me.

"Seriously?" Tao groans. "Can people not read my sign? We are closed until October one. Right now, not October one. I'll go tell dem to go away."

"Wait," I whisper. "It could be the Royals. They might have tracked us here."

"I'll check." Li narrows her eyes at the ceiling in the direction of the front door. "Three large men, and they don't look like they're here for herbal medicines."

Thud! Thud! It's louder this time.

"Shit," I mutter.

"Should we fake like we aren't here?" Tao asks.

"No," Li says. "These guys look like they'll let themselves in if we don't first."

Tao closes the photo album. "Quick! I'll hide the pictures. You hide the kids."

It takes me a second to realize that *the kids* is referring to me and Arella.

Li clutches Arella's other arm. "Follow me."

Practically leaping over the many boxes on the floor, Li takes us to the farthest back corner under the stairs. It's dimmer back here. A bunch of glass jars are stacked on bookshelves. In the corner against the wall stands a freezer chest that Li shoves aside to reveal a dusty floor. She steps onto one of the wood planks, and up pops a square section of the floor. It's just wide enough for a person to crawl through.

"Get in," Li says.

Using the questionable wood ladder, Arella climbs down first. I follow shortly after. The second my head clears the flooring, Li shuts the trapdoor and we're surrounded by black. There isn't a single crack of light with how sealed it is. The floor rumbles above us as Li returns the freezer chest back to its spot.

"Can you make me immune?" I ask.

Arella grabs my hand. "Done."

I imagine a tiny flame on the tip of my finger, and it appears. My little fire illuminates the space that's just tall enough for me to reach up and barely touch the trapdoor. It's not wide enough for me to lie down though—not that I'd want to. It's dustier than hell, with cobwebs hanging along all four walls.

I move my little flame to see Arella. Her face is crumpled with concern.

"Don't worry, baby," I whisper. "I won't let anyone hurt you." She hasn't given me permission to call her pet names again, but I won't correct myself this time.

Without warning, she slams her front against mine and circles her arms around my back. Then she buries her face in my chest. I'm so shocked that I can't move. A heavy weight lifts off my shoulders as her warmth envelops me.

Eventually, I regain my composure and wrap my arm around her too, squeezing her so tight, she exhales a little breath. The relief that eases through me almost makes me tear up. It's been eating at me that Arella no longer trusted me or felt safe around me. This is proof that she knows I'll do anything to protect her. If any of those men lay a finger on her, I won't hesitate to kill 'em.

Things are quiet for a minute before some heavy pairs of footsteps come stomping down the stairs.

"Then you won't mind if we look around," a deep voice sneers.

"Excuse me," Li says sternly, "we are closed."

"Dat is what I told dem," Tao says. "Dey not listening."

"We aren't here to shop, ma'am. We're looking for fugitives. Have you seen either of these two?"

"No. I have been in my shop all day since seven this morning. I have seen no one except my husband because everybody else actually reads the sign that says we're closed. We're in the middle of remodeling."

"I can tell," a second guy scoffs. "It's a fucking shit show in here."

The first guy speaks again. "This will only take a minute."

"You can't just barge into someone's business and trample around like you own the place!" Li shouts. "Get out of here before I call the Enforcers."

"We *are* the Enforcers," a third voice says.

"Are not." The confidence in Li's tone is unmatched.

"Yes, we are. See?"

Li chuckles. "Fake badge. Also, I'm a Detector. The alarm in my head is going off right now. So you have three seconds to get out before I call the *real* Enforcers."

A pair of footsteps tramp on the floor above us. I put out my flame as if the man can see it. Blackness engulfs us as Arella curls into me, gripping my shirt. I clench her tighter, just in case the man has the power to reach through the floor and snatch her from me. Zordi powers don't normally work between surface level and underground, but I'm not taking any chances.

"Three," Li counts like an annoyed mother.

"We're almost done, old lady. Chill the fuck out."

"Two."

The man above us isn't moving. What is he looking at? Can he see us through the floor?

"I think you liars are forgetting what the consequences are for impersonating an Enforcer," Li says. "What is it? Five to ten years? I hear they drug you up good with perrizo in z-prison. Do you need me to finish counting to one?"

The man above us sighs. "Come on, boys. They ain't here. Let's go."

I don't let out a breath until I hear their footsteps trudge up the stairs and out the door. A moment later, a gentle pair of feet shuffles back down. I imagine it's Tao after relocking the door.

Arella and I remain silent, still hunched into each other as we wait to be released. Our freedom doesn't come right away. Instead, Li and Tao speak to each other in Chinese for a while. I'm fluent in English, conversational in French and Spanish, and I know enough American Sign Language to get by. Whatever Chinese language they're speaking has now made it to the top of my list of languages to learn. I'm going to assume they have a reason for not immediately releasing us, and although I only met them within the last hour, I trust them.

Arella tilts her head up and brushes her lips against the base of my neck. A bright beam of light shines inside me, filling the dark hollow hole where my heart used to be. It's not just that she's breathing on me and almost kissing me that's got me reeling; it's that she's doing it so tenderly, willingly, and unprompted.

Mere hours ago, we were on a flying tire, where she told me she never wanted to see me again. She meant it so much that she even tried to lose me at a gas station. Now she's letting me hold her like I'm the only person she wants holding her forever.

My little fireball reappears on my fingertip again, and I move it near her face. She gazes up at me with her big brown eyes, the fear in them from earlier dissolved. Replacing it is that lustful trusting look I've wanted to see for days. It's the look she used to give me before all this shit happened.

I free my hand that was glued to the small of her back, to push some of her hair behind an ear. She closes her eyes and melts into my touch the way I always melt into hers. Before I even realize I'm doing it, I lean down to plant a heavy kiss against her forehead. When she doesn't pull away, that light in my chest shines brighter. Then she sighs and squeezes her arms around me tighter, making me choke up a little.

If I never have to leave this dusty, dirty, cobweb-infested underground hideaway, I'll be happy. It's like a sanctuary down here when I've got my girl back in my arms.

26

TREY

"I APOLOGIZE THAT IT TOOK SO LONG," LI SAYS THROUGH THE opening of the trapdoor. "They lingered outside our shop for a while. I kept watching them through the walls, reading their lips. From what I could catch, they're convinced you're in the area. They've gone scouring to find you but have made plans to return later. They think you're waiting until nightfall to come here for healing. You should go before they come back."

I help Arella climb up the wooden ladder first, then I do the same. Li shuts the trapdoor, then Tao shoves the freezer chest back over it.

"Is it still light outside?" I ask, taking a breath of clean, not-musty air.

Li glares up at the ceiling, then nods. "Yes. The sun is starting to set though."

"Could we stay here until it's dark?"

"What if they return and you're still here?"

"We'll take that chance."

Arella places an affectionate hand over my forearm. I'm living for any moment when she willingly touches me.

"Are you sure?" she asks me. "If they've gone out to look

for us, that means they aren't around here. This might be our chance."

I scratch the back of my head. "Um, so, I'm not trying to be dramatic or anything, but if we leave now, I'm gonna die."

The three of them scrutinize me with their eyebrows dipped.

I should probably explain. "Yesterday, well, I think it was yesterday—all my days are blending together. Anyway, it doesn't matter what day it was. The point is that Katie, a Premonitioner, told me that she saw my death. It was right outside that shop selling all those waving cats. The Royals stab me and kidnap Arella in the daylight. So, if we could stay here until dark, that'd be great."

With a firm nod, Li claps her hands together. "Who wants some duck?"

A half hour later, Arella and I are sitting at a small dining table with some bowls of rice, roast duck, and a side of brothy soup. Our gracious hosts took their meals to eat upstairs. They said that if the Royals come back, they'll stomp on the floor three times as a signal for us to hide. In the meantime, they'll work on putting their store back together since it'll help make it look like they're not hiding people in their basement.

I finish my meal within ten minutes. Arella cleans out her bowls shortly after I do. As I wash up our dishes, she dries them and puts them back into the cabinets.

The next time I see Katie, I'll have to thank her profusely. Not only did she help save Arella's life, she saved mine too. Without her knowledge, we definitely would have left earlier. Then the Royals would have found us outside and Katie's premonition would have come true.

To continue waiting out the sunlight, Arella and I head to the love seat to rest. So far, we haven't heard any stomping, and I hope we never do.

For a while, Arella cuddles with me in silence. She's sitting between my legs with her back flush against my front and her head resting against my chest. Tenderly, I play with her hands, grateful to be this close to her again.

Things are quiet as I enjoy the feel of her body against mine, especially since my ribs no longer ache. Earlier, when she fell asleep on my shoulder on the bus, it hurt like hell to stay in that position, but I didn't care. I would have rather ached as her pillow than been more comfortable away from her.

I've never been one to enjoy silence. It's hard for me to be alone with my thoughts. Whenever I am, my mind spirals into reminding me what a worthless human I am, walking around without a reason to live. I felt that way until Arella came into my life. With her, I not only enjoy silence but prefer it. She calms my mind in ways I can't explain. With her, I have a purpose. She's my reason to live.

Arella breaks the silence. "Why didn't you tell me earlier?"

"Tell you what?"

"That Katie had a premonition about your death. You freaked out when you saw those waving cats, and you said nothing."

"I didn't wanna scare you."

She tilts her head back to look at me. "Trey, how am I supposed to protect you when you keep information like that from me?"

"*I'm* the one who's supposed to protect *you*."

Her mouth draws into a hard frown. "Why can't we protect each other?"

"I don't want you to worry about me."

She turns around to straddle my lap, and I'm not mad about it. I even pull her in closer, keeping my hands around her hips. Gently, she caresses the back of my head with her nails, sending tingles down my spine. "Will you make me a promise?"

My gut instinct is to say yes because I want to give this woman anything she wants, but I can't lie to her. There are certain things I won't promise her, and they mostly involve anything that goes against her safety. "Depends what it is."

"Will you promise me that from now on, we'll be a team? You protect me, and I'll protect you."

Something is tugging at my lips, because I can't stop them from smiling. "Is it really that important to you to protect me?"

She creases her face together like I'm an idiot. "Victor got me to project my immunity onto you by trying to murder you in front of me. What does that tell you?"

Good point. "I'll make you that promise on one condition."

"What?"

"You have to promise me that we'll be a team—forever. I protect you, and you protect me—forever. Deal?"

She beams and nods. "Deal."

"Oh, and also, promise me that if someone's throwing an element ball at me, you won't jump in front of it."

"Deal."

"And promise me that you'll never try to abandon me at a gas station ever again."

She nods again. "Deal."

"Great. Now can I also go back to calling you *babe*?"

Her lips curve into a warm smile. "I'd like that."

I don't realize my hand is clutching her face, guiding her toward me, until my mouth is already consuming hers. My kisses start off tender—light pressure, short breaths, and gentle touches—until suddenly, I'm not gentle anymore. I pant as I claw at her body to come closer to mine, because even when she's straddling me, she's not close enough.

"Trey . . ." She moans as I lay her over the couch cushions and climb on top of her. I put a leg on either side of her hips, then attack her neck with my lips. Her soft hands reach under my shirt, clawing at my abs.

I melt into her touch, groaning against her collarbone. "Arella."

I kiss up her neck as she arches her head back. I've missed this so much. The taste of her sweetness. The smell of her intoxicating scent. The way she lets out breathless whimpers as I keep sucking on her skin.

Naturally, I grind my hard cock against her inner thigh. She digs her fingernails into my back, making me let out an uncontrollable grunt. The things this woman does to me. The power she has over me with just one touch. I'm hers. For as long as she wants me, for whatever she wants me for, I'm hers. All hers.

My lips travel upward until I find her mouth again. Panting hard, we return to what can only be described as an animalistic make-out session. We scratch at each other's clothes. She breathlessly moans my name over and over. I thrust my hips against her, attempting to find any sort of release from the torment we've been going through.

I know this chaos isn't over, but for now, right here, I have Arella. She's alive, she's safe, and she's allowing me back into her heart. This is all that matters. This is what I risked my life to get back. This is my reason to keep risking it all.

I love this woman with every part of my soul. To be without her is to be without sunlight and air and food and water and whatever else I need to survive. I'm never going to allow someone to take her away from me ever again. I'll spend the rest of my life fighting to be with her if that's what it takes.

"Arella?" I whisper against her lips.

"Mmm?"

"I love you."

She doesn't hesitate. "I love you too."

I might pass out from how happy I am to hear those words from her. A rush of flutters fills me to the brim. I've never felt so full like this. So completely and utterly full.

I lean down to plant one long, hard kiss against her lips, then pull back again. "Do you think you can ever forgive me?"

"For what?"

"You know, blowing your tire so I had an excuse to meet you. Trying to use you to make my dead parents proud. Spending three days passed out in an infirmary while you were trapped in a place with people you didn't know. Putting your life in danger. Should I go on?"

"Trey, most of that wasn't your fault. Actually, none of it was. Now that I know the whole story, I would have done the same thing if I were you. Fake-date someone to find out information that could result in taking down the people who killed my parents? And to stop those people from killing more people? When that's all it was supposed to be, I would have taken that mission in a heartbeat. You never meant for me or anyone to get hurt. The only thing you did wrong was trust the wrong people. I forgive you for what happened, but I think the more important question is, do you forgive yourself?"

I don't have to think about my answer. "No, but maybe someday."

Arella grabs my face and pulls my mouth to hers. She kisses me so long and hard, it takes my breath away.

I pant for air as I do a push-up over her. "I really don't want this to stop, but I think we should get going."

Twenty-some minutes later, I've got our heavy backpack over my shoulders. Tao filled it with a fuck-ton of Healing Water, Healing Goo, and Healing Spray. I hope we won't need it, but it'll be good to have.

"Come back to visit anytime, okay?" Li says as she leads us to the back door of their shop. "Don't wait twenty years this time."

I chuckle lightly. "I won't. Thank you again for everything. Seriously. You guys saved our lives."

Li stops at the door, then turns to give me a smile and pinch my cheeks. Her eyes glisten a little. "I'm so proud of you, Trey Grant. You've grown up to be such a strong and handsome good boy."

My insides flutter as Arella and I exit their shop. Li will

never know how much her words mean to me. That's the first time someone other than Liz has ever told me they're proud of me. Hearing it from Li is like hearing it from my mother.

Tao's black SUV is exactly where he said it would be: two spots away from the dumpster. With his key, I unlock it with a *beep*. Arella and I climb in, I toss our backpack onto the backseat, then we're off.

"I can't believe they just *gave* us their car." Arella shifts to get comfy in the passenger seat. "I mean, it's a freaking Lincoln."

"I bet they'll have enough money on their next royalty check to buy another." I glance into the rearview mirror. So far, so good. "Also, I'll come back some other time and thank them tenfold."

"Are we going to go search for your parents' safe house now?"

"Yep." I check the rearview mirrors again. There's a car behind us. An elderly lady is driving with an elderly man in the passenger side. Probably not Royals. Also, their emotions are pretty content.

"How do we know that Victor doesn't know about your parents' safe house? Now that we've discovered he and your mom were a thing, what if she told him about it?"

"I thought about that earlier, and I think we're okay. My parents' message said that the only person I should trust is Aunt Debbie. That tells me Victor wasn't on the *trustworthy list* for a while. Probably since the day Aunt Jodi left him and he broke things off with my mom.

"Now that I think about it, it was around that time when my parents started bringing me out to Julian, California. I remember because Victor had just started treating me like a plague-ridden toad. Whenever my parents brought me out there to stargaze, I'd wish on all the stars that my Uncle V would find another wife. I wanted him to be happy so he'd be nice to me again."

All the emotions I had as a kid during those days come rushing back to me. Victor used to be my favorite person in the world. He was the one I'd beg my parents to let me call, so I could ask him to come play with me. He was the one I'd look forward to seeing every weekend. He was the one who taught me how to swim and to roller-skate.

We were so close that we had a secret word. Whenever either of us said *crystal*, it meant that whatever just happened stayed between us. It started one Christmas morning when Victor and I snuck downstairs to the decorated tree and opened one of my presents early.

In the midst of shooting Uncle V with my new Nerf guns, I bumped into the Christmas tree and one of my mom's precious crystal angel ornaments fell. The wings broke off, and there was no fixing it. My mom never found out where her angel ornament went, because Victor and I made a pact to never tell anyone. From then on, whenever we had to keep something a secret, we'd say *crystal*.

That was the last Christmas I ever spent with Victor. Suddenly, he stopped coming by to take me out for late-night ice cream and walks around the neighborhood. My loud nights filled with Victor and me wrestling on the carpet while I avoided Aunt Jodi's glares became quiet nights with just my parents, asking them when Uncle V would come back to visit.

"Let me see if I've got this right." Arella ticks off her points on each finger. "Victor was in love with your mom but was married to Jodi. After Jodi left him for another man, Victor's so heartbroken that he dumps your mom. Then he starts treating his own son like trash?"

I purse my lips and nod. "Sounds about right."

"That doesn't make any sense. With Jodi gone, wouldn't he have felt more free to be with your mom? What if your dad —or the person you thought was your dad—found out about the affair and threatened to hurt Victor if he kept seeing your mom?"

"That's possible, I guess. Either way, I'm not gonna try to make it make sense. The only person who can tell us why he did what he did is Victor, and to say we're not on the best *let's sit down and hash out the past* terms is putting it lightly."

Arella and I talk for a bit longer before she eventually falls asleep.

When we finally arrive in Julian, California, it's well past three in the morning. The sky is black, the roads are quiet, and the emotions coming to my head are mostly muted.

Arella's eyes flutter open as I tap her awake.

"We're here," I say as I gesture toward the Y-shaped tree my parents always parked their car at. I shut the Lincoln off, then grab the backpack.

After locking the car, I take Arella's hand and lead her through the woods.

"If we don't find it," I say as my fireball floats in front of us, "we could go to my cabin in Colorado. It's not underground, but it can be a good transition place while we figure out our next steps."

While the cabin property is under my name, I don't think Victor knows I have it. I bought that cabin well after I moved out. Then again, he could easily look up properties I own and send his men there. *Maybe my cabin isn't a good idea.*

"We *are* going to find this safe house," Arella says with a hell of a lot more confidence than I have. She's gripping my hand pretty tight to ensure that her immunity works on me.

I'm not anywhere closer to understanding her magic more than I was on day one. From what she told me in the car before she fell asleep, she doesn't even have to think that hard about projecting it anymore. She said it's been coming pretty easily to her. This woman is truly extraordinary.

I step over a fallen tree, then help Arella over it too. "What makes you so sure we'll find it?"

"Because we're not leaving until we do."

I've told myself that countless times. Every time, I've

always left with dirt all over my jeans and no safe house. If Arella's that confident, though, I'll try to be too.

A while later, we arrive at the big rock.

"*This* is your secret rock?" Arella knocks on it with her knuckles. "It looks like any other big ol' rock on the ground."

"Because it is. I think my parents put this here to help my seven-year-old brain remember where Cheesy is." I point toward the holey tree a few steps over.

Together, Arella and I take one hundred steps away from Cheesy. The whole time she counts, I expand my Empath power out to cover the woods. No one is nearby, which means we're safe. I've never been so grateful for this gift until now.

"Ninety-nine," Arella says. "One hundred."

We reach the same area I've always come to. There's nothing here but nature.

"Can I assume all these former holes in the ground are yours?" Arella gestures toward all the patches of dirt around us.

"What can I say? I was determined. Now as you can see, there's nothing here. No safe house. No bunker. No trapdoor. No sign. No nothin'."

"Let me look around for a bit. Keep holding my hand and move your fireball with me so I can see, please."

"Yes, ma'am." I salute her like she's my drill sergeant.

For a while, I follow Arella wherever she goes as she scours the woods. When she finds nothing, as I've been telling her, she says, "We took a hundred adult steps. Where do you usually end up when you take a hundred kid steps?"

"About twenty paces back." Hand in hand, I lead her there as my fireball follows us.

"Next to this tree?" She places a hand against the bark of a skinny box elder.

"Yep, and I've looked everywhere around this tree. There's nothing here. My parents' message said *inside and underground*. You see all these dirt patches? I've dug almost fifteen feet down starting from the base of this tree and all around it. I've even drilled into the trunk to see if there's anything inside it. It's a regular tree."

Arella steps around the trunk, running her hand along the rough bark. I move my flames to follow her gaze.

She tilts her head back and squints her eyes. "Have you ever looked for anything up in the branches?"

"No. The safe house is *underground*, remember?"

"And your mom's song says to 'look to the sky when you feel down.' Haven't you ever done an escape room?"

"A what?"

"An escape room," she says as if saying it again means I'll suddenly know exactly what she means. "Seriously? Javina and I love them. It's a fun place where someone locks you and your friends in a room, and you have to solve puzzles in under an hour to get out. I think your mom is hinting for you to look up. Can you move your fireball that way so I can see better?"

I do as I'm told, even though there's no way in hell my mom would have given me a hard puzzle to solve. I was a kid when she died. Still, I float my fireball up the trunk and stop once the flames get too close to the leaves. "Any higher and I'll light this thing up."

"That's close enough. Walk around the tree with me."

Again, I do as I'm told, even though—I gasp. Right there, way up in the bark of one of the thick branches, is a carving.

"What?" Arella asks.

"There's something carved into the bark."

"Where?"

I point up. "Right there."

She squints. "I don't see anything."

"Babe, it's right—" I slap a palm against my forehead. "Oh, did you know that Zordi eyes are different from Ordi eyes?"

"How so?"

"Zordis can see things farther out than Ordinaries can. It's like our eyes have the zoom and focus function of a camera. Maybe I can see it but you can't."

"Well, what's the carving of?"

I bring my fireball down. "212E."

"What's that mean?"

"No fucking clue. You're the escape-room genius here. You tell me."

From her pocket, Arella pulls out the two receipts she wrote on the back of. "Look to the sky when you feel down. Know that things will turn around. Work twice as hard to the finish line. Now it's your time to shine." She taps the receipts against her thigh as she thinks to herself. "Turn around. Twice as hard to the finish line."

"Are you thinkin' we need to turn around?"

She nods. "Toward the east. Four hundred and twenty-four steps."

"Why four hund—Oh! Twice the steps! Wow. Maybe my mom's song *was* a hint. This whole time, I just thought it was her way of telling me to keep my head up because things will turn around as long as I work hard."

"I'm sure she meant the song that way too. Now which way is east, because I have no idea."

Finally! Something I can contribute! I point to our right. "It's that way."

Four hundred and twenty-four steps feels like a lot as an adult. I can't imagine how I would have felt as a kid. When my parents said I should bring Aunt Debbie with me, I think it was more of a request than a suggestion: one, because I needed someone to drive me here, and, two, because they must have told Aunt Debbie that my mom's song included instructions.

"Four twenty-two, four twenty-three, four twenty-four." Arella stops taking her kid-size steps and glances at the huge tree standing in front of us. Its long branches loom above our heads like an umbrella. The trunk is so large, it would probably take at least three of my arms to wrap around it. Any other time, any other place, I'd see this tree and think nothing of it. Tonight, I've got a feeling this is it.

"What now?" I ask.

Arella paces around the tree, towing me with her. "I'm not seeing anything. Can you use your special eyeballs to check up top?"

My special eyeballs? I let out a light laugh, then do as I'm told. We walk around the tree twice, but I find nothing.

"Hmm." Arella squats to examine the base of the tree.

I move my flames closer to help her see. "Anything?"

"Not yet."

Suddenly, something shiny catches my eye. *Now it's your time to shine.* The last line of my mother's song. I wave at my fireball, and it floats back up to my eye level. The flames illuminate a shiny reflective device inside a little hole in the tree. It's the same size as the hole in the rocky entrance to Shadow Ridge. I'm about to stick my index finger into the slot when Arella grabs my arm.

"What are you doing?" She gapes at me like I'm crazy. "You see a mysterious hole and you're just going to stick your finger into it? What if you get your finger chopped off?"

"Relax. I think it's a fingerprint scanner."

"How do you know?"

"It looks like the same kind we use to open the door to the Ridge." I stick my finger straight into the hole.

Nothing happens. No beeping. No ten-foot door sliding open. No guards greeting me with scowls on the other side. I glance around to see if there's something off in the distance I might be missing. I don't see a trapdoor that's popped up from the ground, or an opening of any sort.

"What's supposed to happen?" Arella asks.

"I'm not sure. Maybe I'll try a different finger." I stick my middle finger into the hole. Nothing happens. I try my ring finger. My thumb. My pinky. Same thing. I hope this isn't the part I needed Aunt Debbie for, because her fingers are long gone.

"Try your index finger again," Arella says. "Harder this time."

After I blow some dirt out of the hole and wipe my finger clean on my sweatpants, I stick my index finger back in. Something clicks inside the tree, then a large part of the bark pops forward. I pull the bark back to reveal a hollowed-out tree trunk.

"It worked." Arella's jaw drops. "This is so cool. Like a real-life escape room, except we're trying to get in, not out."

It's nice that she finds this amusing. I guide my fireball up the hollow. It's a tight space, barely big enough for my broad shoulders. Downward is a flight of stairs. I flick my wrist, and my flames travel all the way down until they hit a metal hatch door.

"Me first," I say as I step into the hollow. Our backpack hanging on my shoulders hits the walls of the tiny space. "Stay close, okay? And don't let go of my hand."

"Trey, we haven't stopped holding hands this entire time. I'm not planning on going anywhere."

And I hope she never does.

27

ARELLA

One-handed, Trey turns the hatch door's wheel. It squeals as it twists to the open position. Together, we lift the heavy door. Trey waves his hand, making his fireball float down the hatch, revealing a set of stairs and a living room. I can't see much else beyond that.

"I'll go first to make sure it's safe," Trey says. Finally, we release each other's hands. "Don't come down until I say so, 'kay?"

After I nod, he heads down and disappears into the darkness. The wooden stairs creak under his feet.

A minute later, he pops his head up the hatch and holds a hand out to me. "Watch your step, babe."

Once my feet touch the carpet, Trey points at the hatch door. It shuts with a light thump, drowning us in pitch black. A new fireball brightens the room. He tosses it into the air, then searches the wall until he finds a light switch. The ceiling lights flicker on with a light buzzing sound.

I spin to examine our surroundings. "How is there electricity down here?"

"No clue." Trey slashes a hand in the air, then his fireball disappears.

Against the wall sits a small couch with a recliner next to it. They are covered with protective plastic sheets. In the middle of the room stands a coffee table with a layer of dust on it so thick, I can't see the surface. Everything looks like it hasn't been touched in years. Probably as many years as Trey's parents have been gone.

Trey drops our backpack onto the dirty carpet at his feet. "Let's look around."

I follow him toward the small kitchen, where a thick layer of dust and dirt covers everything from the countertops to the appliances. He peels the fridge open. The inside looks like a science experiment gone wrong. It smells like it too. Whatever was in there before is now unrecognizable lumps of black goo.

Trey slams the fridge shut. "Let's never open that again."

"Agreed."

We head down a hall, where he flips on another light. Trey opens a door on the right to reveal a small bathroom with a sink, a toilet, and a one-person shower.

"How is there plumbing down here?" I ask.

"Babe, did you forget that *you're* the one who found this place? I'm seeing it for the first time, just like you are. I don't understand how anything works down here."

I point at my chest. "*I* didn't find this. *We* found it together."

"I couldn't have done it without you solving my mom's riddle."

"And I couldn't have gotten here without you telling me which way is east."

He smirks handsomely. "Glad I could contribute."

Across the hall is another door that creaks as he opens it. A bedroom greets us with two queen beds covered with protective plastic. A large dresser stands against the opposite wall. Trey pulls open the drawers. They're full of clothes for an adult man and an adult woman. The bottom drawers are full of clothes for a seven-year-old boy.

"It's good to know they weren't *trying* to abandon me," Trey says. "That doesn't change the fact that they set up this entire safe house because they knew there was a chance they *could* die but continued on with their mission anyway."

"You also knew there was a chance you could die when you came back to the Ridge to save me, yet you did it anyway."

Trey shakes his head as he slams the drawers shut. "That's different."

"How so?"

"I don't have a child waiting for me at home."

That's a good point. I can't imagine what it's like to be Trey, to have lost his parents at a young age in a traumatic way, only to discover that they chose their jobs over him. I don't know the full story, so that statement might be oversimplifying his parents' decision, but the bottom line is that they chose to risk their lives, knowing they could be abandoning their son in the end. What could have possibly been more important than him?

I leave Trey's side to go explore the nightstands. In one of the drawers are some passports and ID cards. I recognize Trey's mom in one of the passports, but the name next to her face isn't Suzie Grant; it's Linda Johnson. Trey's dad—I mean, the man he thought was his dad—is pictured in the other passport. The name next to his face is Michael Johnson. There are two other passports as well. One is for Aunt Debbie, and the other is for seven-year-old Trey. They have fake names next to their faces too.

"Looks like your parents were prepared to leave the country," I say.

Trey comes up behind me and glances over my shoulder. "Daniel Johnson? What? Do I look like a fucking Daniel to you?"

I place the passports back where I found them, then head toward the closet. I slide the doors open to reveal an air mattress, extra pillows, linens, towels, and cleaning supplies.

Trey doesn't waste a second to grab the towels. "Let's clean this bedroom up so we can sleep in it."

I roll out the vacuum. "Good idea."

Together, we work to remove the layer of dirt and grime from . . . well, everywhere. I vacuum the carpet three times over, but it still feels grimy on my feet. Meanwhile, Trey wipes off every surface in the bedroom and cleans the bathroom.

"At least we can sleep now," Trey says a while later from the bedroom doorway.

I'm gathering all the dirty towels into a pile on the floor. "How long do you think we should stay here?"

"Until we figure out what to do next. We'll have to resurface for some food in the morning. I found cans of soup and beans in the kitchen cabinets, but I refuse to let you consume anything in here. It's all probably so toxic, one bite will kill your baby."

My body stills. I didn't realize Trey still thinks I'm pregnant. I suppose he has no reason to think otherwise. I haven't had much free time to think about the loss of our baby, let alone explain it to him. We've been a little too preoccupied with running for our lives for the baby topic to even come up.

"Are you hungry?" Trey asks.

"I can wait until the morning."

"Okay. I'm gonna use the bathroom. When I come back, I have something to tell you."

I have something to tell you too . . .

With a sigh, I stand back to take a look at our cleaning job. The bedroom looks and smells less musty than before. The protective cover that was over one of the beds is now lying in a heap on the floor.

I don't waste a second getting under the covers. As I lay my head against the weird-smelling pillow, my eyes get heavy. My exhausted body is ready for a long, uninterrupted night of rest. The last places I slept were handcuffed to a lumpy bed, the dirty floor of a barn, a rocky bus, and the front seat of a Lincoln. I'm excited to sleep in an actual bed tonight—without the handcuffs.

Trey reenters the bedroom with damp hands, patting them off on his shirt. "I dirtied up all the towels while cleaning. Didn't think about saving one for our hands." With a plop, his sweatpants fall to his ankles, then he drags his shirt over his head.

My eyes don't leave his abs and muscular shoulders as he joins me under the covers. I'm used to seeing him in only his boxers. This is how he normally sleeps. So why are my insides tingling this much?

Trey props himself up on an elbow and tenderly tucks some of my hair behind an ear. "You look cozy."

I lean into his touch, hoping he'll continue to do it. "I'm exhausted, and this bed is comfy."

"Would you rather we talk in the morning?"

"No." I sit up and prop my pillow against the wall behind me. "I'm curious about what you have to tell me."

He sighs deeply, and it makes my body tense. The blankets ruffle as he sits up. "There's no easy way to say this, so I'm just gonna say it. Do you remember when you told me about your parents? About how they were driving home on a rainy night in September of '95 and drove right over a cliff?"

Of all the things I thought Trey had to tell me, I didn't think it would relate to my parents. I side-eye him. "Yeah?"

"Well . . ." He scratches the back of his neck. "I researched them. Aries and Bella Rance, right?"

"Right."

He bites his lip and stares at his hands for a moment before looking back up at me. "The reason I thought to research them in the first place is because my parents also died on a rainy night in September of '95."

I blink as I process that information. "Are you saying they died the exact same month?"

"No, babe. I'm saying they died the exact same *night*."

"What?"

"Yeah, that was my reaction too. At first, I couldn't find anything on an Aries Rance or a Bella Rance online. After some digging, I ended up Googling for deaths over a cliff in September of 1995. Turns out, there was only one couple that happened to, and it happened on the same night my parents were killed. And here's the other part: It happened in Three Rivers, near the same mountain range Shadow Ridge is hidden under."

I gasp with a hand over my mouth. "Do you think there's a connection?"

"I don't know exactly what, but there's gotta be one. Back then, ZIRDA was already doing research on Immunes. My parents were some of the researchers. The subjects were told it was part of a top-secret medical study put on by the government. My theory is that *you* were one of my parents' research subjects."

"I suppose that's plausible." I hope the tests being performed at that time were more humane than the ones Victor was doing.

"It would explain why your family was around Shadow Ridge that night. Now, are you ready for the next part?"

The next part? My heart's still thrashing over finding out that my parents died on the same night as Trey's parents. Do I really want to hear more? "I'm going to assume by the hesitation in your tone that this next part is crazier."

"It is. I think the Royals who killed my parents are the same ones who killed yours. Somehow, the Royals found out about ZIRDA studying some rare Ordinaries and they wanted to take the Immunes for themselves. On that rainy night, they shoved your parents down a cliff to make it look like a car accident so they could kidnap you. My theory is that my parents saved you from them."

I gasp as it all clicks together. "That's why they showed up at your house that night. They were looking for me."

"Most likely. My parents must have handed you off to another ZIRDA agent to take you to your grandparents before they rushed home. That's why I think your grandparents know something. Why else would they have moved you around every year?"

"You think they moved me around to hide me from the Royals?"

"One hundred percent."

I ponder that for a moment, then say, "Why keep me in California though? If there were people coming after me in this state, why keep me here?"

"Unfortunately, the Royals don't only reside in California. They've got people everywhere, all around the world. Unless your grandparents were going to hide you in a hole your entire life, no matter where they took you, the Royals would have found you."

"Wow. This is a lot to process."

"I know, and I'm sorry to throw this all on you at once, but are you ready for the last part?"

My eyes bulge. "There's more?"

"Last thing, I promise. The articles I read about your parents' car going off a cliff weren't about an Aries and Bella Rance. The couple's names were Stanley and Robyn Calder. And . . ." Trey clears his throat. "Their three-year-old daughter, Hannah Calder, supposedly died with them."

Three-year-old daughter? Hannah? Died? If what Trey is saying is true, then there's a lot more to that night in September of '95 than I thought. This whole time, I thought my parents' death was just a tragic car accident. Do my grandparents know what really happened? Was my name Hannah at one point?

For the next hour, Trey and I talk through theories of what could have happened that rainy night. The only thing that comes out of our conversation is that we have more questions than answers.

Trey yawns, and it's the first time I've ever seen him do it. "Are you ready to sleep now, babe?" he asks.

"Actually"—my heart rate kicks up—"I have something to tell you too."

He fixes his attention onto me. "What's up?"

I haven't had a chance to plan out my words. Like Trey said earlier, there's no easy way to say it, so I come out with it. "I lied to you."

His expression remains impassive. "About what?"

"There was never some guy from college."

He presses his eyebrows together and tilts his head to the side. "Huh?"

"I never cheated on you. There was never a guy from college. I only told you that because you told me you needed a reason to let me go, so I gave it to you."

"What? When did I say that?"

"When you were drunk."

He pauses to think, then stares at my belly. "But—"

I put a hand up before he can say anything about us not being able to conceive. "You said your powers are passed down by genetics, right?"

"Yeah?"

"Maybe you don't know because it might go back a few generations, but was there ever someone in your family who could sense other people's emotions?"

"Yes?" His eyes narrow. "Why?"

"Well, um, because, the baby—um, since the baby could do it, so could I. I sensed your heartache that night you were drunk. That was the first time. Then I could sense all those people in the Ridge too."

He inhales a sharp breath. "What?"

"At first it was only the people who were within a few feet of me. Later, the baby could sense people farther out. It could tell exactly where someone was by sensing what direction the emotions were coming from and how strong they were."

"You . . . you're preg—oh my god! And it's . . . it's mine!" Trey shoots off the bed and rakes his hands through his hair. It's not in frustration, the way he typically does it. He looks more confused than anything. "But—but how is that possible? To have a half-Zordi, half-Ordi child? That's not—wait. Who cares how it's possible? My baby's an Empath, just like me. Holy shit! I'm gonna be a dad!"

My eyes go wide. "Oh, Trey. Hold on."

He doesn't hear me. He climbs back into bed, rips the blanket off my legs, then presses his ear to my stomach.

"Trey, I—"

His shuddering body stops me. He grips onto my legs, then lets out a cry.

I place my palms over his back as his shoulders tremble. "Are you okay?"

It takes a few heartbeats before he arches his head back, and I can finally see the tears rushing down his face. "Arella, I'm more than okay! I'm gonna be a dad! I've always wanted a family. I haven't had one in so long. I'm gonna work so hard, baby. I promise you. I'm gonna work so hard to be the best dad this little baby could ever have."

I burst into tears. *This* was the reaction I wanted when I was scared to tell him I was pregnant. *This* is what every woman dreams of seeing from her man the second she gets that positive pregnancy test.

Trey swipes his thumb under my wet eyes. "I'm gonna teach them how to play guitar and piano. You can teach them how to bake and how to be a good person. We'll do things like go to amusement parks. I've never been to one. That's something good dads do with their kids, right? I'll take them to baseball games and out for movies. Disney World. The zoo. Oh, god. I've always wanted to go to a zoo."

"Trey . . ." I say through tears as I try to find the right words.

"Look, I know I don't know anything about babies, but I'm gonna learn. I'll take classes. I'll read books, and do lots of Googling. I'll take really good care of this baby. I'll take really good care of you too, Arella. I promise."

"Trey, stop."

"I can't. I'm so fucking happy right now. Fuck, I'm even crying. I don't think I've ever cried from happiness before. Look at me. I'm such a goddamn sap, and I don't even care. I'm gonna be a dad! I'm gonna be—"

"Trey!" I finally find the strength to shout through my tears. "Listen to me!"

Ultimately, he settles, taking my hands into his. "What, baby?"

"Oh, honey. You just made it harder for me to tell you."

"Tell me what?"

I've never seen anyone so wholesomely happy about being a dad before. I squeeze his hands to give him reassurance that everything will be okay. "Honey, the baby is gone."

28

ARELLA

I EXPECT HIM TO BURST OUT WITH A LOUD *WHAT?* BUT HE doesn't. Instead, he stares at me with a deadpan look like he doesn't understand the language I'm speaking.

"I'm sorry, Trey. Maybe I should have started with that." I didn't because I needed him to know that I had never cheated on him. I needed him to know the baby was his. I didn't expect him to react so strongly about being a father.

"W-what do you mean, *gone?*"

"As in, I'm not pregnant anymore." I'm surprised by how well I'm keeping myself together. I wasn't sure if I could say it out loud without crying. However, after seeing how happy Trey was just now, I think he's going to lose it, and at least one of us has to stay strong.

He squeezes my hands tighter in his. "No! That's . . . no! But—you . . . H-how? How do you know?"

"Because the morning after I was electrocuted, I couldn't sense other people's emotions anymore."

"Electrocuted?"

"Yes. While you were in the infirmary, Victor sent me to a lab. There, a lady did a bunch of tests on me. One of them was dropping lightning balls on me to try to get me to shield myself from them. I couldn't do it, and I'm pretty sure that's what caused the baby to—"

I'm right. He does lose it. He flies off the bed and heaves a hand through his hair. Now *that* is in the manner I'm used to seeing. "No! This can't be. I—Goddammit! Victor! That fucking . . . There's not even a word horrible enough to describe what I feel about him right now."

Trey paces the room. "He's probably the goddamn Royal who organized the murder of my parents. He kidnapped my girl, then he killed my baby. How can one man cause so much damage? Why? What did I ever do to him?"

The blanket Trey ripped off me hovers into the air. I grab it as the dresser drawers open and all their contents float out. Shirts, pants, and boxers drift around the room. "Trey."

He's not even looking my way. "And he's supposedly my biological father? You've gotta be fucking kidding me! If he really was my father, why would he kill my mother? A woman he supposedly loved?"

"Trey," I say louder as I grab a pillow from the air, trying to keep it against the bed.

He continues pacing the other side of the room. "I can't allow him to keep tormenting me. Everything that man does is toxic. He's going to keep hurting people if I don't stop him. He'll keep coming after my girl too. You'll always be in danger for as long as he's alive. I can't let that happen."

The pillow I'm holding down bursts into flames. My scream makes Trey spin around as I toss it onto the floor.

"Oh, shit!" He waves a shaky hand at the flaming pillow. The flames don't stop. "Fuck."

"Trey, make it stop."

"I—I'm trying." His chest rises and falls as he gasps for air. He has that desolate look in his eyes again—the same look he got after Li told him that Victor is his real father.

Suddenly, I know exactly what I need to do. I jump off the bed. The second I take his face into my palms, everything in the air falls to the carpet. The flames consuming the pillow disappear into plumes of smoke. It takes a minute for Trey's breathing to slow. The entire time, my hands never leave his face.

After several deep breaths, he finally makes eye contact with me. That desolate look is gone, replaced by sorrow. He wraps his muscular arms tight around my waist. "I'm sorry, babe. Are you hurt?"

"I'm okay. Are you?"

He nods slightly, and I don't need Li's lie-detecting power to know he's lying.

I drop my hands, then turn to find what's left of that pillow in a burnt heap on the floor. The carpet beneath it is scorched too. It hits me that the bedroom I was locked inside of at the Ridge was probably Trey's at one point.

"Good thing we have extra pillows," I say.

"Good thing we're underground."

"Good thing the fire didn't spread."

With a tender finger, he tucks some of my hair behind an ear. "Good thing I've got you. Did you know you have a special power where every time you touch me, it calms me?"

"I've noticed."

Trey leans down to kiss my forehead. "Thank you for being everything I never knew I needed."

My heart swoons. He's everything I never knew I needed too.

I leave him to grab a new pillow from the closet and toss it onto the bed. "This has happened before, hasn't it?"

His gaze falls to the carpet. "Yeah, lots. It started after my parents died, then it stopped sometime after I turned sixteen. It hasn't happened since until today. I don't know what it is or how to prevent it."

"When does it usually happen?" I ask, even though I know the answer.

"Whenever I get too emotional, or anxious, or depressed."

"I think they're panic attacks."

"Hmm" is all he says. Then he spends a moment staring at the carpet.

Eventually, we get back under the covers. Trey pats his shoulder, then gestures for me to scoot closer. I don't hesitate to nestle into the crook of his arm. As he wraps his limbs around me, his hand bumps my gauze. It doesn't hurt.

"It's been long enough," he says. "Can I take this off for you?"

"Sure." I expect him to peel it off. Instead, he points at my arm. The gauze flies away and lands on the floor. My skin under it looks brand new.

Trey inspects my arm, then nods his approval. I let out a sigh as I nuzzle deeper into him and rest a hand over his pec. He points at the light switch, and it flips with a click. The room goes dark. A night-light plugged in on the other side of the room illuminates everything just enough for me to not feel like I'm stuck in a box with no exit.

For a while, neither of us says anything. All that fills my ears are the sounds of our soft breaths. I shut my eyes and relish the warmth of being in Trey's arms again.

I'm about to drift off to sleep when he says, "Babe?"

I don't open my eyes. "Mmm?"

"I think you're right."

"About what?"

His chest rumbles against my face as he says, "The panic attacks. I think that's what they are too."

"I'm no doctor, but I'm, like, ninety-nine percent sure that's what it is. You exhibit all the signs of it. Short breaths. Shaky hands. A blank look in your eyes. You said it started after your parents were killed, which means it probably stems from that trauma."

"How do I stop it?"

"There's no way to *stop* it, really. I think it's something you just learn to live through and manage until they go away on their own. In the meantime, you could go see a therapist and see if that helps."

"I'd have to see a zerapist, but yeah, I'll think about doing that."

"Ahh," I say when it clicks. "Because you can't talk about your world with Ordinaries."

"Exactly. And because we have different bodily functions, we have to see people like zoctors and zutritionists."

"But if your car breaks down, can you see a regular mechanic?"

"Yes. There are no such things as zechanics because there aren't special cars just for Zordis."

Now that I think about it, that all makes sense.

Trey shifts under the blanket until he's on top of me. He opens his palm, and a little fireball appears in it. He tosses it into the air, and it hovers above us as he caresses my cheek. I'm grateful that he brought out the flames. I wouldn't be able to see the intense look in his eyes otherwise.

"I love being able to openly talk to you about my world, baby. I love you so much—with all my heart. I want to marry you and have babies with you and grow old with you. I want it all with you. Say you want it with me too."

I don't hesitate. "I do."

He grips the back of my neck as he drops his mouth over mine. His lips are as eager as his tongue. My hands caress down his bare back as he peppers tender kisses over my neck. I arch my head back and moan as he sucks my skin into his mouth.

In a low voice against my collarbone, he says, "We're meant to be together, Arella. I know it within the depths of my soul. You're it for me, and I'll spend the rest of my life convincing you that I'm it for you too."

"I don't need to be convinced, Trey. I already know you're the one for me."

He shifts onto his side and props himself up on an elbow.

His other hand caresses me behind my ear in little circles. Shadows from his fireball dance across his features as he says, "When this is all over, I'm gonna get you a ring. It'll be so big, the fucking astronauts will be able to see it from space."

"That sounds great, honey, but what about—"

"No. Don't say it. I know there are logistics, but I don't care. No zovernment is going to keep me away from you. We can't get married legally, but I'd love to at least see a ring on your finger. We'll know what it means, and that's what matters to me. If you want to have a small ceremony with some friends and your family, we can do that too, just without the paperwork. We can do it wherever you want. I'll buy everyone plane tickets to Paris if that's your dream wed—oh!" Trey pops up and slides off the bed. "That reminds me. I have something for you."

He flips the light on, using his hand this time, then his hovering fireball smokes out. He digs through our backpack to pull out his leather jacket. From the inner pocket, he drags out something shiny.

"My necklace! How did you—"

"Katie gave it to me. She said she had a vision that made her think Victor might have stolen it, so she took it before he could."

That Katie, saving the day again. "We owe that girl."

Trey scoffs. "No kidding."

Once I've got all my long waves pulled up, Trey rejoins me in bed and hooks the jewelry around my neck. The entire time, he stares me in the eyes like he wants to devour me. Maybe he does. I wouldn't mind.

I let my hair back down, then run my fingers along the diamond. "Have I ever told you how much I love this thing? It's stupid because it's just a necklace, but it means so much to me because it came from you."

"*You* mean so much to me."

Roughly, I grab the back of his neck and pull him on top

of me. He comes willingly and goes straight for my lips. His kisses are hard and desperate. Mine are just the same. The way we move so in sync only solidifies how perfect we are for each other.

I drag my shirt over my head, then shove my pants down. Once my bra is off, Trey doesn't waste a second wrapping his tongue around my nipple. I arch my head back and moan toward the ceiling as I cup the back of his head and wrench him closer.

"Oh, baby," he says against my breast. "You taste so good."

He keeps licking me as he rolls my other nipple between his thumb and fingers. I claw my way down his back until I reach his boxers and pull them down just enough to give me access to his dick. He groans into my chest as I stroke his thick shaft up and down.

"Don't be gentle with me," I say breathlessly.

As if that's what he's been waiting to hear all day, he shoves his boxers down all the way, then pulls my legs up. I rest them against his shoulders.

He slides his tip against my damp opening and moans. "Fuck. You're so wet."

"You did that to me." I gasp as he plunges into me, no warning or anything. My fingernails dig into his arms as I let out a yelp. I know I asked him not to be gentle, but I didn't expect him to shove it in *that* hard.

He plants a hand on either side of my head. "Fuck, baby. You're so tight."

I half moan, half scream as he draws back and shoves it into me again.

He stills. "Are you okay, babe?"

"Yeah," I lie through a pant. "Give me more."

He draws back and thrusts again. This time, the pain is partly pleasure. With each of his thrusts, he kisses my neck and grunts into it. His deep, guttural sounds turn me into a puddle.

I grip his shoulders as I eventually stretch to his size. After a while, the pain transforms into satisfying bliss. With each pump, his chest slides up and down mine as if he needs to be as close to me as possible. His deep groans mix with my breathless whimpers and the sounds of our bodies smacking together. I wanted it rough, but I'll accept these slow and steady thrusts for now.

"I love you, Arella," he whispers into my ear. "I love you so fucking much."

"I love you too, Trey," I say as my head bangs against the pillow over and over.

His breaths send warm air down my shoulder. "I promise I'll always love you—no matter what. And I'll always fight for you. And protect you. And treat you right. And make love to you with my whole heart like I am right now."

"Yes, Trey," I moan. "I want that. All of it. But harder."

"Harder?" He pushes himself up. "You want it harder?"

"Yes, Trey. Fuck me."

His mouth parts, then he licks his bottom lip. "Beg for it."

"Please!" I scream. "Fuck me!"

"Again."

"Please! Give it to me as hard as you can."

"Good girl." He slaps a hand on either side of my hips and keeps me against him as he gets to his knees. Then he slams his cock into me over and over. With each thrust, he yanks my hips into him so our bodies meet as hard as they can. I scream his name to the ceiling and clench my hands into the sheets.

"Fuuuck . . ." he says between grunts. "You're taking it so good, baby."

I can't respond. Not when he's pounding into me so hard like this. It's taking all my energy just to keep up with him. The mattress creaks beneath us again and again. I screw my eyes shut as the pleasure consumes all my senses. Just when I think it can't get any better, his thumb finds my clit.

"I need you to come for me," he says through moans. "I need to feel your emotions rush through my head."

I have no idea what he means by that, and now is not the time to ask, because I can't think about anything except the feel of his thumb rubbing me to my climax. Like he has before, he goes in little circles, using the perfect amount of pressure. I head straight for the edge.

"Oh, god," I breathe out. "That feels amazing."

"Tell me how you want it, baby."

"Just like that. Don't stop."

He doesn't. He doesn't go any harder or faster either. He just keeps his rhythm as he continues pumping his cock back and forth inside me and rubbing my clit. I keep my eyes closed and take in every ounce of pleasure he's giving me until I reach the edge and jump over it.

I scream out as the pleasure ripples through me. I pulse around his shaft as tingles shoot down my legs in waves. He continues rubbing me until my breathing slows into long pants and my body relaxes.

When I open my eyes, I find him staring at me through dazed blue-grays. Without wasting another second, he pulls my legs up higher and relentlessly drives into me. I grip onto his firm arms to hold myself as still as possible for him. His pumps feel even better after my orgasm. I'm so sensitive, I can feel every vein of his cock against my inner walls.

"Fuck, babe," he says through deep grunts, "I'm gonna come."

"Come inside me."

"Oh, god." He thrusts into me harder. "Beg for it, baby."

"Come inside me, Trey. Please!"

"Beg some more."

"Please! Come for me!"

"Fuuuck . . ." He thrusts a few more times before he stills, then fills me with his load. He pulsates over and over, grunting as he drains his final drops inside me. His hands lock my hips against his as if he needs to make sure I can't get away.

Don't worry, honey. I don't plan to.

After one last pump, he collapses over my chest. Together, we pant until our breaths slow.

I'm sweaty, but he's not, which is nothing new. I'll assume that has something to do with the way his body functions differently from mine.

"That was amazing," he says against my breast. "Whenever you orgasm, your emotions rush through my head."

"How?"

"I have no idea. Your immunity walls just come down— only for a few seconds though."

Interesting. "I better never fake it, then."

He chuckles a little. "I'll know it if you do."

I grab his face and guide him up to kiss me. Then I whisper against his lips, "Do you want to do that again?"

He pulls out, making me gasp. "Hell yeah."

29

ARELLA

I jolt awake, gasping for air. Everything is dark except for the little night-light in the corner. It takes me a second to remember where I am. I've been waking up in a lot of strange places lately.

Trey places a gentle hand over my waist and gives me a tender squeeze. "You're okay, babe. I'm right here."

I relax my shoulders and flop my head back over the pillow. "I had another nightmare."

"About what?"

"Lightning balls and spiky spheres of ice."

He leans in closer to caress my face. "I'm sorry, angel. I hope these nightmares don't stick around like the spider ones have."

"Me too." I let out a little sigh. "What time is it?"

"Earlier, the clock on the microwave said it was just past noon, but I have no clue if that's accurate or not."

"How long have you been awake?"

"Not long. Maybe a half hour."

I sit up and rub my eyes. "Could you turn the light on?"

Trey sits up too, and points at the light switch. It clicks, then the room brightens to life.

I squint and blink a few times before my eyes adjust to find my man in a gray polo and a pair of light wash jeans. He doesn't normally wear polos or light wash jeans. It was probably the closest thing to what he prefers to wear that he could find in here. "Telekinesis is a really cool power to have. I wish I had that."

"You have a power that's waaay cooler than mine."

"My immunity isn't a *power*, and it's not as useful as being able to move things with your mind."

"First off, your immunity *is* a power. It's not a Zordi power, but it's still a power—a powerful one at that. Second, telekinesis is my *body* power. So, it's mostly my hands doing the work. My mind plays a huge part, but without my hands, it couldn't happen."

I take a moment to let that information settle in. "There's still a lot for me to learn about the Zordi world, isn't there?"

"You know, my plan once I got you to Paris was to tell you everything about my world. I didn't wanna tell you in advance because I didn't want you to freak out and leave me before I could get you somewhere safe. You seem to be taking all this pretty well. Maybe I should have just told you. We might have avoided all this."

"No, you did the right thing by not telling me. If you had, I definitely would have left you. When I first saw people using their powers, I was terrified."

"I'm so sorry." He takes my hands into his and gives me a light peck on the knuckles. "What's the first power you saw?"

"Whatever power Victor has that makes his eyes go black."

Trey thinks, then his face scrunches together. "He doesn't have a power that makes his eyes go black."

"Yes, he does."

"Victor is an Aero, an Animal Empath, and he has enhanced taste. None of those can make his eyes go black."

"I know what I saw, Trey. He held me down, stared at my

face, then this creepy black cloud took over the whites of his eyes. I saw it multiple times."

"Hmm." His eyes gloss over in deep thought.

"While you think about that, I'm gonna go brush my teeth." I slide off the bed and head toward the bathroom.

After I've got fresh breath, I join Trey back in the bedroom. He stands in front of the nightstand with the drawer open, holding his fake passport, staring at it with a far-off look in his eyes.

I rub a palm over his shoulder. "What're you thinking about?"

He continues staring at the name *Daniel Johnson* before he sighs and sets the passport down. Then he shuts the drawer, takes my hands into his, and leads me to sit on the edge of the bed with him.

"Babe," he says through a long sigh, "I'm gonna say something to you, and it's gonna sound crazy."

"Is it crazier than telling me that our parents were killed on the same night, and that the media said I died with them, and that my name was probably Hannah Calder at one point?"

"This is equally as crazy."

I'm not sure if I can handle any more bad news, but . . . "Okay, let's hear it."

"I'm gonna go back."

I freeze as I try to comprehend what he means. "Go back?"

"I thought about it all last night and some more when I woke up this morning. Katie told me that Victor's been running tests on Immunes for the last nineteen years. Do you wanna take a wild guess as to what happened to the others?"

"I don't have to guess. I already know."

"I have to stop him. Otherwise, he'll continue killing more innocent people. So, I have to go back."

I swallow thickly. "What are you going to do?"

He stares at me without blinking. "You already know, so please don't make me say it out loud. The idea of having to do it is already making me nauseous."

I'm not going to make him say it, because he's right: I do know. I'd like to think I'm the type of person who'll talk him out of this, but seeing how the Royals at the gas station didn't hesitate to kill an innocent man, I have no compassion for them.

"Judge me if you want, but I've made my decision."

I give his hands a loving squeeze. "I'm not judging you, honey. Actually, I think this is very heroic of you."

He scoffs lightly. "I'm not doing this to be a hero. Honestly, the root of this decision is pretty selfish. We can't hole up down here for the rest of our lives. You deserve better than that, and as long as Victor is alive, you won't be safe. So, selfishly, I'm doing this for me. For you. For us. For our future family together. I won't be able to sleep knowing someone is searching for us with the intent to hurt you. And if we have kids, then what? Our babies could never live a normal life if we're always on the run. I don't want that."

I had these same thoughts yesterday when we were in Tao's Lincoln. While Trey drove, I asked myself, *When can we stop running?* After some deep thought, the answer was clear: As long as Victor is breathing, I won't be safe. I'll always have to run. The only way to stop running is to stop Victor.

I give Trey a firm nod as I make my decision too. "Okay. Let's go."

He gapes at me. "What?"

"I said, let's go."

He lets out a humorless chuckle. "No, no, no. *You're* not going. *I* am."

"I'm coming with you."

He jumps to his feet and slashes a hand through the air. "Hell no! Not in a million years. It could be dangerous."

"And that's exactly why I need to go. You won't stand a

chance against Victor and his Royal minions without my immunity protecting you."

"No. Fuck no." He shakes his head with a look in his eyes that says he won't back down. "Abso-fucking-lutely not."

I'm not going to back down either. "I said I'm coming."

"Arella, this is not the time to be difficult."

"You promised we'd be a team, remember? You protect me, and I'll protect you."

"This *is* me protecting you. You need to stay here until I come back."

I get to my feet as I cross my arms over my chest. "And what if you don't come back?"

"Then at least you'll be alive."

"But that means you aren't, which means I'm still in danger. If I go with you, at least we'll have a *chance* at winning."

He points a hand toward the ceiling. "We don't know what the situation looks like up there. When we left, the Royals had just gotten through the cavern entrance and people were dying. Then once we got through the tunnel, we were attacked by a swarm of Royals. Pixie, Ruby, and Katie held them back to give me a chance to get you to safety. They risked their lives to save you. The last thing I'm gonna do is bring you straight back to the place we fought to get you out of. Also, I have no idea which side won. If it was Victor's side, that probably means the Ridge is crawling with hundreds of Royals by now."

I put a hand over my hip. "All the more reason why I *need* to come. If it's you against hundreds, we might as well say our goodbyes now because you're definitely not coming back."

Trey's body stiffens. I know *goodbye* is a trigger word for him. I didn't mean to use it against him like that. Still, if given the choice, I wouldn't take it back. I'm right, and he knows it. If he leaves without me, it'll be the last time we ever see each other.

"Arella," he says, choking up, "I can't lose you again."

"I can't lose you either."

Roughly, he yanks me to him and smashes me against his chest. We stand there for a while, just holding each other. He doesn't say anything. He doesn't move either. This reminds me of the night he held me for the first time. It was right after he fought Nathan in my apartment, and it was the first time I had felt safe in a man's arms in years.

I tilt my head back to look at him. "Last night, you promised you'd always fight for me, right?"

"Yeah."

"How about we fight together?"

He captures my face between his hands, then plants his mouth over mine. His kiss is full of agony. As he slips his tongue between my lips, it feels like he's using me to heal himself, like he needs my kiss to quell his anxieties and kill off his demons all at once. I'll gladly be his emotional Healing Goo if it means he'll always kiss me like this.

He's about to pull away when I grab him by the collar of his polo and drag him back toward me. We embrace again until we're panting and my lips are numb.

Trey presses his forehead against mine. "All right, babe. Let's go find something to eat while we make a plan."

30

TREY

The waterfall concealing Shadow Ridge's cavern pours into a small lake. Crickets chirp throughout the darkness as Arella and I crouch behind a bush overlooking the shimmery water. I can't believe I allowed her to come. Earlier, when we stopped at a drive-thru, she went inside to use the bathroom, and I almost put that Lincoln into drive and left her there. It's not like she could have found her way to the Ridge without me. The only reason I didn't take off is because she's right. Without her immunity protecting me, I'd be waltzing straight into a death trap.

"You need me to go over the plan again?" I ask in a low voice.

"Nope. I've got it all up here." She taps her temple three times.

"Do you remember what the most important part is?"

"Yes. If you die, I need to get out of there as fast as possible."

"Right. Don't try to save me. Don't try to stop the bleeding. Just go."

She gives me a curt nod, but that defiant look in her eyes tells me she only agreed to my terms to shut me up. She's already proven that she won't leave me behind if there's even a *chance* I'll make it, and that's the part that worries me the most. If I'm about to die, I need her to forget about me and save herself.

"All right. Stay close and—" Suddenly, a bunch of people's emotions cloud my head, all coming from inside the cavern.

Arella stills, but she doesn't say anything. She just watches me with wide eyes, wondering why I've frozen up.

More emotions invade my head as ten—no, fifteen—no, twenty-some people come marching out the Ridge's entrance.

"I sense people coming out," I whisper. "They're walking through the cave now, toward the waterfall."

"How many?" she whispers back.

"Maybe close to thirty."

"Do you think they saw us on the camera feeds and are coming out to kill us?"

"I'm not sure, but they're not in a rush, nor do their emotions feel urgent." Which is why I'm so confused.

We remain where we are as I continue sensing the large group approaching the waterfall.

"Get your fucking hands off me!" a man shouts.

I'd know that voice anywhere. It's Victor, and he sounds lethal.

"Keep it moving, asshole," a woman yells back. She steps out from behind the waterfall first, making my heart drop. She's not just any woman. She's an Enforcer, a fully uniformed zovernment official, with her blonde hair tied into a tight bun at the top of her head.

From her holster, the Enforcer whips out a gun. "I said to keep it moving! Otherwise, I'll shoot you with another dose of perrizo to knock you out. Then I'll drag your ass across the ground instead. Is that what you want?"

I grip Arella's arm and hold her tight as if the Enforcer is threatening her, not Victor.

In silence, Victor steps out from behind the waterfall. He's handcuffed and attached to a long chain. On that chain are the rest of the people I sense, marching out of the cave behind him, cuffed at the wrists and fixed to the long chain. I recognize a few of the people as the leftover ZIRDA agents from before. The others, I don't recognize at all. I can only assume that means they're on Victor's side.

Three men step out from behind the waterfall, wearing the same light-blue uniform as the Enforcer woman. How many Enforcers are here? And how did they find this ZIRDA base? ZIRDA hides from the zovernment just as much as they hide from everyone else. Did someone call the Enforcers here as an attempt to get Victor arrested? If that's the case, why are the Enforcers arresting *everybody*?

"Stop at that tree and don't move," the female Enforcer yells at Victor, then marches past all the chained people and shouts down the cavern. "Did you get everyone?"

A deep male voice from behind the waterfall answers her. "We're gonna go back to do one more sweep."

"Great." The female Enforcer points at the three men in uniforms. "You guys keep an eye on these delinquents. I'm gonna go help with the sweep." As she heads back into the cave, the last people on the long chain step out.

I recognize Ruby and Katie right away. Neither woman looks too banged up. *Thank fuck.* But where is Pixie?

Just as a *whoosh* of air blows Arella's hair into my face, someone's emotions pop up behind me. Then something sharp pricks my neck, making everybody's emotions disappear from my head.

Arella yelps as she slaps a hand over her neck. "Ow."

Suddenly, my wrists are heavy. A pair of thick cuffs has appeared around them. Arella's wrists are cuffed too. They're so heavy, they make her fall over into the grass.

Another *whoosh*, then a slender Hispanic man in a light-blue uniform stops running in front of me. He presses a finger against the wired device in his ears. "I found two more hiding in the woods. They were on their way back in when they saw us coming out." The man pauses for a moment, then says, "Yes, ma'am. I'll add them to the chain."

"Wait, no," I say. "We're not with them."

"Yeah, sure. I've *never* heard that one before." In a mocking, high-pitched voice, he says, "No! I'm not a Royal. I haven't committed any crimes or killed any Ordinaries."

"We haven't."

"Yeah, yeah. Good try. Now, get up, and don't try to run. You won't get far."

Even if this man wasn't a Speeder, I wouldn't try to run. I've been trying to make a fireball appear in my hands while he talked, and I haven't seen a single spark.

Katie gapes at me and Arella as we step out of the tree line with the Enforcer behind us. "Trey?"

"What the hell are you two doing back here?" Ruby says.

"Where's Pixie?" I ask because that's the more important question.

Ruby shakes her head. In a choked voice, she says, "At least she went down doing what she loved most—kicking a Royal's ass."

A little piece of my heart breaks for that strong woman I barely knew. She spent more time torturing the hell outta my ears than anything, but in the end, she helped save me and Arella. She's a fucking hero in my book.

The Speeder attaches Arella to the chain first, then he does the same to me.

"You okay, babe?" I ask.

She offers me a slight nod. "You?"

I nod back. Physically, yes, I'm okay. Emotionally, I'm fucking terrified. *How the hell are we gonna get outta this one?*

The Speeder presses a finger to the device in his ears. "Y'all almost done in there?" A pause. "Cool. I'll do another sweep of the perimeter."

With a *whoosh*, the man is gone.

I eye the other three Enforcers guarding the people in cuffs. Each Enforcer looks like he could easily toss a tank over a building.

I turn to Katie and ask in a whisper, "What happened after I left?"

"We kept those Royals away from you for as long as we could. But after they killed Pixie and knocked Ruby unconscious, I surrendered. By that point, it was six against one, and all I could do was hope that you'd gotten far enough away. After that, Victor ordered his people to lock up all the agents in the cells. In case you can't tell, there aren't many of us left."

I cock my head to the side. "The cells?"

"You know, like, jail cells?" She flashes me a *duh* look. "That's where Victor has contained us for the last day or so."

"I didn't know there were jail cells here." Which is stupid, because I lived here for almost eleven years. Victor probably keeps the cells hidden in one of the many areas he forbade me from wandering around.

Katie continues, "We think he was keeping us alive for a possible ransom from ZIRDA or to torture us for information. We were in the middle of plotting an escape when the Ridge got raided by the Enforcers. They think this is a Royals hideout. We tried telling them that we're ZIRDA agents, until the Royals started doing the same. Since the Enforcers can't tell who is on what side, they're taking us all to z-prison. They said once we prove our innocence, we'll be released."

"That's right," the biggest Enforcer says from where he stands. "We'll be interrogating you all thoroughly, so you bestah get yo stories straight."

"Settle down, Cameron," the Enforcer closest to Victor says.

"Don't you tell me to settle down," Cameron says. "A Royal killed my son. I live for moments like this."

From inside the cavern, a woman babbles words so fast, I can't make them out.

"Please, you have to believe me," the woman says. "You—"

"I told you, lady," a man says, cutting her off, "you can prove your innocence to the Keepers."

"But you have to listen to me," the lady says. "I'm not a criminal."

When she steps out from behind the waterfall, I can't believe my eyes. "Aunt Jodi?"

Her skin looks unhealthily pale, and she's skinnier and more frail-looking than I remember, but it's definitely her. I'd recognize her anywhere, because that's the face of the woman who used to glare at me just for walking past her.

Jodi continues rambling as an Enforcer secures her handcuffs to the end of the chain behind me. "No, please! You have to listen to me. That man over there is not who he says he is."

I can't believe it's really her. I haven't seen her since I was six.

"I've been imprisoned here for twenty years!" she shouts as the Enforcer ignores her and huffs his way back into the cave. "I'm not a criminal!"

Is that true? Has Victor really kept his wife locked up here this whole time? Victor told my parents that Jodi packed up all her stuff and left, leaving behind only a note about finding her soul mate. I guess since that story came from Victor's lips, none of it is to be trusted.

"Aunt Jodi?" I say, cutting into whatever she's yelling to the Enforcers.

She flicks her attention to me, then her entire face drops. At first, she doesn't say anything; she just stares. The way she's looking at me isn't the way she used to look at me when I was a kid. There's no disgust, no loathing, not even an ounce of hatred in her eyes. Instead, she's looking at me like she's trying to figure out if I'm real.

"Trey?" My name leaves her mouth in a soft whisper.

"Yep," I say with a nod.

"Oh, god." She chokes up as tears stream down her pale cheeks. "Trey. You—you're so grown up."

"Well," I say dryly, "it's been, like, twenty fucking years."

She places her hands on my forearm, and it takes everything in me not to throw her off. "Trey, listen to me. You have to believe me, because these damn Enforcers won't."

"Shut up, Jodi!" Victor shouts from the front of the chain. "Shut your goddamn mouth."

Jodi ignores him. "Listen, I'm not Jodi. She's a fucking liar, and so are her goddamn parents. They lied about her mind power because it's on the Extinction List. Jodi doesn't have a photographic memory, like they made everyone believe. She's a Mind Swapper. Twenty years ago, she stole my body. I haven't seen a single ray of sunshine until just now. Please, you have to believe me."

I suck in a long breath as I muster up the courage to ask the question I think I already know the answer to. "If you're not Jodi, then who are you?"

"I'm Victor."

31

TREY

"Sʜᴜᴛ ʏᴏᴜʀ ᴍᴏᴜᴛʜ, Jᴏᴅɪ, ᴏʀ I'ʟʟ ꜰᴜᴄᴋɪɴɢ ᴋɪʟʟ ʏᴏᴜ," Victor shouts. The chains rattle as he points a stern finger at me. "I'll kill him too."

Jodi shakes my forearm to grab my attention back. "Remember that one time we made a blanket fort? We ate spray cheese out of the can, and you told me you had a crush on a girl at your Zordi school. Oh, what was her name? God, I can't remember. Maybe that's not the best way to prove—"

"Don't listen to her," Victor says. "She's a goddamn liar."

Jodi ignores him again. "One time, I took you to the zoo. It was just you and me. When we got to the open aviary, you grabbed one of the small birds walking around and stuck it down your shirt. You wanted to take it home. No matter what I said to you, you refused to let the bird go. Eventually, the zookeepers got the bird out of your grasp, and they kicked us out. Do you remember that?"

I shake my head. "I don't remember ever going to a zoo."

"That's because she's a liar!" Victor says. "She's making this all up to try to save her skin."

All thirty-ish people hooked to this long chain between me and Victor gawk at us with wide eyes and silent mouths. The

335

three Enforcers guarding us are silent too. Like me, they're probably unsure what to believe.

Jodi takes her hands off me and runs them through her greasy, matted hair. The chains clink against her thick handcuffs as she thinks. "Oh! I know! One Christmas morning, I came over early and we snuck down to the tree. We opened up those Nerf guns I got you. While we played, you bumped into the tree and—"

"Stop!" I shout so loudly, it makes Arella jolt back a step. I lock my attention onto Victor. "What happened next?"

"Huh?" he says.

"If you're really Victor, then you'll know what happened after I bumped into the Christmas tree."

He scoffs condescendingly. "Of course I know what happened. You tipped it over."

I turn my attention back to Jodi, whom I'm now pretty sure isn't Jodi. "What happened next?"

"You broke your mama's crystal angel ornament."

"And?"

"The wings broke off. We spent the rest of that morning trying to glue it back together but ended up breaking the head off too, so we dumped the thing in the neighbor's trash bin and made a pact to never tell anyone. That's how we came up with our secret word."

"Which is?"

Jodi doesn't hesitate. "Crystal."

I choke up as the realization sinks in. This whole time, it wasn't my sweet Uncle V who abused me and called me names. It was Jodi in Victor's body. Now that I think about it, it makes sense. It was always Jodi who treated me like shit, not Victor. This whole time, I thought he started treating me like that because he was sad about losing his wife. Turns out, he did it because his wife stole his goddamn body. *What the fuck?*

"So?" Cameron says, breaking the silence. "Who got it right?"

"Yeah," another Enforcer says from behind me, "we wanna know."

"Jodi is correct," I say, then shake my head. "I mean Victor. More specifically, Victor in Jodi's body."

Cameron chuckles to himself, shaking his head. "Damn. The Keepers gon' have a heyday with this one. A Mind Swapper? I thought them fuckers was extinct by now."

This explains why Arella saw Victor's eyes go black. It was Jodi trying to swap minds with Arella. I can't imagine what would happen if it had worked. For someone as toxic as Jodi to have immunity? I don't want to know all the things she'd do with that ability.

My dad places his female hands over my forearm again. "Jodi told me your mama's dead. Is that true?"

The pain in his eyes makes me think about lying, but I can't do that to him. "Jodi blew her up. She blew up both my parents."

"I didn't blow up anyone," Jodi sneers from Victor's body. It's disgusting that her mind has been living in my dad's head for this long and no one knew it. "They blew themselves up. My men's orders were only to detain Suzie and Andy. I had plans to torture them in front of Victor. Whatever happened that night, they killed themselves and took my men with them. I had nothing to do with it."

It's official: Jodi is a fucking nutcase. Abusing me is one thing, but keeping her husband locked up for twenty years, with plans to torture people in front of him for her pure enjoyment? Nutcase.

"Why didn't you kill me when you could?" I shout at Jodi. "I was seven. It would have been easy to get rid of me. Why keep me around for so long?"

If she tells me she kept me around just to torture me too, I won't be surprised.

Jodi chuckles deep from Victor's throat. "I had just killed Debbie and made it look like an overdose. That same night, your parents blew themselves up. How was I supposed to kill you too without raising suspicion? One death is an accident. Two is tragic. Three is a pattern. With the cops and social workers up my ass, it was either keep you alive or get investigated."

"What?" my dad shouts. "You told me Debbie took Trey in! You fucking lied!"

"Of course I did! I couldn't tell you that he was living on the floor right above you."

"What?" my dad turns to me. "Trey, you—you lived here?"

"Yep," I say. "From the day after the explosion, I lived here until the day I turned eighteen, when she kicked me out."

My dad gapes at me, then at Jodi. "You heartless bitch!" He runs at her with his fists up. He doesn't get very far though. The chains connecting him to me and thirty-some other people stop him. "You stole my body, locked me up for twenty years, and the whole time, you kept my son away from me right above my head!"

The Enforcers on the sidelines aim a perrizo gun at my dad, but they don't shoot him.

"You're a psycho!" my dad says. "A deranged lunatic!"

"And you were screwing around with your sister-in-law behind my back!" Jodi shouts. "Then you had a fucking baby with her and tried to hide it from me. I knew the second you laid eyes on Trey that he was yours. Nobody looks at a little boy like that unless they know it's their son."

Everything makes sense now. That's why Jodi always treated me like I was diseased. The whole time, she knew about Victor's affair. She knew I was his son.

Jodi glares at me. "Why don't you look surprised?"

I shrug nonchalantly. "Because I already knew."

"That Victor is your real father?"

"Yep."

My dad drops his jaw—well, technically, he drops Jodi's jaw. "How long have you known?"

"Since yesterday. Li and Tao told me."

"I knew it!" Jodi sneers. "Those chinks must have been hiding you underground somewhere."

My opinion of Jodi was already low based on my memories of her. It dipped even lower after I found out she's a Royal who stole my real father's body. Now she's racist too? What's next? Is she a pedophile? A Nazi? An animal abuser? I wouldn't be surprised by any of those.

In the corner of my eye, I see Cameron press a finger against his earpiece. "Nah, he ain't back yet." A pause, then he turns to one of the other Enforcers. "How long do ya think Eduardo's been gone for?"

The man shrugs. "A few minutes?"

"Hmm. He doesn't usually take that long to run the perimeter. Apparently, he's not responding to—"

BOOM!

The tree behind Cameron explodes, rocketing chunks of wood through the air. Cameron falls over and doesn't get back up. Screams echo around me as I instinctively leap in front of Arella and cover her with my body.

"We're under attack!" an Enforcer shouts.

A mass of people burst out from the tree line. Lightning balls sizzle through the air. A flaming fireball hits an Enforcer in the back and sets him on fire.

"Send backup now!" the Enforcer behind me shouts.

The chain line explodes with a deafening *BOOM!*, releasing everyone from it. With my cuffs still on, I grab Arella's arm and yank her toward me.

Then I shout at Katie over the screaming. "Please tell me these people are from your ZIRDA base!"

"No!" Katie yells over another loud *BOOM!* "They're Royals! Look!"

My attention whips to where she's pointing. A woman with

short brown hair opens her palms toward Jodi's cuffs. With a smaller *boom!*, the cuffs fall off Jodi's wrists. With each small explosion, the heavy metal falls off all the Royals' wrists.

"Grab the Immune!" Jodi shouts, pointing at Arella.

My heart sinks as a bunch of large men charge toward my girl. Ruby and Katie step in front of her with their cuffed fists up. I know exactly which side people are on by the way they either help protect Arella or try to fight their way past the human wall surrounding me and her.

I keep Arella close to me as a fireball flies straight toward Katie's face. She screams with her arms up to block it. The fireball stops barely an arm away from her, then rolls to the ground and smokes out.

Katie's eyes bulge as another fireball rockets toward her face. The flames hit the same invisible wall, fall to the grass, then smoke out.

I gawk at Arella, who's got her eyes trained on the other element balls launching toward the people surrounding her. Each ball stops in the air, then disappears.

"What the hell?" a Royal shouts.

"It's you, isn't it?" Ruby says to Arella.

"I don't know how long I can do this," Arella says as she stops an ice ball from crashing over Katie's head. It falls to the ground and shatters into pieces.

"Keep that up!" Ruby says, then she runs toward the guy running at her with a knife in his hands. She ducks his weapon, then turns and kicks him in the back. Using her heavy metal cuffs, she bangs him on the head, and he drops to the ground.

As the Royals close in on us, the people surrounding Arella use their cuffs to keep the Royals away from her. People shout and cry out as they fight each other. From the corner of my eye, I see two men in cuffs charge at me, each one holding a knife in his hands. Katie tackles one to the ground while I kick the other in his gut. Then I bash my cuffs against his face. It only takes one hit for him to drop his knife, but it takes another hit for him to slump to the ground.

"Get off me, asshole!" Katie struggles with the man straddling her. He's trying to dig his knife into her neck. I rush up beside him and bang my cuffs against the side of his face. He yelps, then falls onto his shoulder. Katie picks up the knife he dropped and drives it straight into his stomach. He cries out again.

A woman charges at me with a water ball in her palm. It hits me in the face, drenching me with an icy-cold liquid. Agony explodes up my jaw as she punches me, then kicks me in the stomach.

"Get away from my son!" My dad tackles the woman into the grass. Then they roll around, punching at each other. The woman straddles my dad's frail body and drenches his face with a steady stream of water.

I'm about to help him when Arella screams out from behind me. I twist around on my heel, then gasp. A thick man has Arella by her neck in one hand and a knife in his other. As I run to save her, the man draws the knife back and aims it at her stomach.

"No!" Katie shoves Arella out of the way. Then she screams as the man drives the knife straight into her side. She cries out as the man pulls the knife back and aims for her throat.

I grab the man by the back of his shirt and yank him away from her. He stumbles, falling onto his ass. Then I heave my cuffs into his face.

Then again.

And again.

Once he limply thuds onto the ground, I stop.

"Trey!" Arella is hunched over Katie, putting pressure over the knife wound in Katie's stomach. "Help me! We have to save her!"

I kneel at Katie's side. The glint of bloody metal sticking

out of her neck makes my lungs stop working. Her body shakes as she gurgles, then she goes limp and her head droops over.

Of all the people to die, I never wanted any of them to be Katie.

"Come on, Trey!" Arella cries. "Help me!"

I choke up as I grab Arella by her arm. "Babe, she's gone."

"No! She can't be!"

I drag Arella off the grass to meet my eyes. Her bloody hands tremble against my shirt. "We can't save her, Arella. She's gone."

"No!" Tears stream down her face as her knees buckle. "Katie!"

"I'm so s—" The wind gets knocked out of me as someone tackles me into the dirt. Jodi in Victor's body climbs on top of me and jabs something sharp into my side. I gasp for air as pain ripples through my stomach and down my leg. I feel every agonizing inch of the dagger as Jodi slides it out of my body.

She raises the weapon into the air again and spits into my face. "You worthless piece of shit! I never should have—" She flies off me as someone yanks her away.

"That's my son!" My dad climbs on top of Jodi and bashes his cuffs against her face. Then he grabs Jodi's dagger and drives it into her chest.

"Trey!" Arella drops to her knees at my side, putting pressure over my wound. "Oh, god!"

I groan in pain as Jodi kicks my dad's skinny body off her. Then she straddles my dad and stabs him in the stomach with the same dagger she just pulled out of her chest.

"No!" I scream as Jodi stabs him again, then again, and again.

My dad screams until his female body goes limp. Then he's not screaming anymore.

"Nooo!" I jerk upright, then everything stills. I try to stand up, but I can't. I can't even blink. All the screaming around me stops, and the air goes silent like we're in a library.

Jodi freezes on top of my dad. Her knife hand is drawn back, but she's not making a single move. A fireball flying above me is frozen in midair. The flames don't dance. The wind doesn't blow the trees. The crickets don't chirp.

Arella's mouth falls open at the hush surrounding us.

"Holy shit!" a man shouts from barely ten steps away. "That one just moved."

"That's impossible," a woman says. "I just froze everything except us within a quarter-mile radius."

"I swear, I saw that girl move."

"Which one?"

Arella stills, but her hands tremble against my wound. I reach out to protect her, but my arms don't budge. My heart races as two pairs of footsteps stomp their way toward us.

A male Enforcer I haven't seen before steps into my view and points a firm finger at Arella. "It was this woman right here."

The female Enforcer at his side produces a water ball in her hand, then drops it over Arella's head.

Arella gasps for air as the chilly liquid drenches her and drips onto my chest. I can feel the bitter cold, but my body doesn't react to it.

"What?" The female Enforcer grabs Arella by her arm and drags her onto her feet.

"Let me go!" Arella screams, making my heart thrash against my tight lungs.

"How are you doing that?" the female Enforcer asks, then gasps. "Oh my god! She's an Ordinary."

The male Enforcer presses a finger against the device in his ears. "Yes, we just arrived. Everything is under control now. Everyone's been immobilized. We're ready for the other Porters." A pause. "Sounds good. And boss, you're not gonna believe this, but there's an Ordinary here, and she's moving." Another pause. "I mean exactly what I said. I'm standing right next to her, and my zense isn't activating. Not only that, but she can move, even after the immobilization." Another pause. This time, it's longer. "Aye. We'll take her in for a scrub."

"No!" Arella tries hitting the female Enforcer with her cuffs, but it's no use.

The female Enforcer shoves Arella to her knees, then points a gun at her neck. I try to protect her, but my limbs won't budge.

"Stay down," she says, then turns to her partner. "What if the scrub doesn't work on her like my immobilization isn't?"

The male Enforcer shrugs. "I guess we'll find out."

SCRUBBED MIND

SECRETS TRILOGY: BOOK 3

A ZORDI WORLD NOVEL
SECRETS
TRILOGY
3
SCRUBBED MIND
THEY TOOK HER AWAY.
NOW HE'S TAKING HER BACK.
MELISSA LAM

1

TREY

I bang a fist against the wood table. "Where is she?"

The Keeper sitting across from me sighs. With the long sleeve of his navy-blue uniform, he rubs the fingerprints off the golden nameplate pinned to his upper chest. It reads ORTIZ. "Mr. Grant, if you don't want to cooperate with me, I'm happy to ask the Enforcers to put you back behind bars until you do. Now answer my question."

I burst out of my metal chair. It falls behind me with a *clank!* against the hard floor of this stuffy interrogation room. This bullshit little space is barely bigger than a bathroom stall. Plus, it's musty, it's windowless, and, most of all, it's Arella-less.

"I've been cooperating with you for the last three days!" I shout at the useless example of a Superior in front of me. "Now I'm done cooperating, because every time I ask you where she is, you refuse to answer. If you don't tell me now, I'll tear this whole place apart until I find her!" *And that's a fucking promise.*

Ortiz leans back in his chair and chuckles. "This prison is packed with Enforcers whose powers aren't subdued by perrizo—while yours are. How do you plan to tear this place apart without your gifts?"

Each injection of perrizophine forced onto every inmate is supposed to last twelve hours. To ensure there's never a chance an inmate's perrizo has worn off before their next injection, doses are handed out like candy every eight hours.

I never realized how much I relied on my Empath power until now. I have to pay attention to people's facial expressions and body language to guess how they're feeling. Even then, it's just a guess. When I get outta here, I'm never talking shit about my mind power ever again. And I say *when* because it's a matter of when, not if.

Three days ago, I woke up in a large holding cell, surrounded by the remaining ZIRDA (Zordinary Innovations Research and Development Agency) agents and double that number of Royals, the chaotic assholes who think all Zordis are better than Ordinaries, just because we were born with powers—something outside of our control. The Enforcers stated that if we could prove we hadn't broken any laws, they'd let us go.

One by one, they took us into an interrogation room. Depending on our answers to their questions, a Detector on the other side of the wall either confirmed that our words are true or that we've lied.

On day one, every Royal was taken out of the holding cell, interrogated, then relocated to separate cells to await their trials that will determine how long they'll be incarcerated for. Depending on the severity of their crimes, they could be trapped in prison for the rest of their lives. I hope that's the case for all of them.

As for the ZIRDA agents, they were also interrogated on day one, then released within twenty minutes of their interrogations starting. I'm not that great at math, but I'm good enough to know that three days is a hell of a lot longer than twenty minutes.

The first ZIRDA agent to be freed was Ruby. She was also the only person left I knew by name. Everyone else I knew by name had been killed: Dash the Speeder, who helped me get Arella out of Shadow Ridge by making sure the hidden tunnel was safe. Carlos the security guard, who helped fend off the Royals while I got Arella to safety. Pixie the Ear Blower, who was barely twenty years old and one of the bravest people I've ever known.

The youngest to die was Katie. She's the one I owe the most. She preloaded some perrizo guns for me, which was crucial in our escape. Katie is also the one who pushed Arella out of the way when a Royal tried to stab her with a knife. Sadly, Katie ended up on the other end of that knife.

I barely had time to process Katie's death before Aunt Jodi, in Victor's body, stabbed me in the side. Then Victor, in Jodi's body, tackled her to the ground. They tried to kill each other until the Enforcers showed up seconds later, but it was too late. Victor—who I thought for all my life was my uncle but was really my dad—had already stopped breathing.

Jodi had suffered some injuries too—a few blows to the head and a dagger to the chest. She didn't make it long enough to see the prison's Healer. I did, though, and now I don't even have a scar to memorialize that battle.

I'd like to say I've had a moment to mourn the loss of my dad, but I've been too busy trying to figure out what the zovernment has done with my girl and wondering why they're still keeping me here when they've already deemed me innocent.

They're not holding me for being a Royal, nor are they holding me for committing crimes as a ZIRDA agent. Surprisingly, they aren't holding me for exposure to an Ordinary either. After their many questions, all of which I answered with the truth, they determined that since I used my powers to protect Arella and only did it *after* she'd already found out about the existence of Zordinaries, they're dropping the charges.

So if I'm not being convicted for anything, why am I still

here? More importantly, why am I talking to a Keeper? Keepers are high-level zovernment officials who make the laws. Enforcers are the ones who enforce those laws. The people who were arrested with me were all interrogated by Enforcers, which makes sense because this is mid-level Enforcer work. So why is there a *Keeper* sitting in front of me?

Ortiz points at my knocked-over chair. "Pick that up, sit your ass down, and answer my question."

Glaring at the man, I scoop up my chair and set it upright with a *clank!* Then I plant myself back onto the metal and cross my arms with a huff.

"What else do you know about her immunity?" Ortiz asks for the third time. Since he's so insistent about getting my answer to this question, I'm gonna assume *this* is why they're still keeping me around. Arella must be an anomaly to the zovernment too.

"I've already told you everything I know."

Like it did the last two times I said that, a device on the wall glows red with the word LIE. Whoever that Detector is who keeps pressing that LIE button on the other side of that wall needs to stop.

This Keeper already knows I was sent on a mission to find out the source of Arella's immunity. He also knows I never found it. I told him that she was able to project her immunity onto me multiple times. I even told him the way she did it was by imagining waves of water drenching me. I've told him everything I know—except one thing.

What I haven't told him is that I was able to break through Arella's immunity walls by making her orgasm. I don't want the zovernment knowing that, for two reasons: First, I don't want them to take advantage of that knowledge and scrub her memories. Second, they've already let me off the hook for fake-dating an Ordinary. I doubt they'll be as relenting if they find out I had sex with her too.

Sadly, getting locked up for that is the least of my worries.

My biggest concern is that they'll find out Arella and I were able to conceive, even though it's biologically impossible for us to do so. I still have no idea how that happened, and it doesn't matter. What matters now is that the Keepers don't find out about it. Who knows what they'll do with that information. If it's anything close to dissecting Arella to study her reproductive organs, fuck that. This is why I need to know where she is, because if they've already locked her up for research, then I need to bust her out.

"You can't tell lies in here." Ortiz folds his hands together over the table. "So how about you stop wasting—"

Knock-knock.

The door unlocks, then opens to reveal a slender Asian woman in a fancy-ass burgundy suit. Her heels clack against the floor as she lets herself into the room. "Thank you for your time, Mr. Ortiz. You may dismiss yourself."

Ortiz lets out a scoff and wrinkles his face together. "Excuse me? I'm in the middle of an interrogation. Who are you?"

In a sweet tone, the twenty-something woman says, "I'm Mia Wang, Executive Keeper."

"Executive Keeper?" Ortiz chuckles under his breath. "Yeah, right. Those people never come out from behind their desks."

"I assure you, Mr. Ortiz, when needed, we do *come out from behind our desks*. I am here to speak to Mr. Grant. Therefore, you are no longer needed." Mia gestures a shooing hand out the door again.

Ortiz remains in his seat. "You can't be serious. Where is your badge?"

Without hesitation, Mia pulls back the left collar of her silky shirt and suit jacket. Right over her heart is the *official crest of the Keepers* branded into her skin. It's something I've only ever seen in books. Only the highest level Executive Keepers get that symbol branded onto their skin. They're the

Executive Keepers who are allowed more information than the other executives and the lower level Keepers—like this toe-jam sniffer who's just dropped his jaw.

It doesn't take more than a second for Ortiz to hop onto his feet and scurry out the door. With an apologetic smile, he closes and locks my precious exit behind him.

Mia makes her way to Ortiz's newly vacated chair and sits. With a smile, she says, "How are you today, Mr. Grant?"

I'm not fooled by her gentle voice or the way she just asked that question like she actually cares about my answer. "Been better."

"I hear you've been pretty concerned about the Ordinary the Enforcers found you with."

Concerned is not the right word for it. Obsessively tormented over her well-being is more accurate. "Where is she?"

Like Ortiz, Mia doesn't answer me. "I only have one question, Mr. Grant. Once you answer it, you'll be free to go."

My heart thrashes like it's trying to escape from my chest. Whatever this lady wants to ask me can't be good. "What do you mean by *free to go*?"

"As in, you're welcome to leave." She says that too casually. Like, *waaay* too casually.

"After I proved my innocence, you Supes have kept me drugged up here for three days while interrogating me for hours on end. All of a sudden, an Executive Keeper with the official crest shows up and tells me I just have to answer one question, then I'll be *free to go*?"

"Yes, sir."

I can't think of what information this woman wants from me that would grant me my freedom. "What's your question?"

"My question is: When Miss Rance was kidnapped, did you feel the glimmer?"

My eyes go wide because that is the farthest thing from what I expected her to ask me.

Since falling in love with Arella, I've felt the glimmer three times. The first time was when she was attacked by spiders. The second time was when she was in a bad car accident. The third time was after she realized she was kidnapped. Each time, nausea took over my body, my limbs went numb, and my chest felt tight like someone had a vise grip on it.

"Your honesty is important, Mr. Grant." Mia stares me down with an impassive look.

Without my Empath power, I can't even begin to figure out what this woman is up to. A Zordi can only feel the glimmer when their *soul mate* is in danger. We're taught in Zordi school that our kind is meant to be with *only* our kind. So why did this Keeper even think to ask if I felt the glimmer with an *Ordinary*?

Does the zovernment already know it's possible for us to be soul mates with Ordinaries? Does that mean they also know it's possible for our kinds to reproduce together? Based on what this Keeper is asking me, yes.

Why does it not surprise me to find out that the zovernment spreads false information? I guess after finding out that Aunt Jodi stole Victor's body for over twenty years and that my uncle is actually my biological father, nothing can shock me now.

I must be taking too long to answer, because Mia says, "I'm just looking for a simple yes or no, Mr. Grant. Did you feel the glimmer when Miss Rance was kidnapped?"

Should I lie? If I do, that stupid device on the wall will glow red again. Why does knowing if Arella is my soul mate or not matter anyway? And why is it so important that they had to send an Executive Keeper to ask me about it? In America, the Executive Keepers are based in New York City. Did this lady come to California all the way from New York just to ask me *one* question?

I repeat her words in my head. *When Miss Rance was*

kidnapped, did you feel the glimmer? Suddenly, it hits me: The keyword here is *when.*

"No," I say, because technically, I didn't. Arella was sedated in her sleep before she was taken, so she didn't know she was in danger until *after* she woke up. The glimmer doesn't activate if the person in danger doesn't know they're in danger.

Mia glances at the wall, where a light glows green with the word TRUTH. She narrows her eyes at me as she thinks for a moment. She's smarter than I thought, because within a few heartbeats, she clears her throat and asks, "Did you ever feel the glimmer *after* she was kidnapped? Maybe once she woke up from the sedatives the Royals injected her with?"

I go silent again. How do they know Arella was drugged? Did they interrogate her too?

My hesitation makes Mia stare at me. "Again, Mr. Grant, your honesty is important."

I lean back into my chair and side-eye her. "Important for what?"

"That's classified information."

"Classified?" I scoff. "Like how you Keepers are keeping millions of Zordis away from their possible Ordi soul mates?"

A slight smile turns up the corners of Mia's lips. "So you admit you felt the glimmer?"

I lean over the table and lower my voice. "How can you live with yourself? We have the right to be with our soul mates, even if they're Ordis."

Mia leans toward me as she, too, lowers her voice. "That's a small price to pay to keep our kind safe, don't you think? Can you imagine what would happen if we openly told the general public that it's possible for Ordinaries to be our soul mates? Our kind would expose themselves left and right in retaliation. Then once the Ordinaries find out about us, they'll want to get rid of us again.

"Our kind cannot survive another mass genocide. Plus, it'll

be harder for our Scrubbers to do another worldwide scrub. People have more technology now than they did back then. The Ordinaries will come after us with more than just poison. Knowing where Miss Rance is will be the least of your worries."

I hate to admit it, but this Keeper is right. Ordinaries are not ready to know about the Zordi world again. They're too fearful of anything they don't understand. There would be more than just murders and genocides. The world would erupt into chaos.

Mia presses her back against her chair. "Final question, Mr. Grant, then I will see you out the door."

"You said I only had to answer one question, then I was free to go. I've answered it. Now let me go."

She ignores me. "Did you know she was pregnant with your child?"

I try to keep my face impassive because I don't want to give her an answer. Unfortunately, my silence and lack of shock are all the answer she needs.

Mia's chair squeals as she pushes it back and stands up. "Thank you for your time today, Mr. Grant. I'll walk you outside."

I stay where I am. "That's it?"

"Yes, sir. That's it." Her heels *clack-clack-clack* as she heads toward the door.

What is going on? This Keeper just found out that I broke the second most enforced Zordi law—to never engage in sexual activities with an Ordinary—and now she's just gonna let me go? Wait . . . why the hell am I questioning this? If she's freeing me, why am I still sitting here?

Fifteen minutes later, I'm out of my z-prison jumpsuit and wearing the clothes I was arrested in: some light-wash jeans and a gray polo with a slit in the side from where Aunt Jodi stabbed me. All the bloodstains have been washed out, which I'm not mad about. Some of that blood was Katie's, and I don't need to walk around with a display of sacrifice all over me.

When I step out of the bathroom in my laundered outfit, Mia says, "Follow me."

At the prison's main entrance, a gray-haired man in a light-blue Enforcer uniform waits for us with my leather jacket neatly folded in his palms. On top of my jacket is my wallet.

"Thank you," I say as I shove my wallet into my back pocket, then slip into my jacket. With it on, I feel closer to normal, although I won't feel completely normal until I'm holding Arella again. That's why the moment the Enforcer disappears behind a door marked MAIN OFFICE, I turn to Mia.

"Where is she?"

As if she can't hear me, Mia opens one of the double doors, then holds it wide for me. Sunlight shines onto my shoes, the first glimpse of the outside I've had since being arrested. I'm about to take a step out when I stop. What if this is a trick? Having sex with an Ordinary is a huge offense. To the zovernment, *for a ZIRDA mission* is not a valid excuse for breaking the law. Why are they just letting me go?

"Are you hesitating because you'd rather stay behind bars?" Mia asks.

Fuck that. I step out into the bright September sun and squint. It only takes a second for my Zordi eyes to adjust, then I can see clearly. I'm no expert, but based on where the sun is, I'd say it's three o'clockish.

Mia joins me outside, then clicks the door shut behind her. "What time was your last dose of perrizophine?"

"Around ten this morning."

"Great. That dose should wear off around ten tonight. When it does, drink lots of Healing Water. It'll help counteract some of the side effects from coming off a long period of being under perrizo. Since your time here was short, I expect your side effects to be minor compared to the people who leave z-prison after decades of being locked up. If the side effects become unbearable, try eating some bananas. For some reason, they help."

Healing Water. Bananas. Got it. Now back to the important stuff. Since the way I asked my question before didn't yield results, I reword it. "Do you know where Arella is?"

Mia ignores my question again. "Do you know where *you* are?"

"The z-prison in Corcoran."

"Correct. On the outside of these brick walls is a van waiting to take you home. We don't normally give inmates rides. Given your situation, I pulled some strings to arrange it for you."

My situation? What does that mean? Is she talking about how I didn't know I was going to be released today, or that I don't have any family to come pick me up? Either way, I appreciate the ride.

Mia continues, "The driver has specific instructions to take you home and nowhere else, so don't even try."

"In other words, don't ask him to take me to wherever you're keeping Arella?"

Mia lets out a big sigh. "Mr. Grant, we aren't keeping Miss Rance anywhere. She's safe at home, where she has been since this morning."

Since this morning? That means they've kept her for the last three days too. Is that why they're finally letting me go? They finished their studies on her, and now they don't need to keep me locked up anymore? That's some bullshit.

I try not to sound angry. "Why did you guys keep her for that long?"

Mia blinks up at me with an expression I can't read. For a second, I think she's about to answer my question, until she turns back toward the doors and opens one. "If you know what's good for you, Mr. Grant, you'll stay away from her."

My anger comes out this time. "Why did you guys keep her for that long?"

"Don't forget about the bananas, okay? They really do help." Without another word, she disappears behind the door, and it clicks shut.

I think about rushing back in and demanding that she tell me what they did with Arella for three whole days, but I doubt that will help anything. Plus, now that I know where my girl is, I feel a pull to head straight there.

Three and a half torturous hours later, the van driver drops me off outside my home. No matter what I said to him, he refused to take me to Arella's apartment.

I race to open my garage. The loud door lifts to reveal only my car. *Shit.* I'd forgotten I ditched my motorcycle on the side of a road after I got Arella out of Shadow Ridge. My bike would have been faster, but my car will do.

Since running inside to find my keys will waste precious time, I plant myself behind the steering wheel and wave a hand at the ignition. Nothing happens, so I do it again. Then I facepalm myself. *I'm such an idiot.* If my empathy power isn't working, then my telekinesis isn't either.

I sprint through my house to find my keys. Once I do, I'm back in my car with the engine started.

———

THE OUTSIDE OF ARELLA'S APARTMENT LOOKS THE SAME AS IT always does. The car I bought for her is parked in her usual spot. I pull my Lexus right up next to it, then half run, half stumble toward her door.

Knock-knock-knock.

My hands shake against my leg as I wait for the door to open. I'm itching to hold her. I need my world to feel right again.

When the barrier keeping her from me finally opens, my heart fills with relief. There she is, and she looks unharmed. Her long chestnut hair cascades down her shoulders in soft waves. The hem of her white sundress falls just above her knees. Her eyes are warm and gentle—the way they always are. She looks like an angel. Partly because she's so beautiful, partly because I can't believe she's finally standing in front of me.

"Arella." Her name comes out breathily as I scoop her into my arms and crush her against my chest. "I've been so worried about you. Are you okay? Please tell me you're okay."

She doesn't return my hug or melt into my body the way she normally does. Instead, she goes stiff. Then she pushes herself out of my grasp and takes a step back. "Um, yeah? I'm okay."

I keep examining her arms and legs, looking for any signs of cuts or bruises. "Did they hurt you?"

She cocks her head to the side and creases her eyebrows together. "Um, no?"

I slap a palm over my heart. "Oh, thank fuck. I'm so glad you're—"

A movement on Arella's couch catches my attention. Someone I've never seen before stands up and stares at me with narrowed eyes and a crumpled forehead. White male in his early twenties, light brown hair, looks like he keeps up with his workouts, and he's got a french fry sticking out of his mouth. Two fast food bags sit on Arella's coffee table along with two fountain drinks.

I hook my thumb toward the guy. "Who the fuck is he?"

Arella blinks at me. "Better question: Who are *you*?"

ACKNOWLEDGMENTS

To my **husband, Joe**:
I never knew someone could love another person as much as
you love me. I'll be the first to admit that my personality is
about as chaotic as this book, but somehow, you make me feel
like I'm always worth it. To me, you've always been easy to
love. Now lie back and let me open up that *treasure chest.* ;)

To my **beta readers** *who read this entire trilogy:*
Even though I told you all upfront that there would be
another cliff-hanger, your jaws dropped to the floor anyway.
Thanks for being the first people to hop on this wild ride with
me. Kaycee Racer, Priscillah Bancy, Kelsey Davis, Whitney
Tanner, Mads Arlow, and Annie.

To my **readers**:
Thank you for continuing Trey and Arella's story. As you
move on to *Scrubbed Mind*, know that it was the easiest and
fastest for me to write, and also my favorite in this trilogy.

To **Enchanted Ink Publishing**:
Natalia and Greg, for gracefully answering all of my never-
ending questions. Stephanie, for always letting me know when
something makes you laugh. Christian, for taking my
undetailed concept of "blue lightning with two daggers" and
making it look amazing. Lisa, for catching all of the tiniest
mistakes and missing spaces. My eyes could never.

To my **Secret Keepers**:
They say that strangers can be more supportive of your dreams than your own friends and family. With my street team, this rings true. You ladies go above and beyond to help me grow, and I appreciate you all so much!

To **the three babies I lost in the womb trying to have my first baby**:
Your little brother made it, and he's happily thriving in the world.

To **anyone who has ever lost a pregnancy or child**:
You are not alone, and it was not your fault.

ABOUT THE AUTHOR

Melissa Lam loves reading and writing romance books that take the reader on an emotional roller coaster full of mystery, suspense, and heartache.

As an extroverted introvert who doesn't like to leave the house (because it requires wearing pants), Melissa enjoys playing strategic board games and taking long showers. When she does find the will to put pants on, she can be found traveling, enjoying bubble tea, or experiencing the world through food.

TL;DR I like to eat and write about heartbreaking shit.

Website: authormelissalam.com
Instagram: instagram.com/authormelissalam
Facebook: facebook.com/authormelissalam
Newsletter: authormelissalam.com/newsletter

SUPPORT INDIE AUTHORS

The best way to support indie authors is to leave reviews, because it helps other readers discover us! If you enjoyed this book, please consider leaving your feedback on Amazon, Goodreads, and anywhere else readers hang out.

Grab the next book in this series at
www.authormelissalam.com